The Book of Wizards

Stories of Enchantment from Near and Far

The Book of Wizards

Stories of Enchantment from Near and Far

edited by Jennifer Schwamm Willis

Thunder's Mouth Press
New York

THE BOOK OF WIZARDS: *Stories of Enchantment from Near and Far*

Compilation copyright © 2004 by Jennifer Schwamm Willis
Introduction copyright © 2004 by Jennifer Schwamm Willis

Published by
Thunder's Mouth Press
An Imprint of Avalon Publishing Group Inc.
245 West 17th Street, 11th floor
New York, NY 10011

Library of Congress Cataloging-in-Publication Data is available.

ISBN: 1-56025-588-9

Book design: Michael Walters
Printed the United States of America
Distributed by Publishers Group West

For Kevin

A magical boy who cast a spell on me long ago

Table of Contents

Introduction

The word "wizard" comes from the Middle English word for "wise" (wys), and originally meant "philosopher" or "sage". Wizards are wise beings who see through illusion to truth; appearances do not fool them. Wizards see through disguises and recognize evil in the most handsome prince—or goodness in the most misshapen crone. Our favorite wizards often use their magic powers sparingly, finding much of their power in wisdom. Their knowledge of the natural world—including human nature—empowers them to defeat evil.

Wizards often inhabit the form of an ordinary person or an animal, and they can turn up anywhere. The wizards who appear in this collection of stories come in various shapes and from various places—including India, China, South America, New York City, England, Persia and Hawaii, as well as imaginary places like Earthsea, Hoarsbreath and a town called New Duddleston.

Many wizards pass along their knowledge to apprentices, who become caretakers of their master's knowledge—which often involves words: spells and incantations that may reside in closely guarded books.

Like wizards, storytellers pass on the accumulated wisdom of families and cultures and civilizations. They help us to conjure up surprising worlds that live on in our understanding and memory. The best stories change our lives, and may help us to overcome great difficulties—just as a wizard might change a dragon into a flower (or a vegetarian).

Readers of good stories are sorcerer's apprentices: we pursue our own learning in the shadow of a master or mistress whose understanding may at times seem beyond our own. Our work is to open our hearts and minds to such wisdom—the wisdom we find in each other's best stories. When we do that, we make our own magic and become storytellers and wizards ourselves.

—*Jennifer Schwamm Willis*

The Bones of
the Earth

by Ursula K. Le Guin

Ursula K. Le Guin's father was an anthropologist and her mother was a writer. The family's house in Berkeley, California, was filled with books and all kinds of interesting people. Ursula grew up to become one of the world's foremost writers of contemporary fantasy. This story tells of the strong bond between an old wizard and his apprentice.

It was raining again, and the wizard of Re Albi was sorely tempted to make a weather spell, just a little, small spell, to send the rain on round the mountain. His bones ached. They ached for the sun to come out and shine through his flesh and dry them out. Of course he could say a pain spell, but all that would do was hide the ache for a while. There was no cure for what ailed him. Old bones need the sun. The wizard stood still in the doorway of his house, between the dark room and the rain-streaked open air, preventing himself from making a spell, and angry at himself for preventing himself and for having to be prevented.

He never swore—men of power do not swear, it is not safe—but he cleared his throat with a coughing growl, like a bear. A moment later a thunderclap rolled off the hidden upper slopes of Gont Mountain, echoing round from north to south, dying away in the cloud-filled forests.

A good sign, thunder, Dulse thought. It would stop raining soon. He pulled up his hood and went out into the rain to feed the chickens.

He checked the henhouse, finding three eggs. Red Bucca was setting. Her eggs were about due to hatch. The mites were bothering her, and she looked scruffy and jaded. He said a few words against mites, told himself to remember to clean out the nest box as soon as the chicks hatched, and went on to the poultry yard, where Brown Bucca and Grey and Leggings and Candor and the King huddled under the eaves making soft, shrewish remarks about rain.

"It'll stop by midday," the wizard told the chickens. He fed them and squelched back to the house with three warm eggs. When he was a child he had liked to walk in mud. He remembered enjoying the cool of it rising between his toes. He still liked to go barefoot, but no longer enjoyed mud; it was sticky stuff, and he disliked stooping to clean his feet before going into the house. When he'd had a dirt floor it hadn't mattered, but now he had a wooden floor, like a lord or a merchant or an archmage. To keep the cold and damp out of his bones. Not his own notion. Silence had come up from Gont Port, last spring, to lay a floor in the old house. They had had one of their arguments about it. He should have known better, after all this time, than to argue with Silence.

"I've walked on dirt for seventy-five years," Dulse had said. "A few more won't kill me!"

To which Silence of course made no reply, letting him hear what he had said and feel its foolishness thoroughly.

"Dirt's easier to keep clean," he said, knowing the struggle already lost. It was true that all you had to do with a good hard-packed clay floor was sweep it and now and then sprinkle it to keep the dust down. But it sounded silly all the same.

"Who's to lay this floor?" he said, now merely querulous.

Silence nodded, meaning himself.

The boy was in fact a workman of the first order, carpenter, cabinetmaker, stonelayer, roofer; he had proved that when he lived up here as Dulse's student, and his life with the rich folk of Gont Port had not softened his hands. He brought the boards from Sixths mill in Re Albi, driving Gammers ox team; he laid the floor and polished it the next day, while the old wizard was up at Bog Lake gathering simples. When

Dulse came home there it was, shining like a dark lake itself. "Have to wash my feet every time I come in," he grumbled. He walked in gingerly. The wood was so smooth it seemed soft to the bare sole. "Satin," he said. "You didn't do all that in one day without a spell or two. A village hut with a palace floor. Well, it'll be a sight, come winter, to see the fire shine in that! Or do I have to get me a carpet now? A fleecefell, on a golden warp?"

Silence smiled. He was pleased with himself.

He had turned up on Dulse's doorstep a few years ago. Well, no, twenty years ago it must be, or twenty-five. A while ago now. He had been truly a boy then, long-legged, rough-haired, soft-faced. A set mouth, clear eyes. "What do you want?" the wizard had asked, knowing what he wanted, what they all wanted, and keeping his eyes from those clear eyes. He was a good teacher, the best on Gont, he knew that. But he was tired of teaching, didn't want another prentice underfoot. And he sensed danger.

"To learn," the boy whispered.

"Go to Roke," the wizard said. The boy wore shoes and a good leather vest. He could afford or earn ship's passage to the school.

"I've been there."

At that Dulse looked him over again. No cloak, no staff.

"Failed? Sent away? Ran away?"

The boy shook his head at each question. He shut his eyes; his mouth was already shut. He stood there, intensely gathered, suffering: drew breath: looked straight into the wizard's eyes.

"My mastery is here, on Gont," he said, still speaking hardly above a whisper. "My master is Heleth."

At that the wizard whose true name was Heleth stood as still as he did, looking back at him, till the boy's gaze dropped.

In silence Dulse sought the boy's name, and saw two things: a fir cone, and the rune of the Closed Mouth. Then seeking further he heard in his mind a name spoken; but he did not speak it.

"I'm tired of teaching and talking," he said. "I need silence. Is that enough for you?"

The boy nodded once.

"Then to me you are Silence," the wizard said. "You can sleep in the nook under the west window. There's an old pallet in the woodhouse. Air it. Don't bring mice in with it." And he stalked off towards the Overfell, angry with the boy for coming and with himself for giving in; but it was not anger that made his heart pound. Striding along—he could stride, then—with the sea wind pushing at him always from the left and the early sunlight on the sea out past the vast shadow of the mountain, he thought of the Mages of Roke, the masters of the art of magic, the professors of mystery and power. "He was too much for em, was he? And he'll be too much for me," he thought, and smiled. He was a peaceful man, but he did not mind a bit of danger.

He stopped then and felt the dirt under his feet. He was barefoot, as usual. When he was a student on Roke, he had worn shoes. But he had come back home to Gont, to Re Albi, with his wizard's staff, and kicked his shoes off. He stood still and felt the dust and rock of the cliff-top path under his feet, and the cliffs under that, and the roots of the island in the dark under that. In the dark under the waters all islands touched and were one. So his teacher Ard had said, and so his teachers on Roke had said. But this was his island, his rock, his dirt. His wizardry grew out of it. "My mastery is here," the boy had said, but it went deeper than mastery. That, perhaps, was something Dulse could teach him: what went deeper than mastery. What he had learned here, on Gont, before he ever went to Roke.

And the boy must have a staff. Why had Nemmerle let him leave Roke without one, empty-handed as a prentice or a witch? Power like that shouldn't go wandering about unchanneled and unsignaled.

My teacher had no staff, Dulse thought, and at the same moment thought, The boy wants his staff from me. Gontish oak, from the hands of a Gontish wizard. Well, if he earns it I'll make him one. If he can keep his mouth closed. And I'll leave him my lore-books. If he can clean out a henhouse, and understand the Glosses of Danemer, and keep his mouth closed.

The new student cleaned out the henhouse and hoed the bean

patch, learned the meaning of the Glosses of Danemer and the Arcana of the Enlades, and kept his mouth closed. He listened. He heard what Dulse said; sometimes he heard what Dulse thought. He did what Dulse wanted and what Dulse did not know he wanted. His gift was far beyond Dulse's guidance, yet he had been right to come to Re Albi, and they both knew it.

Dulse thought sometimes in those years about sons and fathers. He had quarreled with his own father, a sorcerer-prospector, over his choice of Ard as his teacher. His father had shouted that a student of Ard's was no son of his, had nursed his rage, died unforgiving.

Dulse had seen young men weep for joy at the birth of a first son. He had seen poor men pay witches a year's earnings for the promise of a healthy boy, and a rich man touch his gold-bedizened baby's face and whisper, adoring, "My immortality!" He had seen men beat their sons, bully and humiliate them, spite and thwart them, hating the death they saw in them. He had seen the answering hatred in the sons' eyes, the threat, the pitiless contempt. And seeing it, Dulse knew why he had never sought reconciliation with his father.

He had seen a father and son work together from daybreak to sundown, the old man guiding a blind ox, the middle-aged man driving the iron-bladed plough, never a word spoken. As they started home the old man laid his hand a moment on the son's shoulder.

He had always remembered that. He remembered it now, when he looked across the hearth, winter evenings, at the dark face bent above a lore-book or a shirt that needed mending. The eyes cast down, the mouth closed, the spirit listening.

"Once in his lifetime, if he's lucky, a wizard finds somebody he can talk to." Nemmerle had said that to Dulse a night or two before Dulse left Roke, a year or two before Nemmerle was chosen Archmage. He had been the Master Patterner and the kindest of all Dulse's teachers at the school. "I think, if you stayed, Heleth, we could talk."

Dulse had been unable to answer at all for a while. Then, stammering, guilty at his ingratitude and incredulous at his obstinacy—"Master, I would stay, but my work is on Gont. I wish it was here, with you—"

"It's a rare gift, to know where you need to be, before you've been to all the places you don't need to be. Well, send me a student now and then. Roke needs Gontish wizardry. I think we're leaving things out, here, things worth knowing. . . ."

Dulse had sent students on to the school, three or four of them, nice lads with a gift for this or that; but the one Nemmerle waited for had come and gone of his own will, and what they had thought of him on Roke Dulse did not know. And Silence, of course, did not say. It was evident that he had learned there in two or three years what some boys learned in six or seven and many never learned at all. To him it had been mere groundwork.

"Why didn't you come to me first!?" Dulse had demanded. "And then go to Roke, to put a polish on it?"

"I didn't want to waste your time."

"Did Nemmerle know you were coming to work with me?"

Silence shook his head.

"If you'd deigned to tell him your intentions, he might have sent a message to me."

Silence looked stricken. "Was he your friend?"

Dulse paused. "He was my master. Would have been my friend, perhaps, if I'd stayed on Roke. Have wizards friends? No more than they have wives, or sons, I suppose . . . Once he said to me that in our trade it's a lucky man who finds someone to talk to . . . Keep that in mind. If you're lucky, one day you'll have to open your mouth."

Silence bowed his rough, thoughtful head.

"If it hasn't rusted shut," Dulse added.

"If you ask me to, I'll talk," the young man said, so earnest, so willing to deny his whole nature at Dulse's request that the wizard had to laugh.

"I asked you not to," he said. "And it's not my need I spoke of. I talk enough for two. Never mind. You'll know what to say when the time comes. That's the art, eh? What to say, and when to say it. And the rest is silence."

The young man slept on a pallet under the little west window of

Dulse's house for three years. He learned wizardry, fed the chickens, milked the cow. He suggested, once, that Dulse keep goats. He had not said anything for a week or so, a cold, wet week of autumn. He said, "You might keep some goats."

Dulse had the big lore-book open on the table. He had been trying to reweave one of the Acastan spells, much broken and made powerless by the Emanations of Fundaur centuries ago. He had just begun to get a sense of the missing word that might fill one of the gaps, he almost had it, and—"You might keep some goats," Silence said.

Dulse considered himself a wordy, impatient man with a short temper. The necessity of not swearing had been a burden to him in his youth, and for thirty years the imbecility of prentices, clients, cows, and chickens had tried him sorely. Prentices and clients were afraid of his tongue, though cows and chickens paid no attention to his outbursts. He had never been angry at Silence before. There was a very long pause.

"What for?"

Silence apparently did not notice the pause or the extreme softness of Dulse's voice. "Milk, cheese, roast kid, company," he said.

"Have you ever kept goats?" Dulse asked, in the same soft polite voice.

Silence shook his head.

He was in fact a town boy, born in Gont Port. He had said nothing about himself, but Dulse had asked around a bit. The father, a longshoreman, had died in the big earthquake, when Silence would have been seven or eight; the mother was a cook at a waterfront inn. At twelve the boy had got into some kind of trouble, probably messing about the magic, and his mother had managed to prentice him to Elassen, a respectable sorcerer in Valmouth. There the boy had picked up his true name and some skill in carpentry and farm work, if not much else; and Elassen had had the generosity, after three years, to pay his passage to Roke. That was all Dulse knew about him.

"I dislike goat cheese," Dulse said.

Silence nodded, acceptant as always.

From time to time in the years since then, Dulse remembered how he hadn't lost his temper when Silence asked about keeping goats; and each time the memory gave him a quiet satisfaction, like that of finishing the last bite of a perfectly ripe pear.

After spending the next several days trying to recapture the missing word, he had set Silence to studying the Acastan Spells. Together they finally worked it out, a long toil. "Like ploughing with a blind ox," Dulse said.

Not long after that he gave Silence the staff he had made for him of Gontish oak.

And the Lord of Gont Port had tried once again to get Dulse to come down to do what needed doing in Gont Port, and Dulse had sent Silence down instead, and there he had stayed.

And Dulse was standing on his own doorstep, three eggs in his hand and the rain running cold down his back.

How long had he been standing here? Why was he standing here? He had been thinking about mud, about the floor, about Silence. Had he been out walking on the path above the Overfell? No, that was years ago, years ago, in the sunlight. It was raining. He had fed the chickens, and come back to the house with three eggs, they were still warm in his hand, silky brown lukewarm eggs, and the sound of thunder was still in his mind, the vibration of thunder was in his bones, in his feet. Thunder?

No. There had been a thunderclap, a while ago. This was not thunder. He had had this queer feeling and had not recognised it, back—when? long ago, back before all the days and years he had been thinking of. When, when had it been?—before the earthquake. Just before the earthquake. Just before a half mile of the coast at Essary slumped into the sea, and people died crushed in the ruins of their villages, and a great wave swamped the wharfs at Gont Port.

He stepped down from the doorstep onto the dirt so that he could feel the ground with the nerves of his soles, but the mud slimed and fouled any messages the dirt had for him. He set the eggs down on the doorstep, sat down beside them, cleaned his feet with rain water from the pot by the step, wiped them dry with the rag that hung on the handle of the pot, rinsed and rung out the rag and hung it on the handle of the pot, picked up the eggs, stood up slowly, and went into his house.

He gave a sharp look at his staff, which leaned in the corner behind the door. He put the eggs in the larder, ate an apple quickly because he was hungry, and took up his staff. It was yew, bound at the foot with copper, worn to satin at the grip. Nemerle had given it to him.

"Stand!" he said to it in its language, and let go of it. It stood as if he had driven it into a socket.

"To the root," he said impatiently, in the language of the Making. "To the root!"

He watched the staff that stood on the shining floor. In a little while he saw it quiver very slightly, a shiver, a tremble.

"Ah, ah, ah," said the old wizard.

"What should I do?" he said aloud after a while.

The staff swayed, was still, shivered again.

"Enough of that, my dear," Dulse said, laying his hand on it. "Come now. No wonder I kept thinking about Silence. I should send for him . . . send to him . . . No. What did Ard say? Find the center, find the center. That's the question to ask. That's what to do . . ." As he muttered on to himself, routing out his heavy cloak, setting water to boil on the small fire he had lighted earlier, he wondered if he had always talked to himself, if he had talked all the time when Silence lived with him. No. It had become a habit after Silence left, he thought, with the bit of his mind that went on thinking the ordinary thoughts of life, while the rest of it made preparations for terror and destruction.

He hard-boiled the three new eggs and one already in the larder and put them into a pouch along with four apples and a bladder of resinated wine, in case he had to stay out all night. He shrugged arthritically into his heavy cloak, took up his staff, told the fire to go out, and left.

He no longer kept a cow. He stood looking into the poultry yard, considering. The fox had been visiting the orchard lately. But the chickens would have to forage if he stayed away. They must take their chances, like everyone else. He opened their gate a little. Though the rain was no more than a misty drizzle now, they stayed hunched up under the henhouse eaves, disconsolate. The King had not crowed once this morning.

"Have you anything to tell me?" Dulse asked them.

Brown Bucca, his favorite, shook herself and said her name a few times. The others said nothing.

"Well, take care. I saw the fox on the full-moon night," Dulse said, and went on his way.

As he walked he thought; he thought hard; he recalled. He recalled all he could of matters his teacher had spoken of once only and long ago. Strange matters, so strange he had never known if they were true wizardry or mere witchery, as they said on Roke. Matters he certainly had never heard about on Roke, nor had he ever spoken about them there, maybe fearing the Masters would despise him for taking such things seriously, maybe knowing they would not understand them, because they were Gontish matters, truths of Gont. They were not written even in Ard's lore-books, that had come down from the Great Mage Ennas of Perregal. They were all word of mouth. They were home truths.

"If you need to read the Mountain," his teacher had told him, "go to the Dark Pond at the top of Semere's cow pasture. You can see the ways from there. You need to find the center. See where to go in."

"Go in?" the boy Dulse had whispered.

"What could you do from outside?"

Dulse was silent for a long time, and then said, "How?"

"Thus." And Ard's long arms stretched out and upward in the invocation of what Dulse would know later was a great spell of Transforming. Ard spoke the words of the spell awry, as teachers of wizardry must do lest the spell operate. Dulse knew the trick of hearing them aright and remembering them. When Ard was done, Dulse had repeated the words in his mind in silence, half-sketching the strange, awkward gestures that were part of them. All at once his hand stopped.

"But you can't undo this!" he said aloud.

Ard nodded. "It is irrevocable."

Dulse knew no transformation that was irrevocable, no spell that could not be unsaid, except the Word of Unbinding, which is spoken only once.

"But why—"

"At need," Ard said.

Dulse knew better than to ask for explanation. The need to speak such a spell could not come often; the chance of his ever having to use it was very slight. He let the terrible spell sink down in his mind and be hidden and layered over with a thousand useful or beautiful or enlightening mageries and charms, all the lore and rules of Roke, all the wisdom of the books Ard had bequeathed him. Crude, monstrous, useless, it lay in the dark of his mind for sixty years, like the cornerstone of an earlier, forgotten house down in the cellar of a mansion full of lights and treasures and children.

The rain had ceased, though mist still hit the peak and shreds of cloud drifted through the high forest. Though not a tireless walker like Silence, who would have spent his life wandering in the forests of Gont Mountain if he could, Dulse had been born in Re Albi and knew the roads and ways around it as part of himself. He took the shortcut at Rissi's well and came out before midday on Semere's high pasture, a level step on the mountainside. A mile below it, all in sunlight now, the farm buildings stood in the lee of a hill across which a flock of sheep moved like a cloud-shadow. Gont Port and its bay were hidden under the steep, knotted hills that stood inland above the city.

Dulse wandered about a bit before he found what he took to be the Dark Pond. It was small, half mud and reeds, with one vague, boggy path to the water, and no tracks on that but goat hoofs. The water was dark, though it lay out under the bright sky and far above the peat soils. Dulse followed the goat tracks, growling when his foot slipped in the mud and he wrenched his ankle to keep from falling. At the brink of the water he stood still. He stooped to rub his ankle. He listened.

It was absolutely silent.

No wind. No birdcall. No distant lowing or bleating or call of voice. As if all the island had gone still. Not a fly buzzed. He looked at the dark water. It reflected nothing. Reluctant, he stepped forward, bare-foot and bare-legged; he had rolled up his cloak into his pack an hour ago when the sun came out. Reeds brushed his legs. The mud was soft and sucking under his feet, full of tangling reed-roots. He made no noise as he moved slowly out into the pool, and the circles of ripples from his movement were slight and small. It was shallow for a long way. Then his cautious foot felt no bottom, and he paused.

The water shivered. He felt it first on his thighs, a lapping like the tickling touch of fur; then he saw it, the trembling of the surface all over the pond. Not the round ripples he made, which had already died away, but a ruffling, a roughening, a shudder, again, and again.

"Where?" he whispered, and then said the word aloud in the language all things understand that have no other language.

There was the silence. Then a fish leaped from the black, shaking water, a white-grey fish the length of his hand, and as it leaped it cried out in a small, clear voice, in that same language, "Yaved!"

The old wizard stood there. He recollected all he knew of the names of Gont, brought all its slopes and cliffs and ravines into his mind, and in a minute he saw where Yaved was. It was the place where the ridges parted, just inland from Gont Port, deep in the knot of hills above the city. It was the place of the fault. An earthquake centered there could shake the city down, bringing avalanche and tidal wave, close the cliffs of the bay together like hands clapping. Dulse shivered, shuddered all over like the water of the pool.

He turned and made for the shore, hasty, careless where he set his feet, and not caring if he broke the silence by splashing and breathing hard. He slogged back up the path through the reeds till he reached dry ground and course grass, and heard the buzz of midges and crickets. He sat down then on the ground, hard, for his legs were shaking.

"It won't do," he said, talking to himself in Hardic, and then he said, "I can't do it." Then he said, "I can't do it by myself."

He was so distraught that when he made up his mind to call Silence he could not think of the opening of the spell, which he had known for sixty years; then when he thought he had it, he began to speak a

Summoning instead, and the spell had begun to work before he realized what he was doing and stopped and undid it word by word.

He pulled up some grass and rubbed at the slimy mud on his feet and legs. It was not dry yet, and only smeared about on his skin. "I hate mud," he whispered. Then he snapped his jaws and stopped trying to clean his legs. "Dirt, dirt," he said, gently patting the ground he sat on. Then, very slow, very careful, he began to speak the spell of calling.

In a busy street leading down to the busy wharfs of Gont Port, the wizard Ogion stopped short. The ship's captain beside him walked on several steps and turned to see Ogion talking to the air.

"But I will come, master!" he said. And then after a pause, "How soon?" And after a longer pause, he told the air something in a language the ship's captain did not understand, and made a gesture that darkened the air about him for an instant.

"Captain," he said, "I'm sorry, I must wait to spell your sails. An earthquake is near. I must warn the city. Do you tell them down there, every ship that can sail make for the open sea. Clear out past the Armed Cliffs! Good luck to you." And he turned and ran back up the street, a tall, strong man with rough greying hair, running now like a stag.

Gont Port lies at the inner end of a long narrow bay between steep shores. Its entrance from the sea is between two great headlands, the Gates of the Port, the Armed Cliffs, not a hundred feet apart. The people of Gont Port are safe from sea-pirates. But their safety is their danger: the long bay follows a fault in the earth, and jaws that have opened may shut.

When he had done what he could to warn the city, and seen all the gate guards and port guards doing what they could to keep the few roads out from becoming choked and murderous with panicky people, Ogion shut himself into a room in the signal tower of the Port, locked the door, for everybody wanted him at once, and sent a sending to the Dark Pond in Semere's cow pasture up on the Mountain.

His old master was sitting in the grass near the pond, eating an apple. Bits of eggshell flecked the ground near his legs, which were caked with drying mud. When he looked up and saw Ogion's sending he smiled a wide, sweet smile. But he looked old. He had never looked so old. Ogion had not seen him for over a year, having been busy; he was always busy in Gont Port, doing the business of the lords and people, never a chance to walk in the forests on the mountainside or to come sit with Heleth in the little house at Ri Albi and listen and be still. Heleth was an old man, near eighty now; and he was frightened. He smiled with joy to see Ogion, but he was frightened.

"I think what we have to do," he said without preamble, "is try to hold the fault from slipping much. You at the Gates and me at the inner end, in the mountain. Working together, you know. We might be able to. I can feel it building up, can you?"

Ogion shook his head. He let his sending sit down in the grass near Heleth, though it did not bend the stems of the grass where it stepped or sat. "I've done nothing but set the city in a panic and send the ships out of the bay," he said. "What is it you feel? How do you feel it?"

They were technical questions mage to mage. Heleth hesitated before answering.

"I learned about this from Ard," he said and paused again.

He had never told Ogion anything about his first teacher, a sorcerer of no fame even in Gont, and perhaps of ill fame. Ogion knew only that Ard had never gone to Roke, had been trained on Perregal, and that some mystery or shame darkened the name. Though he was talkative for a wizard, Heleth was silent as a stone about some things. And so Ogion, who respected silence, had never asked him about his teacher.

"It's not Roke magic," the old man said. His voice was dry, a little forced. "Nothing against the balance, though. Nothing sticky."

That had always been his word for evil doings, spells for gain, curses, black magic: "Sticky stuff."

After a while, searching for words, he went on: "Dirt. Rocks. It's a dirty magic. Old. Very old. As old as Gont Island."

"The old powers?" Ogion murmered.

Heleth said, "I'm not sure."

"Will it control the earth itself?"

"More a matter of getting in with it, I think. Inside." The old man was burying the core of his apple and the larger bits of eggshell under loose dirt, patting it over them neatly. "Of course I know the words, but I'll have to learn what to do as I go. That's the trouble with the big spells, isn't it? You learn what you're doing while you do it. No chance to practice." He looked up. "Ah—there! You feel that?"

Ogion shook his head.

"Straining," Heleth said, his hand still absently, gently patting the dirt as one might pat a scared cow. "Quite soon now, I think. Can you hold the Gates open, my dear?"

"Tell me what you'll be doing—"

But Heleth was shaking his head: "No," he said. "No time. Not your kind of thing." He was more and more distracted by whatever it was he sensed in the earth or air, and through him Ogion too felt that gathering, intolerable tension.

They sat unspeaking. The crisis passed. Heleth relaxed a little and even smiled. "Very old stuff," he said, "what I'll be doing. I wish now I'd thought about it more. Passed it on to you. But it seemed a bit crude. Heavy handed . . . She didn't say where she'd learned it. Here, of course . . . There are different kinds of knowledge, after all."

"She?"

"Ard. My teacher." Heleth looked up, his face unreadable, its expression possibly sly. "You didn't know that? No, I suppose I never mentioned it. I wonder what difference it made to her wizardry, her being a woman. Or to mine, my being a man . . . What matters, it seems to me, is whose house we live in. And who we let enter the house. This kind of thing—There! There again—"

His sudden tension and immobility, the strained face and inward look, were like those of a woman in labor when her womb contracts. That was Ogion's thought, even as he asked, "What did you mean, 'in the Mountain'?"

The spasm passed; Heleth answered, "Inside it. There at Yaved." He pointed to the knotted hills below them. "I'll go in, try to keep things from sliding around, eh? I'll find out how when I'm doing it, no doubt. I think you should be getting back to yourself. Things are tightening up." He stopped again, looking as if he were in intense pain, hunched and clenched. He struggled to stand up. Unthinking Ogion held out his hand to help him.

"No use," said the old wizard grining, "you're only wind and sunlight. Now I'm going to be dirt and stone. You'd best go on. Farewell, Aihal. Keep the—keep the mouth open, for once, eh?"

Ogion, obedient, bringing himself back to himself in the old stuffy, tapestried room in Gont Port, did not understand the old man's joke until he turned to the window and saw the Armed Cliffs down at the end of the long bay, the jaws ready to snap shut. "I will," he said, and set to it.

"What I have to do, you see," the old wizard said, still talking to Silence because it was a comfort to talk to him even if he was no longer there, "is get into the mountain, right inside. But not the way a sorcerer-prospecter does, not just slipping about between things and looking and tasting. Deeper. All the way in. Not the veins, but the bones. So," and standing there alone in the high pasture in the noon light, Heleth opened his arms wide in the gesture of invocation that opens all the greater spells; and he spoke.

Nothing happened as he said the words Ard had taught him, his old witch-teacher with her bitter mouth and her long, lean arms, the words spoken awry then, spoken truly now.

Nothing happened and he had time to regret the sunlight and the sea wind, and to doubt the spell, and to doubt himself, before the earth rose up around him, dry, warm, and dark.

In there he knew he should hurry, that the bones of the earth ached to move, and that he must become them to guide them, but he could not hurry. There was on him the bewilderment of any transformation. He had in his day been fox, and bull, and dragonfly, and knew what it was to change being. But this was different, this slow enlargement. I am vastening, he thought.

He reached out towards Yaved, towards the ache, the suffering. As he came closer to it he felt a great strength flow into him from the west, as if Silence had taken him by the hand after all. Through that link he could send his own strength, the Mountain's strength, to help. I didn't tell him I wasn't coming back, he thought, his last words in Hardic, his last grief, for he was in the bones of the mountain now. He knew the arteries of fire, and the beat of the great heart. He knew what to do. It was in no tongue of man that he said, "Be quiet, be easy. There now, there. Hold fast. So, there. We can be easy."

And he was easy, he was still, he held fast, rock in rock and earth in earth in the fiery dark of the mountain.

It was their mage Ogion whom the people saw stand alone on the roof of the signal tower on the wharf, when the streets ran up and down in waves, the cobbles bursting out of them, and walls of clay brick puffed into dust, and the Armed Cliffs leaned together, groaning. It was Ogion they saw, his hands held out before him, straining, parting: and the cliffs parted with them, and stood straight, unmoved. The city shuddered and stood still. It was Ogion who stopped the earthquake. They saw it, they said it.

"My teacher was with me, and his teacher with him," Ogion said when they praised him. "I could hold the Gate open because he held the Mountain still." They praised his modesty and did not listen to him. Listening is a rare gift, and men will have their heroes.

When the city was in order again, and the ships had all come back, and the walls were being rebuilt, Ogion escaped from praise and went up into the hills above Gont Port. He found the queer little valley called Trimmer's Dell, the true name of which in the Language of the Making was Yaved, as Ogion's true name was Aihal. He walked about there all one day, as if seeking something. In the evening he lay down on the ground and talked to it. "You should have told me. I could have said goodbye," he said. He wept then, and his tears fell on the dry dirt among the grass stems and made little spots of mud, little sticky spots.

He slept there on the ground, with no pallet or blanket between him and the dirt. At sunrise he got up and walked by the high road over to Re Albi. He did not go into the village, but past it to the house that stood alone north of the other houses at the beginning of the Overfell. The door stood open.

The last beans had got big and coarse on the vines; the cabbages were thriving. Three hens came clucking and pecking around the dusty dooryard, a red, a brown, a white; a grey hen was setting her clutch in the henhouse. There were no chicks, and no sign of the cock, the King, Heleth had called him. The king is dead, Ogion thought. Maybe a chick is hatching even now to take his place. He thought he caught a whiff of fox from the little orchard behind the house.

He swept out the dust and leaves that had blown in the open doorway across the floor of polished wood. He set Heleth's mattress and blanket in the sun to air. "I'll stay here a while," he thought. "It's a good house." After a while he thought, "I might keep some goats."

Aladdin and the Wonderful Lamp

by Andrew Lang

Born in Scotland, Andrew Lang (1844–1912) was a poet, novelist and critic. He is remembered best for his work collecting, compiling and translating hundreds of folk and fairy tales from around the world. This is his version of the classic tale of Aladdin and his magic lamp.

There once lived a poor tailor who had a son called Aladdin, a careless, idle boy who would do nothing but play all day long in the streets with little idle boys like himself. This so grieved the father that he died; yet, in spite of his mother's tears and prayers, Aladdin did not mend his ways. One day, when he was playing in the streets as usual, a stranger asked him his age, and if he were not the son of Mustapha the tailor.

'I am, sir,' replied Aladdin; 'but he died a long while ago.'

On this the stranger, who was a famous African magician, fell on his neck and kissed him, saying, 'I am your uncle and I knew you from your likeness to my brother. Go to your mother and tell her I am coming.'

Aladdin ran home and told his mother of his newly found uncle.

'Indeed, child,' she said, 'your father had a brother, but I always thought he was dead.'

However, she prepared supper and bade Aladdin seek his uncle, who came laden with wine and fruit. He presently knelt and kissed the place where Mustapha used to sit, bidding Aladdin's mother not to be surprised at not having seen him before, as he had been forty years out of the country.

He then turned to Aladdin and asked him his trade, at which the boy hung his head, while his mother burst into tears. On learning that Aladdin was idle and would learn no trade, he offered to take a shop for him and stock it with merchandise. Next day he bought Aladdin a fine suit of clothes and took him all over the city, showing him the sights, and brought him home at nightfall to his mother, who was overjoyed to see her son so fine.

Next day the magician led Aladdin into some beautiful gardens a long way outside the city gates. They sat down by a fountain, and the magician pulled a cake from his girdle, which he divided between them. They then journeyed onward till they almost reached the mountains. Aladdin was so tired that he begged to go back, but the magician beguiled him with pleasant stories and led him on in spite of himself.

At last they came to two mountains divided by a narrow valley. 'We will go no farther,' said the false uncle. 'I will show you something wonderful; only do you gather up sticks while I kindle a fire.'

When the fire was lit the magician threw on it a powder he had with him, at the same time saying some magical words. The earth trembled a little and opened in front of them, disclosing a square flat stone with a brass ring in the middle to raise it by. Aladdin tried to run away, but the magician caught him and gave him a blow that knocked him down.

'What have I done, Uncle?' he said piteously.

Whereupon the magician said more kindly, 'Fear nothing, but obey me. Beneath this stone lies a treasure which is to be yours, and no one else may touch it, so you must do exactly as I tell you.'

At the word treasure, Aladdin forgot his fears and grasped the ring as he was told, saying the names of his father and grandfather. The stone came up quite easily and some steps appeared.

'Go down,' said the magician. 'At the foot of those steps you will find an open door leading into three large halls. Tuck up your gown and go through them without touching anything, or you will die instantly. These halls lead into a garden of fine fruit trees. Walk on till you come to a niche in a terrace where stands a lighted lamp. Pour out the oil it contains and bring it to me.' He drew a ring from his finger and gave it to Aladdin, bidding him prosper.

Aladdin found everything as the magician had said, gathered some fruit off the trees and, having got the lamp, arrived at the mouth of the cave.

The magician cried out in a great hurry, 'Make haste and give me the lamp.' This Aladdin refused to do until he was out of the cave. The magician flew into a terrible passion, and throwing some more powder on the fire, he said something, and the stone rolled back into its place.

The magician left Persia forever, which plainly showed that he was no uncle of Aladdin's, but a cunning sorcerer who had read in his magic books of a wonderful lamp which would make him the most powerful man in the world. Though he alone knew where to find it, he could only receive it from the hand of another. He had picked out the foolish Aladdin for this purpose, intending to get the lamp and kill him afterward.

For two days Aladdin remained in the dark, crying and lamenting. At last he clasped his hands in prayer, and in so doing rubbed the ring, which the magician had forgotten to take from him.

Immediately an enormous and frightful genie rose out of the earth, saying, 'What wouldst thou with me? I am the slave of the ring and will obey thee in all things.'

Aladdin fearlessly replied, 'Deliver me from this place,' whereupon the earth opened, and he found himself outside. As soon as his eyes could bear the light he went home, but fainted on the threshold. When he came to himself he told his mother what had passed, and showed her the lamp and the fruits he had gathered in the garden, which were in reality precious stones. He then asked for some food.

'Alas, child,' she said, 'I have nothing in the house, but I have spun a little cotton and will go and sell it.'

Aladdin bade her keep her cotton, for he would sell the lamp instead. As it was very dirty she began to rub it, that it might fetch a higher price. Instantly a hideous genie appeared and asked what she would have.

She fainted away, but Aladdin, snatching the lamp, said boldly, 'Fetch me something to eat!'

The genie returned with a silver bowl, twelve silver plates containing rich meats, two silver cups, and a bottle of wine.

Aladdin's mother, when she came to herself, said, 'Whence comes this splendid feast?'

'Ask not, but eat,' replied Aladdin.

So they sat at breakfast till it was dinner time, and Aladdin told his mother about the lamp. She begged him to sell it and have nothing to do with genii.

'No,' said Aladdin, 'since chance has made us aware of its virtues, we will use it and the ring likewise, which I shall always wear on my finger.' When they had eaten all the genie had brought, Aladdin sold one of the silver plates, and so on till none were left. He then had recourse to the genie, who gave him another set of plates, and thus they lived for many years.

One day Aladdin heard an order from the sultan proclaiming that everyone was to stay at home and close his shutters while the princess, his daughter, went to and from the bath. Aladdin was seized by a desire to see her face, which was very difficult as she always went veiled. He hid himself behind the door of the bath and peeped through a chink.

The princess lifted her veil as she went in, and looked so beautiful that Aladdin fell in love with her at first sight. He went home so changed that his mother was frightened. He told her he loved the princess so deeply he could not live without her and meant to asked her in marriage of her father. His mother, on hearing this, burst out laughing, but Aladdin at last prevailed upon her to go before the sultan and carry his request. She fetched a napkin and laid in it the magic fruits from the enchanted garden, which sparkled and shone like the most beautiful jewels. She took these with her to please the sultan and set out, trusting in the lamp. The grand vizir and the lords of council had just gone in as she entered the hall and placed herself in front of the sultan. He, however, took no notice of her. She went every day for a week and stood in the same place.

When the council broke up on the sixth day the sultan said to his vizir, 'I see a certain woman in the audience chamber every day, carrying something in a napkin. Call her next time that I may find out what she wants.'

Next day, at a sign from the vizir, she went up to the foot of the throne and remained kneeling till the sultan said to her, 'Rise, good woman, and tell me what you want.'

She hesitated, so the sultan sent away all but the vizir and bade her speak freely, promising to forgive her beforehand for anything she might say. She then told him of her son's violent love for the princess.

'I prayed him to forget her,' she said, 'but in vain; he threatened to do some desperate deed if I refused to go and ask Your Majesty for the hand of the princess. Now I pray you to forgive not me alone but my son Aladdin.'

The sultan asked her kindly what she had in the napkin, whereupon she unfolded the jewels and presented them.

He was thunderstruck, and turning to the vizir, said, 'What sayest thou? Ought I not to bestow the princess on one who values her at such a price?'

The vizir, who wanted her for his own son, begged the sultan to withhold her for three months, in the course of which he hoped his son would contrive to make him a richer present. The sultan granted this and told Aladdin's mother that, though he consented to the marriage, she must not appear before him again for three months.

Aladdin waited patiently for nearly three months, but after two had elapsed his mother, going into the city to buy oil, found everyone rejoicing and asked what was going on.

'Do you not know,' was the answer, 'that the son of the grand vizir is to marry the sultan's daughter tonight?'

Breathless, she ran and told Aladdin, who was overwhelmed at first, but presently bethought him of the lamp. He rubbed it, and the genie appeared, saying, 'What is thy will?'

Aladdin replied, 'The sultan, as thou knowest, has broken his promise to me, and the vizir's son is to have the princess. My command is that tonight you bring hither the bride and bridegroom.'

'Master, I obey,' said the genie.

Aladdin then went to his chamber where, sure enough at midnight, the genie transported the bed containing the vizir's son and the princess.

'Take this new-married man,' Aladdin said, 'and put him outside in the cold and return at daybreak.'

Whereupon the genie took the vizir's son out of bed, leaving Aladdin with the princess.

'Fear nothing,' Aladdin said to her; 'you are my wife, promised to me by your unjust father, and no harm shall come to you.'

The princess was too frightened to speak and passed the most miserable night of her life, while Aladdin lay down beside her and slept soundly. At the appointed hour the genie fetched in the shivering bridegroom, laid him in his place, and transported the bed back to the palace.

Presently the sultan came to wish his daughter good morning. The unhappy vizir's son jumped up and hid himself, while the princess would not say a word and was very sorrowful.

The sultan sent her mother to her, who said, 'How comes it, child, that you will not speak to your father? What has happened?'

The princess sighed deeply, and at last told her mother how, during the night, the bed had been carried into some strange house, and what had passed there. Her mother did not believe her in the least but bade her rise and consider it an idle dream.

The following night exactly the same thing happened, and next morning, on the princess' refusing to speak, the sultan threatened to cut off her head. She then confessed all, bidding him ask the vizir's son if it were not so. The sultan told the vizir to ask his son, who owned the truth; adding that, dearly as he loved the princess, he had rather die than go through another such fearful night and that he wished to be separated from her. His wish was granted, and there was an end of feasting and rejoicing.

When the three months were over, Aladdin sent his mother to remind the sultan of his promise. She stood in the same place as

before, and the sultan, who had forgotten Aladdin, at once remembered him and sent for her. On seeing her poverty the sultan felt less
inclined than ever to keep his word and asked the vizir's advice, who
counseled him to set so high a value on the princess that no man living
could come up to it.

The sultan then turned to Aladdin's mother, saying, 'Good woman,
a sultan must remember his promises and I will remember mine, but
your son must first send me forty basins of gold brimful of jewels, carried by forty black slaves, led by as many white ones, splendidly
dressed. Tell him that I await his answer.'

The mother of Aladdin bowed low and went home, thinking all was
lost. She gave Aladdin the message, adding, 'He may wait long enough
for your answer!'

'Not so long, Mother, as you think,' her son replied. 'I would do a
great deal more than that for the princess.' He summoned the genie,
and in a few moments the eighty slaves arrived and filled up the small
house and garden.

Aladdin made them set out to the palace, two and two, followed by
his mother. They were so richly dressed, with such splendid jewels in
their girdles, that everyone crowded to see them and the basins of gold
they carried on their heads.

They entered the palace and, after kneeling before the sultan, stood
in a half-circle round the throne with their arms crossed, while
Aladdin's mother presented them to the sultan.

He hesitated no longer but said, 'Good woman, return and tell your
son that I wait for him with open arms.'

She lost no time in telling Aladdin, bidding him make haste. But
Aladdin first called the genie.

'I want a scented bath,' he said, 'a richly embroidered habit, a horse
surpassing the sultan's, and twenty slaves to attend me. Besides this I
desire six slaves, beautifully dressed, to wait on my mother; and lastly,
ten thousand pieces of gold in ten purses.'

No sooner said than done. Aladdin mounted his horse and passed
through the streets, the slaves strewing gold as they went. Those who

had played with him in his childhood knew him not, he had grown so handsome.

When the sultan saw him, he came down from his throne, embraced him, and led him into a hall where a feast was spread, intending to marry him to the princess that very day. But Aladdin refused, saying, 'I must build a palace fit for her,' and took his leave.

Once home, he said to the genie, 'Build me a palace of the finest marble, set with jasper, agate, and other precious stones. In the middle you shall build me a large hall with a dome, its four walls of massy gold and silver, each side having six windows whose lattices, all except one, which is to be left unfinished, must be set with diamonds and rubies. There must be stables and horses and grooms and slaves. Go and see about it!'

The palace was finished by next day, and the genie carried him there and showed him all his orders faithfully carried out, even to the laying of a velvet carpet from Aladdin's palace to the sultan's. Aladdin's mother then dressed herself carefully and walked to the palace with her slaves. The sultan sent musicians with trumpets and cymbals to meet them and the air resounded with music and cheers.

Aladdin's mother was taken to the princess, who saluted her and treated her with great honor. At night the princess said good-bye to her father and set out on the carpet for Aladdin's palace, with his mother at her side, and followed by the hundred slaves. She was charmed at the sight of Aladdin who ran to receive her.

'Princess,' he said, 'blame your beauty for my boldness if I have displeased you.'

She told him that, having seen him, she willingly obeyed her father in this matter. After the wedding had taken place, Aladdin led her into the hall where a feast was spread, and she supped with him, after which they danced till midnight.

Next day Aladdin invited the sultan to see the palace. On entering the hall with the four-and-twenty windows, with their rubies, diamonds, and emeralds, he cried, 'It is a world's wonder! There is only one thing that surprises me. Was it by accident that one window was left unfinished?'

'No, sir, by design,' returned Aladdin. 'I wished Your Majesty to have the glory of finishing this palace.'

The sultan was pleased and sent for the best jewelers in the city. He showed them the unfinished window and bade them fit it up like the others.

'Sir,' replied their spokesman, 'we cannot find jewels enough.' The sultan had his own fetched, which they soon used, but to no purpose, for in a month's time the work was not half done. Aladdin, knowing that their task was vain, bade them undo their work and carry the jewels back, and the genie finished the window at his command. The sultan was surprised to receive his jewels again and visited Aladdin, who showed him the window finished. The sultan embraced him, the envious vizir meanwhile hinting that it was the work of enchantment.

Aladdin had won the hearts of the people by his gentle bearing. He was made captain of the sultan's armies and won several battles for him, but remained modest and courteous as before and lived thus in peace and content for several years.

But far away in Africa the magician remembered Aladdin, and by his magic arts discovered that Aladdin, instead of perishing miserably in the cave, had escaped and had married a princess, with whom he was living in great honor and wealth. He knew that the poor tailor's son could only have accomplished this by means of the lamp and traveled night and day till he reached the capital of China, bent on Aladdin's ruin. As he passed through the town he heard people talking everywhere about a marvelous palace.

'Forgive my ignorance,' he asked, 'what is this palace you speak of?'

'Have you not heard of Prince Aladdin's palace,' was the reply, 'the greatest wonder of the world? I will direct you if you have a mind to see it.'

The magician thanked him who spoke and, having seen the palace, knew that it had been raised by the genie of the lamp and became half mad with rage. He determined to get hold of the lamp and again plunge Aladdin into the deepest poverty.

Unluckily, Aladdin had gone hunting for eight days, which gave the magician plenty of time. He bought a dozen copper lamps, put them into a basket, and went to the palace, crying, 'New lamps for old!' followed by a jeering crowd.

The princess, sitting in the hall of four-and-twenty windows, sent a slave to find out what the noise was about. The slave came back laughing, so the princess scolded her.

'Madam,' replied the slave, 'who can help laughing to see an old fool offering to exchange fine new lamps for old ones?'

Another slave, hearing this, said, 'There is an old one on the cornice there which he can have.'

Now this was the magic lamp, which Aladdin had left there, as he could not take it out hunting with him. The princess, not knowing its value, laughingly bade the slave take it and make the exchange. She went and said to the magician, 'Give me a new lamp for this.'

He snatched it and bade the slave take her choice, amid the jeers of the crowd. Little he cared, but left off crying his lamps, and went out of the city gates to a lonely place, where he remained till nightfall, when he pulled out the lamp and rubbed it. The genie appeared and at the magician's command carried him, together with the palace and the princess in it, to a lonely place in Africa.

Next morning the sultan looked out of the window toward Aladdin's palace and rubbed his eyes, for it was gone. He sent for the vizir and asked what had become of the palace. The vizir looked out, too, and was lost in astonishment. He again put it down to enchantment and this time the sultan believed him and sent thirty men on horseback to fetch Aladdin in chains. They met him riding home, bound him, and forced him to go with them on foot.

The people, however, who loved him, followed, armed, to see that he came to no harm. He was carried before the sultan, who ordered the executioner to cut off his head. The executioner made Aladdin kneel down, bandaged his eyes, and raised his scimitar to strike. At that instant the vizir, who saw that the crowd had forced their way into the courtyard and were scaling the walls to rescue Aladdin, called to the executioner to stay his hand. The people, indeed, looked so threatening that the sultan gave way and ordered Aladdin to be unbound, and pardoned him in the sight of the crowd.

Aladdin now begged to know what he had done.

'False wretch!' said the sultan, 'come hither,' and showed him from the window the place where his palace had stood. Aladdin was so amazed that he could not say a word.

'Where is the palace and my daughter?' demanded the sultan. 'For the first I am not so deeply concerned, but my daughter I must have and you must find her or lose your head.'

Aladdin begged for forty days in which to find her, promising if he failed, to return and suffer death at the sultan's pleasure. His prayer was granted, and he went forth sadly from the sultan's presence. For three days he wandered about like a madman, asking everyone what had become of his palace, but they only laughed and pitied him.

He came to the banks of a river and knelt down to say his prayers before throwing himself in. In so doing he rubbed the magic ring he still wore. The genie he had seen in the cave appeared and asked his will.

'Save my life, genie,' said Aladdin, 'and bring my palace back.'

'That is not in my power,' said the genie. 'I am only the slave of the ring, you must ask the slave of the lamp.'

'Even so,' said Aladdin, 'but thou canst take me to the palace, and set me down under my dear wife's window.' He at once found himself in Africa, under the window of the princess, where he fell asleep from sheer weariness.

He was awakened by the singing of the birds and his heart was lighter. He saw plainly that all his misfortunes were owing to the loss of the lamp and vainly wondered who had robbed him of it.

That morning the princess rose earlier than she had since she had been carried into Africa by the magician, whose company she was forced to endure once a day. She, however, treated him so harshly that he dared not live there altogether. As she was dressing, one of her women looked out and saw Aladdin. The princess ran and opened the window, and at the noise she made Aladdin looked up. She called him to come to her, and great was their joy at seeing each other again.

After he had kissed her Aladdin said, 'I beg of you, Princess, before we speak of anything else, for your own sake and mine, tell me what has become of an old lamp I left on the cornice in the hall of four-and-twenty windows, when I went hunting.'

'Alas,' she said, 'I am the innocent cause of our sorrows,' and told him of the exchange of the lamp.

'Now I know,' cried Aladdin, 'that we have to thank the African magician for this! Where is the lamp?'

'He carries it about with him,' said the princess. 'I know, for he pulled it out of his robe to show me. He wishes me to break my faith with you and marry him, saying that you were beheaded by my father's command. He is forever speaking ill of you, but I only reply by my tears. If I persist, I doubt not that he will use violence.'

Aladdin comforted her and left her for a while. He changed clothes with the first person he met in the town and, having bought a certain powder, returned to the princess, who let him in by a little side door.

'Put on your most beautiful dress,' he said to her, 'and receive the magician with smiles, leading him to believe that you have forgotten me. Invite him to sup with you and say you wish to taste the wine of his country. He will go for some and while he is gone I will tell you what to do.'

She listened carefully to Aladdin and, when he left her, arrayed herself gaily for the first time since she left China. She put on a girdle and headdress of diamonds, and seeing in a glass that she looked more beautiful than ever, received the magician, saying to his great amazement, 'I have made up my mind that Aladdin is dead and that all my tears will not bring him back to me, so I am resolved to mourn no more and therefore invite you to sup with me. But I am tired of the wines of China and would fain taste those of Africa.'

The magician flew to his cellar and the princess put the powder Aladdin had given her in her cup. When he returned she asked him to drink her health in the wine of Africa, handing him her cup in exchange for his as a sign she was reconciled to him.

Before drinking, the magician made her a speech in praise of her beauty, but the princess cut him short, saying, 'Let me drink first, and you shall say what you will afterward.' She set her cup to her lips while the magician drained his to the dregs and fell back lifeless.

The princess then opened the door to Aladdin and flung her arms round his neck, but Aladdin put her away, bidding her to leave him, as he had more to do. He then went to the dead magician, took the lamp out of his vest, and bade the genie carry the palace and all in it back to China. This was done, and the princess in her chamber only felt two slight shocks and little thought she was at home again.

The sultan, who was sitting in his closet, mourning for his lost daughter, happened to look up and rubbed his eyes, for there stood the palace as before! He hastened thither, and Aladdin received him in the hall of the four-and-twenty windows, with the princess at his side. Aladdin told him what had happened and showed him the dead body of the magician, that he might believe. A ten days' feast was proclaimed, and it seemed as if Aladdin might now live the rest of his life in peace; but it was not to be.

The African magician had a younger brother, who was, if possible, more wicked and cunning than himself. He traveled to China to avenge his brother's death and went to visit a pious woman called Fatima, thinking she might be of use to him. He entered her cell and clapped a dagger to her breast, telling her to rise and do his bidding on pain of death. He changed clothes with her, colored his face like hers, put on her veil, and murdered her that she might tell no tales.

Then he went toward the palace of Aladdin, and all the people, thinking he was the holy woman, gathered round him, kissing his hands and begging his blessing. When he reached the palace there was such a noise round him that the princess bade her slave look out of the window and ask what was the matter. The slave said it was the holy woman, curing people of their ailments by her touch, whereupon the princess, who had long desired to see Fatima, sent for her.

On coming to the princess, the magician offered up a prayer for her health and prosperity. When he had done the princess made him sit by her and begged him to stay with her always. The false Fatima, who wished for nothing better, consented but kept his veil down for fear of discovery. The princess showed him the hall and asked him what he thought of it.

'It is truly beautiful,' said the false Fatima. 'In my mind it wants but one thing.'

'And what is that?' said the princess.

'If only a roc's egg,' replied he, 'were hung up from the middle of this dome, it would be the wonder of the world.'

After this the princess could think of nothing but a roc's egg, and when Aladdin returned from hunting he found her in a very ill humor. He begged to know what was amiss, but she told him that all her pleasure in the hall was spoilt for the want of a roc's egg hanging from the dome.

'If that is all,' replied Aladdin, 'you shall soon be happy.'

He left her and rubbed the lamp, and when the genie appeared commanded him to bring a roc's egg. The genie gave such a loud and terrible shriek that the hall shook.

'Wretch,' he cried, 'is it not enough that I have done everything for you, but you must command me to bring my master and hang him up in the midst of this dome? You and your wife and your palace deserve to be burnt to ashes, but this request does not come from you but from the brother of the African magician whom you destroyed. He is now in your palace disguised as the holy woman—whom he murdered. He it was who put that wish into your wife's head. Take care of yourself, for he means to kill you.' So saying the genie disappeared.

Aladdin went back to the princess, saying his head ached and requesting that the holy Fatima should be fetched to lay her hands on it. But when the magician came near, Aladdin, seizing his dagger, pierced him to the heart.

'What have you done?' cried the princess. 'You have killed the holy woman!'

'Not so,' replied Aladdin, 'but a wicked magician,' and told her of how she had been deceived.

After this Aladdin and his wife lived in peace. He succeeded the sultan when he died, and reigned for many years, leaving behind him a long line of kings.

The Sixty-two Curses of
Caliph Arenschadd

by Patricia C. Wrede

Girls often are the protagonists in Patricia C. Wrede's many books and stories about wizards and magicians. This humorous tale pits a clever young girl against a powerful wizard with a nasty temper.

The worst thing about Caliph Arenschadd is that he's a wizard. At least that's what my Father says. Mother says the worst thing about the caliph is his temper, and that it's a good thing he's a wizard because if he were just an ordinary caliph he'd cut people's heads off when they displeased him, instead of cursing them.

I tend to agree with Mother. Cutting someone's head off is permanent; a curse, you can break. Of course, it usually takes something nasty and undignified to do it, but everything about curses is supposed to be unpleasant. Father doesn't see it that way. I think he'd prefer to be permanently dead than temporarily undignified.

Father is Caliph Arensdhadd's grand vizier, which is the reason all of us have opinions about the caliph and his curses. You see, a long time ago the caliph decided that he would lay a curse on anyone who displeased him, thus punishing the person and displaying the caliph's magical skill at the same time. (Mother also says Caliph Arenschadd likes to show off.) He found out very quickly that it was hard work coming up with a new curse every time someone made him unhappy, but by then he'd had a proclamation issued and he couldn't back down. So he shut himself up in one of the palace minarets for weeks, and when he came out he had a list of sixty-two curses he could cast at a moment's notice.

From then on, every time someone has done something the caliph doesn't like, the caliph has hauled out his list of curses and slapped one on whoever-it-was. Everyone starts at the first curse on the list and works their way down, so you can tell how long someone's been at court by whether his fingernails are three feet long or his eyelids stuck together. Father's been at court longer than anybody, so we've worked our way through an awful lot of curses.

I say *we* because Caliph Arenschadd doesn't just curse the particular person he's annoyed with. His curses get the person's whole family as well. I don't think that's fair, but Mother says it's just like him. She's been mad at the caliph ever since the eleventh curse, which made all three of us lose our voices for a week right in the middle of the Enchantresses and Sorceresses Annual Conference. Mother was supposed to present a paper, but she had to cancel it because she couldn't talk, and she's never forgiven Caliph Arenschadd.

I have to admit that some of the curses are fun. I enjoyed being bright green, and having monkey's paws was quite useful (I like climbing things, and the peaches had just turned ripe). Having my eyelids stuck together was boring, though. Things even out. It's best when you know what to expect, but after Father passed the forty-second curse there wasn't anyone ahead of us anymore to let us know what came next. We muddled through curses number forty-three through forty-seven with only a little more trouble than usual, and Caliph Arenschadd actually seemed pleased. We went for almost three months without any curses at all. Then one day Father came home from the palace looking grim and solemn.

Mother took one look at him and said, "O my husband and light of my eyes, not *again!*" in the exasperated tone she usually saves for me when I've put a rip in my skirts.

"I'm afraid so, Mirza," Father said. "He was in an awful mood today, but I simply couldn't put off asking him about those water rights for the caravaners any longer. So we're going to find out about number forty-eight." Father never says the word *curse* when he's talking about one of Caliph Arenschadd's; he only refers to them by number.

"Someone should take that caliph in hand," Mother said.

"Are you offering?" Father demanded.

I could tell there was an argument starting, so I got up and slipped out of the room before they could get me in on it. Mother and Father usually have an argument right after Caliph Arenschadd puts another curse on us; I think it relieves their feelings or something. It never lasts long, and as soon as they're finished they start looking for the way to break the curse. They're very good at it. Most of the curses last less than a week, and the longest one only went nine days. It's never much fun to be around for the arguing part, though, which is why I left.

I went to visit my best friend, Tumpkin. Tumpkin isn't his real name; I call him that because the first time I met him he wouldn't tell me who he was and I had to call him something. I ran into him in one of the private gardens at the palace, so I figured he was one of the caliph's pages, poking around where he wasn't supposed to be. He's about the same age as I am and he's nearsighted and sort of pudgy— just the kind of kid that gets picked on all the time. That's why I started calling him Tumpkin; it seemed to fit.

I didn't have to spend much time looking for Tumpkin on the first day of the forty-eighth curse. He was in his favorite spot, under a bush behind a gold garden seat. He heard me coming and looked up. When he saw who it was, he grinned at me in relief. "Imani!" he said. "I was just thinking about you."

"You ought to be thinking about your duties," I told him. "Someone's going to catch you shirking one of these days, and then you'll really be in trouble."

"Do *you* have to tell me what to do, too?" Tumpkin said grumpily. He waved in the direction of the palace. "You sound just like everyone in there."

"No, I sound like my father," I said, flopping down on the bench. "Sorry, it's been a rough day."

Tumpkin stopped looking grumpy and looked interested and sympathetic instead. "What happened?"

"Father picked up another curse, and he and Mother are arguing about it," I said.

"Another one?" Tumpkin said. "How many does that make?"

"Forty-eight," I said gloomily. "And we don't have even a tiny hint of what it is this time."

"I could try and find out for you," Tumpkin offered diffidently.

"Don't bother," I said. "Caliph Arenschadd takes better care of his list of curses than he does of the crown jewels. If you got caught, he'd probably slap four or five curses on you at once."

"He can't," Tumpkin said smugly. "They only work one at a time. And besides—"

"It's all *right*, Tumpkin," I said hastily. "We'll find out soon enough what number forty-eight is; you don't have to risk moving yourself up the list."

"Well, actually—" Tumpkin said, and stopped, looking very uncomfortable.

"Tumpkin!" I said, staring at him. "Do you mean to say the caliph has never put *any* of his curses on you?"

"I guess so," Tumpkin said. "I mean, no, he hasn't."

"You must be really good at keeping out of the way," I said with considerable admiration. "I've never heard of anyone who didn't make it through at least five curses during his first six weeks at court, and you've been around for nearly a year!"

"Longer than that, but I spend a lot of time out here." Tumpkin sounded more uncomfortable than ever, so I let the subject drop and went back to talking about my parents and curse number forty-eight. After a while Tumpkin relaxed, but he didn't make a second offer to sneak a look at Caliph Arenschadd's list of curses.

I stayed with Tumpkin for most of the afternoon, and there was still no sign of the curse when I started for home. That worried me. The longer Caliph Arenschadd's curses take to have an effect, the nastier they tend to be. I could tell that Mother and Father were worried, too; neither of them said much at dinner.

That evening I had the first dream. I was running and running through the night, and the wind was in my hair, and a silver moon shone high in the sky. I woke up just as I realized that I was running on four feet, like a dog. The thin crescent of the waxing moon was framed in the window at the foot of my bed. I sat staring at it for a long time before I fell asleep again.

I had the same dream the following night. I didn't worry about it much at the time; I was far more concerned about the forty-eighth curse. There still didn't seem to be any signs of it taking hold, at least none that I could see, and I'd never known one of Caliph Arenschadd's curses to take this long to affect someone. I stayed inside most of the time, figuring that I'd rather not have to try to get home with my feet turned backward or my knees stuck together if the curse hit all of a sudden. I didn't even go to the palace to see Tumpkin.

Two nights later, the dream got stronger. I ran and ran, with the wind down my back and the ground flowing past my feet and the sweet smell of grass at night in my nostrils. And a silver moon hung round and perfect in the sky above me.

I dreamed again the following night, and every night after that. Always it was the same dream, of running strong and free and wild in the wind and the moonlight. And always I woke with the moon shining through the window at the foot of my bed. At first it was just a crescent-shaped sliver of silver light, but every day the sliver grew wider. My dream became more and more vivid as the moon waxed, until I could close my eyes even in the day and see moonlight shining on sharp blades of grass. I began looking forward to the night, because I knew that then I would dream of running in the wind.

I didn't tell anyone about the dream. Mother and Father were still puzzling over the curse, and I didn't want to distract them. Besides, the dream was a private, special thing. I didn't want to share it with anyone, not even Tumpkin.

Not that I'd been seeing much of Tumpkin. At first I didn't go to the palace because I didn't want the curse to catch up with me while I was away from home. By the time I decided I didn't care about the curse, I didn't want to go anywhere. I probably would have stayed home forever if Mother hadn't chased me out after a week so she could work on some delicate enchantments.

Tumpkin was glad to see me. In fact, he practically pounced on me the minute I came into the garden. "You're back!" he said. "Did your parents figure out how to break it already? What was it, anyway?"

"What was what?" I asked crossly.

"The forty-eighth curse," Tumpkin said. He frowned worriedly at me. "Don't you remember?"

"Of course I remember!" I snapped. "No, Mother and Father haven't broken it, because they still don't know what it is."

"They don't know?"

"That's what I said. Didn't you listen? I think they should give up. If nothing's happened yet, the curse probably didn't take and we don't have anything to worry about."

"Something's happened," Tumpkin muttered.

"What did you say?" I said. "Why are you staring at me like that?"

"I said, something has happened," Tumpkin replied quickly. "Your eyebrows are getting thicker."

I snorted. "Well, if that's all curse forty-eight amounts to, I think Mother and Father should quit wasting time trying to break it. Who cares what my eyebrows look like?"

He didn't have an answer for that, so he told me about the latest book he was reading instead. I was feeling restless and impatient, but I knew Mother would be annoyed if I came home too early, so I made myself listen politely. At least I didn't have to say anything myself as long as Tumpkin was talking.

Tumpkin kept giving me speculative looks whenever he thought I wasn't looking. Finally I couldn't stand it any longer, and I left. I dawdled all the way home, and then when I arrived Mother and Father were talking and hardly even noticed me.

" . . . beyond the bounds of reason this time," Mother was saying as I came in. "Even you have to admit that."

"I'm sure the caliph has a reason," Father said in the stiff tone he uses when he knows he's wrong but can't say so.

"For a curse like this? We aren't talking about a petty inconvenience, Selim. This is a danger to everyone in the city. And there's no cure for lycanthropy."

"Caliph Arenschadd wouldn't endanger his people," Father said, even more stiffly than before.

"Maybe not if he thought about it first," Mother retorted. "But I don't think he's thought about this at all. Lycanthropy—"

"Imani!" Father said, spotting me at last. He shot Mother a look that was half warning, half relief. "When did you come in?"

"Just now," I said. I looked up at him. His eyebrows were getting thicker; they nearly met in the middle. Mother's were thicker, too. "What's lycanthropy?"

Mother and Father looked at each other. "You might as well explain, Selim," Mother said. "If we don't tell her, she'll just look it up in the dictionary."

Father sighed. "*Lycanthropy* means the assumption by human beings of the form and nature of wolves," he said, and looked down. "That's what the forty-eighth curse is, Imani. We've become werewolves."

"Well, I don't see what's so terrible about that," I said. I thought of my dream of running in the moonlight. "I think I'm going to like being a wolf."

They stared at me as if they'd never seen me before. Then Mother got a grim look on her face. "You'll find out soon enough," she said.

Mother was right. Two nights later I woke up well after midnight, feeling strange and tingly all over. I slipped out of bed and went out onto the balcony that overlooks our private garden. It was deep in shadow, because the moon was still on the other side of the house, rising. I could see the edge of the shadow creeping nearer as the moon rose, and I shivered in anticipation. I sat on the edge of the balcony, watching the line of moonlight come nearer, and waited.

The moon came over the domed roof of the house. I leaned into the silvery light and felt myself change. It was strange and exciting and scary all at once, though it didn't hurt at all. A moment later I stood on four paws and shook myself all over. Then I sat back and howled at the moon.

I heard answering howls from the corner of the house, and then, two adult wolves came padding into sight below my window. Mother had turned into a slender, coal black female; Father was dark gray and more solidly built. He had white hairs in his muzzle. I leaped down from the balcony to join them, and Mother cuffed me with her paw. I snarled, and she cuffed me again. Then Father made a sharp barking noise and we turned. Together we jumped over the garden wall and into the city streets.

The first thing I noticed was the smells. The whole city reeked of garbage and people and cooking spices and cats and perfumes. It was awful. I cringed and whined very softly. Mother bared her teeth in sympathy, and even Father coughed once or twice. Then we faded into the shadows and headed for the edge of town.

If it hadn't been for the smells, sneaking through the city like that would have been a lot of fun. As it was, I was glad we lived outside the city wall. Nobody saw us but a couple of dogs, and they ran when Father snarled at them. And then we passed the last of the houses and came out into the fields.

It was even better than my dream, to begin with. We ran and ran, and I could feel the wind in my fur and smell the fresh grass and the flowers and the little animals that had hidden as we approached. Now and then we'd stop and howl for the sheer joy of it. And all the while, the moonlight poured down around us in silver sheets.

Then we ran over the rabbit. Literally ran over it; the stupid thing was too scared to move when it heard us coming, and Father tripped over it. *Then* it ran, or rather, tried to. Mother caught it before it got very far. She trotted back with it while Father was picking himself up, and we split it between us.

The moon was getting low in the sky, and we began to feel a need to return home. I tried to fight it; I didn't want to go anywhere near that awful-smelling place again. But all I could do was whine and shuffle and edge closer. Mother cuffed me a couple of times because I wasn't going fast enough to suit her, and finally she nipped my tail. I yelped and gave up, and we ran back toward town.

As we passed the first house, we heard a baby crying inside. Mother and Father stopped and exchanged glances, just the way they'd done when they were people, Father looked up at the sky. The moon was close to setting; we had to get home. He growled and leaped forward, and Mother and I followed. A few minutes later, we reached our house and jumped over the garden wall.

Jumping back up to my balcony was harder than jumping down; I had to try twice, and I almost didn't make it in time. The moon set just as I scrabbled over the balcony rail, and I sprawled on the floor as a girl instead of a wolf. I sat up, remembering the wild run I'd just had.

Then I was sick to my stomach. Raw rabbit may be great when you're a wolf, but it's pretty disgusting to think about when you're a person.

I didn't get much sleep the rest of that night. I had too much to think about. I felt as if I'd been suckered: all those dreams about running in the moonlight, and not one about raw rabbit. I wondered how many other nasty surprises were in store for me. I thought of the way Mother and Father had looked at each other when they heard the baby cry. A cold shiver ran down my back, and I decided I didn't want to find out any more about being a werewolf. Then I remembered Mother's voice saying, "There's no cure for lycanthropy," and I shivered again.

Mother and Father were late to breakfast the next morning, and when they came in they were arguing. "It's the only thing we can do," Mother insisted. "And after last night, we have to do *something*. If Imani hadn't slowed us down coming home, that baby might have been—"

"There has to be another alternative," Father interrupted. He sounded desperate.

"Suggest one," Mother said. "Bearing in mind that the moon still isn't completely full, so we'll have at least another three or four nights like the last one unless we solve this problem right away."

I looked up. "Mother! You've found a way to break the curse?"

"Not quite," Mother said. "But we've come up with something we hope will work just as well."

I looked from Mother to Father. "What are you going to do?"

Father sighed. "I'm going to apologize to Caliph Arenschadd," he said reluctantly.

Mother insisted that both of us go along with Father to apologize to the caliph. I'm not sure whether she was worried about Father's ability to be tactful or whether she thought Caliph Arenschadd would be more likely to relent if he were faced with all three of us at once, but she was very firm. So I had to spend all morning having my hair washed and perfumed and my hands painted, and putting on my best clothes. Then I had to wait while Mother and Father finished doing the same things. I had to sit practically without moving so I wouldn't muss my hair or tear my skirts or rub any of the paint off my hands. I hate court appearances.

When we got to court, we were ushered into the caliph's presence for a private audience. Father bowed and started in on the obligatory courtesies. I didn't bother listening; all that O-Radiant-Light-of-the-Universe stuff bores me. I looked around the audience chamber instead, and that was why I saw Tumpkin sneaking in at the back. I stiffened. *Nobody* is supposed to be at a private audience except the caliph, whoever he's seeing, and the deaf guards the caliph hires especially for private audiences. Tumpkin would be in real trouble if anyone else noticed him.

Father finished his apology. "Very nicely put," the caliph said, smiling. "Accepted. Was there anything else?"

"O Commander of Legions, the curse yet remains," Father said delicately. "That is, the forty-eighth curse of your renowned list of curses, which you in your great and no-doubt-justified anger cast over me and my wife and daughter."

"Of course it remains," the caliph said. He sounded a little testy. "When I curse someone, they stay cursed until they break it."

"O Fountain of Wisdom, you have said it better than your humble servant ever could," Father replied. "That is our difficulty precisely. For nowhere in all the scrolls and tomes and works of magic is written the cure for your forty-eighth curse, and so we have come to you to beg your mercy."

"You want me to lift the curse, is that it?" the caliph said, frowning. "I don't like the idea; it would set a bad precedent."

Father wiped his forehead with the end of his sleeve. "O Auspicious and Merciful Caliph, what is wrong with establishing that a man's punishment ends when he humbly acknowledges his error? Display your justice before the whole court, and remove this dreadful curse from me and mine."

"Well . . ."

"O Just and Sagacious Monarch, let me add my entreaties to my husband's," Mother said. She stepped forward and knelt gracefully in front of Caliph Arenschadd. "Have pity! Or if your heart is hardened against us, think of your subjects who huddle within their doors each night in fear while wolves prowl the streets. Think of them, and lift the curse."

"Get up, Mirza, get up," the caliph said. "You know that sort of thing makes me uncomfortable."

"O Caliph of Compassion, I cannot," Mother said, bowing her head so he couldn't see the annoyance on her face. "My limbs will not support both my body and the curse that weighs on me. Lift the curse, and I will stand."

"I can't," said the caliph.

"What?" said Mother and Father together.

"I didn't work out how to lift all the curses I made up," Caliph Arenschadd said self-consciously. "I didn't think I needed to."

"You mean you were too lazy to bother," Mother muttered. Father gave her a horrified look, but fortunately Caliph Arenschadd hadn't heard.

"O Powerful Sovereign, what then are we to do?" Father said.

"You'll just have to find a way to break it yourselves," Caliph

Arenschadd said. He was trying to sound airy and unconcerned, but I could see that he was really embarrassed and worried. He wasn't much better than Father at pretending he was right when he knew he wasn't.

"But Commander of Legions, there *is* no cure for lycanthropy!" Father said.

"Not usually," Tumpkin said from behind the caliph. "But I think I know one that will work this time."

I shut my eyes, wondering what Caliph Arenschadd would do to Tumpkin for sneaking into a private audience and whether Tumpkin would be able to tell us how to break the curse before Caliph Arenschadd did it. Nothing happened, so after a moment I opened my eyes again. Mother, Father, and the caliph were all staring at Tumpkin, who looked pleased and proud and a little embarrassed by all the attention he was getting. Nobody seemed to be angry.

"My son, how can this be?" said Caliph Arenschadd. "You are still a beginner in wizardry. *How* can you do what my grand vizier"—he waved at Father—"his skilled and intelligent wife"—he gestured at Mother—"and myself cannot achieve?"

"It's not wizardry, Father," Tumpkin said. "It's just logic."

" 'Father'?" I said indignantly. "You mean you're the *prince*? Why didn't you *tell* me?"

"Imani!" Mother said sharply. "Mind your manners! Pray forgive the impulsiveness of her youth, Your Highness."

"It's all right," Tumpkin said. "We've known each other for a long time."

"You seem to have many secrets I was not aware of, my son," said Caliph Arenschadd, but he couldn't keep from sounding proud instead of reproachful. "Therefore, tell us how you think to break this curse.

"It's just a theory," Tumpkin said. "But you told me once that your curses only work one at a time. If you cast another curse on the grand vizier, wouldn't that take the place of this one?"

Mother and Father and Caliph Arenschadd all stared at Tumpkin some more. I stared, too, thinking furiously. If Caliph Arenschadd put the next curse on Father, we'd be in the same situation we'd been in when Father got the forty-eighth curse, not knowing what the curse was or how to break it. Curse forty-nine could be just as bad as all this werewolf business. But if somebody *else* made the caliph mad . . .

"That's the stupidest thing I've ever heard," I said loudly.

Everyone turned to look at me. Mother and Father looked horrified; the caliph looked startled and unbelieving. Tumpkin grinned, and I knew he'd figured out what I was up to.

"Imani!" Mother said automatically.

"What was that you said, girl?" Caliph Arenschadd asked ominously.

I swallowed hard and said, "I said that that list of curses was a stupid idea. And it was even stupider not to figure out how to break them all. Stupid and lazy. And sticking in a werewolf curse was the stupidest thing of all. *Everybody* knows you can't break a werewolf curse, but I bet you didn't even think about it."

I paused for breath. The caliph was positively purple with rage; the minute I stopped talking, he pointed three fingers at me and said something that sounded like "Donny-skazle frampwit!"

I looked at Mother and Father. They were bright green.

I heaved a sigh of relief; I hadn't been quite sure that Caliph Arenschadd would start over with the first curse on the list for me. I studied Mother and Father again more closely. Their eyebrows were back to normal.

"It worked!" I said. I *grinned* at Tumpkin, then looked at Caliph Arenschadd. "Sorry about that, Your Majesty; I was just trying to make you mad."

"Imani . . ." Mother sounded as if she didn't know whether to laugh or scold me.

I shrugged. "Well, *somebody* had to do it. And I wasn't sure it would work right if the caliph wasn't really mad at somebody. 'Scuse me, Your Majesty."

"I believe I understand," the caliph said slowly. He looked from me to Tumpkin and back. "Just don't do it again, young woman. Audience concluded."

I went straight outside and walked backward around the palace three times, and that took care of being green. Then Mother and Father took me home and fussed over me. Father said I was quick-witted enough to make a fine diplomat, if I'd just learn a little tact, and he'd start my training tomorrow. Mother said that Father was a fine one to talk about tact, and she wasn't going to let him waste my abilities in politics. She was going to start teaching me sorcery that evening.

I left them arguing and went to see Tumpkin. He was waiting in the garden, just as I expected.

"You took awhile getting here," he said.

"My parents wanted to argue," I explained. "Why didn't you tell me you were the prince?"

"I didn't think you'd believe me," Tumpkin said. "I don't look much like a prince, you know."

I snorted. "What's that got to do with anything?"

"It seems to matter a lot to some people," Tumpkin said, and neither of us said anything for a little.

"How did you figure out what to do about the curse?" I asked finally.

"I don't know," Tumpkin said. "I just thought about it a lot, after I found out it was a werewolf curse. I knew it was going to take something unusual to get rid of it, or your Mother and Father would have figured it out weeks ago."

"They'd never have thought of getting rid of one curse by replacing it with another," I said.

Tumpkin looked at me sidelong. "Was it very bad?" he asked.

"Some of it," I said shortly, thinking of the rabbit and the way the city streets smell to a wolf. Then I thought about running through the grass. "Some of it was wonderful."

Tumpkin didn't ask any more questions, and he never has. I think he understands, but he won't make me tell him about the details until I want to. That's why we're such good friends. I still call him Tumpkin, even though now I know he's really the prince.

A couple of weeks ago Caliph Arenschadd issued a new proclamation about punishing people who offend him. He's decided to turn them blue. The more times someone offends him, the bluer they get and the longer it lasts. Father talked him into it by pointing our that it's rather difficult to do most of the jobs in the palace with your eyelids stuck shut or three-foot fingernails, but no one will have to stop working just because he's blue. So no one else will ever work up to curse forty-eight, and we won't ever have to worry about werewolves in town.

Which is a good thing, I suppose. But sometimes I still dream about moonlight and the wind in my fur as I run, and run, and run forever through endless, sweet-smelling grass.

from

The Phoenix and the Carpet

by E. Nesbit

Edith Nesbit (1858–1924) wrote wonderful stories about children who follow their curiosity and who stumble into magical worlds. *The Phoenix and the Carpet* is the second book in the well-loved trilogy that began with *Five Children and It*. The children in this excerpt happen upon a magic carpet that conceals a strange egg.

It began with the day when it was almost the Fifth of November, and a doubt arose in some breast—Robert's, I fancy—as to the quality of the fireworks laid in for the Guy Fawkes celebration.

'They were jolly cheap,' said whoever it was, and I think it was Robert, 'and suppose they didn't go off on the night? Those Prosser kids would have something to snigger about then.'

'The ones *I* got are all right,' Jane said; 'I know they are, because the man at the shop said they were worth thribble the money—'

'I'm sure thribble isn't grammar,' Anthea said.

'Of course it isn't,' said Cyril; 'one word can't be grammar all by itself, so you needn't be so jolly clever.'

Anthea was rummaging in the corner-drawers of her mind for a very disagreeable answer, when she remembered what a wet day it was, and how the boys had been disappointed of that ride to London and back on the top of the tram, which their mother had promised them as a reward for not having once forgotten, for six whole days, to wipe their boots on the mat when they came home from school.

So Anthea only said, 'Don't be so jolly clever yourself, Squirrel. And the fireworks look all right, and you'll have the eightpence that your tram fares didn't cost to-day, to buy something more with. You ought to get a perfectly lovely Catharine wheel for eightpence.'

'I daresay,' said Cyril, coldly; 'but it's not *your* eight-pence anyhow—'

'But look here,' said Robert, 'really now, about the fireworks. We don't want to be disgraced before those kids next door. They think because they wear red plush on Sundays no one else is any good.'

'I wouldn't wear plush if it was ever so—unless it was black to be beheaded in, if I was Mary Queen of Scots,' said Anthea, with scorn.

Robert stuck steadily to his point. One great point about Robert is the steadiness with which he can stick.

'I think we ought to test them,' he said.

'You young duffer,' said Cyril, 'fireworks are like postage-stamps. You can only use them once.'

'What do you suppose it means by "Carter's tested seeds" in the advertisement?'

There was a blank silence. Then Cyril touched his forehead with his finger and shook his head.

'A little wrong here,' he said. 'I was always afraid of that with poor Robert. All that cleverness, you know, and being tops in algebra so often—it's bound to tell—'

'Dry up,' said Robert, fiercely. 'Don't you see? You can't *test* seeds if you do them *all*. You just take a few here and there, and if those grow you can feel pretty sure the others will be—what do you call it?—Father told me—"up to sample". Don't you think we ought to sample the fire-works? Just shut our eyes and each draw one out, and then try them.'

'But it's raining cats and dogs,' said Jane.

'And Queen Anne is dead,' rejoined Robert. No one was in a very good temper. 'We needn't go out to do them; we can just move back the table, and let them off on the old tea-tray we play toboggans with. I don't know what *you* think, but *I* think it's time we did something, and that would be really useful; because then we shouldn't just *hope* the fireworks would make those Prossers sit up—we should *know*.'

'It *would* be something to do,' Cyril owned with languid approval.

So the table was moved back. And then the hole in the carpet, that had been near the window till the carpet was turned round, showed most awfully. But Anthea stole out on tip-toe, and got the tray when cook wasn't looking, and brought it in and put it over the hole.

Then all the fireworks were put on the table, and each of the four children shut its eyes very tight and put out its hand and grasped something. Robert took a cracker, Cyril and Anthea had Roman candles; but Jane's fat paw closed on the gem of the whole collection, the Jack-in-the-box that had cost two shillings, and one at least of the party—I will not say which, because it was sorry afterwards—declared that Jane had done it on purpose. Nobody was pleased. For the worst of it was that these four children, with a very proper dislike of anything even faintly bordering on the sneakish, had a law, unalterable as those of the Medes and Persians, that one had to stand by the results of a toss-up, or a drawing of lots, or any other appeal to chance, however much one might happen to dislike the way things were turning out.

'I didn't mean to,' said Jane, near tears. 'I don't care, I'll draw another—'

'You know jolly well you can't,' said Cyril, bitterly. 'It's settled. It's Medium and Persian. You've done it, and you'll have to stand by it—and us too, worse luck. Never mind. *You'll* have your pocket-money before the Fifth. Anyway, we'll have the Jack-in-the-box *last*, and get the most out of it we can.'

So the cracker and the Roman candles were lighted, and they were all that could be expected for the money; but when it came to the Jack-in-the-box it simply sat in the tray and laughed at them, as Cyril said. They tried to light it with paper and they tried to light it with matches; they tried to light it with Vesuvian fuses from the pocket of father's second-best overcoat that was hanging in the hall. And then Anthea slipped away to the cupboard under the stairs where the brooms and dustpans were kept, and the rosiny firelighters that smell so nice and like the woods where pine-trees grow, and the old newspapers, and the bees-wax and turpentine, and the horrid stiff dark rags that are used for cleaning brass and furniture, and the paraffin for the lamps. She came back with a little pot that had once cost sevenpence-halfpenny when it was full of red-currant jelly; but the jelly had been all eaten long ago, and now Anthea had filled the jar with paraffin. She came in, and she threw the paraffin over the tray just at the moment when Cyril was trying with the twenty-third match to light the Jack-in-the-box. The Jack-in-the-box did not catch fire any more than usual, but the paraffin acted quite differently, and in an instant a hot flash of flame leapt up and burnt off Cyril's eyelashes, and scorched the faces of all four before they could spring back. They backed, in four instantaneous bounds, as far as they could, which was to the wall, and the pillar of fire reached from floor to ceiling.

'My hat,' said Cyril, with emotion, 'you've done it this time, Anthea.'

The flame was spreading out under the ceiling like the rose of fire in Mr Rider Haggard's exciting story about Allan Quatermain. Robert and Cyril saw that no time was to be lost. They turned up the edges of the carpet, and kicked them over the tray. This cut off the column of fire, and it disappeared and there was nothing left but smoke and a dreadful smell of lamps that have been turned too low. All hands now rushed to the rescue, and the paraffin fire was only a bundle of trampled carpet, when suddenly a sharp crack beneath their feet made the amateur firemen start back. Another crack—the carpet moved as if it had had a cat wrapped in it; the Jack-in-the-box had at last allowed itself to be lighted, and it was going off with desperate violence inside the carpet.

Robert, with the air of one doing the only possible thing, rushed to the window and opened it. Anthea screamed, Jane burst into tears, and Cyril turned the table wrong way up on top of the carpet heap. But the firework went on, banging and bursting and spluttering even underneath the table.

Next moment mother rushed in, attracted by the howls of Anthea, and in a few moments the firework desisted and there was a dead silence, and the children stood looking at each other's black faces, and, out of the corners of their eyes, at mother's white one.

The fact that the nursery carpet was ruined occasioned but little surprise, nor was any one really astonished that bed should prove the immediate end of the adventure. It has been said that all roads lead to Rome; this may be true, but at any rate, in early youth I am quite sure that many roads lead to *bed*, and stop there—or *you* do.

The rest of the fireworks were confiscated, and mother was not pleased when father let them off himself in the back garden, though he said, 'Well, how else can you get rid of them, my dear?'

You see, father had forgotten that the children were in disgrace, and that their bedroom windows looked out on to the back garden. So that they all saw the fireworks most beautifully, and admired the skill with which father handled them.

Next day all was forgotten and forgiven; only the nursery had to be deeply cleaned (like spring-cleaning), and the ceiling had to be whitewashed.

And mother went out; and just at tea-time next day a man came with a rolled-up carpet, and father paid him, and mother said—

'If the carpet isn't in good condition, you know, I shall expect you to change it.' And the man replied—

'There ain't a thread gone in it nowhere, mum. It's a bargain, if ever there was one, and I'm more'n 'arf sorry I let it go at the price; but we can't resist the lydies, can we, sir?' and he winked at father and went away.

Then the carpet was put down in the nursery, and sure enough there wasn't a hole in it anywhere.

As the last fold was unrolled something hard and loud-sounding bumped out of it and trundled along the nursery floor. All the children scrambled for it, and Cyril got it. He took it to the gas. It was shaped like an egg, very yellow and shiny, half-transparent, and it had an odd sort of light in it that changed as you held it in different ways. It was as though it was an egg with a yolk of pale fire that just showed through the stone.

'I *may* keep it, mayn't I, mother?' Cyril asked. And of course mother said no; they must take it back to the man who had brought the carpet, because she had only paid for a carpet, and not for a stone egg with a fiery yolk to it.

So she told them where the shop was, and it was in the Kentish Town Road, not far from the hotel that is called the Bull and Gate. It was a poky little shop, and the man was arranging furniture outside on the pavement very cunningly, so that the more broken parts should show as little as possible. And directly he saw the children he knew them again, and he began at once, without giving them a chance to speak.

'No you don't,' he cried loudly; 'I ain't a-goin' to take back no carpets, so don't you make no bloomin' errer. A bargain's a bargain, and the carpet's puffik throughout.'

'We don't want you to take it back,' said Cyril; 'but we found something in it.'

'It must have got into it up at your place, then,' said the man, with indignant promptness, 'for there ain't nothing in nothing as I sell. It's all as clean as a whistle.'

'I never said it wasn't *clean*,' said Cyril, 'but—'

'Oh, if it's *moths*,' said the man, 'that's easy cured with borax. But I expect it was only an odd one. I tell you the carpet's good through and through. It hadn't got no moths when it left my 'ands—not so much as an hegg.'

'But that's just it,' interrupted Jane; 'there *was* so much as an egg.'

The man made a sort of rush at the children and stamped his foot.

'Clear out, I say!' he shouted, 'or I'll call for the police. A nice thing for customers to 'ear you a-coming 'ere a-charging me with finding things in goods what I sells. 'Ere, be off, afore I sends you off with a flea in your ears. Hi! Constable—'

The children fled, and they think, and their father thinks, that they couldn't have done anything else. Mother has her own opinion. But father said they might keep the egg.

'The man certainly didn't know the egg was there when he brought the carpet,' said he, 'any more than your mother did, and we've as much right to it as he had.'

So the egg was put on the mantelpiece, where it quite brightened up the dingy nursery. The nursery was dingy, because it was a basement room, and its windows looked out on a stone area with a rockery made of clinkers facing the windows. Nothing grew in the rockery except London pride and snails.

The room had been described in the house agent's list as a 'convenient breakfast-room in basement,' and in the daytime it was rather dark. This did not matter so much in the evenings when the gas was alight, but then it was in the evening that the blackbeetles got so sociable, and used to come out of the low cupboards on each side of the fireplace where their homes were, and try to make friends with the children. At least, I suppose that was what they wanted, but the children never would.

On the Fifth of November father and mother went to the theatre, and the children were not happy, because the Prossers next door had lots of fireworks and they had none.

They were not even allowed to have a bonfire in the garden.

'No more playing with fire, thank you,' was father's answer, when they asked him.

When the baby had been put to bed the children sat sadly round the fire in the nursery.

'I'm beastly bored,' said Robert.

'Let's talk about the Psammead,' said Anthea, who generally tried to give the conversation a cheerful turn.

'What's the good of *talking*?' said Cyril. 'What I want is for something to happen. It's awfully stuffy for a chap not to be allowed out in the evenings. There's simply nothing to do when you've got through your homers.'

Jane finished the last of her home-lessons and shut the book with a bang.

'We've got the pleasure of memory,' said she. 'Just think of last holidays.'

Last holidays, indeed, offered something to think of—for they had been spent in the country at a white house between a sand-pit and a gravel-pit, and things had happened. The children had found a Psammead, or sand-fairy, and it had let them have anything they wished for—just exactly anything, with no bother about its not being really for their good, or anything like that. And if you want to know what kind of things they wished for, and how their wishes turned out you can read it all in a book called *Five Children and It* (*It* was the Psammead). If you've not read it, perhaps I ought to tell you that the fifth child was the baby brother, who was called the Lamb, because the first thing he ever said was 'Baa!' and that the other children were not particularly handsome, nor were they extra clever, nor extraordinarily good. But they were not bad sorts on the whole; in fact, they were rather like you.

'I don't want to think about the pleasures of memory,' said Cyril; 'I want some more things to happen.'

'We're very much luckier than any one else, as it is,' said Jane. 'Why, no one else ever found a Psammead. We ought to be grateful.'

'Why shouldn't we *go on* being, though?' Cyril asked—'lucky, I mean; not grateful. Why's it all got to stop?'

'Perhaps something will happen,' said Anthea, comfortably. 'Do you know, sometimes I think we are the sort of people that things *do* happen to.'

'It's like that in history,' said Jane: 'some kings are full of interesting things, and others—nothing ever happens to them, except their being born and crowned and buried, and sometimes not that.'

'I think Panther's right,' said Cyril: 'I think we are the sort of people things do happen to. I have a sort of feeling things would happen right enough if we could only give them a shove. It just wants something to start it. That's all.'

'I wish they taught magic at school,' Jane sighed. 'I believe if we could do a little magic it might make something happen.'

'I wonder how you begin?' Robert looked round the room, but he got no ideas from the faded green curtains, or the drab Venetian blinds, or the worn brown oil-cloth on the floor. Even the new carpet suggested nothing, though its pattern was a very wonderful one, and always seemed as though it were just going to make you think of something.

'I could begin right enough,' said Anthea; 'I've read lots about it. But I believe it's wrong in the Bible.'

'It's only wrong in the Bible because people wanted to hurt other people. I don't see how things can be wrong unless they hurt somebody, and we don't want to hurt anybody; and what's more, we jolly well couldn't if we tried. Let's get the *Ingoldsby Legends*. There's a thing about Abracadabra there,' said Cyril, yawning. 'We may as well play at magic. Let's be Knights Templars. They were awfully gone on magic. They used to work spells or something with a goat and a goose. Father says so.'

'Well, that's all right,' said Robert, unkindly; 'you can play the goat right enough, and Jane knows how to be a goose.'

'I'll get *Ingoldsby*,' said Anthea, hastily. 'You turn up the hearthrug.'

So they traced strange figures on the linoleum, where the hearthrug had kept it clean. They traced them with chalk that Robert had nicked from the top of the mathematical master's desk at school. You know, of course, that it is stealing to take a new stick of chalk, but it is not wrong to take a broken piece, so long as you only take one. (I do not know the reason of this rule, nor who made it.) And they chanted all the gloomiest songs they could think of. And, of course, nothing happened. So then Anthea said, 'I'm sure a magic fire ought to be made of sweet-smelling wood, and have magic gums and essences and things in it.'

'I don't know any sweet-smelling wood, except cedar,' said Robert; 'but I've got some ends of cedar-wood lead pencil.'

So they burned the ends of lead pencil. And still nothing happened.

'Let's burn some of the eucalyptus oil we have for our colds,' said Anthea.

And they did. It certainly smelt very strong. And they burned lumps of camphor out of the big chest. It was very bright, and made a horrid black smoke, which looked very magical. But still nothing happened. Then they got some clean tea-cloths from the dresser drawer in the kitchen, and waved them over the magic chalk-tracings, and sang 'The Hymn of the Moravian Nuns at Bethlehem', which is very impressive. And still nothing happened. So they waved more and more wildly, and Robert's tea-cloth caught the golden egg and whisked it off the mantelpiece, and it fell into the fender and rolled under the grate.

'Oh, crikey!' said more than one voice.

And every one instantly fell down flat on its front to look under the grate, and there lay the egg, glowing in a nest of hot ashes.

'It's not smashed, anyhow,' said Robert, and he put his hand under the grate and picked up the egg. But the egg was much hotter than any one would have believed it could possibly get in such a short time, and Robert had to drop it with a cry of 'Brother!' It fell on the top bar of the grate, and bounced right into the glowing red-hot fire.

'The tongs!' cried Anthea. But, alas, no one could remember where they were. Every one had forgotten that the tongs had last been used to fish up the doll's teapot from the bottom of the water-butt, where the Lamb had dropped it. So the nursery tongs were resting between the water-butt and the dustbin, and cook refused to lend the kitchen ones.

'Never mind' said Robert. 'We'll get it out with the poker and the shovel.'

'Oh, stop,' cried Anthea. 'Look at it! Look! look! look! I do believe something *is* going to happen!'

For the egg was now red-hot, and inside it something was moving. Next moment there was a soft cracking sound; the egg burst in two, and out of it came a flame-coloured bird. It rested a moment among the flames, and as it rested there the four children could see it growing bigger and bigger under their eyes.

Every mouth was a-gape, every eye a-goggle.

The bird rose in its nest of fire, stretched its wings, and flew out into the room. It flew round and round, and round again, and where it passed the air was warm. Then it perched on the fender. The children looked at each other. Then Cyril put out a hand towards the bird. It put its head on one side and looked up at him, as you may have seen a parrot do when it is just going to speak, so that the children were hardly astonished at all when it said, 'Be careful; I am not nearly cool yet.'

They were not astonished, but they were very, very much interested.

They looked at the bird, and it was certainly worth looking at. Its feathers were like gold. It was about as large as a bantam, only its beak was not at all bantam-shaped. 'I believe I know what it is,' said Robert. 'I've seen a picture—'

He hurried away. A hasty dash and scramble among the papers on father's study table yielded, as the sum-books say, 'the desired result'. But when he came back into the room holding out a paper, and crying, 'I say, look here,' the others all said, 'Hush!' and he hushed obediently and instantly, for the bird was speaking.

'Which of you,' it was saying, 'put the egg into the fire?'

'He did,' said three voices, and three fingers pointed at Robert.

The bird bowed; at least it was more like that than anything else.

'I am your grateful debtor,' it said with a high-bred air.

The children were all choking with wonder and curiosity—all except Robert. He held the paper in his hand, and he *knew*. He said so. He said—

'*I* know who you are.'

And he opened and displayed a printed paper, at the head of which was a little picture of a bird sitting in a nest of flames.

'You are the Phoenix,' said Robert; and the bird was quite pleased.

'My fame has lived then for two thousand years,' it said. 'Allow me to look at my portrait.'

It looked at the page which Robert, kneeling down, spread out in the fender, and said—

'It's not a flattering likeness. . . . And what are these characters?' it asked, pointing to the printed part.

'Oh, that's all dullish; it's not much about *you*, you know,' said Cyril, with unconscious politeness; 'but you're in lots of books—'

'With portraits?' asked the Phoenix.

'Well, no,' said Cyril; 'in fact, I don't think I ever saw any portrait of you but that one, but I can read you something about yourself, if you like.'

The Phoenix nodded, and Cyril went off and fetched Volume X of the old *Encyclopedia*, and on page 246 he found the following:—

'Phoenix—in ornithology, a fabulous bird of antiquity.'

'Antiquity is quite correct,' said the Phoenix, 'but fabulous—well, do I look it?'

Every one shook its head. Cyril went on—

'The ancients speak of this bird as single, or the only one of its kind.'

'That's right enough,' said the Phoenix.

'They describe it as about the size of an eagle.'

'Eagles are of different sizes,' said the Phoenix; 'it's not at all a good description.'

All the children were kneeling on the hearth-rug, to be as near the Phoenix as possible.

'You'll boil your brains,' it said. 'Look out, I'm nearly cool now;' and with a whirr of golden wings it fluttered from the fender to the table. It was so nearly cool that there was only a very faint smell of burning when it had settled itself on the table-cloth.

'It's only a very little scorched,' said the Phoenix, apologetically; 'it will come out in the wash. Please go on reading.'

The children gathered round the table.

'The size of an eagle,' Cyril went on, 'its head finely crested with a beautiful plumage, its neck covered with feathers of a gold colour, and the rest of its body purple; only the tail white, and the eyes sparkling like stars. They say that it lives about five hundred years in the wilderness, and when advanced in age it builds itself a pile of sweet wood and aromatic gums, fires it with the wafting of its wings, and thus burns itself; and that from its ashes arises a worm, which in time grows up to be a Phoenix. Hence the Phoenicians gave—'

'Never mind what they gave,' said the Phoenix, ruffling its golden feathers. 'They never gave much, anyway; they always were people who gave nothing for nothing. That book ought to be destroyed. It's most inaccurate. The rest of my body was *never* purple, and as for my tail— well, I simply ask you, *is* it white?'

It turned round and gravely presented its golden tail to the children.

'No, it's not,' said everybody.

'No, and it never was,' said the Phoenix. 'And that about the worm is just a vulgar insult. The Phoenix has an egg, like all respectable birds.

It makes a pile—that part's all right—and it lays its egg, and it burns itself; and it goes to sleep and wakes up in its egg, and comes out and goes on living again, and so on for ever and ever. I can't tell you how weary I got of it—such a restless existence; no repose.'

'But how did your egg get *here?*' asked Anthea.

'Ah, that's my life-secret,' said the Phoenix. 'I couldn't tell it to any one who wasn't really sympathetic. I've always been a misunderstood bird. You can tell that by what they say about the worm. I might tell *you,*' it went on, looking at Robert with eyes that were indeed starry. '*You* put me on the fire—'

Robert looked uncomfortable.

'The rest of us made the fire of sweet-scented woods and gums, though,' said Cyril.

'And—and it was an accident my putting you on the fire,' said Robert, telling the truth with some difficulty, for he did not know how the Phoenix might take it. It took it in the most unexpected manner.

'Your candid avowal,' it said, 'removes my last scruple. I will tell you my story.'

'And you won't vanish, or anything sudden will you?' asked Anthea, anxiously.

'Why?' it asked, puffing out the golden feathers, 'do you wish me to stay here?'

'Oh *yes,*' said every one, with unmistakable sincerity.

'Why?' asked the Phoenix again, looking modestly at the table-cloth.

'Because,' said every one at once, and then stopped short; only Jane added after a pause, 'you are the most beautiful person we've ever seen.'

'You are a sensible child,' said the Phoenix, 'and I will *not* vanish or anything sudden. And I will tell you my tale. I had resided, as your book says, for many thousand years in the wilderness, which is a large, quiet place with very little really good society, and I was becoming weary of the monotony of my existence. But I acquired the habit of laying my egg and burning myself every five hundred years—and you know how difficult it is to break yourself of a habit.'

'Yes,' said Cyril; 'Jane used to bite her nails.'

'But I broke myself of it,' urged Jane, rather hurt, 'you know I did.'

'Not till they put bitter aloes on them,' said Cyril.

'I doubt,' said the bird, gravely, 'whether even bitter aloes (the aloe, by the way, has a bad habit of its own, which it might well cure before seeking to cure others; I allude to its indolent practice of flowering but once a century), I doubt whether even bitter aloes could have cured *me*. But I *was* cured. I awoke one morning from a feverish dream—it was getting near the time for me to lay that tiresome fire and lay that tedious egg upon it—and I saw two people, a man and a woman. They were sitting on a carpet—and when I accosted them civilly they narrated to me their life-story, which, as you have not yet heard it, I will now proceed to relate. They were a prince and princess, and the story of their parents was one which I am sure you will like to hear. In early youth the mother of the princess happened to hear the story of a certain enchanter, and in that story I am sure you will be interested. The enchanter—'

'Oh, please don't,' said Anthea. 'I can't understand all these beginnings of stories, and you seem to be getting deeper and deeper in them every minute. Do tell us your *own* story. That's what we really want to hear.'

'Well,' said the Phoenix, seeming on the whole rather flattered, 'to cut about seventy long stories short (though *I* had to listen to them all—but to be sure in the wilderness there is plenty of time), this prince and princess were so fond of each other that they did not want any one else, and the enchanter—don't be alarmed, I won't go into his history—had given them a magic carpet (you've heard of a magic carpet?), and they had just sat on it and told it to take them right away from every one—and it had brought them to the wilderness. And as they meant to stay there they had no further use for the carpet, so they gave it to me. That was indeed the chance of a lifetime!'

'I don't see what you wanted with a carpet,' said Jane, 'when you've got those lovely wings.'

'They *are* nice wings, aren't they?' said the Phoenix, simpering and spreading them out. 'Well, I got the prince to lay out the carpet, and I laid my egg on it; then I said to the carpet, "Now, my excellent carpet, prove your worth. Take that egg somewhere where it can't be hatched for two thousand years, and where, when that time's up, some one will light a fire of sweet wood and aromatic gums, and put the egg in to hatch;" and you see it's all come out exactly as I said. The words were no sooner out of my beak than egg and carpet disappeared. The royal lovers assisted to arrange my pile, and soothed my last moments. I burnt myself up and knew no more till I awoke on yonder altar.'

It pointed its claw at the grate.

'But the carpet,' said Robert, 'the magic carpet that takes you anywhere you wish. What became of that?'

'Oh, *that?*' said the Phoenix, carelessly—'I should say that that is the carpet. I remember the pattern perfectly.'

It pointed as it spoke to the floor, where lay the carpet which mother had bought in the Kentish Town Road for twenty-two shillings and ninepence.

At that instant father's latch-key was heard in the door.

'*Oh,*' whispered Cyril, 'now we shall catch it for not being in bed!'

'Wish yourself there,' said the Phoenix, in a hurried whisper, 'and then wish the carpet back in its place.'

No sooner said than done. It made one a little giddy, certainly, and a little breathless; but when things seemed right way up again, there the children were, in bed, and the lights were out.

They heard the soft voice of the Phoenix through the darkness.

'I shall sleep on the cornice above your curtains,' it said. 'Please don't mention me to your kinsfolk.'

'Not much good,' said Robert, 'they'd never believe us. I say,' he called through the half-open door to the girls; 'talk about adventures and things happening. We ought to be able to get some fun out of a magic carpet *and* a Phoenix.'

'Rather,' said the girls, in bed.

'Children,' said father, on the stairs, 'go to sleep at once. What do you mean by talking at this time of night?'

No answer was expected to this question, but under the bedclothes Cyril murmured one.

'Mean?' he said. 'Don't know what we mean. I don't know what *any-thing* means—'

'But we've got a magic carpet *and* a Phoenix,' said Robert.

'You'll get something else if father comes in and catches you,' said Cyril. 'Shut up, I tell you.'

Robert shut up. But he knew as well as you do that the adventures of that carpet and that Phoenix were only just beginning.

Father and mother had not the least idea of what had happened in their absence. This is often the case, even when there are no magic carpets or Phoenixes in the house.

Baba Yaga and the Sorcerer's Son

by Patricia A. McKillip

Contemporary fantasy writer Patricia A. McKillip's story is about Baba Yaga, a witch from traditional Russian folklore whose hut stands on two enormous chicken legs.

Long ago, in a vast and faraway country, there lived a witch named Baba Yaga. She was sometimes very wise and sometimes very wicked, and she was so ugly mules fainted at the sight of her. Most of the time she dwelled in her little house in the deep woods. Occasionally, she dipped down Underearth as easily as if the earth were the sea and the sea were air: down to the World Beneath the Wood.

One morning when she was vacationing Underground, she had an argument with her house, which was turning itself around and around on its chicken legs and wouldn't stop. Baba Yaga, who had stepped outside to find a plump morsel of something for breakfast, couldn't get back in her door. She had given her house chicken legs to cause wonder and consternation in passersby. Nobody was around now but Baba Yaga, her temper simmering like a soup pot, and yet there it was, turning and swaying on its great bony legs in the greeny, underwater light of Underearth, looking for all the world like a demented chicken watching a beetle run circles around it.

"Stop that!" Baba Yaga shouted furiously. "Stop that at once!" Then she made her voice sweet and said the words that you are supposed to say if you come across her house unexpectedly in the forest, and are brave or foolish or desperate enough to want in: "Little house, turn your back to the trees, and open your door to me." But the house, bewildered perhaps by being surrounded by trees, continued turning and turning. Baba Yaga scolded it until her voice was hoarse and flapped her apron at it as if it really were a chicken. "You stupid house!" she raged, for she still hadn't had her breakfast, or even her morning tea. And then, if that wasn't bad enough, the roof of the world opened up at that moment and hurled something big and dark down at her that missed her by inches.

She was so startled the warts nearly jumped off her nose. She peered down at it, blinking, fumbling in her apron for her spectacles.

A young man lay at her feet. He had black hair and black eyelashes; he was dressed in a dark robe with little bits of mirrors and star dust and cat hairs all over it. He looked dead, but as she stared, a little color came back into his waxen face. His eyes fluttered open.

He gave a good yell, for Baba Yaga at her best caused strong windows to crack and fall out of their frames. Baba Yaga lifted her foot and kicked at a huge chicken foot that threatened to step on him, and he yelled again. By then he had air back in his lungs. He rolled and crouched, staring at the witch and trembling.

Then he took a good look at the house. "Oh," he sighed, "it's you, Baba Yaga." He felt himself: neck bone, shin bone. "Am I still alive?"

"Not for long," Baba Yaga said grimly. "You nearly squashed me flat."

He was silent then, huddled in his robe, eyeing her warily. *Baba Yaga,* mothers said to their children in the world above, *will eat you if you don't eat your supper.* He, unimpressed with the warning, had always fed his peas to the dog anyway. And now look. Here she was as promised, payment for thousands of uneaten peas. Baba Yaga's green, prismed glasses glittered at him like a fly's eyes. He bowed his head.

"Oh, well," he said. "If you don't kill me, my father will. I just blew up his house."

Baba Yaga's spectacles slid to the end of her nose. She said grumpily, "Was it spinning?"

"No. It was just sitting there, being a house, with all its cups in the cupboard, and the potatoes growing eyes in the bin, and dust making fuzzballs under the bed, just doing what houses do—"

"Ha!"

"And I was just . . . experimenting a little, with some magic in the cauldron. Baba Yaga, I swear I did exactly what the Book said to do, except we ran out of Dragon root, so I tossed in some Mandragora root instead—I thought it'd be a good substitute—but . . ." His black eyes widened at the memory. "All of a sudden bricks and boards and I went flying, and here I . . . here I . . . Where am I, anyway?"

"Underground."

"Really?" he whispered without sound. "I blew myself that far. Why," he added a breath later, distracted, "is your house doing that?"

"I don't know."

"Well, isn't—doesn't that make it difficult for you to get in the door?"

"Yes."

"Well, then, why are you letting it—When you talk through your teeth like that, does that mean you're angry?"

Baba Yaga shrieked like a hundred boiling teakettles. The young man's head disappeared. The house continued to spin.

The witch caught her breath. She felt a little better, and there was the matter of the Sorcerer's son's missing head to contemplate. She waited. A wind full of pale colors and light voices sighed through the trees. She smelled roses from somewhere, maybe from a dream somebody was having about the Underwood. The head emerged slowly, like a turtle's head, from the neck of the dark robe. The young man looked pale again, uneasy, but his eyes held a familiar, desperate glint. "Baba Yaga. You must help me. I'll help you."

She snorted. "Do what? Blow my house up?"

"No. Please. You're terrible and capricious, but you know things. You can help me. Down here, rules blur into each other. A dream is real; a word spoken here makes a shape in the world above. If you could just make things go backward, just for a few moments, back to the moment before I reached for the Mandragora root—before I destroyed my father's house—if it could just be whole again—"

"Bosh," Baba Yaga said rudely. "You would blow it up all over again."

"Would I?"

"Besides, what do you think I am? I can't even get my house to stop spinning, and you want me to unspin the world."

He sighed. "Then what am I to do? Baba Yaga, I love my father and I'm very sorry I blew up his house. Isn't there anything I can do? I just—Everything is gone. All his sorcery books, all his lovely precious jars and bottles, potions and elixirs, his dragon tooth, his giant's thumbnail, his narwhal tusk—even his five-hundred-year-old cauldron blew into bits. Not to mention the cups, the beds, his favorite chair, and his cats—if I landed down here, they probably flew clear to China. Baba Yaga, he loves me, I know, but if I were him I might turn me into a toad or something for a couple of months—Maybe I should just run away to sea. Please?"

Baba Yaga felt momentarily dizzy, as if all his babbling were sailing around her head. She said crossly, "What could you possibly do? I don't want my wood stove and my tea towels blown to China."

"I promise, I promise. . . ." The young man got to his feet, stood blinking at the house twirling precariously on its hen legs among the silent, blue-black trees. It was an amazing sight, one he could tell his children and his grandchildren about if he managed to stay alive that long. *When I was a young man, I fell off the world, down, down to the Underneath, where I met the great witch Baba Yaga. She needed help and only I could help her. . . .*

"Little house," he called. "Little house, turn your back to the trees and open your door to me."

The house turned its feet forward, nestled down like a hen over an egg, opened its door, and stopped moving.

Baba Yaga opened her mouth and closed it, opened her mouth and closed it, looking, for a moment, like the ugliest fish in the world. "How did you—how did you—"

The young man shrugged. "It always works in the stories."

Baba Yaga closed her mouth. She shoved her glasses back up her nose and gave the young man, and then the house, an icy, glittering-green glare. She marched into her house without a word and slammed the door.

"Baba Yaga!" the young man cried. "Please!"

A terrible noise rumbled through the trees then. It was thunder; it was an earthquake; it was a voice so loud it made the grass flatten itself and turn silvery, as under a wind. The young man, his robe puffed and tugged every direction, was blown like a leaf against the side of the house.

"Johann!" the voice said. "Johann!"

The young man squeaked.

The wind died. Baba Yaga's head sprang out of her door like a cuckoo in a clock. "NOW WHAT!"

The young man, trembling again, his face white as tallow, gave a whistle of awe. "My father."

Baba Yaga squinted Upward from behind her prisms. She gave a sharp, decisive sniff, took her spectacles off. Then she took her apron off. She disappeared inside once more. When she came out again, she was riding her mortar and pestle.

The young man goggled. Baba Yaga's house slowly turning on its chicken legs among the trees was an astonishing sight indeed. But Baba Yaga whisking through the air in the bowl she used to grind garlic, rapping its side briskly with the pestle as if it were a horse, made the young sorcerer so giddy he couldn't even tell if the mortar had grown huge, or if Baba Yaga had suddenly gotten very small.

"Come!" she shouted, thrusting a broom handle over the side. He caught it; she pulled him up, dumped him on the bottom of the bowl, and yelled to the mortar, "Geeee-ha!"

Off they went.

It was a wondrous ride. The mortar was so fast it left streaks in the air, which the young man swept away, like clouds, with the broom. Each time he swept he saw a different marvel, far below, like another piece of the rich tapestry of the Underwood. He saw twelve white swans light on a stone in the middle of a darkening sea and turn into princes. He saw an old man standing on a cliff, talking to a huge flounder with a crown on its head. He saw two children, lost in a wood, staring hungrily at the sweet gingerbread house of another witch. He saw a princess in a high tower unbraid her hair and shake it loose so that it tumbled down and down the wall like a river of gold to the bottom, where her true love caught it in his hands. He saw a great, silent palace surrounded by brambles thick as a man's wrist, sharp as daggers, and he saw the King's son who rode slowly toward them. He saw rose gardens and deep, dark forests with red dragons lurking in them. He saw hummingbirds made of crystal among trees with leaves of silver and pearls. He saw secret, solitary towers rising out of the middle of lovely lakes, or from the tops of mountain crags. He whispered, enchanted, as every sweep of the broom filled his eyes with wonders, "There is more magic here than in all my father's books. . . . I could stay here. . . . Maybe I'll stay here. . . . I will stay. . . ." He saw a small pond with a fish in it, as gold as the sun, that spoke once every hundred years. It rose up to the surface as he passed. Its eyes were blue fire; its mouth was full of delicate bubbles like a precious hoard of words. It broke the surface, leaped into the light. It said—

"Johann!"

The mortar bucked in the air like a boat on a wave. The young man sat down abruptly. Baba Yaga said irritably to the sky, "Stop shouting, he's coming. . . ."

"Baba Yaga," the young sorcerer whispered. "Baba Yaga." Still sprawled at the bottom of the mortar, he gripped the hem of her skirt. "Where are you taking me?"

"Home."

"I stopped—" he whispered, for his voice was gone. "I stopped your house. I helped you."

"Indeed," the witch said. "Indeed you did. But I am Baba Yaga, and no one ever knows from one moment to the next what I will do."

She said nothing more. The young man slumped over himself, not even seeing the Firebird below, with her red beak and diamond eyes, stealing golden apples from the garden of the King. He sighed. Then he sighed again. Then he said, with a magnificent effort, "Oh, well. I suppose I can stand to leave all this behind and be a toad for a few months. It's as much as I deserve. Besides, if I ran away, he'd miss me." He stood up then, and held out his arms to the misty, pastel sky of the world within the World. "Father! It's me! I'm coming back. I'm coming. . . ."

Baba Yaga turned very quickly. She rapped the young sorcerer smartly on the head with her pestle. His eyes closed. She caught him in her arms as he swayed, and she picked him up and tossed him over the side of the mortar. But instead of falling down, he fell up, up into the gentle, opalescent sky, up until Up was Down below the feet of those who dwelled in the world Above.

"And good riddance," Baba Yaga said rudely. But she lingered in her mortar to listen.

"Oh," the young sorcerer groaned. "My head."

"Johann! You're alive!"

"Barely. That old witch Baba Yaga hit me over the head with her pestle—"

"Hush, don't talk. Rest."

"Father, is that you? Am I here?"

"Yes, yes, my son—"

"I'm sorry I blew up your house."

"House, shmouse, you blew up your head, you stupid boy, how many times have I told you—"

"It was the Mandragora root."

"I know. I've told you and told you—"

"Is this my bed? The house is still standing? Father, your cauldron, the cats, the pictures on the wall—"

"Nothing is broken but your head."

"Then I didn't—But how did I—Father, I blew myself clear to the Underwood—I saw Baba Yaga's house spinning and spinning, and I stopped it for her, and she took me for a ride in her mortar and pestle—I saw such wonders, such magics, such a beautiful country. . . . Someday I'll find my way back. . . ."

"Stop talking. Sleep."

"And then she hit me for no reason at all, after I had helped her, and she sent me back here. . . . Did you know she wears green spectacles?"

"She does not!"

"Yes, she does."

"You were dreaming."

"Was I? Was I, really? Or am I dreaming now that the house is safe, and you aren't angry. . . . Which is the true dream?"

"You're making my head spin."

"Mine, too."

The voices were fading. Baba Yaga smiled, and three passing crows fell out of the sky in shock. She beat a drumroll on the mortar with her pestle and sailed back to her kitchen.

from

The Magician's Nephew

by C. S. Lewis

C. S. Lewis (1898–1963) was a university professor and religious scholar, and the author of the captivating seven volume fantasy series *The Chronicles of Narnia*. This selection from the first book in the series introduces us to two children—Polly and Digory—and to Digory's Uncle Andrew, a misguided and selfish wizard who tricks Polly into putting on a magic ring that causes her to vanish.

I t was so sudden, and so horribly unlike anything that had ever happened to Digory even in a nightmare, that he let out a scream. Instantly Uncle Andrew's hand was over his mouth. "None of that!" he hissed in Digory's ear. "If you start making a noise your Mother'll hear it. And you know what a fright might do to her."

As Digory said afterward, the horrible meanness of getting at a chap in *that* way, almost made him sick. But of course he didn't scream again.

"That's better," said Uncle Andrew. "Perhaps you couldn't help it. It *is* a shock when you first see someone vanish. Why, it gave even me a turn when the guinea-pig did it the other night."

"Was that when you yelled?" asked Digory.

"Oh, you heard *that*, did you? I hope you haven't been spying on me?"

"No, I haven't," said Digory indignantly. "But what's happened to Polly?"

"Congratulate me, my dear boy," said Uncle Andrew, rubbing his

hands. "My experiment has succeeded. The little girl's gone—vanished—
right out of the world."

"What have you done to her?"

"Sent her to—well—to another place."

"What *do* you mean?" asked Digory.

Uncle Andrew sat down and said, "Well, I'll tell you all about it.
Have you ever heard of old Mrs. Lefay?"

"Wasn't she a great-aunt or something?" said Digory.

"Not exactly," said Uncle Andrew. "She was my godmother. That's
her, there, on the wall."

Digory looked and saw a faded photograph: it showed the face of
an old woman in a bonnet. And he could now remember that he had
once seen a photo of the same face in an old drawer, at home, in the
country. He had asked his Mother who it was and Mother had not
seemed to want to talk about the subject much. It was not at all a nice
face, Digory thought, though of course with those early photographs
one could never really tell.

"Was there—wasn't there—something wrong about her, Uncle
Andrew?" he said.

"Well," said Uncle Andrew with a chuckle, "it depends what you call
wrong. People are so narrow-minded. She certainly got very queer in
later life. Did very unwise things. That was why they shut her up."

"In an asylum, do you mean?"

"Oh no, no, no," said Uncle Andrew in a shocked voice. "Nothing
of that sort. Only in prison."

"I say!" said Digory. "What had she done?"

"Ah, poor woman," said Uncle Andrew. "She had been very unwise.
There were a good many different things. We needn't go into all that.
She was always very kind to me."

"But look here, what has all this got to do with Polly? I do
wish you'd—"

"All in good time, my boy," said Uncle Andrew. "They let old Mrs.
Lefay out before she died and I was one of the very few people whom
she would allow to see her in her last illness. She had got to dislike

ordinary, ignorant people, you understand. I do myself. But she and I were interested in the same sort of things. It was only a few days before her death that she told me to go to an old bureau in her house and open a secret drawer and bring her a little box that I would find there. The moment I picked up that box I could tell by the pricking in my fingers that I held some great secret in my hands. She gave it me and made me promise that as soon as she was dead I would burn it, unopened, with certain ceremonies. That promise I did not keep."

"Well, then, it was jolly rotten of you," said Digory.

"Rotten?" said Uncle Andrew with a puzzled look. "Oh, I see. You mean that little boys ought to keep their promises. Very true: most right and proper, I'm sure, and I'm very glad you have been taught to do it. But of course you must understand that rules of that sort, however excellent they may be for little boys—and servants—and women—and even people in general, can't possibly be expected to apply to profound students and great thinkers and sages. No, Digory. Men like me, who possess hidden wisdom, are freed from common rules just as we are cut off from common pleasures. Ours, my boy, is a high and lonely destiny."

As he said this he sighed and looked so grave and noble and mysterious that for a second Digory really thought he was saying something rather fine. But then he remembered the ugly look he had seen on his Uncle's face the moment before Polly had vanished: and all at once he saw through Uncle Andrew's grand words. "All it means," he said to himself, "is that he thinks he can do anything he likes to get anything he wants."

"Of course," said Uncle Andrew, "I didn't dare to open the box for a long time, for I knew it might contain something highly dangerous. For my godmother was a *very* remarkable woman. The truth is, she was one of the last mortals in this country who had fairy blood in her. (She said there had been two others in her time. One was a duchess and the other was a charwoman.) In fact, Digory, you are now talking to the last man (possibly) who really had a fairy godmother. There! That'll be something for you to remember when you are an old man yourself."

"I bet she was a bad fairy," thought Digory; and added out loud, "But what about Polly?"

"How you do harp on that!" said Uncle Andrew. "As if that was what mattered! My first task was of course to study the box itself. It was very ancient. And I knew enough even then to know that it wasn't Greek, or Old Egyptian, or Babylonian, or Hittite, or Chinese. It was older than any of those nations. Ah—that was a great day when I at last found out the truth. The box was Atlantean; it came from the lost island of Atlantis. That meant it was centuries older than any of the stone-age things they dig up in Europe. And it wasn't a rough, crude thing like them either. For in the very dawn of time Atlantis was already a great city with palaces and temples and learned men."

He paused for a moment as if he expected Digory to say something. But Digory was disliking his Uncle more every minute, so he said nothing.

"Meanwhile," continued Uncle Andrew, "I was learning a good deal in other ways (it wouldn't be proper to explain them to a child) about Magic in general. That meant that I came to have a fair idea what sort of things might be in the box. By various tests I narrowed down the possibilities. I had to get to know some—well, some devilish queer people, and go through some very disagreeable experiences. That was what turned my head gray. One doesn't become a magician for nothing. My health broke down in the end. But I got better. And at last I actually *knew*."

Although there was not really the least chance of anyone over-hearing them, he leaned forward and almost whispered as he said:

"The Atlantean box contained something that had been brought from another world when our world was only just beginning."

"What?" asked Digory, who was now interested in spite of himself.

"Only dust," said Uncle Andrew. "Fine, dry dust. Nothing much to look at. Not much to show for a lifetime of toil, you might say. Ah, but when I looked at that dust (I took jolly good care not to touch it) and thought that every grain had once been in another world—I don't mean another planet, you know; they're part of our world and you could get to them if you went far enough—but a really Other World—another Nature—another universe—somewhere you would never reach even if you traveled through the space of this universe forever and ever—a world that could be reached only by Magic—well!" Here Uncle Andrew rubbed his hands till his knuckles cracked like fireworks.

"I knew," he went on, "that if only you could get it into the right form, that dust would draw you back to the place it had come from. But the difficulty was to get it into the right form. My earlier experiments were all failures. I tried them on guinea-pigs. Some of them only died. Some exploded like little bombs—"

"It was a jolly cruel thing to do," said Digory who had once had a guinea-pig of his own.

"How do you keep getting off the point!" said Uncle Andrew. "That's what the creatures were for. I'd bought them myself. Let me see—where was I? Ah yes. At last I succeeded in making the rings: the yellow rings. But now a new difficulty arose. I was pretty sure, now, that a yellow ring would send any creature that touched it into the Other Place. But what would be the good of that if I couldn't get them back to tell me what they had found there?"

"And what about *them*?" said Digory. "A nice mess they'd be in if they couldn't get back!"

"You will keep on looking at everything from the wrong point of view," said Uncle Andrew with a look of impatience. "Can't you understand that the thing is a great experiment? The whole point of sending anyone into the Other Place is that I want to find out what it's like."

"Well why didn't you go yourself then?"

Digory had hardly ever seen anyone look so surprised and offended as his Uncle did at this simple question. "Me? Me?" he exclaimed. "The boy must be mad! A man at my time of life, and in my state of health, to risk the shock and the dangers of being flung suddenly into a different universe? I never heard anything so preposterous in my life! Do you realize what you're saying? Think what Another World means—you might meet anything—anything."

"And I suppose you've sent Polly into it then," said Digory. His cheeks were flaming with anger now. "And all I can say," he added, "even if you are my Uncle—is that you've behaved like a coward, sending a girl to a place you're afraid to go to yourself."

"Silence, sir!" said Uncle Andrew, bringing his hand down on the table. "I will not be talked to like that by a little, dirty, schoolboy. You don't understand. I am the great scholar, the magician, the adept, who is *doing* the experiment. Of course I need subjects to do it *on*. Bless my soul, you'll be telling me next that I ought to have asked the guinea-pigs' permission before I used *them!* No great wisdom can be reached without sacrifice. But the idea of my going myself is ridiculous. It's like asking a general to fight as a common soldier. Supposing I got killed, what would become of my life's work?"

"Oh, do stop jawing," said Digory. "Are you going to bring Polly back?"

"I was going to tell you, when you so rudely interrupted me," said Uncle Andrew, "that I did at last find out a way of doing the return journey. The green rings draw you back."

"But Polly hasn't got a green ring."

"No," said Uncle Andrew with a cruel smile.

"Then she can't get back," shouted Digory. "And it's exactly the same as if you'd murdered her."

"She can get back," said Uncle Andrew, "if someone else will go after her, wearing a yellow ring himself and taking two green rings, one to bring himself back and one to bring her back."

And now of course Digory saw the trap in which he was caught: and he stared at Uncle Andrew, saying nothing, with his mouth wide open. His cheeks had gone very pale.

"I hope," said Uncle Andrew presently in a very high and mighty voice, just as if he were a perfect Uncle who had given one a handsome tip and some good advice, "I *hope*, Digory, you are not given to showing the white feather. I should be very sorry to think that anyone of our family had not enough honor and chivalry to go to the aid of—er—a lady in distress."

"Oh shut up!" said Digory. "If you had any honor and all that, you'd be going yourself. But I know you won't. All right. I see I've got to go. But you *are* a beast. I suppose you planned the whole thing, so that she'd go without knowing it and then I'd have to go after her."

"Of course," said Uncle Andrew with his hateful smile.

"Very well. I'll go. But there's one thing I jolly well mean to say first. I didn't believe in Magic till today. I see now it's real. Well if it is, I suppose all the old fairy tales are more or less true. And you're simply a wicked, cruel magician like the ones in the stories. Well, I've never read a story in which people of that sort weren't paid out in the end, and I bet you will be. And serve you right."

Of all the things Digory had said this was the first that really went home. Uncle Andrew started and there came over his face a look of such horror that, beast though he was, you could almost feel sorry for him. But a second later he smoothed it all away and said with a rather forced laugh, "Well, well, I suppose that is a natural thing for a child to think—brought up among women, as you have been. Old wives' tales, eh? I don't think you need worry about *my* danger, Digory. Wouldn't it be better to worry about the danger of your little friend? She's been gone some time. If there are any dangers Over There—well, it would be a pity to arrive a moment too late."

"A lot *you* care," said Digory fiercely. "But I'm sick of this jaw. What have I got to do?"

"You really must learn to control that temper of yours, my boy," said Uncle Andrew coolly. "Otherwise you'll grow up to be just like your Aunt Letty. Now. Attend to me."

He got up, put on a pair of gloves, and walked over to the tray that contained the rings.

"They only work," he said, "if they're actually touching your skin. Wearing gloves, I can pick them up—like this—and nothing happens. If you carried one in your pocket nothing would happen: but of course you'd have to be careful not to put your hand in your pocket and touch it by accident. The moment you touch a yellow ring, you vanish out of this world. When you are in the Other Place I expect—of course this hasn't been tested yet, but I *expect*—that the moment you touch a green ring you vanish out of that world and—I expect—reappear in this.

Now. I take these two greens and drop them into your right-hand pocket. Remember very carefully which pocket the greens are in. G for green and R for right. G.R. you see: which are the first two letters of green. One for you and one for the little girl. And now you pick up a yellow one for yourself. I should put it on—on your finger—if I were you. There'll be less chance of dropping it."

Digory had almost picked up the yellow ring when he suddenly checked himself.

"Look here," he said. "What about Mother? Supposing she asks where I am?"

"The sooner you go, the sooner you'll be back," said Uncle Andrew cheerfully.

"But you don't really know whether I can get back."

Uncle Andrew shrugged his shoulders, walked across to the door, unlocked it, threw it open, and said:

"Oh very well then. Just as you please. Go down and have your dinner. Leave the little girl to be eaten by wild animals or drowned or starved in the Otherworld or lost there for good, if that's what you prefer. It's all one to me. Perhaps before tea time you'd better drop in on Mrs. Plummer and explain that she'll never see her daughter again; because you were afraid to put on a ring."

"By gum," said Digory, "don't I just wish I was big enough to punch your head!"

Then he buttoned up his coat, took a deep breath, and picked up the ring. And he thought then, as he always thought afterward too, that he could not decently have done anything else.

from

The Magic of Oz

by L. Frank Baum

H e first set up a small silver tripod and placed a gold basin at the top of it. Into this basin he put two powders—a pink one and a sky-blue one—and poured over them a yellow liquid from a crystal vial. Then he mumbled some magic words, and the powders began to sizzle and burn and send out a cloud of violet smoke that floated across the river and completely enveloped both Trot and Cap'n Bill, as well as the toadstools on which they sat, and even the Magic Plant in the gold flower-pot. Then, after the smoke had disappeared into air, the Wizard called out to the prisoners:

"Are you free?"

Both Trot and Cap'n Bill tried to move their feet and failed.

"No!" they shouted in answer.

The Wizard rubbed his bald head thoughtfully and then took some other magic tools from the bag.

First he placed a little black ball in a silver pistol and shot it toward the Magic Isle. The ball exploded just over the head of Trot and scattered a thousand sparks over the little girl.

"Oh!" said the Wizard, "I guess that will set her free."

But Trot's feet were still rooted in the ground of the Magic Isle, and the disappointed Wizard had to try something else.

For almost ah hour he worked hard, using almost every magic tool in his black bag, and still Cap'n Bill and Trot were not rescued.

"Dear me!" exclaimed Dorothy, "I'm 'fraid we'll have to go to Glinda, after all."

That made the little Wizard blush, for it shamed him to think that his magic was not equal to that of the Magic Isle.

"I won't give up yet, Dorothy," he said, "for I know a lot of wizardry that I haven't yet tried. I don't know what magician enchanted this little island, or what his powers were, but I *do* know that I can break any enchantment known to the ordinary witches and magicians that used to inhabit the Land of Oz. It's like unlocking a door; all you need is to find the right key."

"But s'pose you haven't the right key with you," suggested Dorothy; "what then?"

"Then we'll have to make the key," he answered.

The Glass Cat now came back to their side of the river, walking under the water, and said to the Wizard: "They're getting frightened over there on the island because they're both growing smaller every minute. Just now, when I left them, both Trot and Cap'n Bill were only about half their natural sizes."

"I think," said the Wizard reflectively, "that I'd better go to the shore of the island, where I can talk to them and work to better advantage. How did Trot and Cap'n Bill get to the island?"

"On a raft," answered the Glass Cat. "It's over there now on the beach."

"I suppose you're not strong enough to bring the raft to this side, are you?"

"No; I couldn't move it an inch," said the Cat.

"I'll try to get it for you," volunteered the Cowardly Lion. "I'm dreadfully scared for fear the Magic Isle will capture me, too; but I'll try to get the raft and bring it to this side for you."

"Thank you, my friend," said the Wizard.

So the Lion plunged into the river and swam with powerful strokes across to where the raft was beached upon the island. Placing one paw on the raft, he turned and struck out with his other three legs and so strong was the great beast that he managed to drag the raft from off the beach and propel it slowly to where the Wizard stood on the river bank.

"Good!" exclaimed the little man, well pleased.

"May I go across with you?" asked Dorothy.

The Wizard hesitated.

"If you'll take care not to leave the raft or step foot on the island, you'll be quite safe," he decided. So the Wizard told the Hungry Tiger and the Cowardly Lion to guard the cage of monkeys until he returned, and then he and Dorothy got upon the raft. The paddle which Cap'n Bill had made was still there so the little Wizard paddled the clumsy raft across the water and ran it upon the beach of the Magic Isle as close to the place where Cap'n Bill and Trot were rooted as he could.

Dorothy was shocked to see how small the prisoners had become, and Trot said to her friends: "If you can't save us soon, there'll be nothing left of us."

"Be patient, my dear," counseled the Wizard, and took the little axe from his black bag.

"What are you going to do with that?" asked Cap'n Bill.

"It's a magic axe," replied the Wizard, "and when I tell it to chop, it will chop those roots from your feet and you can run to the raft before they grow again."

"Don't!" shouted the sailor in alarm. "Don't do it! Those roots are all flesh roots, and our bodies are feeding 'em while they're growing into the ground."

"To cut off the roots," said Trot, "would be like cutting off our fingers and toes."

The Wizard put the little axe back in the black bag and took out a pair of silver pincers.

"Grow—grow—grow!" he said to the pincers, and at once they grew and extended until they reached from the raft to the prisoners.

"What are you going to do now?" demanded Cap'n Bill, fearfully eyeing the pincers.

"This magic tool will pull you up, roots and all, and land you on this raft," declared the Wizard.

"Don't do it!" pleaded the sailor, with a shudder. "It would hurt us awfully."

"It would be just like pulling teeth to pull us up by the roots," explained Trot.

"Grow small!" said the Wizard to the pincers, and at once they became small and he threw them into the black bag.

"I guess, friends, it's all up with us, this time," remarked Cap'n Bill, with a dismal sigh.

"Please tell Ozma, Dorothy," said Trot, "that we got into trouble trying to get her a nice birthday present. Then she'll forgive us. The Magic Flower is lovely and wonderful, but it's just a lure to catch folks on this dreadful island and then destroy them. You'll have a nice birthday party, without us, I'm sure; and I hope, Dorothy, that none of you in the Emerald City will forget me—or dear ol' Cap'n Bill,"

Dorothy was greatly distressed and had hard work to keep the tears from her eyes.

"Is that all you can do, Wizard?" she asked the little man.

"It's all I can think of just now," he replied sadly. "But I intend to keep on thinking as long—as long—well, as long as thinking will do any good."

They were all silent for a time, Dorothy and the Wizard sitting thoughtfully on the raft, and Trot and Cap'n Bill sitting thoughtfully on the toadstools and growing gradually smaller and smaller in size.

Suddenly Dorothy said: "Wizard, I've thought of something!"

"What have you thought of?" he asked, looking at the little girl with interest.

"Can you remember the Magic Word that transforms people?" she asked.

"Of course," said he.

"Then you can transform Trot and Cap'n Bill into birds or

bumblebees, and they can fly away to the other shore. When they're there, you can transform 'em into their reg'lar shapes again!"

"Can you do that, Wizard?" asked Cap'n Bill, eagerly.

"I think so."

"Roots an' all?" inquired Trot.

"Why, the roots are now a part of you, and if you were transformed to a bumblebee the whole of you would be transformed, of course, and you'd be free of this awful island."

"All right; do it!" cried the sailor-man.

So the Wizard said slowly and distinctly: "I want Trot and Cap'n Bill to become bumblebees—P y r z q x g l ! "

Fortunately, he pronounced the Magic Word in the right way, and instantly Trot and Cap'n Bill vanished from view, and up from the places where they had been flew two bumblebees.

"Hooray!" shouted Dorothy in delight; "they're saved!"

"I guess they are," agreed the Wizard, equally delighted.

The bees hovered over the raft an instant and then flew across the river to where the Lion and the Tiger waited. The Wizard picked up the paddle and paddled the raft across as fast as he could. When it reached the river bank, both Dorothy and the Wizard leaped ashore and the little man asked excitedly:

"Where are the bees?"

"The bees?" inquired the Lion, who was half asleep and did not know what had happened on the Magic Isle.

"Yes; there were two of them."

"Two bees?" said the Hungry Tiger, yawning. "Why, I ate one of them and the Cowardly Lion ate the other."

"Goodness gracious!" cried Dorothy horrified.

"It was little enough for our lunch," remarked the Tiger, "but the bees were the only things we could find."

"How dreadful!" wailed Dorothy, wringing her hands in despair. "You've eaten Trot and Cap'n Bill."

But just then she heard a buzzing overhead and two bees alighted on her shoulder.

"Here we are," said a small voice in her ear. "I'm Trot, Dorothy."

"And I'm Cap'n Bill," said the other bee. Dorothy almost fainted, with relief, and the Wizard, who was close by and had heard the tiny voices, gave a laugh and said:

"You are not the only two bees in the forest, it seems, but I advise you to keep away from the Lion and the Tiger until you regain your proper forms."

"Do it now, Wizard!" advised Dorothy. "They're so small that you never can tell what might happen to 'em."

So the Wizard gave the command and pronounced the Magic Word, and in the instant Trot and Cap'n Bill stood beside them as natural as before they had met their fearful adventure. For they were no longer small in size, because the Wizard had transformed them from bumblebees into the shapes and sizes that nature had formerly given them. The ugly roots on their feet had disappeared with the transformation.

While Dorothy was hugging Trot, and Trot was softly crying because she was so happy, the Wizard shook hands with Cap'n Bill and congratulated him on his escape. The old sailor-man was so pleased that he also shook the Lion's paw and took off his hat and bowed politely to the cage of monkeys.

Then Cap'n Bill did a curious thing. He went to a big tree and, taking out his knife, cut away a big, broad piece of thick bark. Then he sat down on the ground and after taking a roll of stout cord from his pocket—which seemed to be full of all sorts of things—he proceeded to bind the flat piece of bark to the bottom of his good foot, over the leather sole.

"What's that for?" inquired the Wizard.

"I hate to be stumped," replied the sailor-man; "so I'm goin' back to that island."

"And get enchanted again?" exclaimed Trot, with evident disapproval.

"No; this time I'll dodge the magic of the island. I noticed that my wooden leg didn't get stuck, or take root, an' neither did the glass feet of the Glass Cat. It's only a thing that's made of meat—like man an' beasts—that the magic can hold an' root to the ground. Our shoes are leather, an' leather comes from a beast's hide. Our stockin's are wool, an' wool comes from a sheep's back. So, when we walked on the Magic Isle, our feet took root there an' held us fast. But not my wooden leg. So now I'll put a wooden bottom on my other foot an' the magic can't stop me."

"But why do you wish to go back to the island?" asked Dorothy.

"Didn't you see the Magic Flower in the gold flower-pot?" returned Cap'n Bill.

"Of course I saw it, and it's lovely and wonderful."

"Well, Trot an' I set out to get the magic plant for a present to Ozma on her birthday, and I mean to get it an' take it back with us to the Emerald City."

"That would be fine," cried Trot eagerly, "if you think you can do it, and it would be safe to try!"

"I'm pretty sure it is safe, the way I've fixed my foot," said the sailor, "an' if I *should* happen to get caught, I s'pose the Wizard could save me again."

"I suppose I could," agreed the Wizard. "Anyhow, if you wish to try it, Cap'n Bill, go ahead and we'll stand by and watch what happens."

So the sailor-man got upon the raft again and paddled over to the Magic Isle, landing as close to the golden flower-pot as he could. They watched him walk across the land, put both arms around the flower-pot and lift it easily from its place. Then he carried it to the raft and set it down very gently. The removal did not seem to affect the Magic Flower in any way, for it was growing daffodils when Cap'n Bill picked it up and on the way to the raft it grew tulips and gladioli. During the time the sailor was paddling across the river to where his friends awaited him, seven different varieties of flowers bloomed in succession on the plant.

"I guess the Magician who put it on the island never thought that any one would carry it off," said Dorothy.

"He figured that only men would want the plant, and any man who went upon the island to get it would be caught by the enchantment," added the Wizard.

"After this," remarked Trot, "no one will care to go on the island, so it won't be a trap any more."

"There," exclaimed Cap'n Bill, setting down the Magic Plant in triumph upon the river bank, "if Ozma gets a better birthday present than that, I'd like to know what it can be!"

"It'll s'prise her, all right," declared Dorothy, standing in awed wonder before the gorgeous blossoms and watching them change from yellow roses to violets.

"It'll s'prise ev'rybody in the Em'rald City," Trot asserted in glee, "and it'll be Ozma's present from Cap'n Bill and me."

"I think I ought to have a little credit," objected the Glass Cat. "I discovered the thing, and led you to it, and brought the Wizard here to save you when you got caught."

"That's true," admitted Trot, "and I'll tell Ozma the whole story, so she'll know how good you've been."

The Magic Muntr

by Elizabeth Jamison Hodges

Elizabeth Jamison Hodges adapted this 16th century Venetian tale set in western India to tell the story of a young prince and a powerful spell—a "magic muntr."

Long ago in the Deccan of western India, there lived a young prince who was kind, clever, and full of curiosity. His name was Vicram, and when he inherited the royal throne, he devoted himself with such zeal to the well-being of his people that they spoke of him as "Maharajah," which means "Great King." But personally he was so modest that he never became used to this title.

His queen, called the "Ranee," was named Anarkali, for her lips were rosy like pomegranates and her eyes as black and shining as the seeds of the sitapurl. In addition to being exquisite to look upon, she was a perfect companion to the young king. Her words as well as her flower-like beauty filled him with joy.

But since he little reckoned his own worth, he often thought, "Can this enchanting lady love me for myself? Must she not have been dazzled by the sound of my title and the blaze of my power?"

As for the handsome palace in which he lived, he paid little attention to its colorful paintings, jeweled throne, and ebony furniture. Instead, he busied himself with building a forest temple to Saraswathi, the goddess of learning. It was delicately carved, and he adorned it with a tower of lights so brilliant that, after sunset, their glory swept through the thick jungle like a bath of golden rain. Moreover, when not engaged in affairs of state, Vicram liked to talk with the ranee of poetry, music, or plans for his people, and with wise men about magic or wisdom.

One day two travelers who said they were philosophers came to the gates of the palace. The first was an old and truly learned seer, but the other was a demon rakshas in disguise. Both, however, were made welcome, given robes with golden threads, and a meal of curried rice, sweet figs, and almonds. The next morning, they were presented to the king, who kindly asked what he might do for them.

"O, Noble Maharajah," the rakshas said after he had knelt before the ruler and bowed so low that his chin touched the carpet while his robe flowed out around him, "I have heard that the post of prime minister in your kingdom now is vacant and beg to serve you in that capacity. Be assured that I read a great deal, and to gather wisdom I have traveled many yojanas under the moon."

Vicram thought, I should be fortunate indeed to have a wise philosopher to serve me. So after asking this visitor some difficult questions, all of which he answered without hesitation, the king appointed the rakshas to the post of prime minister with the title of "Prudhan."

The true philosopher likewise bowed very low and said, "I also read a great deal and seeking wisdom have traveled many yojanas under the moon. In so doing I heard everywhere of the kindness and learning of Vicram Maharajah. Nothing, therefore, would please me more than to talk with Your Majesty that happily we may share some jewels of wisdom. As is well known, so marvelous is an exchange of this kind that each of us may keep what we also give away."

Vicram was delighted by these words and consented to his plan.

The rakshas then became the prudhan of the land and immediately began plotting evil mischief, while the elderly philosopher visited the maharajah every day to learn from his store of wisdom. In turn, he told the ruler many strange things he had discovered while walking in cities with busy noise, and while resting in forests with quiet deeps.

One day, Vicram said, "Of all the wonders you have known, pray tell me what seemed to you most marvelous?"

The philosopher thought for just a moment.

"The most wondrous thing I ever saw," he said, his eyes shining like tourmalines, "happened one day when I journeyed toward the regions of the West."

"And what was that?" the king said.

The old seer replied, "While I reposed unobserved in the shade of a banyan tree, I noticed a young man walking alone on a dusty highway. Nearby, a small dog lay asleep. As soon as the young man saw him, he approached the animal on tiptoe, put a hand over its heart and softly said a muntr.

"I could not distinguish the words, Your Majesty, which, I might say, sounded like a hurrying brook or an old demon mumbling in sleep. But they were composed of such powerful magic that they allowed the young man's spirit to slip into that of the dog, leaving his human body lying apparently lifeless beside the road."

"How did you know this had happened?" Vicram asked.

"Because," the philosopher replied, "the dog began to sing and to dance, both in human fashion."

"Amazing indeed!" Vicram said.

"Yes, Your Majesty," continued the philosopher, "and after this had gone on for quite a long time, the animal approached the body of the man, placed one paw over its heart, and barked softly with sounds not unlike the muntr I had heard before. Again, however, the words were not clear enough to be distinguished. But immediately the spirit of the man returned to his own body, for he stood up and walked away, while the little dog, breathing gently, lay asleep just as before."

"What did you do then?" asked the maharajah.

"I arose, Your Majesty, ran after the young man and begged him to teach me the magic muntr. At first he was loath to do so, declaring it was a dangerous saying, but I offered in exchange for the secret to tell him a hundred absorbing tales. So much did he love good stories that he had not the heart to refuse my offer.

"Therefore I traveled with him for many yojanas while the moon waxed seven times and waned. After I had told him one hundred stories he taught me the secret words. I can now, at will, cause my spirit to pass into that of another living creature and continue as long as I choose in its likeness before returning to my own form."

Vicram said, "So amazing is a change about such as you have described that, humbly begging your pardon, I must see it with my own eyes to believe it entirely."

When he heard this, the philosopher said, "In that case, Your Majesty, pray watch, and I shall perform the kind of feat I have just described."

He opened a window. Through it a small sparrow flew into the room and alighted on the carpet. Then very softly, the learned seer crept up behind it. When he had caught the bird he placed one finger lightly over the tiny creature's heart, at the same time saying the muntr in a low voice.

Instantly, in front of the maharajah the body of the old man dropped as if lifeless to the carpet while the little bird flew to Vicram, perched on his hand with a friendly flutter and sang as sweetly as a bulbul bird. When asked by the king to fly from a table to a painting and back to himself, it obeyed perfectly every command.

Finally, after one more song, it settled on top of the philosopher's body right over the heart and softly chirped the strange muntr. Immediately the seer revived, and a moment later, the sparrow's own spirit having returned to its body, the little bird flew out of the window.

The philosopher said to his royal host, "I hope Your Majesty can now believe what I have said."

"I do indeed," replied the maharajah, "for never have I seen any thing so extraordinary. Pray, teach this muntr to me. Though I have now heard it twice, both you and the sparrow spoke so softly and so swiftly that I could not make out the words."

"It is a dangerous saying," the philosopher declared, "but since Your Majesty has been exceedingly kind to men of learning, I shall tell it to you."

This he did, and once the maharajah had learned the muntr, he delighted in going out into the jungle, secretly turning himself into a little owl and in this guise visiting many parts of the kingdom. Sometimes he alighted on roof tops where washing had been hung out to dry by day and where at night women talked of hopes and dreams. Sometimes he visited the cities and heard men both argue and agree in busy bazaars. Thus he came to understand his people better than any maharajah in his land before him, and when he returned to royal shape could rule them with greater wisdom.

Because of this, however, the king was often gone from court. The demon rakshas, who had obtained the position of prudhan, noted his many absences, and one day followed the maharajah into the jungle hiding behind trees as he did so.

It happened that on the same day a sambar came bounding along. This deer had such handsome antlers, held his head so high and pranced through the woods as if filled with so much joy, that Vicram decided it would be great sport to change himself into that happy creature.

He climbed, therefore, part way up an acacia tree, which grew in a hilly part of the jungle, and remained very still. When the sambar passed nearby, the maharajah reached his hands out quickly, held him and placed a finger on his back at a spot over the heart. At the same time he recited the magic muntr in a normal voice, not knowing that his prudhan was lurking close by and could overhear. No sooner had he spoken the words than the king's spirit passed into that of the sambar, while his own body fell lifeless to the ground under the acacia tree.

Now when the rakshas heard the muntr spoken aloud, he stored the words in his memory by saying them over and over to himself. Then after the maharajah, in the shape of the deer, had bounded off into another part of the jungle, the prudhan ran to the monarch's fallen body. Kneeling down, he placed a hand over its heart and firmly spoke the secret words he had just heard. At once, while his own form fell as if lifeless on the ground, the rakshas stood up in the guise of the maharajah, and hurried back to the palace to take the place of the king.

As for Vicram, at first he delighted in his new shape, and when a high and exciting wind streaked through the trees, he romped about the jungle as merry as a fawn. Finally, when the sun set he decided to return to his own body, but the wind had blown so many leaves from the trees that, each one now looked different. Even the prudhan's body was nowhere to be seen. In the gale it had rolled down the hillside and lay buried under a sea of leaves.

So after he had looked a long time, Vicram, feeling himself lost indeed, gave up in despair and wandered through the jungle eating wild plants and fleeing from tigers, jackals, and other animals which chased him. When he laid down to sleep, small ants climbed out of their nests and swarmed over him. When he wished to drink from forest streams, powerful lions bared their teeth and frightened him away.

In this desperate plight, he happened one day to see a parrot which had flown from the top of a banyan tree to a branch near the ground. If I could fly like a bird, Vicram thought, I could escape from these troublesome animals. So he crept up softly behind the parrot which was asleep, placed his chin ever so lightly on the creature over his heart, spoke the magic muntr and forthwith entered the body of the parrot. That of the sambar fell to the ground and lay as if asleep for a few days, until it was found by its own wandering spirit which pranced away with it.

The head of the parrot that Vicram had entered was blue and yellow like a summer sea edged with golden sand. The breast was rosy and the wings green like leaves of a palm tree. Vicram not only felt handsome, but now he could rise above tigers, jackals, lions and other ground creatures. Pleased with his greater freedom, he practiced flying short distances before attempting to search for his palace, and, to have company, he joined a flock of other birds living merrily in the jungle.

With great delight he found that he understood their language, and that they from wide travel could tell him many things. So on warm nights he listened carefully while cicadas sang and the moon slipped over the deeps of sky like a silver ship.

In this way Vicram learned much, not only concerning his own kingdom but about countries far away with rivers of golden fish and about distant oceans rich in pearls. Thus a few days passed not uncomfortably for the former ruler, who delighted in hearing of all that was strange and curious.

One night, however, when it was dark, he fell asleep on a low branch of a sicakai tree, not knowing, so lost had he become, that it was near the temple of Saraswathi. Nor did he awake when the lamps on its tower were lit for the night.

About the same time a fowler came through the woods in search of birds to snare and sell. By the lights of the tower he saw the brilliant plumage of the parrot. So he threw a net over the bird's sleepy head and thus caught Vicram in it.

Delighted with his colorful prize, the fowler put the parrot in a cage where he kept other captured birds and, bolting the door with a little wooden peg, carried them all to the edge of the capital city. But when the fowler went away for a short time, Vicram, with intelligence like a man's, pulled the peg out of its place, and using his beak, pushed open the door.

Next, he watched while with a great squawking, twittering, and flutter of feathers the other birds fought, scrambled, and pell-mell pushed their way out of the cage. Vicram alone remained inside it.

When the fowler returned and found birds gone and the cage open, he wrung his hands and said, "Woe is me, most unfortunate of fowlers. Gone, all gone, like drops of water under a hot sun."

"Cheer up. Not quite all," Vicram said. "I am here."

The fowler looked round about but saw not a single human being nearby.

"I am here in the cage," Vicram said, "the parrot you so admired. See, I have not deserted you."

When the fowler discovered that it was his bird which had spoken so well though it had been caught only that day, he was astounded. Even more was he surprised when the parrot answered difficult questions and of its own accord spoke brightly of golden fish in distant rivers and pearl-rich reefs in faraway oceans.

The birdcatcher thought, I can sell this extraordinary parrot for a good price. So he took it to a bazaar where people bought and sold strange and beautiful things.

Now not far away from where he stopped with Vicram there arose a great surge of angry voices. Placing a branch of a tree against the door of the cage, the fowler ran to the place of dispute to find out why the morning air was rent with such ugly sounds.

After he had worked his way to the inner circle of the crowd, he found a woman, dressed like a farmer's wife, shouting at a handsomely clad young man.

"How dare you treat a poor woman so?" she said, stamping her foot. Then turning to others for sympathy, she said, "Last night I dreamed that this same young man offered to pay me a hundred golden mohurs for seven cartloads of fresh bringals, from my husband's farm. We delivered these vegetables, mind you the freshest we had, and now he refuses to pay even a single anna for them."

The fowler heard a shuffling of feet as all the people murmured, some taking the side of the farmer's wife, others the part of the young man.

Then the birdcatcher raised his voice higher than these sounds, the way the clear notes of a flute soar bravely above the music of drums, and said, "I have a remarkable parrot, with so much sense I am sure he can decide your dispute justly if you will agree to what he says."

At this all the people laughed, but when the fowler said his newly caught parrot could not only ape the speech of humans, but converse most sweetly of distant rivers and faraway oceans, the quarreling pair agreed to ask the strange bird to settle the case.

Thus the matter came before the parrot, and as he sat behind the bars of his cage, he listened carefully while first the young man spoke and then the woman.

Next Vicram asked for a table, a mirror, and from the young man a hundred golden mohurs. When these were brought, he had the mirror propped up on the table with the money placed in front of it. Seeing the coins, the woman's eyes lighted up for she expected they would be hers, but the young man looked at them with much concern.

"Now," Vicram said to the woman, "you may have only the mohurs which you see in the mirror, for since the vegetables you delivered were dream bringals, which could not be eaten by the young man, it is fitting that your payment be only in coins which cannot be spent by you."

When he had spoken these words, the woman cried out in disappointment, but the young man was delighted, and the people laughed and applauded the wisdom of the parrot. Then the story flew in every direction like bees in a field full of sunflowers. Finally it reached the maharajah's palace.

On that day Anarkali, the ranee, was sitting in her own apartments feeling extremely downcast. For many days she had been worried about the ruler in whose body, unknown to her, the rakshas now was living. It seemed to the queen that her husband was so changed he was like another man. She had the royal cooks prepare his favorite foods; peppery curries of rice with onions, tamarind, and cucumbers, but the maharajah would not touch them and demanded strange unsavory dishes he had never requested before.

No longer did he speak to her of music and poetry or of how he might help his people. Instead, his conversation was all of war and of gold. So, very much frightened, she had confined herself to her own apartments, bolting the door against everybody except one woman, a faithful attendant.

She, thinking it might amuse the ranee, now so sad and lonely, told her about the strange bird.

Anarkali was fascinated by the story of the clever parrot. She sent word to the fowler that she would pay a thousand golden mohurs if he would sell it to her.

But when he heard that the ranee had been sad for many days, he said, "Her Majesty may have the parrot as a gift. I do not wish to sell him for I should like to help make her happy. Besides, this bird seems too much like a human being to be bought or sold."

So Anarkali accepted the gift with many thanks and gave a little house and a generous pension to the fowler. After that he never went into the jungle to snare wild birds again.

For her part, the ranee was delighted with the parrot. She admired his colorful feathers and talked to him for a long time every day, marveling at the wonderful things he said. Also, she had built for him a large and spacious cage. It was decked with rubies, lined with red and purple velvet and furnished with silver swings. Round the room in which it was placed, she had several mirrors hung so that, seeing his reflection, he would be less lonely. She also had pictures of trees and flowers brought in, that even away from the jungle he might feel at home.

While the days passed the ranee came to love the parrot more and more. She fed him herself with food from her own table, and every day summoned three musical ladies of the court to play sweet tunes for him on stringed instruments.

Thus passed some time during which Vicram observed that no man came to the queen's apartments. So, full of curiosity about how the country was being governed, he said, "Pray, tell me, Your Majesty, who is the king of this land?"

Anarkali said, "His name is Vicram, and he is called 'Maharajah,' but no longer is he like the man he was a short time ago. Then his words were full of poetry and music, and all his deeds were kindness. One day, however, he went away and on returning, conversed of naught but war and gold. This frightened me so that I have shut myself up here and refused to see him. Nor do I wish to go out again, though he has sent me strings of pearls and purple amethysts and entreats me to wear them before the court."

From these words, Vicram knew someone had taken his royal shape, but he was overjoyed to learn that the queen had not loved the imposter though his appearance, title, and power appeared the same as the real king's. So he told her the story of the magic muntr and of his strange wanderings. But who had taken his body and was now pretending to be Vicram Maharajah, he did not know.

The ranee, overjoyed to learn that her husband was still kind, said, "Dearest Husband, no wonder I felt such love for you even in your present shape as a bird, but who can have stolen your own form?"

Then Vicram asked if anyone was missing from the court the same day the king had first seemed so changed, and the queen remembered that the prudhan went away that very day and did not return. Indeed, the one who came back in the likeness of the king gave out that the prime minister had been lost and probably killed by a wild beast.

"Very likely then," Vicram said, "it is he who has taken my body."

At this the ranee wept and said, "Ö, my dear Husband. Alas! What can we do?"

Vicram said, "It is clear that whoever lives in my shape must also know the magic muntr. I pray you, have a hen brought to this apartment, and then invite hither the one who is called the 'Maharajah.' " He also explained more fully what she should do.

So the woman who attended the ranee was asked to get a hen, and when she brought it, Anarkali sent out word that she would like the maharajah to come to her apartments. The rakshas arrived in the guise of the king, his face shining for joy like a mound of melting butter.

The queen said, "Your Majesty, lately I have been very sad and bored. Pray tell me, can you divert me by doing something remarkable?"

Though much surprised by her question, the rakshas was so eager to please the ranee, who had been very cool to him, that he began to boast.

"I am able to do the most remarkable thing in the world," he said. "I can turn myself into another creature."

"Can you, indeed! Then pray," she said, indicating the hen, "let me see Your Majesty turn yourself into this chicken."

Thereupon, the rakshas picked up the hen, touched her over the heart and whispered the magic muntr. Immediately, the body of the maharajah lay still on the floor while the chicken began to fly round the room, clucking a sort of song as it did so.

Seeing this, the queen opened the door of the cage, and the parrot flew swiftly to the king's body, rested over its heart, and said the muntr. In less time than it takes a kitten to twitch his ears, Vicram resumed his own shape as the maharajah.

Then he caught the hen and put it into the small cage in which the parrot had been brought to the palace. A servant took it away with orders not to release the chicken except in the darkest part of the jungle.

The rakshas, when he had been freed there, flew about for a long time, but never found his own body. He lived the rest of his life a lonely hen in a dismal swamp.

As for Vicram, he appointed the true philosopher to the post of prudhan. And he rejoiced every day, because through the magic muntr and his strange adventures he now knew that Anarkali loved him for his own true self. His happiness made the ranee happy too, and they both lived long and merrily.

Pantoum for a Parrot
How wise the bird which speaks as man!
More royal than the rakshas's seeming,
He overthrows an evil plan
And ends a quarrel spun from dreaming.

More royal than the rakshas's seeming,
His wisdom shines like temple light,
And ends a quarrel spun from dreaming,
Yet knows a sambar's wild delight.

His wisdom shines like temple light;
He overthrows an evil plan,
Yet knows a sambar's wild delight
How wise the bird which speaks as man!

from

The Tempest

by William Shakespeare

Prospero, the Duke of Milan, is a powerful magician. His brother Antonio usurps Prospero's position and casts him and his young daughter Miranda out to sea in a flimsy boat. The pair is marooned on a remote island for many years. One day fortune brings a vessel bearing Antonio and his companions—among them the King's son Ferdinand—near Prospero's island. The magician conjures a storm with the help of his spirit servants Ariel and Caliban and forces the ship to land on the shores of his enchanted domain.

ARIEL

All hail, great master! grave sir, hail! I come
To answer thy best pleasure; be't to fly,
To swim, to dive into the fire, to ride
On the curl'd clouds, to thy strong bidding task
Ariel and all his quality.

PROSPERO

Hast thou, spirit,
Perform'd to point the tempest that I bade thee?

ARIEL

To every article.
I boarded the king's ship; now on the beak,
Now in the waist, the deck, in every cabin,
I flamed amazement: sometime I'ld divide,
And burn in many places; on the topmast,
The yards and bowsprit, would I flame distinctly,
Then meet and join. Jove's lightnings, the precursors
O' the dreadful thunder-claps, more momentary
And sight-outrunning were not; the fire and cracks
Of sulphurous roaring the most mighty Neptune
Seem to besiege and make his bold waves tremble,
Yea, his dread trident shake.

PROSPERO

My brave spirit!
Who was so firm, so constant, that this coil
Would not infect his reason?

ARIEL

Not a soul
But felt a fever of the mad and play'd
Some tricks of desperation. All but mariners
Plunged in the foaming brine and quit the vessel,
Then all afire with me: the king's son, Ferdinand,
With hair up-staring,—then like reeds, not hair,—
Was the first man that leap'd; cried, 'Hell is empty
And all the devils are here.'

PROSPERO

Why that's my spirit!
But was not this nigh shore?

ARIEL

Close by, my master.

PROSPERO

But are they, Ariel, safe?

ARIEL

Not a hair perish'd;
On their sustaining garments not a blemish,
But fresher than before: and, as thou badest me,
In troops I have dispersed them 'bout the isle.
The king's son have I landed by himself;
Whom I left cooling of the air with sighs
In an odd angle of the isle and sitting,
His arms in this sad knot.

PROSPERO

Of the king's ship
The mariners say how thou hast disposed
And all the rest o' the fleet.

ARIEL

Safely in harbour
Is the king's ship; in the deep nook, where once
Thou call'dst me up at midnight to fetch dew
From the still-vex'd Bermoothes, there she's hid:
The mariners all under hatches stow'd;
Who, with a charm join'd to their suffer'd labour,
I have left asleep; and for the rest o' the fleet
Which I dispersed, they all have met again
And are upon the Mediterranean flote,
Bound sadly home for Naples,
Supposing that they saw the king's ship wreck'd
And his great person perish.

PROSPERO

Ariel, thy charge
Exactly is perform'd: but there's more work.
What is the time o' the day?

ARIEL

Past the mid season.

PROSPERO

At least two glasses. The time 'twixt six and now
Must by us both be spent most preciously.

ARIEL

Is there more toil? Since thou dost give me pains,
Let me remember thee what thou hast promised,
Which is not yet perform'd me.

PROSPERO

How now? moody?
What is't thou canst demand?

ARIEL

My liberty.

PROSPERO

Before the time be out? no more!

ARIEL

I prithee,
Remember I have done thee worthy service;
Told thee no lies, made thee no mistakings, served
Without or grudge or grumblings: thou didst promise
To bate me a full year.

PROSPERO

Dost thou forget
From what a torment I did free thee?

ARIEL

No.

PROSPERO

Thou dost, and think'st it much to tread the ooze
Of the salt deep,
To run upon the sharp wind of the north,
To do me business in the veins o' the earth
When it is baked with frost.

ARIEL

I do not, sir.

PROSPERO

Thou liest, malignant thing! Hast thou forgot
The foul witch Sycorax, who with age and envy
Was grown into a hoop? hast thou forgot her?

ARIEL

No, sir.

PROSPERO

Thou hast. Where was she born? speak; tell me.

ARIEL

Sir, in Argier.

PROSPERO

O, was she so? I must
Once in a month recount what thou hast been,
Which thou forget'st. This damn'd witch Sycorax,
For mischiefs manifold and sorceries terrible
To enter human hearing, from Argier,
Thou know'st, was banish'd: for one thing she did
They would not take her life. Is not this true?

ARIEL

Ay, sir.

PROSPERO

This blue-eyed hag was hither brought with child
And here was left by the sailors. Thou, my slave,
As thou report'st thyself, wast then her servant;
And, for thou wast a spirit too delicate
To act her earthy and abhorr'd commands,
Refusing her grand hests, she did confine thee,
By help of her more potent ministers
And in her most unmitigable rage,
Into a cloven pine; within which rift
Imprison'd thou didst painfully remain
A dozen years; within which space she died
And left thee there; where thou didst vent thy groans

As fast as mill-wheels strike. Then was this island—
Save for the son that she did litter here,
A freckled whelp hag-born—not honour'd with
A human shape.

ARIEL

Yes, Caliban her son.

PROSPERO

Dull thing, I say so; he, that Caliban
Whom now I keep in service. Thou best know'st
What torment I did find thee in; thy groans
Did make wolves howl and penetrate the breasts
Of ever angry bears: it was a torment
To lay upon the damn'd, which Sycorax
Could not again undo: it was mine art,
When I arrived and heard thee, that made gape
The pine and let thee out.

ARIEL

I thank thee, master.

PROSPERO

If thou more murmur'st, I will rend an oak
And peg thee in his knotty entrails till
Thou hast howl'd away twelve winters.

ARIEL

Pardon, master;
I will be correspondent to command
And do my spiriting gently.

PROSPERO

Do so, and after two days
I will discharge thee.

ARIEL

That's my noble master!
What shall I do? say what; what shall I do?

PROSPERO

Go make thyself like a nymph o' the sea: be subject
To no sight but thine and mine, invisible
To every eyeball else. Go take this shape
And hither come in't: go, hence with diligence!

Exit Ariel
Awake, dear heart, awake! thou hast slept well; Awake!

MIRANDA

The strangeness of your story put
Heaviness in me.

PROSPERO

Shake it off. Come on;
We'll visit Caliban my slave, who never
Yields us kind answer.

MIRANDA

'Tis a villain, sir,
I do not love to look on.

PROSPERO

But, as 'tis,
We cannot miss him: he does make our fire,
Fetch in our wood and serves in offices
That profit us. What, ho! slave! Caliban!
Thou earth, thou! speak.

CALIBAN

[Within] There's wood enough within.

PROSPERO

Come forth, I say! there's other business for thee:
Come, thou tortoise! when?

Re-enter Ariel like a water-nymph
Fine apparition! My quaint Ariel,
Hark in thine ear.

ARIEL

My lord it shall be done.

Exit

PROSPERO

Thou poisonous slave, got by the devil himself
Upon thy wicked dam, come forth!

Enter Caliban

CALIBAN

As wicked dew as e'er my mother brush'd
With raven's feather from unwholesome fen
Drop on you both! a south-west blow on ye
And blister you all o'er!

PROSPERO

For this, be sure, to-night thou shalt have cramps,
Side-stitches that shall pen thy breath up; urchins
Shall, for that vast of night that they may work,
All exercise on thee; thou shalt be pinch'd
As thick as honeycomb, each pinch more stinging
Than bees that made 'em.

CALIBAN

I must eat my dinner.
This island's mine, by Sycorax my mother,
Which thou takest from me. When thou camest first,
Thou strokedst me and madest much of me, wouldst give me
Water with berries in't, and teach me how
To name the bigger light, and how the less,
That burn by day and night: and then I loved thee
And show'd thee all the qualities o' the isle,
The fresh springs, brine-pits, barren place and fertile:
Cursed be I that did so! All the charms
Of Sycorax, toads, beetles, bats, light on you!
For I am all the subjects that you have,
Which first was mine own king: and here you sty me
In this hard rock, whiles you do keep from me
The rest o' the island.

PROSPERO

Thou most lying slave,
Whom stripes may move, not kindness! I have used thee,
Filth as thou art, with human care, and lodged thee
In mine own cell, till thou didst seek to violate
The honour of my child.

CALIBAN

O ho, O ho! would't had been done!
Thou didst prevent me; I had peopled else
This isle with Calibans.

PROSPERO

Abhorred slave,
Which any print of goodness wilt not take,
Being capable of all ill! I pitied thee,
Took pains to make thee speak, taught thee each hour
One thing or other: when thou didst not, savage,
Know thine own meaning, but wouldst gabble like
A thing most brutish, I endow'd thy purposes
With words that made them known. But thy vile race,
Though thou didst learn, had that in't which
good natures
Could not abide to be with; therefore wast thou
Deservedly confined into this rock,
Who hadst deserved more than a prison.

CALIBAN

You taught me language; and my profit on't
Is, I know how to curse. The red plague rid you
For learning me your language!

PROSPERO

Hag-seed, hence!
Fetch us in fuel; and be quick, thou'rt best,
To answer other business. Shrug'st thou, malice?
If thou neglect'st or dost unwillingly
What I command, I'll rack thee with old cramps,
Fill all thy bones with aches, make thee roar
That beasts shall tremble at thy din.

CALIBAN

No, pray thee.

Aside
I must obey: his art is of such power,
It would control my dam's god, Setebos,
and make a vassal of him.

PROSPERO

So, slave; hence!

Exit Caliban

Re-enter Ariel, invisible, playing and singing; Ferdinand following Ariel's song.

> Come unto these yellow sands,
> And then take hands:
> Courtsied when you have and kiss'd
> The wild waves whist,
> Foot it featly here and there;
> And, sweet sprites, the burthen bear.
> Hark, hark!

Burthen dispersedly, within
The watch-dogs bark!

Burthen Bow-wow
Hark, hark! I hear
The strain of strutting chanticleer
Cry, Cock-a-diddle-dow.

FERDINAND

Where should this music be? i' the air or the earth?
It sounds no more: and sure, it waits upon
Some god o' the island. Sitting on a bank,
Weeping again the king my father's wreck,
This music crept by me upon the waters,
Allaying both their fury and my passion
With its sweet air: thence I have follow'd it,
Or it hath drawn me rather. But 'tis gone.
No, it begins again.

Ariel sings
Full fathom five thy father lies;
Of his bones are coral made;
Those are pearls that were his eyes:
Nothing of him that doth fade
But doth suffer a sea-change
Into something rich and strange.
Sea-nymphs hourly ring his knell

Burthen Ding-dong
Hark! now I hear them,—Ding-dong, bell.

FERDINAND

The ditty does remember my drown'd father.
This is no mortal business, nor no sound
That the earth owes. I hear it now above me.

PROSPERO

The fringed curtains of thine eye advance
And say what thou seest yond.

MIRANDA

What is't? a spirit?
Lord, how it looks about! Believe me, sir,
It carries a brave form. But 'tis a spirit.

PROSPERO

No, wench; it eats and sleeps and hath such senses
As we have, such. This gallant which thou seest
Was in the wreck; and, but he's something stain'd
With grief that's beauty's canker, thou mightst call him
A goodly person: he hath lost his fellows
And strays about to find 'em.

MIRANDA

I might call him
A thing divine, for nothing natural
I ever saw so noble.

PROSPERO

[Aside] It goes on, I see,
As my soul prompts it. Spirit, fine spirit! I'll free thee
Within two days for this.

FERDINAND

Most sure, the goddess
On whom these airs attend! Vouchsafe my prayer
May know if you remain upon this island;

And that you will some good instruction give
How I may bear me here: my prime request,
Which I do last pronounce, is, O you wonder!
If you be maid or no?

MIRANDA

No wonder, sir;
But certainly a maid.

FERDINAND

My language! heavens!
I am the best of them that speak this speech,
Were I but where 'tis spoken.

PROSPERO

How? the best?
What wert thou, if the King of Naples heard thee?

FERDINAND

A single thing, as I am now, that wonders
To hear thee speak of Naples. He does hear me;
And that he does I weep: myself am Naples,
Who with mine eyes, never since at ebb, beheld
The king my father wreck'd.

MIRANDA

Alack, for mercy!

FERDINAND

Yes, faith, and all his lords; the Duke of Milan
And his brave son being twain.

PROSPERO

[Aside] The Duke of Milan
And his more braver daughter could control thee,
If now 'twere fit to do't. At the first sight
They have changed eyes. Delicate Ariel,
I'll set thee free for this.

To Ferdinand
A word, good sir;
I fear you have done yourself some wrong: a word.

MIRANDA

Why speaks my father so ungently? This
Is the third man that e'er I saw, the first
That e'er I sigh'd for: pity move my father
To be inclined my way!

FERDINAND

O, if a virgin,

And your affection not gone forth, I'll make you
The queen of Naples.

PROSPERO

Soft, sir! one word more.

Aside
They are both in either's powers; but this swift business
I must uneasy make, lest too light winning
Make the prize light.

To Ferdinand
One word more; I charge thee
That thou attend me: thou dost here usurp
The name thou owest not; and hast put thyself
Upon this island as a spy, to win it
From me, the lord on't.

FERDINAND

No, as I am a man.

MIRANDA

There's nothing ill can dwell in such a temple:
If the ill spirit have so fair a house,
Good things will strive to dwell with't.

PROSPERO

Follow me.
Speak not you for him; he's a traitor. Come;
I'll manacle thy neck and feet together:
Sea-water shalt thou drink; thy food shall be
The fresh-brook muscles, wither'd roots and husks
Wherein the acorn cradled. Follow.

FERDINAND

No;
I will resist such entertainment till
Mine enemy has more power.

Draws, and is charmed from moving

MIRANDA

O dear father,
Make not too rash a trial of him, for
He's gentle and not fearful.

PROSPERO

What? I say,
My foot my tutor? Put thy sword up, traitor;
Who makest a show but darest not strike, thy conscience
Is so possess'd with guilt: come from thy ward,
For I can here disarm thee with this stick
And make thy weapon drop.

MIRANDA

Beseech you, father.

PROSPERO

Hence! hang not on my garments.

MIRANDA

Sir, have pity;
I'll be his surety.

PROSPERO

Silence! one word more
Shall make me chide thee, if not hate thee. What!
An advocate for an imposter! hush!
Thou think'st there is no more such shapes as he,
Having seen but him and Caliban: foolish wench!
To the most of men this is a Caliban
And they to him are angels.

MIRANDA

My affections
Are then most humble; I have no ambition
To see a goodlier man.

PROSPERO

Come on; obey:
Thy nerves are in their infancy again
And have no vigour in them.

FERDINAND

So they are;
My spirits, as in a dream, are all bound up.
My father's loss, the weakness which I feel,
The wreck of all my friends, nor this man's threats,
To whom I am subdued, are but light to me,
Might I but through my prison once a day
Behold this maid: all corners else o' the earth
Let liberty make use of; space enough
Have I in such a prison.

PROSPERO

[Aside] It works.

To Ferdinand
Come on.
Thou hast done well, fine Ariel!

To Ferdinand
Follow me.

To Ariel
Hark what thou else shalt do me.

MIRANDA

Be of comfort;
My father's of a better nature, sir,
Than he appears by speech: this is unwonted
Which now came from him.

PROSPERO

Thou shalt be free
As mountain winds: but then exactly do
All points of my command.

ARIEL

To the syllable.

PROSPERO

Come, follow. Speak not for him.

Exeunt

Instead of Three Wishes

by Megan Whalen Turner

In this amusing story, Megan Whalen Turner gives a new twist to the traditional tale of the person who is granted three wishes by a magical creature.

Selene and the elf prince met on a Monday afternoon in New Duddleston when she had gone into town to run an errand for her mother. Mechemel was there to open a bank account. He had dressed carefully and anonymously for his trip in a conservative gray suit, a cream-colored shirt, a maroon tie. He was wearing a dark gray overcoat and carried a black leather briefcase. Selene hardly noticed him the first time she saw him.

He was standing on the traffic island in the middle of Route 237 when she went into Hopewell's Pharmacy and was still there when she came out again. She thought he must be cold on a November day with no hat and no gloves. He looked a little panicked out on the median by himself. The traffic light had changed. The walk sign reappeared, but Mechemel remained on the island, rooted to the concrete, with his face white and his pale hair blown up by the wind. Selene walked out to ask if he needed a hand.

"Young woman," he snapped, "I am perfectly capable of crossing a street on my own." Selene shrugged and turned to go, but the light had changed again and she, too, was stranded. While she waited for another chance to cross, the cars sped by. The breeze of their passing pushed Selene and the elf prince first forward, then back. It wasn't a comfortable sensation. When the walk sign reappeared, she was eager to get back to the sidewalk and catch her bus for home. A few steps into the crosswalk, she noticed that the elf prince still had not moved.

Rude old man, she thought, I should leave him here. But she stretched out a hand. Without looking at her, the elf prince put his arm around hers, and they walked to the curb together. Once they were up on the sidewalk, he snatched his arm away, as if it might catch fire.

"Well," he said with a sneer, "I suppose you expect a reward now."

Selene looked at the crosswalk. She looked at the old man. A nut, she thought. Nice suit, though.

"No, thank you," Selene said aloud. "Happy to oblige." She gave him the pleasant but impersonal smile she used on customers when she worked after school at the cafeteria.

"Of course you are." His voice dripped sarcasm, and Selene took a step back. "But I can't let you get away without one, can I?" When he fumbled in the inside pocket of his suit coat, Selene took several more steps back. He pulled out a wallet. From the wallet he extraced three small white cards and pushed them at Selene.

They looked like business cards. Instead of a printed name, a fili-greed gold line wrapped itself in a design in the middle of each white rectangle.

"What are they?" Selene asked.

"Wishes," said the elf prince. "You've got three. Just make a wish and burn a card. It doesn't"—he looked her over with contempt—"require a college education."

"Thanks, but no, thanks," said Selene, and handed the cards back. She'd read about people who were offered three wishes by malevolent sprites. No matter what they wished, something terrible happened. She looked carefully at the man. Behind the nice suit and the tie, he was just as she thought a malevolent sprite might appear.

"What do you mean, 'Thanks, but no, thanks'?" The elf prince was irritated. "They are perfectly good wishes, I assure you. They're not cheap 'wish for a Popsicle' wishes, young woman. They are very high-quality. Here." He pushed them toward her. "Wish for anything. Go ahead."

"I wish for peace on earth," Selene said, and sneaked a look over her shoulder. Her bus was coming up the street but still two blocks away.

"That's not a thing!" snarled the elf prince. "That's an idea. That's a concept. I didn't say wish for a concept. I said a thing. A material object. Go on."

Selene stood her ground. "I'd rather not."

"Look," said the elf prince, "you get a reward for doing me a favor. I can't go around owing you one. What do you want?"

Selene could hear the bus rumbling up behind her. "Why don't you pick something for me?" she asked. "Something you think is appropriate. How would that be?" The bus stopped beside her, and the doors sighed open.

"Well," said the elf prince with some asperity, "I can hardly think—"

"—Of something off the top of your head? I'm like that, too," said Selene. "Tell you what, when you think of something, you can send it to my house. It's easy to find. We live in the New Elegance Estates."

She hopped onto the bus. The doors closed behind her, and the elf prince was left standing on the sidewalk as the bus drove away.

Oh, she thought as she sat down, I wish I hadn't told him where we lived. I wish I hadn't.

Left behind, the elf prince was nonplussed. When he recovered, he propped his elegant briefcase on the top of a postal box and opened it wide enough to pull out a small Persian carpet, which he threw down on the sidewalk. He stepped onto it.

"Home," he snapped, and disappeared.

Selene and her mother lived in a housing development several miles beyond the suburbs of New Duddleston. The builder who had bought up the farm on the outskirts of the city had intended to build an entire community of different-size houses and apartment buildings. He had laid out the roads, and then paved all the driveways. By the time he began building the houses, he had run out of money. Only a few of the smaller ones had been finished when he went bankrupt, leaving the owners of those houses surrounded by vacant lots covered in weeds with driveways that led to no houses and roads that went nowhere.

Selene's mother was one of the owners. She had used her savings to buy the house and had hoped to take in a lodger to help with the mortgage payments, but so far no one had been interested in such a peculiar neighborhood. She and her daughter lived frugally on a monthly insurance check and waited for someone else to buy the land and build houses to go with all the driveways.

"Hello! I'm home!" Selene shouted as soon as she was in the door.

"I'm in the kitchen. Did you have a good day at school?" Her mother had her wheelchair pushed up to the kitchen table. In front of her was a plate of crumbs and one remaining half of a scone.

"Hey," said Selene, "I thought I told you to eat those up yesterday when they were still fresh."

Selene's mother smiled. "I ate as many as I could. And you know that I always think your scones are better the longer I wait."

"That's only because you're hungrier when you finally eat them. I bought the stuff to make more. And I got your prescription filled. Do you want a pill now?" The wrinkles around her mother's eyes showed that she was having a painful day.

"Yes, please, dear," she said. "I'm a little sore. Did you have any trouble getting the prescription filled?"

Selene was reminded of the peculiar man outside the pharmacy. "Not with the prescription," said Selene. "They know me at the pharmacy."

"But you did have a problem?"

"Not a problem, really. But I ran into a nutty old guy." Selene described her encounter with the elf prince. She provided a skillful caricature. "Still, I wish I hadn't told him where we lived."

"I wouldn't worry. He has probably forgotten all about you by now."

• • •

The next morning, as Selene was pulling on her coat before going to school, the doorbell rang. She opened the front door and found a shockingly green small man on the front step.

"Your gift," he said, "from Prince Mechemel of the Elf Realm of South Minney." And he swept a bow all the way down to his toes and waved it out across the stubbly crab-grass to the street. A golden coach and six black horses stood at the curb.

"Zowee," said Selene. "Is that for me?"

"Our master sends it to you and hopes that you will accept it as repayment of his debt to you."

"Oh." Selene paused. "Look," she said, "that's really nice of him, but could you . . . take it back? I really appreciate it and everything. It's very beautiful, but the coach would never fit in the garage, and I don't have anywhere to keep the horses. Tell him I said thank you, though." She carefully closed the door.

By the time she had walked to the living room window that overlooked the front yard, the leprechaun, the coach, and the horses were gone.

"Zow-ee," Selene said again, and went to tell her mother all about it.

"It's a good thing we don't have many neighbors," her mother said. "They'd wonder."

The next day the doorbell rang again. This time when Selene opened the door, there was an elegant woman with deep blue skin and dark green eyes. She was wrapped in a sea green cape that covered her all the way down to her toes and puddled there at her feet. In one thin, beautiful hand she held a set of keys on a silver key ring.

"Our master entreats you to accept these as repayment of his debt to you."

She held out the keys. Selene started to ask what they were for, when she caught sight of the mansion newly arrived on the lot across the street.

"Oh, my," she said. "Is that . . . ?"

"For you," said the blue woman with a happy smile. "Do you like it?"

"It is a beautiful house," said Selene.

"Palace, really," said the hamadryad. "It's got those gates in the front. I don't really remember if that makes it a palace or a château, exactly. I know that if it had a portcullis, it would be a castle, and it doesn't. But it does have those little turrets at the corners, so I think that means it's not a château."

Selene was silent.

"I'd definitely call it a palace," the hamadryad assured her. "You do like it?"

Selene said that she thought it was a lovely palace, she really liked the gold turrets at the corners, but she lived alone with her mother, and they could never use that much room.

The dryad looked so crestfallen that Selene rushed to say, "It's not that I don't like it. It's just that we're really very comfortable here."

"It's got central heating," the dryad said wistfully.

"We couldn't afford to pay the bill," Selene said sadly.

"And really lovely plumbing. Much nicer than we have back at the castle."

"I'm afraid not," said Selene. "But thank you, really. Please tell Mr.— His Highness that all this isn't necessary. He doesn't owe me anything."

She smiled at the dryad, and the dryad smiled sadly back and went away. The lovely white palace with the gold roof dissolved into mist and disappeared.

The next day Selene waited for the doorbell to ring. By the time she decided it wasn't going to, she had made herself late for school. On Thursday afternoons she worked in the school cafeteria baking rolls for school lunches. She didn't get off the bus until almost five-thirty and walked home through the pitch dark. She could see the lights in her house from a long way off.

As she went inside, her mother called from the living room. "Selene, do come meet the delightful young man who's come to marry you."

"Marry me?" She went into the living room. Her mother had her wheelchair pulled up to one side of the coffee table. On the other sat a young man, about Selene's age, in a fitted maroon velvet tunic that was held in place by a wide belt across his thighs. He wore dark green tights and leather slippers punched full of tiny cross-shaped holes. His cape was thrown over one shoulder and artistically draped on the sofa beside him. It was also maroon velvet but was imprinted with a leaf pattern. Green lace leaves in the same pattern trimmed its edges. In his lap was a soft conical hat with a twelve-inch blue feather curling above it.

The prince was very handsome, Selene had to admit. He had dark curly hair and very round blue eyes. He had the very cleft in his chin that is the prerequisite of fairy-tale princes.

He stood up and bowed from the waist. "A great pleasure to make your acquaintance," said the prince.

"It's nice to meet you, too," said Selene. "Did I hear that you're supposed to marry me?"

"Yes," said her mother. "It's what's-his-name's newest idea. He thought any girl would jump at the chance to marry a prince."

"That's the theory," said Selene. She turned back to the prince. "Could you," she said, "tell me a little about yourself?"

They spent a pleasant evening together, Selene, her mother, and Harold. Until her accident, Selene's mother had taught history at the high school. Since then, she had pursued her profession at home, sending Selene to the university library for enormous piles of books on the weekends. Now that she had a genuine fourteenth-century prince on hand, she had endless questions to ask.

Unfortunately, Harold couldn't answer them. He knew quite a bit about the clothes people had been wearing when he'd last been in the human world, but he didn't know anything about treaties or border disputes or religious schisms. All he could say was that he thought that a few heretics had been burned in his day, but he couldn't remember which kind.

"We had ministers to keep track of all those things," Harold explained lamely. "I'm sure that if they were here, they could answer all your questions." He looked around, as if he expected a prime minister or a chargé d'affaires to pop out from behind the sofa.

"What did princes do?" Selene asked.

"We gave treaties the authority of our names," Harold said grandly.
"How?"

"Well." The prince looked uncomfortable. "We signed them, you know, with our names."

They ended up discussing the elf prince's court. Selene asked about the plumbing. Her mother asked about the central heating. Then they asked about the elf prince. Harold was surprised to hear that Selene's impression of him had not been favorable.

"He's mostly really very nice," he insisted. "I once dropped a flagon of red wine in his reflecting pool and he wasn't angry at all." Harold did his best to convince them of Mechemel's kindness, his generosity, and his good humor. Selene was skeptical, but her mother pointed out that anyone who has recently had a fright can be forgiven a lapse in manners.

"I think the passing cars must have disturbed him," she said.

"Are elves really bothered by iron?" asked Selene.

"I don't know that it actually hurts them," said Harold, "but it does, you know, give them the willies."

"Yes, I see," said Selene's mother.

"Of course, automobiles give me the willies, too," admitted the prince. "Things didn't move so fast in my day."

Harold spent the night in the spare bedroom. They sent him back the next morning.

As she closed the door behind him, Selene's mother said, "He was a very nice young man."

"He was sweet," said Selene. "But what in the world would he have done if I'd married him? Gone out to look for a job?"

"Poor boy, can you picture him trying to get one?" Her mother laughed. "What are your qualifications? Well, I look good in velvet and . . ."

"Can't read or write . . ."

"Can't type, can't drive, don't know what electricity is, never heard of a vacuum cleaner."

"He couldn't buy groceries, cook dinner, or pay bills."

"If you wrote out the checks, he could sign his name," Selene's mother reminded her.

"Oh, of course," said Selene, "he would have *ministers* to take care of all that." She added, "He'd do okay if he just came with a pot of gold."

"Oh, no," said her mother. "That's *leprechauns.*"

Selene was late for school again. As she went out the door, she said, "This is the third gift we've rejected. Do you think His Highness the elf prince of wherever will give up?"

Mechemel wasn't giving up. He was getting out the big guns, going to the experts, checking with an authority on humans. He went to talk to his mother. She had a room at the top of the castle with windows on all four walls so that she could lie in bed and look out at the forest. She was old and a little frail, and she didn't get around much, so she passed her time keeping an eye on daily activities in the forest and watching television.

Mechemel climbed up the stairs to her tower. He sat beside her bed and twiddled his thumbs while he explained his difficulty. After a while he grew suspicious of her silence and looked up in outrage.

"You're laughing at me!"

"Mechemel"—his mother's laugh was a lovely sound—"this is the most foolish thing that I have ever heard in my life. I warned you about how fast those iron contraptions can go."

"It's your fault," said Mechemel. "You're the one who wanted to keep your gold in a bank. Who ever heard of fairy gold in a safe-deposit box? Much less a checking account?"

"I know, dear." She smiled apologetically. "But so many of these mail-order companies want to be paid by check or money order, and the sprites were complaining about the lines at the post office. I thought you'd send a leprechaun."

"Leprechauns are unreliable," grumped her son. "They only have to meet one sharp character, and they hand over everything."

"Yes," admitted the fairy queen, "but surely you could have sent a hamadryad, or even one of those human princes that are always hanging around."

"Hamadryads are even worse than leprechauns, and the princes, well . . ." He smiled ruefully at last. "There's no point pretending that any of them were gifted with brains."

"And here you are fussed because the mortal girl thought the same thing. Stop sulking and admit that this is funny."

Mechemel stiffened and then stifled a snort. "You should have seen her face when I pulled out the wishes. She looked afraid for her life."

"She probably was, poor thing."

"What did she think I would do, turn her into a frog?"

"She probably thought that you were a homicidal maniac."

"A what?"

"You don't watch enough television, Mechemel. It's one of those humans that go around murdering other humans for no good reason." She waved one hand at the television set on a stand beside the bed. It stood on a stand of crystal and carefully wrought gold. Its cord ran across the floor and out one window, where it dropped to the ground and was wired directly into one of Ontario Hydroelectric's cross-country power cables.

"I don't understand how you can stand to watch that."

"Oh, it's amusing sometimes. It's so terribly dull, since the humans have stopped coming to court. There's never anyone new to talk to. Watching them talk to each other is the next best thing."

"You should go out more."

The elf queen slipped deeper into her feather pillows. "It's too much trouble. Things have changed too much in the last hundred years. Besides," she added slyly, "look what happened to you."

"It's all very well to snicker about it. The longer I owe her a favor, the more in debt I am. So . . ."

"So what?"

"So tell me what will make her happy."

"I haven't a clue."

"But you're supposed to know!" He threw up his hands. "And stop laughing!"

His mother reached out a hand to pat him on the knee. "Don't worry," she said. "You find out a little more about her, and then we'll think of something."

On Saturday, Selene was out in the front yard, sawing at a dead tree, when the elf prince arrived. The tree had been the builder's one attempt to fulfill a clause in the contract that said "fully landscaped." Stuck into ground packed hard by bulldozers and surrounded by weeds, the little tree had given up immediately and died. Selene didn't mind the weeds—many of them were pretty— but the brittle branches of the dead tree depressed her, so she was cutting it down.

She looked up from her work and realized a man was watching her from the sidewalk. "Are you the next silly idea of that ridiculous elf?"

"No," said Mechemel, and didn't say anything else.

Selene was terribly embarrassed. She looked from her saw to the tree and back to Mechemel.

"Yes," he said, "do stop dismembering that poor bush and invite me in."

"It's a tree, actually."

"Bush," said Mechemel. "*Salix bebbiana.* Or it was. All it is now is dead."

He moved past Selene toward the ramp that led to the front door. "Fortunately uninhabited," he said as he went.

Still carrying the saw, Selene followed him up the ramp and into the house. He waited in the hall while she went to fetch her mother. He looked startled when Selene rolled her in, but collected himself quickly.

"I understand," he said, "that you are willing to take a lodger?"

Selene's mother asked him for references, and he provided them. He told them that he was a visiting professor at the local university.

"Waterloo or Wilfred Laurier?" Selene's mother asked.

"Uh, Waterloo."

"Lovely, perhaps we know the same people. You said you were in the history department?"

Mechemel saw that he was on dangerous ground and retreated

rapidly. He was new there; he didn't know anyone; he wouldn't actually be teaching in the department, just doing research.

"Oh," said Selene's mother, disappointed. "Well, still. I'm sure it will be very nice to have you as a lodger. Did you say that you wanted to take your meals here?" she asked hesitantly.

Mechemel shuddered. "No, thank you," he said.

So Mechemel moved in. Selene and her mother wondered about their new lodger. He came with very little luggage, just the one suitcase. He was always home at dinnertime, but he never seemed to eat. Selene cooked her mother dinner, and the two of them ate at the kitchen table, wondering what Mechemel was doing in his room.

"Maybe he lives on store-bought cookies and soda," said Selene.

"It would be warm soda," her mother pointed out. "He doesn't have a fridge." They didn't see the leprechauns skipping up to the spare bedroom window, carrying trays of covered dishes. Mechemel was willing to sacrifice in order to get his debt paid off, but he was not going to eat whatever humans called food. Before he'd left the castle, his mother had told him dire stories about microwaves and things called burritos.

Mechemel had been staying with Selene and her mother for a week before Selene did any baking. On Friday, Mechemel's rent payment made it possible to buy an extra dozen eggs, baking chocolate, and five pounds of extra-fine cake flour. In the evening, she read through her collection of secondhand cookbooks and decided that she wanted to try a brittle chocolate crème de menthe gâteau.

"It sounds wonderful," said her mother. "Do we have crème de menthe?"

"Somebody brought some to the Christmas party last year. I think it's still in the closet over the oven."

"Now that we are rolling in dough, so to speak, will you not be making any more scones?" In the past, Selene's baking has been limited to a weekly batch of scones because their ingredients were affordable.

"Oh, I'll make those first thing in the morning, then try the cake," said Selene, and she got up early on Saturday in order to have the scones ready for her mother's breakfast. Mechemel woke to the aroma of buttermilk currant scones baking in the oven. He got out of his uncomfortable narrow bed and into his clothes before being pulled irresistibly into the kitchen. Selene was measuring out ingredients for her cake with the precision of a chemist; her mother was having a cup of coffee. Mechemel sniffed, appreciatively.

"Are those scones?" he asked. He suffered from an elfin addiction to sweet things.

"Yes," said Selene, without turning around. There was only half an inch of crème de menthe left in the bottle, and she was looking through the recipe to see if it was enough.

"May I have one?"

"Of course." Selene looked around and smiled at him, before turning back to the recipe. It was not the impersonal smile that she used on customers; it was a real one that she reserved for people she thought she might like.

Mechemel's eyebrows went up in astonishment. He remembered that Harold had said she had a smile that would make flowers bloom early, but he had assumed that Harold was exaggerating, as Harold always did. Mechemel sat down at the table. While Selene's mother watched in amusement, he ate the entire plate of scones. The only one left was the one in Selene's mother's hand.

When Selene was done measuring out the crème de menthe, she looked at the plate, empty of all but crumbs. "You ate them *all?*"

Embarrassment colored Mechemel's face deep pink. "I am terribly sorry. I don't know what came over me. . . . I, um . . . It's been some time," he explained, "since I had scones. And these really are, were," he corrected himself, "delicious."

He grew still pinker when Selene laughed. "It's okay. I can make more," she said, "but see if I offer you any cake."

"You're making a cake?" Mechemel said with delight, then back-tracked hastily. "Well, no, no, I certainly wouldn't trouble you for any." He stood up from the table and tried not to look disappointed.

Selene's mother reached up to pat him on the arm. "No, sit down," she said. "Selene was only teasing."

The elf prince looked at her in surprise. He wasn't used to being teased, and no one but his mother had ever patted him on the arm.

So Mechemel sat at the kitchen table and talked to Selene's mother while Selene made her brittle chocolate crème de menthe gâteau. Selene's mother told him their version of the week's events and ended up saying, "In fact, if you had been a present from the elf prince, you would have been perfect."

Mechemel winced. If he had known, he could have sent them a real lodger. It was too late now.

Selene's mother asked Mechemel about his research project, and he made up answers as well as he could. He gathered that Selene's mother was writing a dissertation on something called the Battle of Hastings. He drew a strange look when he raised one eyebrow and said, "Which one was that?"

"Surely you know the Battle of Hastings. When the English lost to the Norman invaders?"

"Oh, yes, of course. How silly of me, yes. A friend of mine was there." He saw another startled look forming and realized his error. "Last year, at the site, not at the battle itself, of course." After that he thought he had better excuse himself. He went back to his room and didn't come out until the cake was ready. He ate half of it.

On Sunday, Selene made another batch of scones for herself and her mother and one batch for Mechemel to eat all by himself. On Monday, he came home in the evening with a bag of groceries and a jar of cloudberry jam. He said that he didn't think it was fair that they spend all his rent money feeding him.

"The jam is from my mother's pantry."

"Oh, does your mother live near here?"

"Not far," he responded, "as the crow flies."

Every week, Mechemel would bring home a bag of ingredients for scones and other delicacies, and on Saturdays, Selene would bake, experimenting with every recipe in her worn-out cookbooks. On weekdays, when Selene and her mother thought he was going to sit in the library at the University of Waterloo, Mechemel went home to talk with his mother. He described Selene's sugary concoctions in detail and related his conversations with Selene's mother. Then he and his mother tried to pick a gift that would please Selene. His mother suggested a cubic zirconium tennis bracelet that she had seen advertised on the shopping channel.

"She doesn't wear any jewelry. She'd probably sell it to buy cake flour. As nearly as I can tell, baking is the one thing she enjoys."

"Buy her five hundred pounds of cake flour."

"I can't. Every time I give her that sort of thing, she makes more cakes and scones and I eat them."

"Well, I don't know which I envy more, your never-ending supply of sweets or the company of that girl's mother. She seems quite clever."

"She is."

"We haven't had a clever person here in years." Mechemel's mother sighed, and Mechemel promised that when he had taken care of his obligation to Selene, he'd try to find something that would amuse her, maybe a videocassette recorder.

He was always back at the house in New Elegance Estates in the late afternoon to share a cup of tea and a long talk with Selene's mother. While they talked, they ate Selene's scones. They discussed history, more often than not; it was Selene's mother's passion. She was particularly interested in Canadian history, and Mechemel, who had lived through a good part of it, was able to provide eyewitness reports of several events. He, of course, lied about the source of his information.

So a little of Selene's mother's loneliness was relieved, and a little of Mechemel's mother's boredom, but Mechemel got no closer to finding a gift to repay Selene. With each passing day, he was more determined to choose a gift without parallel. Money was too easy. He wanted something better.

In the springtime, New Elegance Estates looked as good as they ever did. All the weeds were blooming. The empty streets were washed clean by nightly rains. Mechemel walked home one evening, avoiding puddles, carrying his bag of groceries. He heard footsteps pounding behind him and turned to wait for Selene. Behind her, the number seventeen bus pulled away.

Selene didn't bother to evade the puddles. As she ran, she stamped heavily into each one in her path, spraying water in circles across the pavement. She slowed down before she reached Mechemel, but several especially motivated droplets landed on his shoes. He leaned to look at them over the top of the grocery bag, then looked at Selene with his eyebrows raised.

"Heavens," she said, "will you melt?"

He watched the drops evaporate before he answered dryly, "I think I'm safe. Did you have a good day at school?" He made a hook with his elbow, and she caught her arm through it. They walked shoulder to shoulder toward home.

"Good enough. Only sixteen more days to go." When they got to the front yard, Mechemel pointed with his chin.

"Your bush has rejuvenated."

Selene was stunned. She had never finished the job that she'd started the day Mechemel arrived. All winter, the tree had stood with its trunk sawed halfway through. Now that the warm weather had come, tiny shoots of green had sprung from the bark below the cut.

"I think you'll find that you can cut away the dead part and those green shoots will grow up into a very pretty bush."

"You said it was a bush before, what did you call it?"

"*Salix bebbiana*. It's one of the diamond-barked willows."

"Goodness, you know a lot."

"Not everything," said Mechemel.

That was the day that the letter came. Selene found it in the mailbox at the top of the ramp to the front door. She dumped her schoolbooks down in the front hall and sat beside them while she read it. Mechemel watched her face grow pink with pleasure and then fade with disappointment.

"What is it?" he asked.

"Oh, it's a letter from the Boston School of Culinary Arts."

"Yes?"

"I sent them my scones by overnight mail. As a sample of my work. They liked my scones, and they say I can enroll in their school." She looked up at Mechemel. "They are very exclusive. It's an honor just to be invited to enroll, especially for the pastry program. Listen," and she read aloud from the letter. " 'We thank you for your application. The judges enjoyed your scones and feel that although their charm is rough, you may have talent worthy of cultivation.' "

"Sounds very pompous," said Mechemel.

"They are, but famous, too."

"Did you want to go study there?"

"Lots."

"Then why aren't you more pleased?"

"No money," said Selene.

"Ah," said Mechemel, suddenly understanding.

"Besides," said Selene as she folded up the letter and put it away, "there's Mother. She'd hate to move to Boston. And I couldn't leave her here on her own, so it's no go either way."

"What will you do instead?"

"Probably take the job they've offered me at the school cafeteria. It's full-time." She collected her books and left Mechemel standing in the front hall.

After a while, he put his bag of groceries down and went back out the door to visit his mother.

The next day was Thursday. Selene came home late, but the sunset was not yet over when she closed the front door behind her.

"Selene," her mother called, "come into the living room."

Selene went to the doorway. "Only fifteen days left," she said to her mother, who had her wheelchair pulled up to the coffee table. Mechemel was sitting on the couch next to her. "What's up?" Selene wanted to know.

"Remember that elf prince?" said her mother.

"Oh, no," said Selene. "He hasn't resurfaced, has he?"

"He has," said Mechemel.

What now? Selene almost said aloud, but thought better of it. She looked at Mechemel and blushed.

"He's been slow," said her mother, "but he has finally selected a present for you." Mechemel handed Selene an envelope. Inside, a piece of parchment, much adorned with ribbons and seals, informed her that she was the recipient of a centennial scholarship awarded for excellence in the Very Fine Art of Scone Making and that the Mechemel Foundation would pay the tuition and board at the School of Culinary Excellence of her choice, so long as it subscribed to the high standards of the foundation.

"But I told you—" Selene directed a fierce look at Mechemel.

"And," her mother interrupted her, "while you are away at school, Mechemel's mother has most graciously invited me to stay with her. For as long as is necessary to complete your education," she emphasized.

"With her?"

"And myself," said Mechemel.

"Yes," said Selene's mother with a smile, "I'll be able to give Harold your regards."

"Zowee."

So Mechemel arranged for a dryad to move into the willow in the front yard and keep an eye on the house. Selene went to Boston, and her mother became great friends with the elf queen. In the evening, they sometimes watched television together, but mostly they talked. Mechemel sometimes stopped in, and the three of them discussed the Meech Lake Accord and the French and Indian War. In the summer, Selene came to visit as well and demonstrated what she'd learned in school: cherry coulis, blancmange, clafoutis, mille-feuille, and puff pastry with fresh strawberries picked in the forest by the sprites. And every afternoon, she made a fresh batch of scones for tea.

from

The Magician's Apprentice

by Tom McGowen

A young street urchin's attempt to rob a magician's house has unexpected results in this excerpt from Tom McGowen's fantasy novel.

A frightened man was hurrying down a dark, silent street in a night-shrouded city. He cast quick, apprehensive glances in all directions as he went, and kept his hand on the hilt of a knife that hung in a sheath at his hip. His clothing marked him as a well-to-do member of the merchant class, and he was mentally cursing the folly that had kept him carousing in a tavern until darkness had closed over the city. For while by day the city's streets were thronged with busy, surging crowds, sundown saw them turn into black, winding ribbons that were shunned by honest folk and prowled by members of the city's underworld—beggars, pickpockets, gangs of youths who took pleasure in beating senseless any lone traveler they encountered, and ruthless men and women who would cut a man's throat for a single iron coin. Praying he would not meet any of these creatures of darkness, the merchant gripped his stone-bladed knife and trotted nervously on his way.

Ahead of him glowed a welcome patch of light cast by a small lantern above the door of a house. Gratefully, the man headed for it, but as he entered the rim of the dim illumination a small ragged figure materialized out of the darkness beyond and darted at him. The merchant gave a squawk of dismay and jerked the knife from its sheath. But a high-pitched voice was whining: "Good man, kind man, please spare a coin, just a bit of iron, for a poor hungry orphan," and the hands that clutched at him reached no higher than his chest. A child.

The merchant jerked his arm away from the softly clutching fingers. "Get away," he said hoarsely, and gave the urchin a shove that sent him sprawling to the ground.

The beggar lay face down in the dim yellow pool of light and sent up a soft, thin wailing. The merchant, his heart pounding from the terror that had momentarily gripped him, broke into a run and vanished from sight in the darkness.

When the man's footfalls had died away in the distance, the boy abruptly ceased his sobbing. He rolled nimbly up to a cross-legged position, and with a quick jerk of his head tossed back the tangle of black hair that had fallen over his eyes. His teeth flashed in a mocking grin as he examined the contents of the money bag he had slipped from the merchant's tunic even as the man had been pushing him away.

The boy sorted out the coins and hissed with pleasure. A dozen irons, four coppers, and a silver! Old Paplo, who had taught him the art of picking pockets, had given him a quota of two irons a day to bring home. If the boy turned in that sum, or more, Paplo fed him and permitted him to sleep in a corner of the tiny hovel that was the old man's dwelling. Less than that, and the boy was cursed, slapped, and turned away to find his food and shelter as best he could. So the contents of this money bag, doled out a little at a time, would keep old Paplo placated, and the boy fed and housed, for a good many days.

Of course, he'd not turn everything over to the old man. He would take the silver piece to a money changer who'd give him at least seven coppers for it, and those he would use for fun—a visit to the Street of Sweetmakers, a seat at a dogfight, and a goodly quantity of skewers of spiced roasted meats and other delicacies he seldom had an opportunity to enjoy.

Hopping lithely to his feet, the boy stuffed the money bag into his ragged smock and prepared to saunter on his way. He had taken no more than a step when a loud cough made him glance toward the doorway over which hung the lantern that spread its little glow upon this patch of street. A man had just emerged from the house and was standing with one hand on the door's handle. He was a tall, fat man, wearing the ankle-length gown of pale blue that marked him as a sage—an astrologer, dream explainer, or some similar occupation that dealt with the realms of knowledge and wisdom. The lantern light showed him to have a youthfully smooth face that seemed at odds with the ring of pure white hair that formed a fringe around a shining bald head. The man directed a brief, incurious glance at the ragged figure of the little boy, then coughed again, noisily, bending over with a fist to his mouth. Then he straightened, unhooked the lantern, and with it swinging in his hand moved off down the street. Being a sage, he, of course, had no fear of the dark and dangerous streets; robbers and brigands left such men alone lest powerful curses be placed on them.

The boy's eyes followed the glimmer of swaying light until it melted into darkness, then he flicked his glance back to the entrance of the house. It seemed to him that the man had left the door ajar without noticing it, and after a moment this was confirmed when the boy became aware of a dim line of light coming from inside the house, marking the narrow opening.

The boy quickly moved to the door. Gently, he pushed it open a bit more and poked his head through the doorway. A thin candle was burning in a wall niche near the door, probably left there by the sage so that he wouldn't have to fumble about in darkness when he returned, but the rest of the house was pitch-black and silent. There did not seem to be anyone within.

The boy licked his lips and pondered for a moment. To enter the home of a sage for the purpose of robbery was to take a dreadful chance. The house might well be protected by a spell that would bring swift death to a burglar. On the other hand, the thought of the treasures he might find acted as a spur to the boy. With a silent prayer to

Durbis, the spirit who watches over thieves, he slipped past the door and closed it behind him.

Digging into the twisted length of cloth that served him both as sash and pocket, he withdrew a stump of candle and lit it from the candle burning in the niche. Holding the light at arm's length, he moved cautiously into the depths of the house.

There were only a few rooms, and he examined them all, peering into every corner. He found nothing of any real value: some clothing in a chest in a room with a sleeping mat; writing materials on a shelf in a room with painted walls; and clay cups, dishes, and cooking pots in a room with an open fireplace. From this room he followed the light into a short hall at the end of which was a door. Pulling open the door, he beheld a flight of irregular stone steps, winding down into darkness.

"Perhaps he keeps his valuables and magical things hidden in the cellar," muttered the boy. His bare feet moved noiselessly on the stairs. The door softly bumped shut behind him.

The steps led down into a single room dug out of the earth and walled with stones and mortar. As the boy moved cautiously forward, the candle revealed a broad wooden table cluttered with clay bottles and beakers and a variety of objects that were totally unfamiliar to him. He looked them over for a moment, then, seeing nothing worth taking, moved toward a large cabinet that stood in one corner.

At that moment there was a faint squeak from the top of the stairs. The door, which the boy knew had closed behind him, had been opened by someone.

Terror flooded the boy, but he did not lose his wits. In an instant he had blown out the candle and wiggled his way as far as he could go beneath the table. Perhaps whoever was coming down the stairs would not see him and he could make his escape later. Heart pounding, he waited.

Heavy footsteps padded down the stairs. A figure, holding the lantern that had hung over the house's doorway, moved ponderously into the cellar. It paused, and the glow of light danced on the walls as the lantern was lifted and moved about. Then the figure came to the table, stooped down, and spilled light upon the small ragged figure crouched there. Sick with fear, the boy stared back into the face that was revealed by the lantern light—a smooth, fleshy face with a fringe of white hair surrounding a bald head. It was the sage.

The man gazed solemnly at the shivering boy. "Now," he said in a deep pleasant voice, "if I were a spider and you were a fly, you'd be in serious trouble—eh?"

The boy's fear dissolved into astonishment. He had expected a bellow of surprise and a rain of blows and kicks, but it was obvious that the man had expected to find him here. The boy considered that. It could only mean that he had been deliberately trapped. The loud coughs had been to attract his attention, the door had been left ajar to entice him—the man had obviously wanted him to enter the house, had given him time to do so, and then had come back to catch him. Why?

The man hooked one foot around the leg of a nearby stool and pulled it to him. With a grunt, he seated himself, the lantern dangling from his hand. "You may come out from under there now," he suggested amiably.

The boy eased his way from beneath the table and warily stood up. His eyes darted about. The man had placed himself in such a way that he blocked the stairs, so escape was out of the question at the moment.

The boy studied his captor. Like the boy himself and most of the other inhabitants of the city, the man was dark-eyed and tan-skinned. His features were fine and regular; he had probably been handsome as a young man. A single earring, a tiny ball of polished blue stone, dangled from a delicate chain in his left ear. Although at first glance he seemed fat and slow-moving, the boy had the feeling that he would be able to move with catlike quickness if he chose and that his bulk was more muscular than flabby. There was an air of calm authority about him, as if he would make himself master of most any situation. And, the boy reflected sourly, he was certainly master of this one.

The man was also studying the boy. His first impression was of a barefoot, undernourished child in soiled leg wrappings and a ragged smock that was far too big. The boy resembled any of the other ill-fed, unclean, uneducated urchins that swarmed in the gutters of Ingarron city. But there were subtle differences. He did not slouch; he held himself erect, with poise. And the dark eyes in the thin face framed by the mop of black hair were alert and intelligent.

"My name," said the man after a time, "is Armindor. Armindor the Magician."

The boy darted him a worried glance but made no reply. Armindor waited for a bit, then said, "And what is your name?"

"Tigg."

"How old are you, Tigg?"

The boy shrugged. "About twelve summers. Maybe half a summer older or younger."

"Have your parents never told you your exact age?" asked the man.

"I have no parents."

"An aunt or uncle? Older sister or brother? Anyone?"

Again the boy shrugged. "There's an old man called Paplo, but I'm not related to him—I don't think. I steal for him so he can get drunk. He gives me food and lets me sleep in his house if I steal enough to satisfy him."

"I see. Then you have no family," said Armindor. It seemed to Tigg that the man was pleased about that.

"What are you going to do to me?" demanded the boy. He knew that he was completely in this man's power and had no illusions as to what that might mean. Armindor could beat him senseless, abuse him in any way he chose, or even kill him. He could sell Tigg into slavery, or turn him over to the city judges, who would have his thumbs cut off so that he could never pick pockets again. But somehow, Tigg felt that the man did not intend any of those things.

"Well, now," said Armindor, in answer to Tigg's question, "I certainly think you must be punished in some way for trying to rob me. Justice demands it. Don't you agree?"

Tigg eyed him. The man's tone was deliberately bantering, and the boy wondered why. He had seen enough of human nature in his young life to be able to sense the intention of malice and cruelty, and he did not sense these things in Armindor's manner. He felt that the man was probing, looking for some special kind of reaction, and Tigg believed this must have something to do with the reason why he had been trapped. He decided to match the magician's bantering manner and see what happened.

He assumed what he knew to be an expression of injured innocence— it had gotten him out of more than one predicament before this, "But, Great Magician, I *didn't* rob you," he pointed out. "You can see for yourself that none of your things are missing. How can you punish me for something that wasn't done? *That* wouldn't be justice, now would it?"

The magician's lips twitched and Tigg inwardly rejoiced; he had apparently chosen the right course. "There is some truth in what you say," said Armindor, nodding. "Very well then, we shall make the punishment fit the situation exactly. You planned to take something from me, but I still have everything that is mine, as you remarked. So, as a punishment I shall take something that is yours—and yet, you too will keep everything you have."

The boy puzzled over this for a moment, trying to fathom Armindor's meaning. "I don't understand," he said.

Armindor leaned forward, causing the stool to creak. "I'll explain. You have three valuable possessions—poise, courage, and wit. I saw the poise when I watched you so neatly relieve that merchant of his money bag. That was when I decided to—invite you into my home. I saw the courage when you didn't break into shrieks and tears when I discovered you under the table. And I saw the wit when you answered my last question. Well, I have been looking for a young person with just those qualities. You see, I have decided that I need an apprentice. And now I have found one—you." He smiled. "Thus your punishment will be effected. As my apprentice you will give me the use of your poise, courage, and wit, while of course continuing to keep them yourself."

Tigg, who had been smirking with pleasure at the magician's praise of his qualities, was suddenly plunged into an abyss of shock. Apprentice? Apprentice to a magician? But that would mean the end of his freedom, the end of his whole way of life! It would mean, he felt sure, work: long hours of work—and probably of *study* as well!

Subduing the grimace he felt like making, he slid a charming smile onto his face. "Why, that would be an honor, Great Magician! What a wonderful bit of luck for me! I always wanted to be a magician's apprentice!" I'll pretend to bow to the old fool's wishes, he thought, and as soon as he's looking the other way I'll skip away from here and never come within a thousand steps of the Street of Sages again!

But Armindor was regarding him with twinkling eyes and the faintest suspicion of a smile twitching at his mouth. The man placed the lantern on the table, then stood up and gently but firmly took hold of Tigg's arm. With the boy in his grip, he moved to the large wooden cabinet that stood against the wall in a corner and opened its doors. He took something from a shelf, nudged the doors shut, and guided Tigg back to the table, where he put down the thing he had taken from the cabinet. Tigg saw that it was a small wax figure, shaped like a human, with arms, legs, and a head.

From the loose sleeve of his gown, Armindor drew forth a small sharp-edged dagger. Before Tigg knew what was happening, the man had grasped a lock of his hair, sawed it off with a quick movement of the knife, and dropped it onto the table beside the wax figure.

"Give me your hand," he commanded.

Tigg did so without thinking, then yelped as the dagger pricked his thumb, drawing forth a bright drop of blood. Armindor picked up the doll and pressed the boy's thumb against it, smearing it with blood. Then he pushed the clump of Tigg's hair into the round lump that served as the doll's head, working the wax with his fingertips until the hair was firmly stuck in place.

"Now," he said, holding the doll under Tigg's nose, "this is *you!* I have your spirit in this simulacrum, Tigg, no matter where you may be. Whatever I do to this will happen to you! If I cut off its arm, *your* arm will shrivel and fall off! If I drop it into a fire, *your* body will burn and melt as the simulacrum burns and melts!"

Tigg stared in terror at the lumpy figure. He knew full well the power that magicians had over people whose simulacrums they possessed. He shivered.

"All right, then," said Armindor softly, smiling and putting the doll gently on the table. "As long as I have this, I'll know that you'll be glad to stay with me and become my apprentice. You wouldn't dream of trying to run away, would you—apprentice?"

Tigg sighed. "No, Great Magician," he agreed. "Just tell me what I have to do."

Tigg took up his abode with Armindor at once. The man showed him to a small room in which there was a thick sleeping mat and bade him good dreams. The boy had never slept on anything but the dirt floor of old Paplo's hovel or the rubbish-strewn bit of riverbank beneath a bridge that provided a roof against the rain, so the mat was a delightful luxury. He stretched out on it, began to ponder his sudden change of fortune, and promptly fell asleep.

He was awakened by Armindor far too early the next morning and arose prepared to be sullen and resentful at his captivity. His sullenness could not hold up against the sight of a breakfast of fried bread and vegetable paste, which Armindor assured him was for him. Breakfast was also a little-known luxury for Tigg; old Paplo had never provided it, and Tigg had usually gone without unless he was able to steal something from a vendor's stall. He was astounded to realize that Armindor intended to give him a breakfast every day, and a small portion of his resentment broke off and went drifting away.

However, it quickly became apparent that, as he had foreseen, a magician's apprentice, like any other kind of apprentice, had to devote most of his waking hours to work and study. But the boy was quite surprised to find this far less unpleasant than he had feared. The work was minimal; it amounted only to keeping the house and cellar moderately tidy, running errands, helping Armindor prepare magical materials, and watching as Armindor dealt with the numerous customers who came to him for magical services. As for the study, to Tigg's amazement, that actually turned out to be sheer pleasure!

At first he was appalled when Armindor informed him that a

magician's apprentice must know how to read and work with numbers. Tigg had never been to school, of course, for there were no schools for ordinary children of the city—much less beggars, thieves, and pickpockets—nor had any of the adults he'd known been capable of reading or doing arithmetic. Those were things done only by priests, sages such as Armindor, and merchant's secretaries. Tigg had never even considered trying to learn to read and write, and it seemed an absolute impossibility. "I can't do it!" he protested.

"Yes, you can," Armindor told him gently. He showed Tigg a flat, thin square of wood upon which a number of painted characters were arranged in rows. "Now, this is called an alphabet. . . ."

When, after a time, Tigg grasped that each mark in the row of marks stood for a sound and that these sound marks could be fitted together to make words, he felt as if a door to a delightful garden had been thrown open and he had been invited to come play in it. There was a longing in him, it seemed, which he hadn't even known about until now, to learn and discover new things.

"Now you are truly on the way to becoming a magician," Armindor told him, "for knowing how to read and write, and do a few other things I shall show you, is the basis of magic." From a pocket within his robe he drew forth a number of sheets of smooth, whitish cloth, all sewn together at one edge and covered with painted words. "This is a book of spells, and every spell in it is one I copied down from some other source. You see, most spells were discovered long, long ago and were preserved by many generations of magicians who carefully copied them down. That is why it is essential for a magician to be able to read and write."

After a few days Armindor introduced Tigg to the other things he had hinted at—the manipulation of numbers. The boy found this, too, to be a source of delight. He knew how to count, up to ten anyway, but he had never dreamed that numbers could be taken apart, put together in different ways, and balanced and juggled as Armindor showed him, using wooden disks. It was like a fascinating game.

There was also the surprising bonus that Armindor never once struck him. Tigg had been prepared for beatings such as he had often received from old Paplo and other adults of his acquaintance, but they never came. Unlike the swarming, poverty-ridden, hovel-dwelling people Tigg had lived among until now, who seemed to spend their lives in a steady grip of rage that frequently flared into curses, blows, and violence, Armindor never lost his temper, never raised his voice. If Tigg made an error at his lessons, the man calmly pointed it out; if the results of Tigg's cleaning tasks were less than satisfactory, Armindor merely suggested that he do them over. Without even being aware of it, Tigg soon slipped into an effort to do his best to please the magician. While he would have resented beatings and scoldings, it became a matter of pride to do things so well that Armindor would never have to mention any shortcomings.

Armindor's magical services seemed to be in great demand; several times each day Tigg watched and listened as the man dealt with someone who sought his help. Many of those who came to him had one of the many sicknesses or maladies that were common throughout the city, and for them Armindor dispensed various potions, pills, and powders with meticulous instructions. "This spell has a sharp and stinging taste the boy will not like," he might tell the mother of a child with a wheezing chest and racking cough, "but you must make him swallow half an eggshellful at dawn, midday, and dusk, to open his throat so that he may breathe properly." At the back of Armindor's dwelling was a small garden in which the magician grew herbs and flowers that were used in making these healing spells, and Tigg learned it would be one of his duties to become familiar with all the plants and their uses.

Other people came to Armindor mainly for knowledge of what their future might hold. For them the magician asked many questions, studied the pattern formed by a number of small, oddly carved bits of bone that he would cast into a bowl, and consulted the complicated charts and diagrams painted on the walls of the room in which he met with his clients. He would then tell the person what to expect and offer advice for countering bad fortune and increasing good. This art, too, Tigg was to learn.

So the boy's days were full and not at all unpleasant. But neverthe-less, Tigg chafed at the feeling that he was not free. He had, after all, been forced into this situation. He was being made to start all over and learn a new profession when he already had a perfectly good profes-sion at which he was highly skilled. He was proud of his ability as a pickpocket and not at all sure that he wanted to become a magician instead. He was often seized with a yearning to go out once more into a crowd of people and pit his clever fingers against the unnoticing stu-pidity of the thronging grown-ups. He sometimes pondered the idea of breaking into the cabinet in Armindor's cellar, stealing the wax image, and carrying it off with him so the magician wouldn't be able to use it to punish him. Then he would find himself thinking of his comfort-able sleeping mat, his regular meals, the rather interesting things he was doing, and the kindness with which Armindor treated him, and he would feel ashamed. The fact was, he didn't know whether to regard Armindor as a kindly rescuer or as a slavemaster.

Nor did he quite know how to regard Armindor's work. Although the man did have a thriving business and plenty of clients, Tigg noticed that he charged most of them, especially those who seemed needy, only nominal sums for his services, and so he seemed to make hardly enough money to get by. Yet he appeared to be almost wealthy. Armindor also had frequent meetings with other blue-robed sages, all of whom, the sharp-eyed Tigg had noticed, wore little blue earrings like the one in Armindor's ear. These men seemed to treat Armindor with considerable respect, and it occurred to Tigg that the man might be something more than just an ordinary magician. The boy sensed a mystery.

When he had been with Armindor for nearly a moon, there was a sudden surprise. He finished breakfast one morning and looked up to see the magician watching him thoughtfully.

"You are doing very well, Tigg. Better than I had even hoped for," the man told him. "I see no reason to wait any longer to carry out the plan I needed you to help me with. In two days a merchant caravan will be leaving on a trip to the city of Orrello on the Silver Sea. You and I will make that trip with the caravan." He stood up. "I must go and make some purchases. While I am gone, you can pack the things we shall need to take to Orrello with us. You'll find them, together with some bags, piled in a corner of the room where I usually meet with clients." Then he strode out of the room, and after a moment Tigg heard the front door close.

The boy's thoughts raced. He knew that Orrello was some twenty days' journey to the north, through uninhabited country. Once he set out on such a journey he was committed to staying with Armindor until the man returned home to this city of Ingarron. Tigg realized this was his chance, and he had to take it *now*, while he could still escape into the streets of Ingarron.

He sprang to his feet, snatched up the burning candle that sat on a shelf nearby, and sped to the cellar. He remembered that the lock on the cabinet in the cellar was a heavy contrivance of intermeshing wooden pegs that was opened with an intricately carved wooden key, but he felt that if he couldn't coax it open somehow he would simply break it or chop it. Down in the cellar he made his way around the littered table and held the candle toward the cabinet door.

The lock was gone. The door was slightly ajar.

Tigg stood motionless with surprise for several seconds. Then he reached out and nudged the door fully open. The candle glow revealed his simulacrum, lying all by itself on the center shelf. All he had to do was pick it up, run upstairs, and dart out the front door, and he would be free again. He could even, if he wished, take a few moments to help himself to some of Armindor's belongings, which would probably fetch a good price in the thieves' market of Ingarron.

But the boy stared at the little waxen figure and gnawed his lip. It was obvious that Armindor had set another trap for him, only this wasn't a trap to ensnare him as the first one had been, it was a trap to force him to make a choice. Armindor was showing him that he could leave if he wished, without any fear of punishment. The man was even offering the thief the chance to rob him, if that was Tigg's wish.

Tigg pondered. Why was Armindor doing this? The boy turned the question over in his mind.

He's left it up to me to decide whether to go or stay, thought Tigg. He's showing me that I really am free. But—he must *want* me to stay, or else he'd have just given me the simulacrum and told me to go. And he's trusting me not to rob him.

He wants me to stay with him. He trusts me.

No one had ever trusted him before. He had never been shown that anyone wanted him before. With strange feelings that he didn't quite understand, Tigg carefully closed the cabinet and hurried upstairs to begin packing.

Magicians of the Way

by Cyril Birch

Cyril Birch is a translator and professor of Chinese literature. Here he retells an old Chinese folktale to paint an amusing and informative picture of magic and wizardry in ancient China.

Buddhist priests shave their heads. But often in a Chinese painting you will see a man, perhaps seated in meditation, whose pious attitude contrasts with his ragged clothes and the mass of unkempt hair on his head. He also will be a holy man, but of the Taoist belief, one who follows the Way or *Tao* of the ancient sage Lao Tzu. Many such men believed that by purifying themselves, or by eating magic herbs or concocting some secret pill or elixir, they could increase their power far beyond the limits of the ordinary human body. Perhaps some of them did so. At any rate, ordinary people heard enough stories about them to believe them the most skilful magicians in the land.

There was the matter of sleep, for instance. A Taoist named Ch'en T'uan, realizing that sleep strengthened both body and mind, set himself to perfect the art. He holds the world record with a sleep of eight hundred years. But he was not always left undisturbed for so long. He lived in seclusion on a mountain called T'ai'huashan. One day he was seen to go down the mountain, and although several months passed he did not return. Other holy men who lived on the mountain told themselves that he had gone to live elsewhere, and returned to their meditations.

Winter drew on, and the stocks of firewood that had been made ready against the cold began to dwindle. The day came when one man was nearing the end of the pile in his woodshed. He took hold of a long thin log and pulled—and discovered that he was grasping a human leg! Horrified, he removed the remaining logs from the top. Then he roared with laughter—to see Ch'en T'uan sit up, rub his eyes, stretch himself and begin to brush the shavings from his person.

On another day, much later, a farmer was scything grass for hay on the lower slope of the mountain. He came to a break in the ground where the dried-up gully of a stream ran down, and there in the gully he was saddened to see a corpse lying. 'Poor fellow,' thought the farmer, and he stooped to take a closer look. Grass and weeds were growing in the soil which had drifted on to the body, and a lark had built its nest between the feet. The farmer was moved to pity. He decided that he would bring a cart to take the corpse away and give it a decent burial. But at this point Ch'en T'uan woke up. Opening wide his eyes he said, 'I was just enjoying a most pleasant nap. Who is this that has disturbed me?'

The farmer recognized the great sage of the mountain. He apologized most humbly for having spoilt the master's rest, and then returned to his scything while Ch'en T'uan strolled slowly off to breakfast.

Liu Ken was a man who devoted himself to Taoism on the mountain Sung-shan. There he acquired many marvellous powers. One of his discoveries was the secret of youth. It was said that when he was over a hundred years old he looked like a boy of fifteen.

Nor did he benefit himself alone. Once a plague broke out in the city of Ying-chuan. Not even the family of the Governor himself was spared. But fortunately the Governor had a high regard for the Way, and when he heard that Liu Ken was in the vicinity he sought his help. Liu Ken at once gave him a piece of paper bearing strangely written characters. It was a charm, which the Governor must paste on the door of his residence at night. The Governor did so: and when morning came, not one member of his family showed any further trace of the dread disease.

But before long Ying-chuan had a change of Governor. The new man, an official named Chang, was very different from his predecessor. He sneered when his subordinates told him of the deeds of Liu Ken. When they persisted with their stories Chang grew angry. He determined to show up this man of marvels, and sent out runners to arrest him. News of this spread quickly through the city. When the runners left the Governor's residence they found the streets blocked by indignant crowds. They themselves had little heart for their task and turned back. But the Governor, nothing daunted, sent troops to break through the crowd and bring Liu Ken to court for questioning.

At length Liu Ken, barefoot and in rags, stood below the gilded chair of the Governor. The court had been cleared of all but the troops, who looked on impassively, determined not to risk their necks by crossing their stern superior. The Governor leant down and addressed Liu Ken in a voice of thunder.

'Are you a magician?' he roared.

Liu Ken's reply showed neither pride nor deference. Calmly he answered, 'Yes.'

'Can you bring down the spirits from the Next World?' the Governor continued.

'I can.'

The Governor was delighted. This was really too easy. This charlatan had fallen straight into his trap. Louder than ever he roared. 'Then let me see some spirits, now in this very court, or you will be punished as an impostor and a swindler.'

Liu Ken glanced to one side, where lay the instruments already prepared for his punishment: the boards for squeezing his ankles, the heavy bamboo rod with which he would be beaten. 'Then he turned back to the Governor, who was amazed to observe a quiet smile on the holy man's face.

'Nothing could be easier,' said Liu Ken softly. He asked for brush, ink-slab, and paper. When a guard had passed them to him he made a few deft strokes on the paper, which he took over to a brazier and committed to the flames. No sooner had the last corner of the paper blackened than the court was filled with the din of trampling hooves and the clatter of armour. The wall at the far end of the court had swung open, to admit a great troop of riders armed with swords and spears. They crowded, four or five hundred of them, into the hall. Then their ranks parted, to reveal a cart in which knelt the two prisoners they were escorting.

Liu ordered the prisoners to be brought out of the cart and led up to the Governor. One was an old man, the other clearly his wife. The old man raised his head and addressed the Governor in tones of stern reproof:

'To think that you, our son, should have brought such disgrace upon us! Do you think your duty to us ended with our death? Or that you can give offence to a holy man without involving us also in your punishment? How can you dare to look us, your dead parents, in the face?'

Ashen-faced, the Governor hastened down from his seat and fell to his knees, weeping, before Liu Ken. He begged him to have mercy, to release his parents.

Liu Ken gave an order, and the Governor looked up to find the court empty save for the holy man and the guards. The far wall was as solid and substantial as ever it had been. And never again did the Governor Chang venture to doubt the powers of those who follow the Way.

Another magician who came up against the authorities was a Taoist named Tso Tz'u, who played a whole series of tricks on the august Duke of Wei. It all began when Tso Tz'u was walking one day along a highway and saw coming towards him a string of a dozen or so coolies, each one laden with a huge basket. Straw packing covered the top of each basket. Tso Tz'u stopped the little procession.

'What have you got in those baskets?' he asked.

'Oranges for the Duke of Wei,' answered the leading porter.

'Oranges!' exclaimed Tso Tz'u. 'How nice for the Duke! But what heavy loads for you poor fellows! Let me help you a little of the way.' And so saying he took the basket from the leading coolie and hoisted it on to his own back. He carried it for a mile or so, then returned it to the first coolie and took over the load of the second. In this way he went right down the line. Now every porter when he received his load back found it lighter than before, and each wondered whether this was merely because of the rest he had had, or whether the Taoist had worked some magic charm for his benefit. When Tso Tz'u had reached the end of the line he took his leave of them, and in due course they reached the Duke's palace and delivered the oranges into the storehouse.

A day or two later the Duke held a small banquet for some visiting noblemen. When all the rich dishes had been disposed of, servants brought in silver dishes laden with luscious golden fruit, and the Duke turned to his guests: 'A rare pleasure, gentlemen! Sweet oranges, freshly brought from the south!'

The mouths of the guests watered as they contemplated the glowing golden fruit. But the first guest to cut one open with the silver knife he was given gaped in dismay—for inside the inviting skin was nothing but empty air. He cast a furtive glance towards the smiling Duke, and wondered fearfully what kind of malice such an insult as this might portend. Then to his surprise he noticed his neighbour looking up in exactly the same way, and then—

'Ancestors bear witness!' roared the Duke in a voice which set all the silver rattling on the tables. 'STEWARD!'

The Duke cursed the steward and his ancestors, and the steward cursed the storekeeper and *his* ancestors, and the storekeeper sought out the chief porter and cursed him and *his* ancestors: for every single one of the whole consignment of oranges was nothing but an empty skin.

Well, of course, the chief porter realized that here was the explanation of the lightness of the loads after Tso Tz'u had carried them for a while, and he told the storekeeper who told the steward who told the Duke that it was all Tso Tz'u's doing. And in no time at all the Duke had Tso Tz'u arrested and thrown into a tiny cell in the state prison.

'He has fed enough at my expense,' said the Duke. 'There is no need to feed him any more.'

And so Tso Tz'u was left to languish and die, and the Duke forgot all about him. He was reminded of the incident only after a year had passed, when one of his earlier guests paid a new visit and asked what punishment had befallen the mischievous Taoist.

'To be sure,' said the Duke, 'it's time his body was taken out and burned.' And he gave orders that this should be done.

But when they lifted the bars and opened the door of the cell, what should meet their eyes but the sight of Tso Tz'u, rapt in meditation, but as ruddy-cheeked and firmly fleshed as ever he had been!

They hardly dared to report their finding to the Duke. But he was not a mean-minded man, and he realized that this was no common malefactor he was dealing with. He gave orders for Tso Tz'u's release and invited him to a dinner. At the end of the dinner Tso Tz'u announced that he was going away, and suggested that the Duke and he should drink a parting cup together. He took a cup of wine and asked for a pin. With the pin he drew a line across the middle of the wine. The wine split down the middle into two portions, which remained separate. Tso Tz'u drank off his portion and handed the Duke the cup, one side of which was still full of wine. But the Duke feared some fresh mischief and would not drink. Tso Tz'u then cheerfully drank up the rest of the wine, and threw up the empty goblet. It did not fall at once, but soared and hovered like a bird below the ceiling of the hall. Everyone watched in astonishment: and when they looked down again, no sign of Tso Tz'u was to be seen.

The tale of these wonders began to spread among the people of Wei, and the Duke grew uneasy at the thought of fresh mishaps that might occur. He regretted his leniency in releasing Tso Tz'u, and gave orders for him to be re-arrested. Soldiers scoured the countryside in search of him. At last a party of troops came across him on a hillside. When Tso Tz'u saw them coming he ran off up the hill. Just above him a flock of sheep were grazing. The soldiers watched him run and started in pursuit. But suddenly, there was no old Taoist to be seen.

'Vanished into thin air,' said the captain of the soldiers in disgust. With pursed lips he surveyed the drifting sheep. Then inspiration seized him. He strode over to a rock on which lay, dozing in the sun, the shepherd of the flock. This man scrambled to his feet as the captain addressed him.

'How many sheep are in your flock?'

'Sixty-nine, sir.'

'Are you sure?' asked the captain.

'Sure? Of course I'm sure. There's Bosseye, and Shaggy, and Twirly-horn, and Flatnose, and . . .'

'I don't want to know all the family!' shouted the captain. 'But we'll see whether you've still got sixty-nine—or seventy!'

And he ordered his men to count them. Unfortunately the sheep wouldn't stand still or form fours to be counted. There were sixteen men in the party, and the captain was given sixteen totals, between forty-two and ninety-three. In desperation he appealed to the shepherd, who was looking on with a grin like a split watermelon. The shepherd gave one glance at the flock, then started in surprise.

'You're right, Captain,' he said. 'There's seventy there. Now who's this come along all uninvited?'

'I know very well who it is,' said the captain. He turned to address the flock. 'Mr Taoist,' he said, 'I do urge you to come along with me. The Duke, my master, is waiting to welcome you.'

There in the middle of the flock, one of the sheep knelt down on the grass and bleated, 'Can I really believe that?'

'That's him,' said the soldiers. They were just making after him—when every sheep in the flock knelt down and bleated, 'Can I really believe that?'

Not wishing to arrest the whole flock, and not at all sure that he would have Tso Tz'u even then, the captain gave up his hopeless task and led his men away.

from

So You Want to Be a Wizard

by Diane Duane

Fantasy author Diane Duane's novel features a lonely New York City girl who discovers a very unusual book at her neighborhood library.

Part *of the problem,* Nita thought as she tore desperately down Rose Avenue, *is that I can't keep my mouth shut.*

She had been running for five minutes now, hopping fences, sliding sideways through hedges, but she was losing her wind. Some ways behind her she could hear Joanne and Glenda and the rest of them pounding along in pursuit, threatening to replace her latest, now-fading black eye. Well, Joanne *would* come up to her with that new bike, all chrome and silver and gearshift levers and speedometer/ odometer and toe clips and water bottle, and ask what she thought of it. So Nita had *told* her. Actually, she had told Joanne what she thought of *her.* The bike was all right. In fact, it had been almost exactly the one that Nita had wanted so much for her last birthday—the birthday when she got nothing but clothes.

Life can be really rotten sometimes, Nita thought. She wasn't really so irritated about that at the moment, however. Running away from a beating was taking up most of her attention.

"Callahan," came a yell from behind her, "I'm gonna pound you up and mail you home in bottles!"

I wonder how many bottles it'll take, Nita thought, without much humor. She couldn't afford to laugh. With their bikes, they'd catch up to her pretty quickly. And then . . .

She tried not to think of the scene there would be later at home— her father raising hands and eyes to the ceiling, wondering loudly enough for the whole house to hear, "Why didn't you hit them *back?*"; her sister making belligerent noises over her new battle scars; her mother shaking her head, looking away silently, because she understood. It was her sad look that would hurt Nita more than the bruises and scrapes and swollen face would. Her mom would shake her head, and clean the hurts up, and sigh. . . .

Crud! Nita thought. The breath was coming hard to her now. She was going to have to try to hide, to wait them out. But where? Most of the people around here didn't want kids running through their yards. There was Old Crazy Swale's house with its big landscaped yard, but the rumors among the neighborhood kids said that weird things happened in there. Nita herself had noticed that the guy didn't go to work like normal people. *Better to get beat up again than go in* there. *But where can I hide?*

She kept on running down Rose Avenue, and the answer presented itself to her: a little brown-brick building with windows warmly alight—refuge, safety, sanctuary. The library. *It's open, it's open. I forgot it was open late on Saturday! Oh, thank Heaven!* The sight of it gave Nita a new burst of energy. She cut across its tidy lawn, loped up the walk, took the five stairs to the porch in two jumps, bumped open the front door, and closed it behind her, a little too loudly.

The library had been a private home once, and it hadn't lost the look of one despite the crowding of all its rooms with bookshelves. The walls were paneled in mahogany and oak, and the place smelled warm and brown and booky. At the thump of the door Mrs. Lesser, the weekend librarian, glanced up from her desk, about to say something sharp. Then she saw who was standing there and how hard she was breathing. Mrs. Lesser frowned at Nita and then grinned. She didn't miss much.

"There's no one downstairs," she said, nodding at the door that led to the children's library in the single big basement room. "Keep quiet and I'll get rid of them."

"Thanks," Nita said, and went thumping down the cement stairs. As she reached the bottom, she heard the bump and squeak of the front door opening again.

Nita paused to try to hear voices and found that she couldn't. Doubting that her pursuers could hear her either, she walked on into the children's library, smiling slightly at the books and the bright posters. She still loved the place. She loved any library, big or little; there was something about all that knowledge, all those facts waiting patiently to be found that never failed to give her a shiver. When friends couldn't be found, the books were always waiting with something new to tell. Life that was getting too much the same could be shaken up in a few minutes by the picture in a book of some ancient temple newly discovered deep in a rain forest, a fuzzy photo of Uranus with its up-and-down rings, or a prismed picture taken through the faceted eye of a bee.

And though she would rather have died than admit it—no respectable thirteen-year-old *ever* set foot down there—she still loved the children's library too. Nita had gone through every book in the place when she was younger, reading everything in sight—fiction and nonfiction alike, fairy tales, science books, horse stories, dog stories, music books, art books, even the encyclopedias.

Bookworm, she heard the old jeering voices go in her head, *four eyes, smart-ass, hide-in-the-house-and-read. Walking encyclopedia. Think you're so hot.* "No," she remembered herself answering once, "I just like to find things out!" And she sighed, feeling rueful. *That* time she had found out about being punched in the stomach.

She strolled between shelves, looking at titles, smiling as she met old friends—books she had read three times or five times or a dozen. Just a title, or an author's name, would be enough to summon up happy images. Strange creatures like phoenixes and psammeads, moving under smoky London daylight of a hundred years before, in company with groups of bemused children; starships and new worlds and the limitless vistas of interstellar night, outer space challenged but never conquered; princesses in silver and golden dresses, princes and heroes carrying swords like sharpened lines of light, monsters rising out of weedy tarns, wild creatures that talked and tricked one another. . . .

I used to think the world would be like that when I got older. Wonderful all the time, exciting, happy. Instead of the way it is. . . .

Something stopped Nita's hand as it ran along the bookshelf. She looked and found that one of the books, a little library-bound volume in shiny red buckram, had a loose thread at the top of its spine, on which her finger had caught. She pulled the finger free, glanced at the title. It was one of those So You Want to Be a . . . books, a series on careers. *So You Want to Be a Pilot* there had been, and *So You Want to Be a Scientist . . . a Nurse . . . a Writer . . .*

But this one said, *So You Want to Be a Wizard.*

A *what?*

Nita pulled the book off the shelf, surprised not so much by the title as by the fact that she'd never seen it before. She thought she knew the whole stock of the children's library. Yet this wasn't a new book. It had plainly been there for some time—the pages had that yellow look about their edges, the color of aging, and the top of the book was dusty. SO YOU WANT TO BE A WIZARD. HEARNSSEN, the spine said: that was the author's name. Phoenix Press, the publisher. And then in white ink in Mrs. Lesser's tidy handwriting, 793.4: the Dewey decimal number.

This has to be a joke, Nita said to herself. But the book looked exactly like all the others in the series. She opened it carefully, so as not to crack the binding, and turned the first few pages to the table of contents. Normally Nita was a fast reader and would quickly have finished a page with only a few lines on it; but what she found on that contents page slowed her down a great deal. "Preliminary Determinations: A Question of Aptitude." "Wizardly Preoccupations and Predilections." "Basic Equipment and Milieus." "Introduction to Spells, Bindings, and

Geasa." "Familiars and Helpmeets: Advice to the Initiate." "Psychotropic Spelling."

Psychowhat? Nita turned to the page on which that chapter began, looking at the boldface paragraph beneath its title.

Warning

Spells of power sufficient to make temporary changes in the human mind are always subject to sudden and unpredictable backlash on the user. The practitioner is cautioned to make sure that his/her motives are benevolent before attempting spelling aimed at . . .

I don't believe this, Nita thought. She shut the book and stood there holding it in her hand, confused, amazed, suspicious—and delighted. If it was a joke, it was a great one. If it wasn't . . .

No, don't be silly.

But if it isn't . . .

People were clumping around upstairs, but Nita hardly heard them. She sat down at one of the low tables and started reading the book in earnest.

The first couple of pages were a foreword.

Wizardry is one of the most ancient and misunderstood of arts. Its public image for centuries has been one of a mysterious pursuit, practiced in occult surroundings, and usually used at the peril of one's soul. The modern wizard, who works with tools more advanced than bat's blood and beings more complex than medieval demons, knows how far from the truth that image is. Wizardry, though exciting and interesting, is not a glamorous business, especially these days, when a wizard must work quietly so as not to attract undue attention.

For those willing to assume the Art's responsibilities and do the work, though, wizardry has many rewards. The sight of a formerly twisted growing thing now growing straight, of a snarled motivation untangled, the satisfaction of hearing what a plant is thinking or a dog is saying, of talking to a stone or a star, is thought by most to be well worth the labor.

Not everyone is suited to be a wizard. Those without enough of the necessary personality traits will never see this manual for what it is. That you have found it at all says a great deal for your potential.

The reader is invited to examine the next few chapters and determine his/her wizardly potential in detail—to become familiar with the scope of the Art—and finally to decide whether to become a wizard.

Good luck!

It's a joke, Nita thought. *Really.* And to her own amazement, she wouldn't believe herself—she was too fascinated. She turned to the next chapter.

Preliminary Determinations

An aptitude for wizardry requires more than just the desire to practice the art. There are certain inborn tendencies, and some acquired ones, that enable a person to become a wizard. This chapter will list some of the better documented of wizardly characteristics. Please bear in mind that it isn't necessary to possess all the qualities listed, or even most of them. Some of the greatest wizards have been lacking in the qualities possessed by almost all others and have still achieved startling competence levels. . . .

Slowly at first, then more eagerly, Nita began working her way through the assessment chapter, pausing only to get a pencil and scrap paper from the checkout desk, so that she could make notes on her aptitude. She was brought up short by the footnote to one page:

> *Where ratings are not assigned, as in rural areas, the area of greatest population density will usually pro- duce the most wizards, due to the thinning of world- walls with increased population concentration. . . .

Nita stopped reading, amazed. "Thinning of worldwalls"—were they saying that there are other worlds, other dimensions, and that things could get through? Things, or people?

She sat there and wondered. All the old fairy tales about people falling down wells into magical countries, or slipping backward in time, or for- ward into it—did this mean that such things could actually happen? If you could actually go into other worlds, other places, and come back again. . . .

Aww—who would believe anybody who came back and told a story like that? Even if they took pictures?

But who cares! she answered herself fiercely. *If only it could be true. . . .*

She turned her attention back to the book and went on reading, though skeptically—the whole thing still felt like a game. But abruptly it stopped being a game, with one paragraph:

> *Wizards love words. Most of them read a great deal, and indeed one strong sign of a potential wizard is the inability to get to sleep without reading something first. But their love for and fluency with words is what makes wizards a force to be reckoned with. Their ability to convince a piece of the world—a tree, say, or a stone—that it's not what it thinks it is, that it's something else, is the very heart of wiz- ardry. Words skillfully used, the persuasive voice, the per- suading mind, are the wizard's most basic tools. With them a wizard can stop a tidal wave, talk a tree out of growing,*

or into it—freeze fire, burn rain—even slow down the
death of the Universe.

That last, of course, is the reason there are *wizards. See
the next chapter.*

Nita stopped short. The universe was running down; all the energy
in it was slowly being used up. She knew that from studing astronomy.
The process was called *entropy*. But she'd never heard anyone talk about
slowing it down before.

She shook her head in amazement and went on to the "correlation"
section at the end of that chapter, where all the factors involved in the
makeup of a potential wizard were listed. Nita found that she had a lot
of them—enough to be a wizard, if she wanted to.

With rising excitement she turned to the next chapter. "Theory and
Implications of Wizardry," the heading said. *"History, Philosophy, and
the Wizards' Oath."*

> *Fifty or sixty eons ago, when life brought itself about, it also
> brought about to accompany it many Powers and Potentialities
> to manage the business of creation. One of the greatest of these
> Powers held aloof for a long time, watching its companions
> work, not wishing to enter into Creation until it could con-
> tribute something unlike anything the other Powers had made,
> something completely new and original. Finally the Lone
> Power found what it was looking for. Others had invented
> planets, light, gravity, space. The Lone Power invented death,
> and bound it irrevocably into the worlds. Shortly thereafter the
> other Powers joined forces and cast the Lone One out.*
>
> *Many versions of this story are related among the many
> worlds, assigning blame or praise to one party or another.
> However, none of the stories change the fact that entropy
> and its symptom, death, are here now. To attempt to halt
> or remove them is as futile as attempting to ignore them.*
>
> *Therefore there are wizards—to handle them.*

A wizard's business is to conserve energy—to keep it from being wasted. On the simplest level this includes such unmagical-looking actions as paying one's bills on time, turning off the lights when you go out, and supporting the people around you in getting their lives to work. It also includes a great deal more.

Because wizardly people tend to be good with language, they can also become skillful with the Speech, the magical tongue in which objects and living creatures can be described with more accuracy than in any human language. And what can be so accurately described can also be preserved—or freed to become yet greater. A wizard can cause an inanimate object or animate creature to grow, or stop growing— to be what it is, or something else. A wizard, using the Speech, can cause death to slow down, or go somewhere else and come back later—just as the Lone Power caused it to come about in the first place. Creation, preservation, destruction, transformation—all are a matter of causing the fabric of being to do what you want it to. And the Speech is the key.

Nita stopped to think this over for a moment. *It sounds like, if you know what something is, truly* know, *you don't have any trouble working with it. Like my telescope—if it acts up, I know every piece of it, and it only takes a second to get it working again. To have that kind of control over—over* everything—*live things, the world, even . . .* She took a deep breath and looked back at the book, beginning to get an idea of what kind of power was implied there.

The power conferred by use of the Speech has, of course, one insurmountable limitation: the existence of death itself. As one renowned Senior Wizard has remarked, "Entropy has us outnumbered." No matter how much preserving we do, the Universe will eventually die. But it will last longer because of our efforts—and since no one knows for sure whether another Universe will be born from the ashes of this one, the effort seems worthwhile.

No one should take the Wizards' Oath who is not committed to making wizardry a lifelong pursuit. The energy invested in a beginning wizard is too precious to be thrown away. Yet there are no penalties for withdrawal from the Art, except the knowledge that the Universe will die a little faster because of energy lost. On the other hand, there are no prizes for the service of Life—except life itself. The wizard gets the delight of working in a specialized area—magic— and gets a good look at the foundations of the Universe, the way things really work. It should be stated here that there are people who consider the latter more of a curse than a blessing. Such wizards usually lose their art. Magic does not live in the unwilling soul. Should you decide to go ahead and take the Oath, be warned that an ordeal of sorts will follow, a test of aptitude. If you pass, wizardry will ensue. . . .

Yeah? Nita thought. *And what if you* don't *pass?*

"Nita?" Mrs. Lessor's voice came floating down the stairs, and a moment later she herself appeared, a large brunette lady with kind eyes and a look of eternal concern. "You still alive?"

"I was reading."

"So what else is new? They're gone."

"Thanks, Mrs. L."

"What was all that about, anyway?"

"Oh . . . Joanne was looking to pick a fight again."

Mrs. Lesser raised an eyebrow at Nita, and Nita smiled back at her shamefacedly. She *didn't* miss much.

"Well, I might have helped her a little."

"I guess it's hard," Mrs. Lesser said. "I doubt *I* could be nice all the time, myself, if I had that lot on my back. That the only one you want today, or should I just have the nonfiction section boxed and sent over to your house?"

"No, this is enough," Nita said. "If my father sees too many books he'll just make me bring them back."

Mrs. Lesser sighed. "Reading one book is like eating one potato chip," she said. "So you'll be back Monday. There's more where that came from. I'll check it out for you."

Nita felt in her pockets hurriedly. "Oh, crud. Mrs. L., I don't have my card."

"So you'll bring it back Monday," she said, handing her back the book as they reached the landing, "and I'll stamp it then. I trust you."

"Thanks," Nita said.

"Don't mention it. Be careful going home," Mrs. Lesser said, "and have a nice read."

"I will."

Nita went out and stood on the doorstep, looking around in the deepening gloom. Dinnertime was getting close, and the wind was getting cold, with a smell of rain to it. The book in her hand seemed to prickle a little, as if it were impatient to be read.

She started jogging toward home, taking a circuitous route—up Washington from Rose Avenue, then through town along Nassau Road and down East Clinton, a path meant to confound pursuit. She didn't expect that they would be waiting for her only a block away from her house, where there were no alternate routes to take. And when they were through with her, the six of them, one of Nita's eyes was blackened and the knee Joanne had so carefully stomped on felt swollen with liquid fire.

Nita just lay there for a long while, on the spot where they left her, behind the O'Donnell's hedge; the O'Donnells were out of town. There she lay, and cried, as she would not in front of Joanne and the rest, as she would not until she was safely in bed and out of her family's earshot. Whether she provoked these situations or not, they kept happening, and there was nothing she could do about them. Joanne and her hangers-on had found out that Nita didn't like to fight, wouldn't try until her rage broke loose—and then it was too late, she was too hurt to fight well. All her self-defense lessons went out of her head with the pain. And they knew it, and at least once a week found a way to sucker her into a fight—or, if that failed, they would simply ambush her. All right, she had purposely baited Joanne today, but there'd been a fight coming anyway, and *she* had chosen to start it rather than wait, getting angrier and angrier, while they baited *her*. But this would keep happening, again and again, and there was nothing she could do about it. *Oh, I wish we could move. I wish Dad would say something to Joanne's father—no, that would just make it worse. If only something could just happen to make it stop!*

Underneath her, where it had fallen, the book dug into Nita's sore ribs. The memory of what she had been reading flooded back through her pain and was followed by a wash of wild surmise. *If there are spells to keep things from dying, then I bet there are spells to keep people from hurting you. . . .*

Then Nita scowled at herself in contempt for actually believing for a moment what couldn't possibly be more than an elaborate joke. She put aside thoughts of the book and slowly got up, brushing herself off and discovering some new bruises. She also discovered something else. Her favorite pen was gone. Her space pen, a present from her Uncle Joel, the pen that could write on butter or glass or upside down, her pen with which she had never failed a test, even in math. She patted herself all over, checked the ground, searched in pockets where she knew the pen couldn't be. No use; it was gone. Or taken, rather—for it had been securely clipped to her front jacket pocket when Joanne and her group jumped her. It must have fallen out, and one of them picked it up.

"Aaaaaagh!" Nita moaned, feeling bitter enough to start crying again. But she was all cried out, and she ached too much, and it was a waste. She stepped around the hedge and limped the little distance home.

Her house was pretty much like any other on the block, a white frame house with fake shutters; but where other houses had their lawns, Nita's had a beautifully landscaped garden. Ivy carpeted the ground, and the flowerbeds against the house had something blooming in every season except the dead of winter. Nita trudged up the driveway without bothering to smell any of the spring flowers, went up the stairs to the back door, pushed it open, and walked into the kitchen as nonchalantly as she could.

Her mother was elsewhere, but the delicious smells of her cooking filled the place; veal cutlets tonight. Nita peered into the oven, saw potatoes baking, lifted a pot lid and found corn on the cob in the steamer.

Her father looked up from the newspaper he was reading at the dining-room table. He was a big, blunt, good-looking man, with startling silver hair and large capable hands—"an artist's hands!" he would chuckle as he pieced together a flower arrangement. He owned the smaller of the town's two flower shops, and he loved his work dearly. He had done all the landscaping around the house in his spare time, and around several neighbors' houses too, refusing to take anything in return but the satisfaction of being up to his elbows in a flowerbed. Whatever he touched grew. "I have an understanding with the plants," he would say, and it certainly seemed that way. It was people he sometimes had trouble understanding, and particularly his eldest daughter.

"My Lord, Nita!" her father exclaimed, putting the paper down flat on the table. His voice was shocked. "What happened?"

As if you don't know! Nita thought. She could clearly see the expressions going across her father's face. *MiGod,* they said, *she's done it again! Why doesn't she fight back? What's wrong with her?* He would get around to asking that question at one point or another, and Nita would try to explain it again, and as usual her father would try to understand and would fail. Nita turned away and opened the refrigerator door, peering at nothing in particular, so that her father wouldn't see the grimace of impatience and irritation on her face. She was tired of the whole ritual, but she had to put up with it. It was as inevitable as being beaten up.

"I was in a fight," she said, the second verse of the ritual, the second line of the scene. Tiredly she closed the refrigerator door, put the book down on the counter beside the stove, and peeled off her jacket, examining it for rips and ground-in dirt and blood.

"So how many of them did you take out?" her father said, turning his eyes back to the newspaper. His face still showed exasperation and puzzlement, and Nita sighed. *He looks about as tired of this as I am. But really, he* knows *the answers.* "I'm not sure," Nita said. "There were six of them."

"Six!" Nita's mother came around the corner from the living room and into the bright kitchen—danced in, actually. Just watching her made Nita smile sometimes, and it did now, though changing expressions hurt. She had been a dancer before she married Dad, and the grace with which she moved made her every action around the house seem polished, endlessly rehearsed, lovely to look at. She glided with the laundry, floated while she cooked. "Loading the odds a bit, weren't they?"

"Yeah." Nita was hurting almost too much to feel like responding to the gentle humor. Her mother caught the pain in her voice and stopped to touch Nita's face as she passed, assessing the damage and conveying how she felt about it in one brief gesture, without saying anything that anyone else but the two of them might hear.

"No sitting up for you tonight, kidlet," her mother said. "Bed, and ice on that, before you swell up like a balloon."

"What started it?" her dad asked from the dining room.

"Joanne Virella," Nita said. "She has a new bike, and I didn't get as excited about it as she thought I should."

Nita's father looked up from the paper again, and this time there was discomfort in his face, and regret. "Nita," he said, "I couldn't afford it this month, really. I thought I was going to be able to earlier, but I couldn't. I *wish* I could have. Next time for sure."

Nita nodded. "It's okay," she said, even though it wasn't really. She'd *wanted* that bike, wanted it so badly—but Joanne's father owned the big five-and-dime on Nassau Road and *could* afford three-hundred-dollar bikes for his children at the drop of a birthday. Nita's father's business was a lot smaller and was prone to what he called (in front of most people) "cash-flow problems" or (in front of his family) "being broke most of the time."

But what does Joanne care about cash flow, or any of the rest of it? I wanted that bike!

"Here, dreamer," her mother said, tapping her on the shoulder and breaking her thought. She handed Nita an icepack and turned back toward the stove. "Go lie down or you'll swell worse. I'll bring you something in a while."

"Shouldn't she stay sitting up?" Nita's father said. "Seems as if the fluid would drain better or something."

"You didn't get beat up enough when you were younger, Harry," her mother said. "If she doesn't lie down, she'll blow up like a basketball. Scoot, Nita."

She scooted, around the corner into the dining room, around the second corner into the living room, and straight into her little sister, bumping loose one of the textbooks she was carrying and scattering half her armload of pink plastic curlers. Nita bent to help pick things up again. Her sister, bent down beside her, didn't take long to figure out what had happened.

"Virella again, huh?" she asked. Dairine was eleven years old, red-headed like her mother, gray-eyed like Nita, and precocious; she was taking tenth-grade English courses and breezing through them, and Nita was teaching her some algebra on the side. Dairine had her father's square-boned build and her mother's grace, and a perpetual, cocky grin. She was a great sister, as far as Nita was concerned, even if she was a little too smart for her own good.

"Yeah," Nita said. "Look out, kid, I've gotta go lie down."

"Don't call me kid. You want me to beat up Virella for you?"

"Be my guest," Nita said. She went on through the house, back to her room. Bumping the door open, she fumbled for the light switch and flipped it on. The familiar maps and pictures looked down at her—the National Geographic map of the Moon and some enlarged Voyager photos of Jupiter and Saturn and their moons.

Nita eased herself down onto the bottom bunk bed, groaning softly—the deep bruises were beginning to bother her now. Lord, she thought, what did I say? If Dari does beat Joanne up, I'll never hear the end of it. Dairine had once been small and fragile and subject to being beaten up—mostly because she had never learned to curb her mouth either—and Nita's parents had sent her to jujitsu lessons at the same time they sent Nita. On Dari, though, the lessons took. One or two overconfident kids had gone after her, about a month and a half into her lessons, and had been thoroughly and painfully surprised. She was protective enough to take Joanne on and, horrors, throw her clear over the horizon. It would be all over school; Nita Callahan's little sister beat up the girl who beat *Nita* up.

Oh no! Nita thought.

Her door opened slightly, and Dari stuck her head in. "Of course," she said, "if you'd rather do it yourself, I'll let her off this time."

"Yeah," Nita said, "thanks."

Dairine made a face. "Here," she said, and pitched Nita's jacket in at her, and then right after it the book. Nita managed to field it while holding the icepack in place with her left hand. "You left it in the kitchen," Dairine said. "Gonna be a magician, huh? Make yourself vanish when they chase you?"

"Sure. Go curl your hair, runt."

Nita sat back against the headboard of the bed, staring at the book. *Why not? Who knows what kinds of spells you could do? Maybe I could turn Joanne into a turkey. As if she isn't one already. Or maybe there's a spell for getting lost pens back.*

Though the book made it sound awfully serious, as if the wizardry were for big things. Maybe it's not right to do spells for little stuff like this—and anyway, you can't do the spells until you've taken the Oath, and once you've taken it, that's supposed to be forever.

Oh, come on, it's a joke! What harm can there be in saying the words if it's a joke? And if it's not, then . . .

Then I'll be a wizard.

Her father knocked on her door, then walked in with a plate loaded with dinner and a glass of cola. Nita grinned up at him, not too widely, for it hurt. "Thanks, Dad."

"Here," he said after Nita took the plate and the glass, and handed her a couple of aspirin. "Your mother says to take these."

"Thanks." Nita took them with the Coke, while her father sat down on the edge of the bed.

"Nita," he said, "is there something going on that I should know about?"

"Huh?"

"It's been once a week now, sometimes twice, for quite a while. Do you want me to speak to Joe Virella and ask him to have a word with Joanne?"

"Uh, no, sir."

Nita's father stared at his hands for a moment. "What should we do, then? I really can't afford to start you in karate lessons again—"

"Jujitsu."

"Whatever. Nita, what *is* it? Why does this keep happening? *Why don't you hit them back?*"

"I *used* to! Do you think it made a difference? Joanne would just get more kids to help." Her father stared at her, and Nita flushed hot at the stern look on his face. "I'm sorry, Daddy, I didn't mean to yell at you. But fighting back just gets them madder, it doesn't help."

"It might help keep you from getting mangled every week, if you'd just keep trying!" her father said angrily. "I hate to admit it, but I'd love to see you wipe the ground up with that loudmouth rich kid."

So would I, Nita thought. *That's the problem.* She swallowed, feeling guilty over how much she wanted to get back at Joanne somehow. "Dad, Joanne and her bunch just don't like me. I don't do the things they do, or play the games they play, or like the things they like—and I don't *want* to. So they don't like me. That's all."

Her father looked at her and shook his head sadly. "I just don't want to see you hurt. Kidling, I don't know . . . if you could just be a little more like them, if you could try to . . ." He trailed off, running one hand through his silver hair. "What am I saying?" he muttered. "Look. If there's anything I can do to help, will you tell me?"

"Yessir."

"Okay. If you feel better tomorrow, would you rake up the backyard a little? I want to go over the lawn around the rowan tree with the aerator, maybe put down some seed."

"Sure. I'll be okay, Dad. They didn't break anything."

"My girl." He got up. "Don't read so much it hurts your eyes, now."

"I won't," Nita said. Her father strode out the door, forgetting to close it behind himself as usual.

She ate her supper slowly, for it hurt to chew, and she tried to think about something besides Joanne or that book.

The Moon was at first quarter tonight; it would be a good night to take the telescope out and have a look at the shadows in the craters. Or there was that fuzzy little comet, maybe it had more tail than it did last week.

It was completely useless. The book lay there on her bed and stared at her, daring her to do something childlike, something silly, something absolutely ridiculous.

Nita put aside her empty plate, picked up the book, and stared back at it.

"All right," she said under her breath. "All right."

She opened the book at random. And on the page to which she opened, there was the Oath.

It was not decorated in any way. It stood there, a plain block of type all by itself in the middle of the page, looking serious and important. Nita read the Oath to herself first, to make sure of the words. Then, quickly, before she could start to feel silly, she read it out loud.

" 'In Life's name, and for Life's sake,' " she read, " 'I say that I will use the Art for nothing but the service of that Life. I will guard growth and ease pain. I will fight to preserve what grows and lives well in its own way; and I will change no object or creature unless its growth and life, or that of the system of which it is part, are threatened. To these ends, in the practice of my Art, I will put aside fear for courage, and death for life, when it is right to do so—till Universe's end.' "

The words seemed to echo slightly, as if the room were larger than it really was. Nita sat very still, wondering what the ordeal would be like, wondering what would happen now. Only the wind spoke softly in the leaves of the trees outside the bedroom window; nothing else seemed to stir anywhere. Nita sat there, and slowly the tension began to drain out of her as she realized that she hadn't been hit by lightning, nor had anything strange at all happened to her. *Now* she felt silly—

and tired too, she discovered. The effects of her beating were catching up with her. Wearily, Nita shoved the book under her pillow, then lay back against the headboard and closed her hurting eyes. So much for the joke. She would have a nap, and then later she'd get up and take the telescope out back. But right now . . . right now. . . .

After a while, night was not night anymore; that was what brought Nita to the window, much later. She leaned on the sill and gazed out in calm wonder at her backyard, which didn't look quite the same as usual. A blaze of undying morning lay over everything, bushes and trees cast light instead of shadow, and she could see the wind. Standing in the ivy under her window, she turned her eyes up to the silver-glowing sky to get used to the brilliance. *How about that,* she said. *The backyard's here, too.* Next to her, the lesser brilliance that gazed up at that same sky shrugged slightly. *Of course,* it said. *This is Timeheart, after all. Yes,* Nita said anxiously as they passed across the yard and out into the bright shadow of the steel and crystal towers, *but did I do right?* Her companion shrugged again. *Go find out,* it said, and glanced up again. Nita wasn't sure she wanted to follow the glance. Once she had looked up and seen—*I dreamed you were gone,* she said suddenly. *The magic stayed, but you went away.* She hurt inside, enough to cry, but her companion flickered with laughter. *No one ever goes away forever,* it said. *Especially not here.* Nita looked up, then, into the bright morning and the brighter shadows. The day went on and on and would not end, the sky blazed now like molten silver. . . .

The Sun on her face woke Nita up as usual. Someone, her mother probably, had come in late last night to cover her up and take the dishes away. She turned over slowly, stiff but not in too much pain, and felt the hardness under her pillow. Nita sat up and pulled the book out, felt around for her glasses. The book fell open in her hand at the listing for the wizards in the New York metropolitan area, which Nita had glanced at the afternoon before. Now she looked down the first column of names, and her breath caught.

Callahan, Juanita L.,
243 E. Clinton Ave.,
Hempstead, NY 11575
(516) 555-6786. (novice, pre-rating)

Her mouth fell open. She shut it.
I'm going to be a wizard! she thought.

The Harrowing of
the Dragon of
Hoarsbreath

by Patricia A. McKillip

Patricia A. McKillip sets this story of young heroes, magic and dragon-slaying on another planet.

O nce, on the top of a world, there existed the ring of an island named Hoarsbreath, made out of gold and snow. It was all mountain, a grim, briney, yellowing ice-world covered with winter twelve months out of thirteen. For one month, when the twin suns crossed each other at the world's cap, the snow melted from the peak of Hoarsbreath. The hardly trees shrugged the snow off their boughs, and sucked in light and mellow air, pulling themselves toward the suns. Snow and icicles melted off the roofs of the miners' village; the snow-tunnels they had dug from house to tavern to storage barn to mineshaft sagged to the ground; the dead-white river flowing down from the mountain to the sea turned blue and began to move again. Then the miners gathered the gold they had dug by firelight out of the chill, harsh darkness of the deep mountain, and took it downriver, across the sea to the mainland, to trade for food and furs, tools and a liquid fire called wormspoor, because it was gold and bitter, like the leavings of dragons. After three swallows of it, in a busy city with a harbor frozen only part of the year, with people who wore rich furs, kept horses and sleds to ride in during winter, and who knew the patterns of the winter stars since they weren't buried alive by the snow, the miners swore they would never return to Hoarsbreath. But the gold waiting in the dark, secret places of the mountain-island drew at them in their dreaming, lured them back.

For two hundred years after the naming of Hoarsbreath, winter followed winter, and the miners lived rich isolated, precarious lives on the pinnacle of ice and granite, cursing the cold and loving it, for it kept lesser folk away. They mined, drank, spun tales, raised children who were sent to the mainland when they were half-grown, to receive their education, and find easier, respectable lives. But always a few children found their way back, born with a gnawing in their hearts for fire, ice, stone, and the solitary pursuit of gold in the dark.

Then, two miners' children came back from the great world and destroyed the island.

They had no intention of doing that. The younger of them was Peka Krao. After spending five years on the mainland, boring herself with schooling, she came back to Hoarsbreath to mine. At seventeen, she was good-natured and sturdy, with dark eyes, and dark, braided hair. She loved every part of Hoarsbreath, even its chill, damp shafts at midwinter and the bone-jarring work of hewing through darkness and stone to unbury its gold. Her instincts for gold were uncanny: she seemed to sense it through her fingertips touching bare rock. The miners called her their good luck. She could make wormspoor, too, one of the few useful things she had learned on the mainland. It lost its bitterness, somehow, when she made it: it aged into a rich, smokey gold that made the miners forget their sore muscles, and inspired marvellous tales out of them that whittled away at the endless winter.

She met the Dragon-Harrower one evening at a cross-section of tunnel between her mother's house and the tavern. She knew all the things to fear in her world: a rumble in the mountain, a guttering torch in the mines, a crevice in the snow, a crack of ice underfoot. There was little else she couldn't handle with a soft word or her own right arm.

Even when he loomed out of the darkness unexpectedly into her taper-light, she wasn't afraid. But he made her stop instinctively, like an animal might stop, faced with something that puzzled its senses.

His hair was dead-white, with strands bright as wormspoor running through it; his eyes were the light, hard blue of dawn during suns-crossing. Rich colors flashed out of him everywhere in her light: from a gold knife-hilt and a brass pack buckle; from the red ties of his cloak that were weighted with ivory, and the blue and silver threads in his gloves. His heavy fur cloak was closed, but she felt that if he shifted, other colors would escape from it into the cold, dark air. At first she thought he must be ancient: the taper-fire showed her a face that was shadowed and scarred, remote with strange experience, but no more than a dozen years older than hers.

"Who are you?" she breathed. Nothing on Hoarsbreath glittered like that in midwinter; its colors were few and simple: snow, damp fur and leather, fire, gold.

"I can't find my father," he said. "Lule Yarrow."

She stared at him, amazed that his colors had their beginnings on Hoarsbreath. "He's dead." His eyes widened slightly, losing some of their hardness. "He fell in a crevice. They chipped him out of the ice at suns-crossing, and buried him six years ago."

He looked away from her a moment, down at the icy ridges of tramped snow. "Winter." He broke the word in two, like an icicle. Then he shifted his pack, sighing. "Do they still have wormspoor on this ice-tooth?"

"Of course. Who are you?"

"Ryd Yarrow. Who are you?"

"Peka Krao."

"Peka. I remember. You were squalling in somebody's arms when I left."

"You look a hundred years older than that," she commented, still puzzling, holding him in her light, though she was beginning to feel the cold. "Seventeen years you've been gone. How could you stand it, being away from Hoarsbreath so long? I couldn't stand five years of it.

There are so many people whose names you don't know, trying to tell you about things that don't matter, and the flat earth and the blank sky are everywhere. Did you come back to mine?"

He glanced up at the grey-white ceiling of the snow-tunnel, barely an inch above his head. "The sky is full of stars, and the gold wake of dragon-flights," he said softly. "I am a Dragon-Harrower. I am trained and hired to trouble dragons out of their lairs. That's why I came back here."

"Here. There are no dragons on Hoarsbreath."

His smile touched his eyes like a reflection of fire across ice. "Hoarsbreath is a dragon's heart."

She shifted, her own heart suddenly chilled. She said tolerantly, "That sounds like a marvellous tale to me."

"It's no tale. I know. I followed this dragon through centuries, through ancient writings, through legends, through rumors of terror and deaths. It is here, sleeping, coiled around the treasures of Hoarsbreath. If you on Hoarsbreath rouse it, you are dead. If I rouse it, I will end your endless winter."

"I like winter." Her protest sounded very small, muted within the thick snow-walls, but he heard it. He lifted his hand, held it lightly against the low ceiling above his head.

"You might like the sky beyond this. At night it is a mine of lights and hidden knowledge."

She shook her head. "I like close places, full of fire and darkness. And faces I know. And tales spun out of wormspoor. If you come with me to the tavern, they'll tell you where your father is buried, and give you lodgings, and then you can leave."

"I'll come to the tavern. With a tale."

Her taper was nearly burned down, and she was beginning to shiver. "A dragon." She turned away from him. "No one will believe you anyway."

"You do."

She listened to him silently, warming herself with wormspoor, as he spoke to the circle of rough, fire-washed faces in the tavern. Even in the light, he bore little resemblance to his father, except for his broad cheekbones and the threads of gold in his hair. Under his bulky cloak, he was dressed as plainly as any miner, but stray bits of color still glinted from him, suggesting wealth and distant places.

"A dragon," he told them, "is creating your winter. Have you ever asked yourselves why winter on this island is nearly twice as long as winter on the mainland twenty miles away? You live in dragon's breath, in the icy mist of its bowels, hoar-frost cold, that grips your land in winter the way another dragon's breath might burn it to cinders. One month out of the year, in the warmth of suns-crossing, it looses its ring-grip on your island, slides into the sea, and goes to mate. Its ice-kingdom begins to melt. It returns, loops its length around its mountain of ice and gold. Its breath freezes the air once more, locks the river into its bed, you into your houses, the gold into its mountain, and you curse the cold and drink until the next dragon-mating." He paused. There was not a sound around him. "I've been to strange places in this world, places even colder than this, where the suns never cross, and I have seen such monsters. They are ancient as rock, white as old ice, and their skin is like iron. They breed winter and they cannot be killed. But they can be driven away, into far corners of the world where they are dangerous to no one. I'm trained for this. I can rid you of your winter. Harrowing is dangerous work, and usually I am highly paid. But I've been looking for this ice-dragon for many years, through its spoor of legend and destruction. I tracked it here, one of the oldest of its kind, to the place where I was born. All I ask from you is a guide."

He stopped, waiting. Peka, her hands frozen around her glass, heard someone swallow. A voice rose and faded from the tavern-kitchen; sap hissed in the fire. A couple of the miners were smiling; the others looked satisfied and vaguely expectant, wanting the tale to continue. When it didn't, Kor Flynt, who had mined Hoarsbreath for fifty years, spat wormspoor into the fire. The flame turned a baleful gold, and then subsided. "Suns-crossing," he said politely, reminding a scholar of a scrap of knowledge children acquired with their first set of teeth, "cause the seasons."

"Not here," Ryd said. "Not on Hoarsbreath. I've seen. I know."

Peka's mother Ambris leaned forward. "Why," she asked curiously, "would a miner's son become a dragon harrower?" She had a pleasant, craggy face; her dark hair and her slow, musing voice were like Peka's. Peka saw the Dragon-Harrower ride between two answers in his mind. Meeting Ambris' eyes, he made a choice, and his own eyes strayed to the fire.

"I left Hoarsbreath when I was twelve. When I was fifteen, I saw a dragon in the mountains east of the city. Until then, I had intended to come back and mine. I began to learn about dragons. The first one I saw burned red and gold under the suns' fire; it swallowed small hills with its shadow. I wanted to call it, like a hawk. I wanted to fly with it. I kept studying, meeting other people who studied them, seeing other dragons. I saw a night-black dragon in the northern deserts; its scales were dusted with silver, and the flame that came out of it was silver. I saw people die in that flame, and I watched the harrowing of that dragon. It lives now on the underside of the world, in shadow. We keep watch on all known dragons. In the green mid-world belt, rich with rivers and mines, forests and farmland, I saw a whole mining town burned to the ground by a dragon so bright I thought at first it was sun-fire arching down to the ground. Someone I loved had the task of tracking that one to its cave, deep beneath the mine-shafts. I watched her die, there. I nearly died. The dragon is sealed into the bottom of the mountain, by stone and by words. That is the dragon which harrowed me." He paused to sip wormspoor. His eyes lifted, not to Ambris, but to Peka. "Now do you understand what danger you live in? What if one year the dragon sleeps through its mating-time, with the soft heat of the suns making it sluggish from dreaming? You don't know it's there, wrapped around your world. It doesn't know you're there, stealing its gold. What if you sail your boats full of gold downriver and find the great white bulk of it sprawled like a wall across your passage? Or worse, you find its eye opening like a third, dead sun to see your hands full of its gold? It would slide its length around the mountain, coil upward and crush you all, then breathe over the whole of the island, and turn it dead-white as its heart, and it would never sleep again."

There was another silence. Peka felt something play along her spine like the thin, quavering, arthritic fingers of wind. "It's getting better," she said, "your tale." She took a deep swallow of wormspoor and added, "I love sitting in a warm, friendly place listening to tales I don't have to believe."

Kor Flynt shrugged. "It rings true, lass."

"It is true," Ryd said.

"Maybe so," she said. "And it may be better if you just let the dragon sleep."

"And if it wakes unexpectedly? The winter killed my father. The dragon at the heart of winter could destroy you all."

"There are other dangers. Rock falls, sudden floods, freezing winds. A dragon is simply one more danger to live with."

He studied her. "I saw a dragon once with wings as softly blue as a spring sky. Have you ever felt spring on Hoarsbreath? It could come."

She drank again. "You love them," she said. "Your voice loves them and hates them, Dragon-Harrower."

"I hate them," he said flatly. "Will you guide me down the mountain?"

"No. I have work to do."

He shifted, and the colors rippled from him again, red, gold, silver, spring-blue. She finished the wormspoor, felt it burn in her like liquid gold. "It's only a tale. All your dragons are just colors in our heads. Let the dragon sleep. If you wake it, you'll destroy the night."

"No," he said. "You will see the night. That's what you're afraid of."

Kor Flynt shrugged. "There probably is no dragon, anyway."

"Spring, though," Ambris said; her face had softened. "Sometimes I can smell it from the mainland, and, and I always wonder . . . Still, after a hard day's work, sitting beside a roaring fire sipping dragon-spit, you can believe anything. Especially this." She looked into her glass at the glowering liquid. "Is this some of yours, Peka? What did you put into it?"

"Gold." The expression in Ryd's eyes made her swallow sudden tears of frustration. She refilled her glass. "Fire, stone, dark, wood-smoke, night air smelling like cold tree-bark. You don't care, Ryd Yarrow."

"I do care," he said imperturbably. "It's the best wormspoor I've ever tasted."

"And I put a dragon's heart into it." She saw him start slightly; ice and hoar-frost shimmered from him. "If that's what Hoarsbreath is." A dragon beat into her mind, its wings of rime, its breath smoldering with ice, the guardian of winter. She drew breath, feeling the vast bulk of it looped around them all, dreaming its private dreams. Her bones seemed suddenly fragile as kindling, and the gold wormspoor in her hands a guilty secret. "I don't believe it," she said, lifting her glass. "It's a tale."

"Oh, go with him, lass," her mother said tolerantly. "There may be no dragon, but we can't have him swallowed up in the ice like his father. Besides, it may be a chance for spring."

"Spring is for flatlanders. There are things that shouldn't be wakened. I know."

"How?" Ryd asked.

She groped, wishing for the first time for a flatlander's skill with words. She said finally, "I feel it," and he smiled. She sat back in her chair, irritated and vaguely frightened. "Oh, all right, Ryd Yarrow, since you'll go with or without me. I'll lead you down to the shores in the morning. Maybe by then you'll listen to me."

"You can't see beyond your snow-world," he said implacably. "It is morning."

They followed one of the deepest mine-shafts, and clambered out of it to stand in the snow halfway down the mountain. The sky was lead grey; across the mists ringing the island's shores, they could see the ocean, a swirl of white, motionless ice. The mainland harbor was locked, Peka wondered if the ships were stuck like birds in the ice. The world looked empty and somber.

"At least in the dark mountain there is fire and gold. Here, there isn't even a sun." She took out a skin of wormspoor, sipped it to warm her bones. She held it out to Ryd, but he shook his head.

"I need all my wits. So do you, or we'll both end up preserved in ice at the bottom of a crevice."

"I know. I'll keep you safe." She corked the skin and added, "In case you were wondering."

But he looked at her, startled out of his remoteness. "I wasn't. Do you feel that strongly?"

"Yes."

"So did I, when I was your age. Now I feel very little." He moved again. She stared after him, wondering how he kept her smoldering and on edge. She said abruptly, catching up with him,

"Ryd Yarrow,"

"Yes."

"You have two names. Ryd Yarrow, and Dragon-Harrower. One is a plain name this mountain gave you. The other you got from the world, the name that gives you color. One name I can talk to, the other is the tale at the bottom of a bottle of wormspoor. Maybe you could understand me if you hadn't brought your past back to Hoarsbreath."

"I do understand you," he said absently. "You want to sit in the dark all your life and drink wormspoor."

She drew breath and held it. "You talk but you don't listen," she said finally. "Just like all the other flatlanders." He didn't answer. They walked in silence awhile, following the empty bed of an old river. The world looked dead, but she could tell by the air, which was not even freezing spangles of breath on her hood-fur, that the winter was drawing to an end. "Suns-crossing must be only two months away," she commented surprisedly.

"Besides, I'm not a flatlander," he said abruptly, surprising her again. "I do care about the miners, about Hoarsbreath. It's because I care that I want to challenge that ice-dragon with all the skill I possess. Is it better to let you live surrounded by danger, in bitter cold, carving half-lives out of snow and stone, so that you can come fully alive for one month of the year?"

"You could have asked us."

"I did ask you."

She sighed. "Where will it live, if you drive it away from Hoarsbreath?"

He didn't answer for a few paces. In the still day, he loosed no colors, though Peka thought she saw shadows of them around his pack. His head was bowed; his eyes were burning back at a memory. "It will find some strange, remote places where there is no gold, only rock; it can ring itself around emptiness and dream of its past. I came across an ice-dragon unexpectedly once, in a land of ice. The bones of its wings seemed almost translucent. I could have sworn it cast a white shadow."

"Did you want to kill it?"

"No. I loved it."

"Then why do you—" But he turned at her suddenly, almost angrily, waking out of a dream.

"I came here because you've built your lives on top of a terrible danger, and I asked for a guide, not a gad-fly."

"You wanted me," she said flatly. "And you don't care about Hoarsbreath. All you want is that dragon. Your voice is full of it. What's a gad-fly?"

"Go ask a cow. Or a horse. Or anything else that can't live on this forsaken, frostbitten lump of ice."

"Why should you care, anyway? You've got the whole great world to roam in. Why do you care about one dragon wrapped around the tiny island on the top of nowhere?"

"Because it's beautiful and deadly and wrapped around my heartland. And I don't know—I don't know at the end of things which of us will be left on Hoarsbreath." She stared at him. He met her eyes fully. "I'm very skilled. But that is one very powerful dragon."

She whirled, fanning snow. "I'm going back. Find your own way to your harrowing. I hope it swallows you."

His voice stopped her. "You'll always wonder. You'll sit in the dark, drinking wormspoor twelve months out of thirteen, wondering what happened to me. What an ice-dragon looks like, on a winter's day, in full flight."

She hovered between two steps. Then, furiously, she followed him.

They climbed deeper into mist, and then into darkness. They camped at night, ate dried meat and drank wormspoor beside a fire in the snow. The night-sky was sullen and starless as the day. They woke to grey mists and travelled on. The cold breathed up around them; walls of ice, yellow as old ivory, loomed over them. They smelled the chill, sweaty smell of the sea. The dead riverbed came to an end over an impassible cliff. They shifted ground, followed a frozen stream downward. The ice-walls broke up into great jewels of ice, blue, green, gold, massed about them like a giant's treasure hoard. Peka stopped to stare at them. Ryd said with soft, bitter satisfaction,

"Wormspoor."

She drew breath. "Wormspoor." Her voice sounded small, absorbed by cold. "Ice-jewels, fallen stars. Down here you could tell me anything and I might believe it. I feel very strange." She uncorked the worm-spoor and took a healthy swig. Ryd reached for it, but he only rinsed his mouth and spat. His face was pale; his eyes red-rimmed, tired.

"How far down do you think we are?"

"Close. There's no dragon. Just mist." She shuddered suddenly at the soundlessness. "The air is dead. Like stone. We should reach the ocean soon."

"We'll reach the dragon first."

They descended hillocks of frozen jewels. The stream they followed fanned into a wide, skeletal filigree of ice and rock. The mist poured around them, so painfully cold it burned their lungs. Peka pushed fur over her mouth, breathed through it. The mist or wormspoor she had drunk was forming shadows around her, flickerings of faces and enormous wings. Her heart felt heavy; her feet dragged like boulders when she lifted them. Ryd was coughing mist; he moved doggedly, as if into a hard wind. The stream fanned again, going very wide before it met the sea. They stumbled down into a bone-searing flow of mist. Ryd disappeared; Peka found him again, bumping into him, for he had stopped. The threads of mist untangled above them, and she saw a strange black sun, hodded with a silvery web. As she blinked at it, puzzled, the web rolled up. The dark sun gazed back at her. She became aware then of her own heartbeat, of a rhythm in the mists, of a faint, echoing pulse all around her: the icy heartbeat of Hoarsbreath.

She drew a hiccup of a breath, stunned. There was a mountain-cave ahead of them, from which the mists breathed and eddied. Icicles dropped like bars between its grainy-white surfaces. Within it rose stones or teeth as milky white as quartz. A wall of white stretched beyond the mists, vast, earthworm round, solid as stone. She couldn't tell in the blur and welter of mist, where winter ended and the dragon began.

She made a sound. The vast, silvery eyelid drooped like a parchment unrolled, then lifted again. From the depths of the cave came a faint, rumbling, a vague, drowsy waking question: Who?

She heard Ryd's breath finally. "Look at the scar under its eye," he said softly. She saw a jagged track beneath the black sun. "I can name the Harrower who put that there three hundred years ago. And the broken eye-tooth. It razed a marble fortress with its wings and jaws; I know the word that shattered that tooth, then. Look at its wing-scales. Rimed with silver. It's old. Old as the world." He turned finally, to look at her. His white hair, slick with mists, made him seem old as winter. "You can go back now. You won't be safe here."

"I won't be safe up there, either," she whispered. "Let's both go back. Listen to its heart."

"Its blood is gold. Only one Harrower ever saw that and lived."

"Please." She tugged at him, at his pack. Colors shivered into the air: sulphur, malachite, opal. The deep rumble came again; a shadow quickened in the dragon's eye. Ryd moved quickly, caught her hands. "Let it sleep. It belongs here on Hoarsbreath. Why can't you see that? Why can't you see? It's a thing made of gold, snow, darkness—" But he wasn't seeing her; his eyes, remote and alien as the black sun, were full of memories and calculations. Behind him, a single curved claw lay like a crescent moon half-buried in the snow.

Peka stepped back from the Harrower, envisioning a bloody moon through his heart, and the dragon roused to fury, coiling upward around Hoarsbreath, crushing the life out of it. "Ryd Yarrow," she whispered. "Ryd Yarrow. Please." But he did not hear his name.

He began to speak, startling echoes against the solid ice around them. "Dragon of Hoarsbreath, whose wings are of hoarfrost, whose blood is gold—" The backbone of the hoar-dragon rippled slightly, shaking away snow. "I have followed your path of destruction from your beginnings in a land without time and without seasons. You have slept one night too long on this island. Hoarsbreath is not your dragon's dream; it belongs to the living, and I, trained and titled Dragon-Harrower, challenge you for its freedom." More snow shook away from the dragon, baring a rippling of scale, and the glistening of its nostrils. The rhythm of its mist was changing. "I know you," Ryd continued, his voice growing husky, strained against the silence. "You were the white death of the fishing-island Klonos, of ten Harrowers in Ynyme, of the winter palace of the ancient lord of Zuirsh. I have harried nine ice-dragons—perhaps your children—out of the known world. I have been searching for you many years, and I came back to the place where I was born to find you here. I stand before you armed with knowledge, experience, and the dark wisdom of necessity. Leave Hoarsbreath, go back to your birthplace forever, or I will harry you down to the frozen shadow of the world."

The dragon gazed at him motionlessly, an immeasurable ring of ice looped about him. The mist out of its mouth was for a moment suspended. Then its jaws crashed together, spitting splinters of ice. It shuddered, wrenched itself loose from the ice. Its white head reared high, higher, ice booming and cracking around it. Twin black suns stared down at Ryd from the grey mist of the sky. Before it roared, Peka moved.

She found herself on a ledge above Ryd's head, without remembering how she got there. Ryd vanished in a flood of mist. The mist turned fiery; Ryd loomed out of them like a red shadow, dispersing them. Seven crescents lifted out of the snow, slashed down at him scarring the air. A strange voice shouted Ryd's name. He flung back his head and cried a word. Somehow the claw missed him, wedged deep into the ice.

Peka sat back. She was clutching the skin of wormspoor against her heart; she could feel her heartbeat shaking it. Her throat felt raw; the strange voice had been hers. She uncorked the skin, took a deep swallow, and another. Fire licked down her veins. A cloud of ice billowed at Ryd.

He said something else, and suddenly he was ten feet away from it, watching a rock where he had stood freeze and snap into pieces.

Peka crouched closer to the wall of ice behind her. From her high point she could see the briny, frozen snarl of the sea. It flickered green, then an eerie orange. Bands of color pinioned the dragon briefly like a rainbow, arching across its wings. A scale caught fire; a small bone the size of Ryd's forearm snapped. Then the cold wind of the dragon's breath froze and shattered the rainbow. A claw slapped at Ryd; he moved a fraction of a moment too slowly. The tip of a talon caught his pack. It burst open with an explosion of glittering colors. The dragon hooded its eyes; Peka hid hers under her hands. She heard Ryd cry out in pain. Then he was beside her instead of in several pieces, prying the wormspoor out of her hands.

He uncorked it, his hands shaking. One of them was seared silver.

"What are they?" she breathed. He poured wormspoor on his burned hand, then thrust it into the snow. The colors were beginning to die down.

"Flame," he panted. "Dragon-flame. I wasn't prepared to handle it."

"You carry it in your pack?"

"Caught in crystals, in fire-leaves. It will be more difficult than I anticipated."

Peka felt language she had never used before clamor in her throat. "It's all right," she said dourly. "I'll wait."

For a moment, as he looked at her, there was a memory of fear in his eyes. "You can walk across the ice to the mainland from here."

"You can walk to the mainland," she retorted. "This is my home. I have to live with or without that dragon. Right now, there's no living with it. You woke it out of its sleep. You burnt its wing. You broke its bone. You told it there are people on its island. You are going to destroy Hoarsbreath."

"No. This will be my greatest harrowing." He left her suddenly, and appeared flaming like a torch on the dragon's skull, just between its eyes. His hair and his hands spattered silver. Word after word came out of him, smoldering, flashing, melting in the air. The dragon's voice thundered; its skin rippled and shook. Its claw ripped at ice, dug chasms out of it. The air clapped nearby, as if its invisible tail had lifted and slapped at the ground. Then it heaved its head, flung Ryd at the wall of mountain. Peka shut her eyes. But he fell lightly, caught up a crystal as he rose, and sent a shaft of piercing gold light at the upraised scales of its underside, burrowing towards its heart.

Peka got unsteadily to her feet, her throat closing with a sudden whimper. But the dragon's tail, flickering out of the mist behind Ryd, slapped him into a snowdrift twenty feet away. It gave a cold, terrible hiss; mist bubbled over everything, so that for a few minutes Peka could see nothing beyond the lip of the ledge. She drank to stop her shivering. Finally a green fire blazed within the white swirl. She sat down again slowly, waited.

Night rolled in from the sea. But Ryd's fires shot in raw, dazzling streaks across the darkness, illuminating the hoary, scarred bulk of dragon in front of him. Once, he shouted endless poetry at the dragon, lulling it until its mist-breath was faint and slow from its maw. It nearly put Peka to sleep, but Ryd's imperceptible steps closer and closer to the dragon kept her watching. The tale was evidently an old one to the dragon; it didn't wait for an ending. Its head lunged and snapped unexpectedly, but a moment too soon. Ryd leaped for shelter in the dark, while the dragon's teeth ground painfully on nothingness. Later, Ryd sang to it, a whining, eerie song that showered icicles around Peka's head. One of the dragon's teeth cracked, and it made an odd, high-pitched noise. A vast webbed wing shifted free to fly, unfolding endlessly over the sea. But the dragon stayed, sending mist at Ryd to set him coughing. A foul ashy-grey miasma followed it, blurring over them. Peka hid her face in her arms. Sounds like the heaving of boulders and the spattering of fire came from beneath her. She heard the dragon's dry roar, like stones dragged against one another. There was a smack, a musical shower of breaking icicles, and a sharp, anguished curse. Ryd appeared out of the turmoil of light and air, sprawled on the ledge beside Peka.

His face was cut, with ice she supposed, and there was blood in his white hair. He looked at her with vague amazement.

"You're still here."

"Where else would I be? Are you winning or losing?"

He scooped up snow, held it against his face. "I feel as if I've been fighting for a thousand years . . . Sometimes, I think I tangle in its memories, as it thinks of other harrowers, old dragon-battles, distant places. It doesn't remember what I am, only that I will not let it sleep . . . Did you *see* its wingspan? I fought a red dragon once with such a span. Its wings turned to flame in the sunlight. You'll see this one in flight by dawn."

She stared at him numbly, huddled against herself. "Are you so sure?"

"It's old and slow. And it can't bear the gold fire." He paused, then dropped the snow in his hand with a sigh, and leaned his face against the ice-wall. "I'm tired, too. I have one empty crystal, to capture the essence of its mist, its heart's breath. After that's done, the battle will be short." He lifted his head at her silence, as if he could hear her thoughts. "What?"

"You'll go on to other dragons. But all I've ever had is this one."

"You never know—"

"It doesn't matter that I never knew it. I know now. It was coiled all around us in the winter, while we lived in warm darkness and firelight. It kept out the world. Is that such a terrible thing? Is there so much wisdom in the flatlands that we can't live without?"

He was silent again, frowning a little, either in pain or faint confusion. "It's a dangerous thing, a destroyer."

"So is winter. So is the mountain, sometimes. But they're also beautiful. You are full of so much knowledge and experience that you forgot how to see simple things. Ryd Yarrow, miner's son. You must have loved Hoarsbreath once."

"I was a child, then."

She sighed. "I'm sorry I brought you down here. I wish I were up there with the miners, in the last peaceful night."

"There will be peace again," he said, but she shook her head wearily.

"I don't feel it." She expected him to smile, but his frown deepened. He touched her face suddenly with his burned hand.

"Sometimes I almost hear what you're trying to tell me. And then it fades against all my knowledge and experience. I'm glad you stayed. If I die, I'll leave you facing one maddened dragon. But still, I'm glad."

A black moon rose high over his shoulder and she jumped. Ryd rolled off the ledge, into the mists. Peka hid her face from the peering black glare. Blue lights smouldered through the mist, the moon rolled suddenly out of the sky and she could breathe again.

Streaks of dispersing gold lit the dawn-sky like the sunrises she saw one month out of the year. Peka, in a cold daze on the ledge, saw Ryd for the first time in an hour. He was facing the dragon, his silver hand outstretched. In his palm lay a crystal so cold and deathly white that Peka, blinking at it, felt its icy stare into her heart.

She shuddered. Her bones turned to ice; mist seemed to flow through her veins. She breathed bitter, frozen air as heavy as water. She reached for the wormspoor; her arm moved sluggishly, and her fingers unfolded with brittle movements. The dragon was breathing in short, harsh spurts. The silvery hoods were over its eyes. Its unfolded wing lay across the ice like a limp sail. Its jaws were open, hissing faintly, but its head was reared back, away from Ryd's hand. Its heartbeat, in the silence, was slow, slow.

Peka dragged herself up, icicle by icicle. In the clear wintry dawn, she saw the beginning and the end of the enormous ring around Hoarsbreath. The dragon's tail lifted wearily behind Ryd, then fell again, barely making a sound. Ryd stood still; his eyes, relentless, spring-blue, were his only color. As Peka watched, swaying on the edge, the world fragmented into simple things: the edges of silver on the dragon's scales, Ryd's silver fingers, his old-man's hair, the pure white of the dragon's hide. They faced one another, two powerful creatures born out of the same winter, harrowing one another. The dragon rippled along its bulk; its head reared farther back, giving Peka a dizzying glimpse of its open jaws. She saw the cracked tooth, crumbled like a jewel she might have battered inadvertently with her pick, and winced. Seeing her, it hissed, a tired, angry sigh.

She stared down at it; her eyes seemed numb, incapable of sorrow.

The wing on the ice was beginning to stir. Ryd's head lifted. He looked bone-pale, his face expressionless with exhaustion. But the faint, icy smile of triumph in his eyes struck her as deeply as the stare from the death-eye in his palm.

She drew in mist like the dragon, knowing that Ryd was not harrowing an old, tired ice-dragon, but one out of his memories who never seemed to yield. "You bone-brained dragon," she shouted, "how can you give up Hoarsbreath so easily? And to a Dragon-Harrower whose winter is colder and more terrible than yours." Her heart seemed trapped in the weary, sluggish pace of its heart. She knelt down, wondering if it could understand her words, or only feel them. "Think of Hoarsbreath," she pleaded, and searched for words to warm them both. "Fire. Gold. Night. Warm dreams, winter tales, silence—" Mist billowed at her and she coughed until tears froze on her cheeks. She heard Ryd call her name on a curious, inflexible note that panicked her. She uncorked the wormspoor with trembling fingers, took a great gulp, and coughed again as the blood shocked through her. "Don't you have any fire at all in you? Any winter flame?" Then a vision of gold shook her: the gold within the dragon's heart, the warm gold of wormspoor, the bitter gold of dragon's blood. Ryd said her name again, his voice clear as breaking ice. She shut her eyes against him, her hands rising through a chill, dark dream. As he called the third time, she dropped the wormspoor down the dragon's throat.

The hoods over its eyes rose; they grew wide, white-rimmed. She heard a convulsive swallow. Its head snapped down; it made a sound between a bellow and a whimper. Then its jaws opened again and it raked the air with gold flame.

Ryd, his hair and eyebrows scored suddenly with gold, dove into the snow. The dragon hissed at him again. The stream beyond him turned fiery, ran towards the sea. The great tail pounded furiously; dark cracks tore through the ice. The frozen cliffs began to sweat under the fire; pillars of ice sagged down, broke against the ground. The ledge Peka stood on crumbled at a wave of gold. She fell with it in a small avalanche of ice-rubble. The enormous white ring of dragon began to move, blurring endlessly past her eyes as the dragon gathered itself. A wing arched up toward the sky, then another. The dragon hissed at the mountain, then roared desperately, but only flame came out of its bowels, where once it had secreted winter. The chasms and walls of ice began breaking apart. Peka, struggling out of the snow, felt a lurch under her feet. A wind sucked at her her hair, pulled at her heavy coat. Then it drove down at her, thundering, and she sat in the snow. The dragon, aloft, its wingspan the span of half the island, breathed fire at the ocean, and its husk of ice began to melt.

Ryd pulled her out of the snow. The ground was breaking up under their feet. He said nothing; she thought he was scowling, though he looked strange with singed eyebrows. He pushed at her, flung her toward the sea. Fire sputtered around them. Ice slid under her; she slipped and clutched at the jagged rim of it. Brine splashed in her face. The ice whirled, as chunks of the mountain fell into the sea around them. The dragon was circling the mountain, melting huge peaks and cliffs. They struck the water hard, heaving the icefloes farther from the island. The mountain itself began to break up, as ice tore away from it, leaving only a bare peak riddled with mine-shafts.

Peka began to cry. "Look what I've done. Look at it." Ryd only grunted. She thought she could see figures high on the top of the peak, staring down at the vanishing island. The ocean, churning, spun the ice-floe toward the mainland. The river was flowing again, a blue-white streak spiralling down from the peak. The dragon was over the mainland now, billowing fire at the harbor, and ships without crews or cargo were floating free.

"Wormspoor," Ryd muttered. A wave ten feet high caught up with them, spilled, and shoved them into the middle of the channel. Peka saw the first of the boats taking the swift, swollen current down from the top of the island. Ryd spat out seawater, and took a firmer grip of the ice. "I lost every crystal, every dragon's fire I possessed. They're at the bottom of the sea. Thanks to you. Do you realize how much work, how many years—"

"Look at the sky." It spun above her, a pale, impossible mass of nothing. "How can I live under that? Where will I ever find dark, quiet places full of gold?"

"I held that dragon. It was just about to leave quietly, without taking half of Hoarsbreath with it."

"How will we live on the island again? All its secrets are gone."

"For fourteen years I studied dragons, their lore, their flights, their fires, the patterns of their lives and their destructions. I had all the knowledge I thought possible for me to acquire. No one—"

"Look at all that dreary flatland—"

"No one," he said, his voice rising, "ever told me you could harrow a dragon by pouring wormspoor down its throat!"

"Well, no one told me, either!" She slumped beside him, too despondent for anger. She watched more boats carrying miners, young children, her mother, down to the mainland. Then the dragon caught her eye, pale against the winter sky, somehow fragile, beautifully crafted, flying into the wake of its own flame.

It touched her mourning heart with the fire she had given it. Beside her, she felt Ryd grow quiet. His face, tired and battered, held a young, forgotten wonder, as he watched the dragon blaze across the world's cap like a star, searching for its winter. He drew a soft, incredulous breath.

"What did you put into that wormspoor?"

"Everything."

He looked at her, then turned his face toward Hoarsbreath. The sight made him wince. "I don't think we left even my father's bones at peace," he said hollowly, looking for a moment less Dragon-Harrower than a harrowed miner's son.

"I know," she whispered.

"No, you don't," he sighed. "You feel. The dragon's heart. My heart. It's not a lack of knowledge or experiences that destroyed Hoarsbreath, but something else I lost sight of: you told me that. The dark necessity of wisdom."

She gazed at him, suddenly uneasy for he was seeing her. "I'm not wise. Just lucky—or unlucky."

"Wisdom is a flatlander's word for your kind of feeling. You put your heart into everything—wormspoor, dragons, gold—and they become a kind of magic."

"I do not. I don't understand what you're talking about, Ryd Yarrow. I'm a miner; I'm going to find another mine—"

"You have a gold-mine in your heart. There are other things you can do with yourself. Not harrow dragons, but become a Watcher. You love the same things they love."

"Yes. Peace and quiet and private places—"

"I could show you dragons in their beautiful, private places all over the world. You could speak their language."

"I can't even speak my own. And I hate the flatland." She gripped the ice, watching it come.

"The world is only another tiny island, ringed with a great dragon of stars and night."

She shook her head, not daring to meet his eyes. "No. I'm not listening to you anymore. Look what happened the last time I listened to your tales."

"It's always yourself you are listening to," he said. The grey ocean swirled the ice under them, casting her back to the bewildering shores of the world. She was still trying to argue when the ice moored itself against the scorched pilings of the harbor.

from

The Story of
the Amulet

by E. Nesbit

E. Nesbit (1858–1924) in *The Story of the Amulet* continues the adventures of Jane, Anthea, Robert, Cyril and their furry friend the psammead, a sand-fairy. The children and the psammead previously appeared in *Five Children and It* and *The Phoenix and the Carpet*.

It was the day after the adventure of Julius Caesar and the Little Black Girl that Cyril, bursting into the bathroom to wash his hands for dinner (you have no idea how dirty they were, for he had been playing shipwrecked mariners all the morning on the leads at the back of the house, where the water-cistern is), found Anthea leaning her elbows on the edge of the bath, and crying steadily into it.

'Hullo!' he said, with brotherly concern, 'what's up now? Dinner'll be cold before you've got enough saltwater for a bath.'

'Go away,' said Anthea fiercely. 'I hate you! I hate everybody!'

There was a stricken pause.

'*I* didn't know,' said Cyril tamely.

'Nobody ever does know anything,' sobbed Anthea.

'I didn't know you were waxy. I thought you'd just hurt your fingers with the tap again like you did last week,' Cyril carefully explained.

'Oh—fingers!' sneered Anthea through her sniffs.

'Here, drop it, Panther,' he said uncomfortably. 'You haven't been having a row or anything?'

'No,' she said. 'Wash your horrid hands, for goodness' sake, if that's what you came for, or go.'

Anthea was so seldom cross that when she was cross the others were always more surprised than angry.

Cyril edged along the side of the bath and stood beside her. He put his hand on her arm.

'Dry up, do,' he said, rather tenderly for him. And, finding that though she did not at once take his advice she did not seem to resent it, he put his arm awkwardly across her shoulders and rubbed his head against her ear.

'There!' he said, in the tone of one administering a priceless cure for all possible sorrows. 'Now, what's up?'

'Promise you won't laugh?'

'I don't feel laughish myself,' said Cyril, dismally.

'Well, then,' said Anthea, leaning her ear against his head, 'it's Mother.'

'What's the matter with Mother?' asked Cyril, with apparent want of sympathy. 'She was all right in her letter this morning.'

'Yes; but I want her so.'

'You're not the only one,' said Cyril briefly, and the brevity of his tone admitted a good deal.

'Oh, yes,' said Anthea, 'I know. We all want her all the time. But I want her now most dreadfully, awfully much. I never wanted anything so much. That Imogen child—the way the ancient British Queen cuddled her up! And Imogen wasn't me, and the Queen was Mother. And then her letter this morning! And about The Lamb liking the salt bathing! And she bathed him in this very bath the night before she went away—oh, oh, oh!'

Cyril thumped her on the back.

'Cheer up,' he said. 'You know my inside thinking that I was doing? Well, that was partly about Mother. We'll soon get her back. If you'll chuck it, like a sensible kid, and wash your face, I'll tell you about it. That's right. You let me get to the tap. Can't you stop crying? Shall I put the door-key down your back?'

'That's for noses,' said Anthea, 'and I'm not a kid any more than you are,' but she laughed a little, and her mouth began to get back into its proper shape. You know what an odd shape your mouth gets into when you cry in earnest.

'Look here,' said Cyril, working the soap round and round between his hands in a thick slime of grey soapsuds. 'I've been thinking. We've only just *played* with the Amulet so far. We've got to *work* it now—work it for all it's worth. And it isn't only Mother either. There's Father out there all among the fighting. *I* don't howl about it, but I *think*—Oh, bother the soap!' The grey-lined soap had squirted out under the pressure of his fingers, and had hit Anthea's chin with as much force as though it had been shot from a catapult.

'There now,' she said regretfully, 'now I shall have to wash my face.'

'You'd have had to do that anyway,' said Cyril with conviction. 'Now, my idea's this. You know missionaries?'

'Yes,' said Anthea, who did not know a single one.

'Well, they always take the savages beads and brandy, and stays, and hats, and braces, and really useful things—things the savages haven't got, and never heard about. And the savages love them for their kind generousness, and give them pearls, and shells, and ivory, and cassowaries. And that's the way—'

'Wait a sec,' said Anthea, splashing. 'I can't hear what you're saying. Shells and—'

'Shells, and things like that. The great thing is to get people to love you by being generous. And that's what we've got to do. Next time we go into the Past we'll regularly fit out the expedition. You remember how the Babylonian Queen froze on to that pocket-book? Well, we'll take things like that. And offer them in exchange for a sight of the Amulet.'

'A sight of it is not much good.'

'No, silly. But, don't you see, when we've seen it we shall know where it is, and we can go and take it in the night when everybody is asleep.'

'It wouldn't be stealing, would it?' said Anthea thoughtfully, 'because it will be such an awfully long time ago when we do it. Oh, there's that bell again.'

As soon as dinner was eaten (it was tinned salmon and lettuce, and a jam tart), and the cloth cleared away, the idea was explained to the others, and the Psammead was aroused from sand, and asked what it thought would be good merchandise with which to buy the affection of say, the Ancient Egyptians, and whether it thought the Amulet was likely to be found in the Court of Pharaoh.

But it shook its head, and shot out its snail's eyes hopelessly.

'I'm not allowed to play in this game,' it said. 'Of course I *could* find out in a minute where the thing was, only I mayn't. But I may go so far as to own that your idea of taking things with you isn't a bad one. And I shouldn't show them all at once. Take small things and conceal them craftily about your persons.'

This advice seemed good. Soon the table was littered over with things which the children thought likely to interest the Ancient Egyptians. Anthea brought dolls, puzzle blocks, a wooden tea-service, a green leather case with *Nécessaire* written on it in gold letters. Aunt Emma had once given it to Anthea, and it had then contained scissors, penknife, bodkin, stiletto, thimble, corkscrew, and glove-buttoner. The scissors, knife, and thimble, and penknife were, of course, lost, but the other things were there and as good as new. Cyril contributed lead soldiers, a cannon, a catapult, a tin-opener, a tie-clip, and a tennis ball, and a padlock—no key. Robert collected a candle ('I don't suppose they ever saw a self-fitting paraffin one,' he said), a penny Japanese pin-tray, a rubber stamp with his father's name and address on it, and a piece of putty.

Jane added a key-ring, the brass handle of a poker, a pot that had held cold-cream, a smoked pearl button off her winter coat, and a key—no lock.

'We can't take all this rubbish,' said Robert, with some scorn. 'We must just each choose one thing.'

The afternoon passed very agreeably in the attempt to choose from the table the four most suitable objects. But the four children could not agree what was suitable, and at last Cyril said—

'Look here, let's each be blindfolded and reach out, and the first thing you touch you stick to.'

This was done.

Cyril touched the padlock.

Anthea got the *Nécessaire*.

Robert clutched the candle.

Jane picked up the tie-clip.

'It's not much,' she said. 'I don't believe Ancient Egyptians wore ties.'

'Never mind,' said Anthea. 'I believe it's luckier not to really choose. In the stories it's always the thing the wood-cutter's son picks up in the forest, and almost throws away because he thinks it's no good, that turns out to be the magic thing in the end; or else someone's lost it, and he is rewarded with the hand of the King's daughter in marriage.'

'I don't want any hands in marriage, thank you.' said Cyril firmly.

'Nor yet me,' said Robert. 'It's always the end of the adventures when it comes to the marriage hands.'

'*Are* we ready?' said Anthea.

'It *is* Egypt we're going to, isn't it?—nice Egypt?' said Jane. 'I won't go anywhere I don't know about—like that dreadful big-wavy burning-mountain city,' she insisted.

Then the Psammead was coaxed into its bag.

'I say,' said Cyril suddenly, 'I'm rather sick of kings. And people notice you so in palaces. Besides the Amulet's sure to be in a Temple. Let's just go among the common people, and try to work ourselves up by degrees. We might get taken on as Temple assistants.'

'Like beadles,' said Anthea, 'or vergers. They must have splendid chances of stealing the Temple treasures.'

'Righto!' was the general rejoinder. The charm was held up. It grew big once again, and once again the warm golden Eastern light glowed softly beyond it.

As the children stepped through it loud and furious voices rang in their ears. They went suddenly from the quiet of the Fitzroy Street dining-room into a very angry Eastern crowd, a crowd much too angry to notice them. They edged through it to the wall of a house and stood there. The crowd was of men, women, and children. They were of all sorts of complexions, and pictures of them might have been coloured by any child with a shilling paint-box. The colours that child would have used for complexions would have been yellow ochre, red ochre, light red, sepia, and indian ink. But their faces were painted already— black eyebrows and lashes, and some red lips. The women wore a sort of pinafore with shoulder straps, and loose things wound round their heads and shoulders. The men wore very little clothing—for they were the working people—and the Egyptian boys and girls wore nothing at all, unless you count the little ornaments hung on chains round their necks and waists. The children saw all this before they could hear anything distinctly. Everyone was shouting so.

But a voice sounded above the other voices, and presently it was speaking in a silence.

'Comrades and fellow workers,' it said, and it was the voice of a tall, coppery-coloured man who had climbed into a chariot that had been stopped by the crowd. Its owner had bolted, muttering something about calling the Guards, and now the man spoke from it. 'Comrades and fellow workers, how long are we to endure the tyranny of our masters, who live in idleness and luxury on the fruit of our toil? They only give us a bare subsistence wage, and they live on the fat of the land. We labour all our lives to keep them in wanton luxury. Let us make an end of it!'

A roar of applause answered him.

'How are you going to do it?' cried a voice.

'You look out,' cried another, 'or you'll get yourself into trouble.'

'I've heard almost every single word of that,' whispered Robert, 'in Hyde Park last Sunday!'

'Let us strike for more bread and onions and beer, and a longer midday rest,' the speaker went on. 'You are tired, you are hungry, you are thirsty. You are poor, your wives and children are pining for food. The barns of the rich are full to bursting with the corn we want, the corn our labour has grown. To the granaries!'

'To the granaries!' cried half the crowd; but another voice shouted clear above the tumult, 'To Pharaoh! To the King! Let's present a petition to the King! He will listen to the voice of the oppressed!'

For a moment the crowd swayed one way and another—first towards the granaries and then towards the palace. Then, with a rush like that of an imprisoned torrent suddenly set free, it surged along the street towards the palace, and the children were carried with it. Anthea found it difficult to keep the Psammead from being squeezed very uncomfortably.

The crowd swept through the streets of dull-looking houses with few windows, very high up, across the market where people were not buying but exchanging goods. In a momentary pause Robert saw a basket of onions exchanged for a hair comb and five fish for a string of beads. The people in the market seemed better off than those in the crowd; they had finer clothes, and more of them. They were the kind of people who, nowadays, would have lived at Brixton or Brockley.

'What's the trouble now?' a languid, large-eyed lady in a crimped, half-transparent linen dress, with her black hair very much braided and puffed out, asked of a date-seller.

'Oh, the working-men—discontented as usual,' the man answered. 'Listen to them. Anyone would think it mattered whether they had a little more or less to eat. Dregs of society!' said the date-seller.

'Scum!' said the lady.

'And I've heard *that* before, too,' said Robert.

At that moment the voice of the crowd changed, from anger to doubt, from doubt to fear. There were other voices shouting; they shouted defiance and menace, and they came nearer very quickly. There was the rattle of wheels and the pounding of hoofs. A voice shouted, 'Guards!'

'The Guards! The Guards!' shouted another voice, and the crowd of workmen took up the cry. 'The Guards! Pharaoh's Guards!' And swaying a little once more, the crowd hung for a moment as it were balanced. Then as the trampling hoofs came nearer the workmen fled dispersed, up alleys and into the courts of houses, and the Guards in their embossed leather chariots swept down the street at the gallop, their wheels clattering over the stones, and their dark-coloured, blue tunics blown open and back with the wind of their going.

'So *that* riot's over,' said the crimped-linen-dressed lady; 'that's a blessing! And did you notice the Captain of the Guard? What a very handsome man he was, to be sure!'

The four children had taken advantage of the moment's pause before the crowd turned to fly, to edge themselves and drag each other into an arched doorway.

Now they each drew a long breath and looked at the others.

'We're well out of *that*,' said Cyril.

'Yes,' said Anthea, 'but I do wish the poor men hadn't been driven back before they could get to the King. He might have done something for them.'

'Not if he was the one in the Bible he wouldn't,' said Jane. 'He had a hard heart.'

'Ah, that was the Moses one,' Anthea explained. 'The Joseph one was quite different. I should like to see Pharaoh's house. I wonder whether it's like the Egyptian Court in the Crystal Palace.'

'I thought we decided to try to get taken on in a Temple,' said Cyril in injured tones.

'Yes, but we've got to know someone first. Couldn't we make friends with a Temple doorkeeper—we might give him the padlock or something. I wonder which are temples and which are palaces,' Robert added, glancing across the market-place to where an enormous gateway with huge side buildings towered towards the sky. To the right and left of it were other buildings only a little less magnificent.

'Did you wish to seek out the Temple of Amen Rä?' asked a soft voice behind them, 'or the Temple of Mut, or the Temple of Khonsu?'

They turned to find beside them a young man. He was shaved clean from head to foot, and on his feet were light papyrus sandals. He was clothed in a linen tunic of white, embroidered heavily in colours. He was gay with anklets, bracelets, and armlets of gold, richly inlaid. He wore a ring on his finger, and he had a short jacket of gold embroidery something like the Zouave soldiers wear, and on his neck was a gold collar with many amulets hanging from it. But among the amulets the children could see none like theirs.

'It doesn't matter which Temple,' said Cyril frankly.

'Tell me your mission,' said the young man. 'I am a divine father of the Temple of Amen Rä and perhaps I can help you.'

'Well,' said Cyril, 'we've come from the great Empire on which the sun never sets.'

'I thought somehow that you'd come from some odd, out-of-the-way spot,' said the priest with courtesy.

'And we've seen a good many palaces. We thought we should like to see a Temple, for a change,' said Robert.

The Psammead stirred uneasily in its embroidered bag.

'Have you brought gifts to the Temple?' asked the priest cautiously.

'We *have* got some gifts,' said Cyril with equal caution. 'You see there's magic mixed up in it. So we can't tell you everything. But we don't want to give our gifts for nothing.'

'Beware how you insult the god,' said the priest sternly. 'I also can do magic. I can make a waxen image of you, and I can say words which, as the wax image melts before the fire, will make you dwindle away and at last perish miserably.'

'Pooh!' said Cyril stoutly,' that's nothing. *I* can make *fire* itself!'

'I should jolly well like to see you do it,' said the priest unbelievingly.

'Well, you shall,' said Cyril, 'nothing easier. Just stand close round me.'

'Do you need no preparation—no fasting, no incantations?' The priest's tone was incredulous.

'The incantation's quite short,' said Cyril, taking the hint; 'and as for fasting, it's not needed in my sort of magic. Union Jack, Printing Press, Gunpowder, Rule Britannia! Come, Fire, at the end of this little stick!'

He had pulled a match from his pocket, and as he ended the incantation which contained no words that it seemed likely the Egyptian had ever heard he stooped in the little crowd of his relations and the priest and struck the match on his boot. He stood up, shielding the flame with one hand.

'See?' he said, with modest pride. 'Here, take it into your hand.'

'No, thank you,' said the priest, swiftly backing. 'Can you do that again?'

'Yes.'

'Then come with me to the great double house of Pharaoh. He loves good magic, and he will raise you to honour and glory. There's no need of secrets between initiates,' he went on confidentially. 'The fact is, I am out of favour at present owing to a little matter of failure of prophecy. I told him a beautiful princess would be sent to him from Syria, and, lo! a woman thirty years old arrived. But she *was* a beautiful woman not so long ago. Time is only a mode of thought, you know.'

The children thrilled to the familiar words.

'So you know that too, do you?' said Cyril.

'It is part of the mystery of all magic, is it not?' said the priest. 'Now if I bring you to Pharaoh the little unpleasantness I spoke of will be forgotten. And I will ask Pharaoh, the Great House, Son of the Sun, and Lord of the South and North, to decree that you shall lodge in the Temple. Then you can have a good look round, and teach me your magic. And I will teach you mine.'

This idea seemed good—at least it was better than any other which at that moment occurred to anybody, so they followed the priest through the city.

The streets were very narrow and dirty. The best houses, the priest explained, were built within walls twenty to twenty-five feet high, and such windows as showed in the walls were very high up. The tops of palm-trees showed above the walls. The poor people's houses were little square huts with a door and two windows, and smoke coming out of a hole in the back.

'The poor Egyptians haven't improved so very much in their building since the first time we came to Egypt,' whispered Cyril to Anthea.

The huts were roofed with palm branches, and everywhere there were chickens, and goats, and little naked children kicking about in the yellow dust. On one roof was a goat, who had climbed up and was eating the dry palm-leaves with snorts and head-tossings of delight. Over every house door was some sort of figure or shape.

'Amulets,' the priest explained, 'to keep off the vile eye.'

'I don't think much of your "nice Egypt",' Robert whispered to Jane; 'it simply not a patch on Babylon.'

'Ah, you wait till you see the palace,' Jane whispered back.

The palace was indeed much more magnificent than anything they had yet seen that day, though it would have made but a poor show beside that of the Babylonian King. They came to it through a great square pillared doorway of sandstone that stood in a high brick wall. The shut doors were of massive cedar, with bronze hinges, and were studded with bronze nails. At the side was a little door and a wicket gate, and through this the priest led the children. He seemed to know a word that made the sentries make way for him.

Inside was a garden, planted with hundreds of different kinds of trees and flowering shrubs, a lake full of fish, with blue lotus flowers at the margin, and ducks swimming about cheerfully, and looking, as Jane said, quite modern.

'The guard-chamber, the store-houses, the Queen's house,' said the priest, pointing them out.

They passed through open courtyards, paved with flat stones, and the priest whispered to a guard at a great inner gate.

'We are fortunate,' he said to the children. 'Pharaoh is even now in the Court of Honour. Now, don't forget to be overcome with respect and admiration. It won't do any harm if you fall flat on your faces. And whatever you do, don't speak until you're spoken to.'

'There used to be that rule in our country,' said Robert, 'when my father was a little boy.'

At the outer end of the great hall a crowd of people were arguing with and even shoving the Guards, who seemed to make it a rule not to let anyone through unless they were bribed to do it. The children heard several promises of the utmost richness, and wondered whether they would ever be kept.

All round the hall were pillars of painted wood. The roof was of cedar, gorgeously inlaid. About half-way up the hall was a wide, shallow step that went right across the hall; then a little farther on another; and then a steep flight of narrower steps, leading right up to the throne on which Pharaoh sat. He sat there very splendid, his red. and white double crown on his head, and his sceptre in his hand. The throne had a canopy of wood and wooden pillars painted in bright colours. On a low, broad bench that ran all round the hall sat the friends, relatives, and courtiers of the King, leaning on richly-covered cushions.

The priest led the children up the steps till they all stood before the throne; and then, suddenly, he fell on his face with hands outstretched. The others did the same. Anthea falling very carefully because of the Psammead.

'Raise them,' said the voice of Pharaoh, 'that they may speak to me.' The officers of the King's household raised them.

'Who are these strangers?' Pharaoh asked, and added very crossly. 'And what do you mean, Rekh-marā, by daring to come into my presence while your innocence is not established?'

'Oh, great King,' said the young priest, 'you are the very image of Rä, and the likeness of his son Horus in every respect. You know the thoughts of the hearts of the gods and of men, and you have divined that these strangers are the children of the children of the vile and conquered Kings of the Empire where the sun never sets. They know a magic not known to the Egyptians. And they come with gifts in their hands as tribute to Pharaoh, in whose heart is the wisdom of the gods, and on his lips their truth.'

'That is all very well,' said Pharaoh, 'but where are the gifts?'

The children, bowing as well as they could in their embarrassment at finding themselves the centre of interest in a circle more grand, more golden and more highly coloured than they could have imagined possible, pulled out the padlock, the *Nécessaire*, and the tie-clip. 'But it's not tribute all the same,' Cyril muttered. 'England doesn't pay tribute!'

Pharaoh examined all the things with great interest when the chief of the household had taken them up to him. 'Deliver them to the Keeper of the Treasury,' he said to one near him. And to the children he said—

'A small tribute, truly, but strange, and not without worth. And the magic, O Rekh-marā?'

'These unworthy sons of a conquered nation . . .' began Rekh-marā.

'Nothing of the kind!' Cyril whispered angrily.

'. . . of a vile and conquered nation, can make fire to spring from dry wood—in the sight of all.'

'I should jolly well like to see them do it,' said Pharaoh, just as the priest had done.

So Cyril, without more ado, did it.

'Do more magic,' said the King, with simple appreciation.

'He cannot do any more magic,' said Anthea suddenly, and all eyes were turned on her, 'because of the voice of the free people who are shouting for bread and onions and beer and a long mid-day rest. If the people had what they wanted, he could do more.'

'A rude-spoken girl,' said Pharaoh. 'But give the dogs what they want,' he said, without turning his head. 'Let them have their rest and their extra rations. There are plenty of slaves to work.'

A richly-dressed official hurried out.

'You will be the idol of the people,' Rekh-marā whispered joyously; 'the Temple of Amen will not contain their offerings.'

Cyril struck another match, and all the court was overwhelmed with delight and wonder. And when Cyril took the candle from his pocket and lighted it with the match, and then held the burning candle up before the King the enthusiasm knew no bounds.

'Oh, greatest of all, before whom sun and moon and stars bow down,' said Rekh-marā insinuatingly, 'am I pardoned? Is my innocence made plain?'

'As plain as it ever will be, I daresay,' said Pharaoh shortly. 'Get along with you. You are pardoned. Go in peace.' The priest went with lightning swiftness.

'And what,' said the King suddenly, 'is it that moves in that sack? Show me, oh strangers.'

There was nothing for it but to show the Psammead.

'Seize it,' said Pharaoh carelessly. 'A very curious monkey. It will be a nice little novelty for my wild beast collection.'

And instantly, the entreaties of the children availing as little as the bites of the Psammead, though both bites and entreaties were fervent, it was carried away from before their eyes.

'Oh, *do* be careful!' cried Anthea. 'At least keep it dry! Keep it in its sacred house!'

She held up the embroidered bag.

'It's a magic creature,' cried Robert; 'it's simply priceless!'

'You've no right to take it away,' cried Jane incautiously. 'It's a shame, a barefaced robbery, that's what it is!'

There was an awful silence. Then Pharaoh spoke.

'Take the sacred house of the beast from them,' he said, 'and imprison all. Tonight after supper it may be our pleasure to see more magic. Guard them well, and do not torture them—yet!'

'Oh, dear!' sobbed Jane, as they were led away. 'I knew exactly what it would be! Oh, I wish you hadn't!'

'Shut up, silly,' said Cyril. 'You know you *would* come to Egypt. It was your own idea entirely. Shut up. It'll be all right.'

'I thought we should play ball with queens,' sobbed Jane, 'and have no end of larks! And now everything's going to be perfectly horrid!'

The room they were shut up in *was* a room, and not a dungeon, as the elder ones had feared. That, as Anthea said, was one comfort. There were paintings on the wall that at any other time would have been most interesting. And a sort of low couch, and chairs.

When they were alone Jane breathed a sigh of relief.

'Now we can get home all right,' she said.

'And leave the Psammead?' said Anthea reproachfully.

'Wait a sec. I've got an idea,' said Cyril. He pondered for a few moments. Then he began hammering on the heavy cedar door. It opened, and a guard put in his head.

' Stop that row,' he said sternly, ' or—'

'Look here,' Cyril interrupted, 'it's very dull for you isn't it? Just doing nothing but guard us. Wouldn't you like to see some magic? We're not too proud to do it for you. Wouldn't you like to see it?'

'I don't mind if I do,' said the guard.

'Well then, you get us that monkey of ours that was taken away, and we'll show you.'

'How do I know you're not making game of me?' asked the soldier. 'Shouldn't wonder if you only wanted to get the creature so as to set it on me. I daresay its teeth and claws are poisonous.'

'Well, look here,' said Robert. 'You see we've got nothing with us? You just shut the door, and open it again in five minutes, and we'll have got a magic—oh, I don't know—a magic flower in a pot for you.'

'If you can do that you can do anything,' said the soldier, and he went out and barred the door.

Then, of course, they held up the Amulet. They found the East by holding it up, and turning slowly till the Amulet began to grow big, walked home through it, and came back with a geranium in full scarlet flower from the staircase window of the Fitzroy Street house.

'Well!' said the soldier when he came in. 'I really am—!'

'We can do much more wonderful things than that—oh, ever so much,' said Anthea persuasively, 'if we only have our monkey. And here's twopence for yourself.'

The soldier looked at the twopence.

'What's this?' he said.

Robert explained how much simpler it was to pay money for things than to exchange them as the people were doing in the market. Later on the soldier gave the coins to his captain, who, later still, showed them to Pharaoh, who of course kept them and was much struck with the idea. That was really how coins first came to be used in Egypt. You will not believe this, I daresay, but really, if you believe the rest of the story, I don't see why you shouldn't believe this as well.

'I say,' said Anthea, struck by a sudden thought, 'I suppose it'll be all right about those workmen? The King won't go back on what he said about them just because he's angry with us?'

'Oh, no,' said the soldier, 'you see, he's rather afraid of magic. He'll keep to his word right enough.'

'Then *that's* all right,' said Robert; and Anthea said softly and coaxingly—

'Ah, do get us the monkey, and then you'll see some lovely magic. Do—there's a nice, kind soldier.'

'I don't know where they've put your precious monkey, but if I can get another chap to take on my duty here I'll see what I can do,' he said grudgingly, and went out.

'Do you mean,' said Robert, 'that we're going off without even *trying* for the other half of the Amulet?'

'I really think we'd better,' said Anthea tremulously.

'Of course the other half of the Amulet's here somewhere or our half wouldn't have brought us here. I do wish we could find it. It is a pity we don't know any *real* magic. Then we could find out. I do wonder where it is—exactly.'

If they had only known it, something very like the other half of the Amulet was very near them. It hung round the neck of someone, and that someone was watching them through a chink, high up in the wall, specially devised for watching people who were imprisoned. But they did not know.

There was nearly an hour of anxious waiting. They tried to take an interest in the picture on the wall, a picture of harpers playing very odd harps and women dancing at a feast. They examined the painted plaster floor, and the chairs were of white painted wood with coloured stripes at intervals.

But the time went slowly, and everyone had time to think of how Pharaoh had said, 'Don't torture them—*yet*.'

'If the worst comes to the worst,' said Cyril, 'we must just bunk, and leave the Psammead. I believe it can take care of itself well enough. They won't kill it or hurt it when they find it can speak and give wishes. They'll build it a temple, I shouldn't wonder.'

'I couldn't bear to go without it,' said Anthea, 'and Pharaoh said "After supper", that won't be just yet. And the soldier was curious. I'm sure we're all right for the present.'

All the same, the sounds of the door being unbarred seemed one of the prettiest sounds possible.

'Suppose he hasn't got the Psammead?' whispered Jane.

But that doubt was set at rest by the Psammead itself; for almost before the door was open it sprang through the chink of it into Anthea's arms, shivering and hunching up its fur.

'Here's its fancy overcoat,' said the soldier, holding out the bag, into which the Psammead immediately crept.

'Now,' said Cyril, 'what would you like us to do? Anything you'd like us to get for you?'

'Any little trick you like,' said the soldier. 'If you can get a strange flower blooming in an earthenware vase you can get anything, I suppose,' he said. 'I just wish I'd got two men's loads of jewels from the King's treasury. That's what I've always wished for.'

At the word 'wish' the children knew that the Psammead would attend to that bit of magic. It did, and the floor was littered with a spreading heap of gold and precious stones.

'Any other little trick?' asked Cyril loftily. 'Shall we become invisible? Vanish?'

'Yes, if you like,' said the soldier; 'but not through the door, you don't.'

He closed it carefully and set his broad Egyptian back against it.

'No! no!' cried a voice high up among the tops of the tall wooden pillars that stood against the wall. There was a sound of someone moving above.

The soldier was as much surprised as anybody.

'That's magic, if you like,' he said.

And then Jane held up the Amulet, uttering the word of Power. At the sound of it and at the sight of the Amulet growing into the great arch the soldier fell flat on his face among the jewels with a cry of awe and terror.

The children went through the arch with a quickness born of long practice. But Jane stayed in the middle of the arch and looked back. The others, standing on the dining-room carpet in Fitzroy Street, turned and saw her still in the arch. 'Someone's holding her,' cried Cyril. 'We must go back.'

But they pulled at Jane's hands just to see if she would come, and, of course, she did come.

Then, as usual, the arch was little again and there they all were.

'Oh, I do wish you hadn't!' Jane said crossly. 'It *was* so interesting. The priest had come in and he was kicking the soldier, and telling him he'd done it now, and they must take the jewels and flee for their lives.'

'And did they?'

' I don't know. You interfered,' said Jane ungratefully. ' I *should* have liked to see the last of it.'

The Spell of the Magician's Daughter

by Evelyn Sharp

Writer and journalist Evelyn Sharp (1869–1955) was a dedicated pacifist and a founding member of the United Suffragists. This fairy tale is about Firefly, a magician's daughter who discovers her true powers through the use of her imagination.

There was once a magician, who lived in a pine forest and frightened everyone who came near him. This did not matter so much as it might have done, perhaps, for it was such a very thick forest that nobody ever did come near him; still, a magician is a magician, as all the world knows, and there is no doubt that he would have been an extremely frightening magician, if he could have found anybody to frighten. As it was, he had to be a nice, fatherly magician instead; for most of his time was taken up in teaching his four daughters to be witches. Now, the three elder daughters were very anxious to be witches; they thought it would be good fun to turn people into frogs and toads, and to go to the christenings of Princes uninvited, and to do all the uncomfortable things that witches love to do. But the magician's youngest daughter was of a very different opinion.

"It is too much trouble to be a witch," she said with a pout. "Who wants to learn a lot of stupid spells and things? Besides, I haven't the right kind of chin; it is round instead of hooked, and nobody could possibly be a witch without a hooked chin."

"The magician will alter the shape of your chin, if you ask him," suggested her eldest sister.

"Oh, but I do not want to ask him!" said little Firefly, hastily; and she stroked her small pink chin with her finger.

"What are you going to do when you grow up?" asked her three sisters. "You must do something, if you are not a witch."

Firefly rose to her feet and gave her short red frock a tug, to try and make it as long as a grown-up person's frock.

"If I must do something," she said in a resigned tone, "I will marry the King's son." And when her three sisters burst out laughing at the idea, she turned and walked away indignantly into the forest.

Now, of course, the magician's forest was by no means an ordinary forest; and one of the most remarkable things about it was the way it managed to suit the mood of everybody who went into it. So when the magician's youngest daughter took her crossness and her grievances into the wood, that afternoon, the sunshine brought her the warm strong scent of the pine trees, and the breeze brought her the sound that lives at the top of the pine trees, and the fairies brought her the secrets of the grass at her feet—and Firefly was a nice little girl again. Then, just as the last bit of her crossness went floating away into nothing at all, the forest suddenly changed into quite another sort of forest. A small white cloud dropped over the sun like a thin muslin curtain, and the trees stopped putting their heads together, which is a favourite habit of pine trees, and the bees stopped whirring; and there was no doubt whatever that something was really going to happen. And the very next minute it did happen, for there came a crackling and a rustling in the underwood; and out into the open, just in front of the little girl in the short red frock, sprang a tall, eager-looking boy.

"Dear me!" exclaimed Firefly, for it was most unusual to meet anyone in the magician's forest. "What are you doing here?"

"I am running away from home," answered the boy, breathlessly. "I am running as fast as ever I can. Do you not see what a tremendous hurry I am in?"

"Why are you running away from home?" demanded the magician's daughter. "It seems to me a very stupid thing to do."

"It is not half so stupid as staying at home, when your country is being enchanted by a most objectionable giant," retorted the boy. Then he looked at her and sighed. "It is a pity," he said in a disappointed tone, "that you are only a girl."

"I do not think it is a pity at all," cried Firefly. "I would *much* rather be a girl, thank you."

"Well, you see," explained the boy, "if you were not a girl you might help me to disenchant my country; as it is, I am only wasting my time in talking to you." Then he made her a very grand bow and ran away again.

Firefly called after him to stop. "It is very evident," she exclaimed in an offended tone, "that you do not know who I am."

The boy looked round impatiently. "Of course I don't," he said; "but it doesn't matter, does it?"

"It matters very much," replied Firefly, stamping her foot angrily; "for I am the magician's daughter."

The boy came back at once. "Why did you not say so before?" he inquired. "Girls are so fond of wasting other people's time! All this while, you might have been helping me to disenchant my country."

Firefly was not at all sure that she knew how to disenchant anybody's country, and she consequently found herself in an awkward fix, which is what may happen to any of us if we do not learn our lessons properly. However, she did her best to look as wise as a magician's daughter should, and she asked the boy to tell her all about the giant.

"The wymps sent him," he explained sadly. "They had a grudge against the King, because he told tales about them in Fairyland when they played tricks with his fruit trees. No doubt, it was very annoying for the King to see all his apples and pears ripening on one side and not on the other, just because it amused the wymps to make the sun shine only on one side of the royal orchard; but it is ever so much worse to be obliged to put up with a giant who won't go away, and lives on nothing but fruit. There he sits in his castle on the top of the biggest hill in the kingdom, and every orchard in the place is being stripped in order to give him enough to eat. You have no idea how difficult it is to feed a giant who never touches anything but fruit! A cartload of strawberries is only just enough for his breakfast, and he eats a melon as we should eat a grape. All the houses are being pulled down and the streets are being made into orchards and gardens, so that the giant may have his food; and if any ordinary person is found swallowing so much as a red currant, he is instantly beheaded. You must agree that it is not pleasant to live in a country with a giant of this description."

"It must be most unpleasant," agreed Firefly; "but why do you not starve the giant instead of feeding him? Perhaps, he would go away if he had no fruit to eat."

The boy shook his head. "The King thought of that," he answered; "but the giant pointed out, most politely, that when he could not get any fruit to eat he always ate kings and other members of the royal family, so his Majesty instantly dropped the subject. Then we sent the whole of the army to kill him, and the giant thought it was a review, and he looked out of the window with great interest until the soldiers told him why they had come. He did not seem to mind the idea of being killed at all, but he explained to them that there were plenty of other giants in the world, and that the next one might eat babies or schoolboys or something like that; so of course the army marched back again. After that, we tried to make terms with the wymps; and they gave in so far as to say that they would remove the giant, if any one could invent a joke that would make him laugh."

"That would surely not be difficult," remarked the magician's daughter.

"It is more difficult than you think," said the boy. "To begin with, the giant is of such a melancholy disposition that any ordinary joke merely depresses him. I have known him to weep bitterly for hours at one of the King's very best jokes, so there is not much chance for any one else in the country."

"Have *you* not tried to make a joke for the giant?" asked Firefly.

"It would be no good," sighed the boy; "everybody says I am much too stupid. But I thought I might find a joke if I came out into the world to look for it, and then I could take it back and disenchant the kingdom, you see. I did not know," he added with a little smile, "that

I should be so lucky as to meet a real magician's daughter. Now I have met you, no doubt you will be good enough to tell me what I must do in order to meet with a joke."

Firefly tried harder than ever to look like a magician's daughter, and she gave her frock another tug to show how important she was feeling. All the same, she could not in the least remember the spell for conjuring up a joke, though the magician had given it her to learn, over and over and over again. So there was nothing for it but to invent a new one, and that was how the magician's youngest daughter came to invent her very first spell.

"To begin with, you must find a girl," she told him, "a really nice sort of girl. And when you have kissed the five fingers of her left hand, she will doubtless tell you the way to the nicest, greenest, and wisest dragon in the world. And when you have told the dragon how nice and green and wise he is, no doubt he will tell you the way to the dwarf who has been trying all his life to make a noise in the world. And if you will assure the dwarf that he is making a most terrific noise in the world, you may be sure that he will tell you the way home again."

"But where shall I find my joke?" demanded the boy, impatiently.

"Oh, well," said Firefly, carelessly, "if you haven't found a joke by that time, you never will."

The boy repeated the spell over again, just to fix it in his mind; then he looked down at the little girl in the short red frock, and a twinkle shone in his eyes.

"Are *you* a really nice sort of girl?" he asked.

Firefly gave a jump. "Oh, I never thought of that," she cried in dismay, quite forgetting that she was supposed to be a witch. "I—I think it ought to be some other girl."

"I don't," laughed the boy, and he promptly took her left hand and kissed it five times on the finger-tips. "Now," he continued, "will you please tell me the way to the nicest, greenest, and wisest dragon in the world?"

Firefly was truly in a fix this time. No doubt the nice, green, wise dragon lived somewhere; but it was quite impossible for a lazy little girl, who had never bothered to learn her lessons, to say where he did live. So she stopped feeling important, and began to pout.

"I never met such a tiresome boy in my life," she complained. "You do nothing but ask questions!"

"But that is exactly what you told me to do," protested the boy.

There was certainly something in what he said, and it was not a bit of good grumbling at the spell she had invented out of her own head; so with a very bad grace she told him to go straight on until he came to the dragon. The boy looked at her suspiciously.

"Your spell is certainly a very funny kind of spell," he remarked. "Are you quite sure you are the magician's daughter?"

Firefly drew herself up and turned her back on him. "If my spells are not good enough for you," she remarked with much dignity, "you can go and try somebody else's spells."

The boy drew near to her and held out his hand coaxingly. "Pray do not be angry," he begged her; "if there is anything odd about your spell, no doubt it is because you are not yet a full-grown magician's daughter."

But Firefly walked straight home to supper, and left him to find the dragon by himself. "Clearly, I must marry the King's son when I grow up," she muttered to herself. "*Anything* would be better than trying to be a witch!" When she reached home, she found her three sisters eating their bread-and-milk, while the magician told them stories about the things that were happening at that very moment in the world beyond the pine forest. That is the best of having a magician for a father; because, of course, any ordinary father can only tell stories about the things that happened yesterday or the day before.

"The country is just being ordered to go into mourning," said the magician, as Firefly sat down with her bowl of bread-and-milk. "The King's son has run away from home in search of a good joke, and he is never expected to return. It is a pity, for, until he does return, my magic tells me that the country will not be disenchanted."

"Was that the King's son?" exclaimed Firefly, in a tone of the greatest astonishment. "Well, I *am* disappointed!"

"Shall you not marry him, little sister, when you grow up?" teased the magician's eldest daughter.

Firefly let her spoon fall into the milk with a splash, and looked away among the tall red trunks of the pine trees. "I have changed my mind," she answered slowly; "perhaps I shall be a witch, after all."

When her three sisters went to bed, she lingered behind and caressed the long white beard of the old magician. "The King's son will never come back," she said, "because I have sent him wandering over the world to work out a spell that isn't a real spell."

The magician smiled, for of course he knew fast enough what she had been doing. "It is a real spell, little daughter," he answered, "because you took it straight from your head and your heart and wove it round the King's son."

"But how can anyone find the nice green dragon and the dwarf who wants to make a noise in the world, when I only invented them myself?" cried Firefly.

"No doubt," admitted the magician, "you must give them time to get there before you can expect anybody to find them; for it always takes longer to find things you have only just invented than it takes to find things that somebody else invented ever so long ago. As for the King's son, he will never find them at all, because the spell is yours and not his. But that is of no consequence."

"N-no," said Firefly, doubtfully; and she looked away again at the tall red trunks of the pine trees. Then she sprang to her feet and gave herself a determined little shake. "If I find the stupid things first, will the King's son be able to find them afterwards?" she demanded.

"He will be very foolish if he doesn't," answered the magician.

"Then I shall go out into the world and search for them, this very minute," declared his little daughter. "That is only fair, since it is my fault that the King's son is looking for things that are not there. All the same," she added with a sigh, "I do wish he were not quite such an unpleasant boy!"

So, the very next morning, as soon as the sun came up and began shining sideways through the tall, straight trunks of the pine trees, the magician's daughter kissed her father and her three sisters, and started on her travels.

"Will you not take a spell or two with you, just to help you on your way?" they called after her. But Firefly shook her head. She had had enough of spells for the present; and besides, she was so ignorant that she would not have known what to do with other people's spells. So she went empty-handed through the forest, and her sisters stayed at home and learned their lessons.

Now, it was all very well to go out into the world to help a King's Son to find a dragon that never need have been invented, but before many days had passed the magician's lazy little daughter began to feel extremely tired of the task she had set herself. "If I had only known that I should have to work out my own spell, I should have made it a *very* different kind of spell," she thought disconsolately. Then she sat down under a hedge, and seriously considered how she should manage to get to her journey's end without any more trouble to herself. "It is quite certain," she reflected, "that I cannot get there by witchcraft, for I have never learned to be a witch. But if I cannot be a witch, there is no reason why I should not pretend to be one." And when a large eagle suddenly swooped down in front of her, as she sat under the hedge, she at once seized the opportunity to pretend she was a witch.

"What a magnificent bird you are!" she began in her softest voice. "How is it that you have grown so handsome and so strong?"

"By eating little girls," answered the eagle, sternly. Firefly secretly trembled; for she was decidedly little, and the eagle was decidedly big. However, she managed to go on smiling, and she reached out her hand and stroked his feathers boldly.

"That is hardly the way to speak to a magician's daughter," she said carelessly. "How would you like to be turned into a soft woolly lamb and carried off by your wife for her supper?"

It was fortunate for her that the eagle did not like it at all, for she certainly could not have done what she threatened. As it was, he shivered all over at the bare idea, and instantly became as polite as possible.

"When I said little girls," he hastened to explain, "I was not referring to any one so important as yourself. Is there anything I can do for you on my way home?"

"Yes," said Firefly, condescendingly, "you may fly with me to the nicest, greenest, and wisest dragon in the world. And you may start this very minute, if you like."

The eagle looked a little crestfallen. "That is not exactly on my way home," he remarked.

"Ah!" smiled Firefly, "then you *do* want to be turned into a nice woolly lamb, do you?"

The eagle immediately gave in, and allowed her to jump on his back; and then he rose into the air and swept up with her to the warm blue sky overhead. For days and days and days the great bird darted onward; and Firefly lay upon his back and wondered what the King's son was doing, and dreamed about so many things that she lost count of the time altogether. At last, the day came when the eagle suddenly bent his head and dived towards the earth, down, down, down, until he touched the ground; and there he lay exhausted, while the magician's daughter slipped off his back and stretched herself.

"If you follow the path down to the sea-shore," panted the bird, "you will find the dragon waiting for you. I cannot carry you any further, for you have grown so tall since we started that my back is not strong enough to bear you. Will you let me go home now?"

"First of all," said Firefly, "you must find the King's son. I do not know where he is, but you will soon meet him somewhere or other. And you must show him the way to the nicest, greenest, and wisest dragon in the world. Then you may go home. But whatever you do, you must not tell the King's son that I sent you."

The eagle promised to obey her, and he rose into the air once more, while the magician's daughter followed the path down to the sea-shore. The first thing she saw was the nicest and the greenest and the wisest dragon in the world. He was lying on the pebbles in the hot sunshine, blinking his eyes at the waves; and he never so much as swished his tail when he saw the little girl in the red frock coming towards him. He was certainly not a very active dragon; but then, a dragon who had been invented by the magician's youngest daughter would naturally be an extremely lazy sort of dragon.

"Why," exclaimed Firefly, "I never expected to find you like this! I always thought that dragons lived in caves."

"So they do when they have been properly invented," answered the dragon, in a hurt tone. "You never said anything about a cave when you invented *me*, you see."

"I'm very sorry," said Firefly, apologetically. "I was in such a hurry at the time that I invented you just anyhow. However, if you will tell me the way to the dwarf who wants to make a noise in the world, I will ask the magician to invent you a cave, directly I get home."

"He lives on the other side of the sea," answered the dragon; and he winked one eye solemnly at the little girl in the red frock. "I am afraid you will have to swim across to get there," he added; and he winked both his eyes at once, as though it amused him to think that someone as lazy as himself was going to do some work.

"I shall do nothing of the sort," answered Firefly; and she walked down to the edge of the water and hailed the first fish that came swimming along. This happened to be a fine handsome young whale with a pleasant smile.

"I should be delighted," he said, when she asked him to carry her across the ocean; "but unfortunately, I am going in the opposite direction."

"Dear me!" remarked Firefly, "one would never think that I was a magician's daughter and could turn you into an octopus at a moment's notice. Do you know what would happen to you, if you were an octopus? Your own father would not know you, and he would eat you up for his supper."

"What a bother it is!" grumbled the whale. "One is never safe from witches nowadays. Would you like to travel on the top of the sea, or along the bottom?"

"The top, please," answered Firefly, arranging herself on his back, "and if you so much as let a drop of water come near me, I will turn you into—"

"All right," said the whale, hastily; and the next moment they were skimming swiftly along the top of the waves. For days and days and days they went on crossing the ocean, and the magician's daughter sat perched on the whale's back, and wondered more than ever what the King's son was doing, and dreamed about so many things that she lost count of the time altogether. At last they arrived on the other side of the sea, and the whale drew a long breath of relief as the little girl in the red frock jumped ashore.

"That's a good thing!" he gasped. "You have grown so much since we started that I could not have carried you another minute."

"That is what the eagle said," thought Firefly. "Have I really grown any taller?" It was quite impossible to know how tall she was, however, without having someone else to measure herself against; so she gave up wondering, and asked the whale where the dwarf lived.

"Follow the path up the beach till you come to him," answered the whale. "May I go home now?"

"First of all, you must look for the King's son," replied Firefly. "You will find him talking to the dragon, and then you will bring him here. After that, you may go home. But whatever you do, you must not tell the King's son that I sent you."

Then the whale went back to fetch the King's son, and the magician's daughter strolled up the beach until she came to the dwarf who wanted to make a noise in the world. She was surprised to find him sitting disconsolately under a gorse bush, with a dissatisfied expression on his face.

"Dear me!" exclaimed Firefly. "What have you done with your house? I always thought that dwarfs lived in neat little houses, with gardens in front of them."

"That depends on the person who invented them," answered the dwarf, crossly. "I was invented so carelessly that I have no home at all. And how am I to make a noise in the world when there is nothing to make a noise with? People ought to be more careful when they invent things!"

"Never mind," said Firefly, soothingly. "If you will wait for the

King's son and tell him to follow the path over the field until he comes to me, I will ask the magician to invent you the neatest little house in the world, directly I get home. And I will make him send you such a pair of creaking boots that you will be heard for miles round whenever you go for a stroll. Won't that be a nice easy way of making a noise in the world?"

The dwarf beamed with joy, for, having been invented by the magician's lazy little daughter, he naturally wanted to make a noise in the world with as little trouble as possible. So he promised to wait for the King's son, and Firefly passed on and followed the path across the field, until it brought her to the foot of the biggest hill in the kingdom. On the top of the hill was a castle, and out of the castle window looked a giant with a melancholy face. All round her stretched the most beautiful country she had ever seen, for there were no crowded streets in it, and no houses, and nothing to make it sad or ugly or dull; it was covered, instead, with the most charming orchards and the most delightful fruit gardens; and all the people in the kingdom lived in the open air, because there was nowhere else to live; and all the children played together under the fruit trees; and everyone was happy and gay from morning till night. Truly, no one would have said that the country was under a spell; but then, it must be remembered that it was the wymps who had bewymped it, and that explains a good deal. As for Firefly, she clapped her hands at the sight of it, for right away at the edge of this beautiful country she could see a line of tall straight pine trees against the blue clear sky.

"I have come home again," she murmured; and then she climbed the hill and sat down by the castle wall to wait for the King's son.

Nobody knows how long she waited, for she thought about him so much that she quite forgot to count the days. But one morning, as she was looking down the hillside as usual, wishing that the boy she was waiting for was not quite such an unpleasant boy, she saw a man striding along the path that led across the field. He was tall and brave-looking, and as he came up the hill-side she saw to her amazement that it was the King's son grown into a man; and she quite forgot that he was the boy who had teased her so unpleasantly in the forest. Now that there was someone to measure herself against, she saw, too, that the bird and the whale had spoken the truth, for she was nearly as tall as the King's son; and when she looked down for her short red frock, she found that it had been changed into a beautiful, soft white gown, fit for a Princess to go to court in.

"What a wonderful witch-woman you are!" said the King's son, as he stooped and kissed the five fingers of her left hand.

"I am not a witch at all," confessed the magician's daughter. "I have only been pretending to be a witch ever since I first saw you. It was extremely hard work," she added dolefully, "for I had to wander round the world in front of you, just to make that tiresome spell come true. I hope I shall never have to invent another spell as long as I live!"

"Then there would not have been a spell at all, unless we had made it up as we went along!" cried the King's son; and the idea tickled him so much that he broke into a peal of laughter. At the same moment a tremendous noise, like several thunder-storms and half-a-dozen gales of wind, sounded from the castle above; and there was the melancholy old giant, laughing just as heartily as the King's son.

"You absurd children!" roared the giant. "That is the best joke I ever heard in my life, and I must go straight off to Wympland to tell it to the wymps."

And without waiting so much as to pack his portmanteau, the giant marched straight out of the country and was never heard of again.

The King's son turned to the magician's daughter, and took her right hand as well, and kissed it five times on the finger-tips.

"Little witch-girl," he murmured, "your spell has disenchanted my country, after all!"

"That is impossible," laughed the magician's daughter, "for it was not a real spell, and I am not a real witch."

Then the King's son answered her as the magician had done, long ago in the pine forest.

"You are a real witch," he declared, "for you took a spell straight from your head and your heart, and you have woven it round the King's son."

Then he took her home and married her; and they chose the finest fruit garden in the kingdom for their own, and they lived in the middle of it, just as all the other people were living in their gardens. But the garden of the King's son was the finest of all, for it was full of baked-apple trees, and preserved-cherry trees, and blackberry-jam bushes, and sugar-candy canes; and best of all, there were almond-and-raisin trees, that always had more almonds than raisins on them.

So the magician's youngest daughter did marry the King's son, when she was grown up. But there is no doubt that she also became a witch, for to this day she can do what she likes with the King's son.

The Dragon of
the North

by Andrew Lang

Andrew Lang (1844-1912) was a Scottish poet, novelist and critic. He is best remembered for his work collecting, compiling and translating hundreds of folk and fairy tales from around the world. This Eastern European tale recounts the story of a magical ring that belonged to King Solomon.

Very long ago, as old people have told me, there lived a terrible monster, who came out of the North, and laid waste whole tracts of country, devouring both men and beasts; and this monster was so destructive that it was feared that unless help came no living creature would be left on the face of the earth. It had a body like an ox, and legs like a frog, two short fore-legs, and two long ones behind, and besides that it had a tail like a serpent, ten fathoms in length. When it moved it jumped like a frog, and with every spring it covered half a mile of ground. Fortunately its habit, was to remain for several years in the same place, and not to move on till the whole neighborhood was eaten up. Nothing could hunt it, because its whole body was covered with scales, which were harder than stone or metal; its two great eyes shone by night, and even by day, like the brightest lamps, and anyone who had the ill luck to look into those eyes became as it were bewitched, and was obliged to rush of his own accord into the monster's jaws. In this way the Dragon was able to feed upon both men and beasts without the least trouble to itself, as it needed not to move from the spot where it was lying. All the neighboring kings had offered rich rewards to anyone who should be able to destroy the monster, either by force or enchantment, and many had tried their luck, but all had miserably failed. Once a great forest in which the Dragon lay had been set on fire; the forest was burnt down, but the fire did not do the monster the least harm. However, there was a tradition amongst the wise men of the country that the Dragon might be overcome by one who possessed King Solomon's signet-ring, upon which a secret writing was engraved. This inscription would enable anyone who was wise enough to interpret it to find out how the Dragon could be destroyed. Only no one knew where the ring was hidden, nor was there any sorcerer or learned man to be found who would be able to explain the inscription.

At last a young man, with a good heart and plenty of courage, set out to search for the ring. He took his way towards the sunrising, because he knew that all the wisdom of old time comes from the East. After some years he met with a famous Eastern magician, and asked for his advice in the matter. The magician answered:

"Mortal men have but little wisdom, and can give you no help, but the birds of the air would be better guides to you if you could learn their language. I can help you to understand it if you will stay with me a few days."

The youth thankfully accepted the magician's offer, and said, "I cannot now offer you any reward for your kindness, but should my undertaking succeed your trouble shall be richly repaid."

Then the magician brewed a powerful potion out of nine sorts of herbs which he had gathered himself all alone by moonlight, and he gave the youth nine spoonfuls of it daily for three days, which made him able to understand the language of birds.

At parting the magician said to him. "If you ever find Solomon's ring and get possession of it, then come back to me, that I may explain the inscription on the ring to you, for there is no one else in the world who can do this."

From that time the youth never felt lonely as he walked along; he always had company, because he understood the language of birds; and in this way he learned many things which mere human knowledge could never have taught him. But time went on, and he heard nothing about the ring. It happened one evening, when he was hot and tired with walking, and had sat down under a tree in a forest to eat his supper, that he saw two gaily-plumaged birds, that were strange to him, sitting at the top of the tree talking to one another about him. The first bird said:

"I know that wandering fool under the tree there, who has come so far without finding what he seeks. He is trying to find King Solomon's lost ring."

The other bird answered, "He will have to seek help from the Witch-maiden, who will doubtless be able to put him on the right track. If she has not got the ring herself, she knows well enough who has it."

"But where is he to find the Witch-maiden?" said the first bird. "She has no settled dwelling, but is here to-day and gone to-morrow. He might as well try to catch the wind."

The other replied, "I do not know, certainly, where she is at present, but in three nights from now she will come to the spring to wash her face, as she does every month when the moon is full, in order that she may never grow old nor wrinkled, but may always keep the bloom of youth."

"Well," said the first bird, "the spring is not far from here. Shall we go and see how it is she does it?"

"Willingly, if you like," said the other.

The youth immediately resolved to follow the birds to the spring; only two things made him uneasy: first, lest he might be asleep when the birds went, and secondly, lest he might lose sight of them, since he had not wings to carry him along so swiftly. He was too tired to keep awake all night, yet his anxiety prevented him from sleeping soundly, and when with the earliest dawn he looked up to the tree-top, he was glad to see his feathered companions still asleep with their heads under their wings. He ate his breakfast, and waited until the birds should start, but they did not leave the place all day. They hopped about from one tree to another looking for food, all day long until the evening, when they went back to their old perch to sleep. The next day the same thing happened, but on the third morning one bird said to the other, "To-day we must go to the spring to see the Witch-maiden wash her face." They remained on the tree till noon; then they flew away and went towards the south. The young man's heart beat with anxiety lest he should lose sight of his guides, but he managed to keep the birds in view until they again perched upon a tree. The young man ran after them until he was quite exhausted and out of breath, and after three short rests the birds at length reached a small open space in the forest, on the edge of which they placed themselves on the top of a high tree. When the youth had overtaken them, he saw that there was a clear spring in the middle of the space. He sat down at the foot of the tree upon which the birds were perched, and listened attentively to what they were saying to each other.

"The sun is not down yet," said the first bird; "we must wait yet awhile till the moon rises and the maiden comes to the spring. Do you think she will see that young man sitting under the tree?"

"Nothing is likely to escape her eyes, certainly not a young man," said the other bird. "Will the youth have the sense not to let himself be caught in her toils?"

"We will wait," said the first bird, "and see how they get on together."

The evening light had quite faded, and the full moon was already shining down upon the forest, when the young man heard a slight rustling sound. After a few moments there came out of the forest a maiden, gliding over the grass so lightly that her feet seemed scarcely to touch the ground, and stood beside the spring. The youth could not turn away his eyes from the maiden, for he had never in his life seen a woman so beautiful. Without seeming to notice anything, she went to the spring, looked up to the full moon, then knelt down and bathed her face nine times, then looked up to the moon again and walked nine times round the well, and as she walked she sang this song:

> Full-faced moon with light unshaded,
> Let my beauty ne'er be faded.

Never let my cheek grow pale!
While the moon is waning nightly,
May the maiden bloom more brightly,
May her freshness never fail!

Then she dried her face with her long hair, and was about to go away, when her eye suddenly fell upon the spot where the young man was sitting, and she turned towards the tree. The youth rose and stood waiting. Then the maiden said, "You ought to have a heavy punishment because you have presumed to watch my secret doings in the moonlight. But I will forgive you this time, because you are a stranger and knew no better. But you must tell me truly who you are and how you came to this place, where no mortal has ever set foot before."

The youth answered humbly: "Forgive me, beautiful maiden, if I have unintentionally offended you. I chanced to come here after long wandering, and found a good place to sleep under this tree. At your coming I did not know what to do, but stayed where I was, because I thought my silent watching could not offend you."

The maiden answered kindly, "Come and spend this night with us. You will sleep better on a pillow than on damp moss."

The youth hesitated for a little, but presently he heard the birds saying from the top of the tree, "Go where she calls you, but take care to give no blood, or you will sell your soul." So the youth went with her, and soon they reached a beautiful garden, where stood a splendid house, which glittered in the moonlight as if it was all built out of gold and silver. When the youth entered he found many splendid chambers, each one finer than the last. Hundreds of tapers burnt upon golden candlesticks, and shed a light like the brightest day. At length they reached a chamber where a table was spread with the most costly dishes. At the table were placed two chairs, one of silver, the other of gold. The maiden seated herself upon the golden chair, and offered the silver one to her companion. They were served by maidens dressed in white, whose feet made no sound as they moved about, and not a word was spoken during the meal. Afterwards the youth and the Witch-maiden conversed pleasantly together, until a woman, dressed in red, came in to remind them that it was bed-time. The youth was now shown into another room, containing a silken bed with down cushions, where he slept delightfully, yet he seemed to hear a voice near his bed which repeated to him, "Remember to give no blood!"

The next morning the maiden asked him whether he would not like to stay with her always in this beautiful place, and as he did not answer immediately, she continued: "You see how I always remain young and beautiful, and I am under no one's orders, but can do just what I like, so that I have never thought of marrying before. But from the moment I saw you I took a fancy to you, so if you agree, we might be married and might live together like princes, because I have great riches."

The youth could not but be tempted with the beautiful maiden's offer, but he remembered how the birds had called her the witch, and their warning always sounded in his ears. Therefore he answered cautiously, "Do not be angry, dear maiden, if I do not decide immediately on this important matter. Give me a few days to consider before we come to an understanding."

"Why not?" answered the maiden. "Take some weeks to consider if you like, and take counsel with your own heart." And to make the time pass pleasantly, she took the youth over every part of her beautiful dwelling, and showed him all her splendid treasures. But these treasures were all produced by enchantment, for the maiden could make anything she wished appear by the help of King Solomon's signet ring; only none of these things remained fixed; they passed away like the wind without leaving a trace behind. But the youth did not know this; he thought they were all real.

One day the maiden took him into a secret chamber, where a little gold box was standing on a silver table. Pointing to the box, she said, "Here is my greatest treasure, whose like is not to be found in the whole world. It is a precious gold ring. When you marry me, I will give you this ring as a marriage gift, and it will make you the happiest of mortal men. But in order that our love may last for ever, you must give me for the ring three drops of blood from the little finger of your left hand."

When the youth heard these words a cold shudder ran over him, for he remembered that his soul was at stake. He was cunning enough, however, to conceal his feelings and to make no direct answer, but he only asked the maiden, as if carelessly, what was remarkable about the ring?

She answered, "No mortal is able entirely to understand the power of this ring, because no one thoroughly understands the secret signs engraved upon it. But even with my half-knowledge I can work great wonders. If I put the ring upon the little finger of my left hand, then I can fly like a bird through the air wherever I wish to go. If I put it on the third finger of my left hand I am invisible, and I can see everything that passes around me, though no one can see me. If I put the ring upon the middle finger of my left hand, then neither fire nor water nor any sharp weapon can hurt me. If I put it on the forefinger of my left hand, then I can with its help produce whatever I wish. I can in a single moment build houses or anything I desire. Finally, as long as I wear the ring on the thumb of my left hand, that hand is so strong that it can break down rocks and walls. Besides these, the ring has other secret signs which, as I said, no one can understand. No doubt it contains secrets of great importance. The ring formerly belonged to King Solomon, the wisest of kings, during whose reign the wisest men lived. But it is not known whether this ring was ever made by mortal hands: it is supposed that an angel gave it to the wise King."

When the youth heard all this he determined to try and get possession of the ring, though he did not quite believe in all its wonderful gifts. He wished the maiden would let him have it in his hand, but he did not quite like to ask her to do so, and after a while she put it back into the box. A few days after they were again speaking of the magic ring, and the youth said, "I do not think it possible that the ring can have all the power you say it has."

Then the maiden opened the box and took the ring out, and it glittered as she held it like the clearest sunbeam. She put it on the middle finger of her left hand, and told the youth to take a knife and try as hard as he could to cut her with it, for he would not be able to hurt her. He was unwilling at first, but the maiden insisted. Then he tried, at first only in play, and then seriously, to strike her with the knife, but an invisible wall of iron seemed to be between them, and the maiden stood before him laughing and unhurt. Then she put the ring on her third finger, and in an instant she had vanished from his eyes. Presently she was beside him again laughing, and holding the ring between her fingers.

"Do let me try," said the youth, "whether I can do these wonderful things."

The maiden, suspecting no treachery, gave him the magic ring.

The youth pretended to have forgotten what to do, and asked what finger he must put the ring on so that no sharp weapon could hurt him?"

"Oh, the middle finger of your left hand," the maiden answered, laughing.

She took the knife and tried to strike the youth, and he even tried to cut himself with it, but found it impossible. Then he asked the maiden to show him how to split stones and rocks with the help of the ring. So she led him into a courtyard where stood a great boulder-stone. "Now," she said, "put the ring upon the thumb of your left hand, and you will see how strong that hand has become. The youth did so, and found to his astonishment that with a single blow of his fist the stone flew into a thousand pieces. Then the youth bethought him that he who does not use his luck when he has it is a fool, and that this was a chance which once lost might never return. So while they stood laughing at the shattered stone he placed the ring, as if in play, upon the third finger of his left hand.

"Now," said the maiden, "you are invisible to me until you take the ring off again."

But the youth had no mind to do that; on the contrary, he went farther off, then put the ring on the little finger of his left hand, and soared into the air like a bird.

When the maiden saw him flying away she thought at first that he was still in play, and cried, "Come back, friend, for now you see I have told you the truth." But the young man never came back.

Then the maiden saw she was deceived, and bitterly repented that she had ever trusted him with the ring.

The young man never halted in his flight until he reached the dwelling of the wise magician who had taught him the speech of birds. The magician was delighted to find that his search had been successful, and at once set to work to interpret the secret signs engraved upon the ring, but it took him seven weeks to make them out clearly. Then he gave the youth the following instructions how to overcome the Dragon of the North: "You must have an iron horse cast, which must have little wheels under each foot. You must also be armed with a spear two fathoms long, which you will be able to wield by means of the magic ring upon your left thumb. The spear must be as thick in the middle as a large tree, and both its ends must be sharp. In the middle of the spear you must have two strong chains ten fathoms in length. As soon as the Dragon has made himself fast to the spear, which you must thrust through his jaws, you must spring quickly from the iron horse and fasten the ends of the chains firmly to the ground with iron stakes, so that he cannot get away from them. After two or three days the monster's strength will be so far exhausted that you will be able to come near him. Then you can put Solomon's ring upon your left thumb and give him the finishing stroke, but keep the ring on your third finger until you have come close to him, so that the monster cannot see you, else he might strike you dead with his long tail. But when all is done, take care you do not lose the ring, and that no one takes it from you by cunning."

The young man thanked the magician for his directions, and promised, should they succeed, to reward him. But the magician answered, "I have profited so much by the wisdom the ring has taught me that I desire no other reward." Then they parted, and the youth quickly flew home through the air. After remaining in his own home for some weeks, he heard people say that the terrible Dragon of the North was not far off, and might shortly be expected in the country. The King announced publicly that he would give his daughter in marriage, as well as a large part of his kingdom, to whosoever should free the country from the monster. The youth then went to the King and told him that he had good hopes of subduing the Dragon, if the King would grant him all he desired for the purpose. The King willingly agreed, and the iron horse, the great spear, and the chains were all prepared as the youth requested. When all was ready, it was found that the iron horse was so heavy that a hundred men could not move it from the spot, so the youth found there was nothing for it but to move it with his own strength by means of the magic ring. The Dragon was now so near that in a couple of springs he would be over the frontier. The youth now began to consider how he should act, for if he had to push the iron horse from behind he could not ride upon it as the sorcerer had said he must. But a raven unexpectedly gave him this advice: "Ride upon the horse, and push the spear against the ground, as if you were pushing off a boat from the land." The youth did so, and found that in this way he could easily move forwards. The Dragon had his monstrous jaws wide open, all ready for his expected prey. A few paces nearer, and man and horse would have been swallowed up by them! The youth trembled with horror, and his blood ran cold, yet he did not lose his courage; but, holding the iron spear upright in his hand, he brought it down with all his might right through the monster's lower jaw. Then quick as lightning he sprang from his horse before the Dragon had time to shut his mouth. A fearful clap like thunder, which could be heard for miles around, now warned him that the Dragon's jaws had closed upon the spear. When the youth turned round he saw the point of the spear sticking up high above the Dragon's upper jaw, and knew that the other end must be fastened firmly to the ground; but the Dragon had got his teeth fixed in the iron horse, which was now useless. The youth now hastened to fasten down the chains to the ground by means of the enormous iron pegs which he had provided. The death struggle of the monster lasted three days and three nights; in his writhing he beat his tail so violently against the ground, that at ten miles" distance the earth trembled as if with an earthquake. When he at length lost power to move his tail, the youth with the help of the ring took up a stone which twenty ordinary men could not have moved, and beat the Dragon so hard about the head with it that very soon the monster lay lifeless before him.

You can fancy how great was the rejoicing when the news was spread abroad that the terrible monster was dead. His conqueror was received into the city with as much pomp as if he had been the mightiest of kings. The old King did not need to urge his daughter to marry the slayer of the Dragon; he found her already willing to bestow her hand upon this hero, who had done all alone what whole armies had tried in vain to do. In a few days a magnificent wedding was celebrated, at which the rejoicings lasted four whole weeks, for all the neighboring kings had met together to thank the man who had freed the world from their common enemy. But everyone forgot amid the general joy that they ought to have buried the Dragon's monstrous body, for it began now to have such a bad smell that no one could live in the neighborhood, and before long the whole air was poisoned, and a pestilence broke out which destroyed many hundreds of people. In this distress, the King's son-in-law resolved to seek help once more from the Eastern magician, to whom he at once traveled through the air like a bird by the help of the ring. But there is a proverb which says that ill-gotten gains never prosper, and the Prince found that the stolen ring brought him ill-luck after all. The Witch-maiden had never rested night nor day until she had found out where the ring was. As soon as she had discovered by means of magical arts that the Prince in the form of a bird was on his way to the Eastern magician, she changed herself into an eagle and watched in the air until the bird she was waiting for came in sight, for she knew him at once by the ring which was hung round his neck by a ribbon. Then the eagle pounced upon the bird, and the moment she seized him in her talons she tore the ring from his neck before the man in bird's shape had time to prevent her. Then the eagle flew down to the earth with her prey, and the two stood face to face once more in human form.

"Now, villain, you are in my power!" cried the Witch-maiden. "I favored you with my love, and you repaid me with treachery and theft. You stole my most precious jewel from me, and do you expect to live happily as the King's son-in-law? Now the tables are turned; you are in my power, and I will be revenged on you for your crimes."

"Forgive me! forgive me!" cried the Prince; "I know too well how deeply I have wronged you, and most heartily do I repent it."

The maiden answered, "Your prayers and your repentance come too late, and if I were to spare you everyone would think me a fool. You have doubly wronged me; first you scorned my love, and then you stole my ring, and you must bear the punishment."

With these words she put the ring upon her left thumb, lifted the young man with one hand, and walked away with him under her arm. This time she did not take him to a splendid palace, but to a deep cave in a rock, where there were chains hanging from the wall. The maiden now chained the young man's hands and feet so that he could not escape; then she said in an angry voice, "Here you shall remain chained up until you die. I will bring you every day enough food to prevent you dying of hunger, but you need never hope for freedom any more." With these words she left him.

The old King and his daughter waited anxiously for many weeks for the Prince's return, but no news of him arrived. The King's daughter often dreamed that her husband was going through some great suffering: she therefore begged her father to summon all the enchanters and magicians, that they might try to find out where the Prince was and how he could be set free. But the magicians, with all their arts, could find out nothing, except that he was still living and undergoing great suffering; but none could tell where he was to be found. At last a celebrated magician from Finland was brought before the King, who had found out that the King's son-in-law was imprisoned in the East, not by men, but by some more powerful being. The King now sent messengers to the East to look for his son-in-law, and they by good luck met with the old magician who had interpreted the signs on King Solomon's ring, and thus was possessed of more wisdom than anyone else in the world. The magician soon found out what he wished to know, and pointed out the place where the Prince was imprisoned, but said: "He is kept there by enchantment, and cannot be set free without my help. I will therefore go with you myself."

So they all set out, guided by birds, and after some days came to the cave where the unfortunate Prince had been chained up for nearly seven years. He recognized the magician immediately, but the old man did not know him, he had grown so thin. However, he undid the chains by the help of magic, and took care of the Prince until he recovered and became strong enough to travel. When he reached home he found that the old King had died that morning, so that he was now raised to the throne. And now after his long suffering came prosperity, which lasted to the end of his life; but he never got back the magic ring, nor has it ever again been seen by mortal eyes.

Now, if YOU had been the Prince, would you not rather have stayed with the pretty witch-maiden?

The Little Black Book of Magic

by Frances Carpenter

Frances Carpenter (1890–1972) as a young woman traveled throughout the world with her father, journalist and photographer Frank Carpenter, whose popular "Carpenter's Geographic Readers" were standard school texts for forty years. Frances herself wrote many books based on the folk and fairy tales she collected during her travels. This story is set in Argentina.

Young Marco lived long ago in the South American land of Argentina. At least, the old people there say that he did. They remember how he found the wizard's little black book of magic. They liked to tell about the exciting adventures it brought him.

In those ancient times, people talked a great deal about wizards and their magic. There was no way of knowing just who might be a wizard. With his magic a wizard could make himself look like an Argentine gaucho, an ordinary cowboy riding over the grassy plains. Or he could change himself into a horse, a rooster, a fish, or a bird.

One could never be sure, either, whether the spirit inside one of these strange forms was good or bad. Even the wickedest wizard of all, the Devil himself, was on the earth then.

There is a wizard in this story. There is also a brave youth who got the best of him.

This clever youth, Marco, was the youngest son of a very poor family. He lived with his crippled father, and his mother and his two brothers in a miserable rancho hut.

Bad luck, too, dwelt under that roof. Marco and his brothers, Lino and Luis, often were hungry. Their ponchos were ragged. Their shabby shirts were not always clean for they had only one each.

It was their ragged clothing that kept Lino and Luis from going to school when they were younger. At least they told everyone that was the reason. Their schoolteacher said it was more because they were lazy.

Like his brothers, Marco also wore ragged clothes. But he went to school just the same. He studied hard, and he learned how to read.

Well, the day came when these three brothers were almost grown-up. They were quite old enough to earn money to help their poor parents. So together they set forth. They went to every rancho in their part of the grass lands of the Argentine pampas. To the big ranchos, and to the small ones they went. But they found no work. Not even one peso did they bring home.

Now and then friends brought small gifts of beef and cornmeal and the good tea called mate. But most of the time there was almost nothing to eat or drink in their poor hut. Things went from bad to worse.

Then one day, Lino, the oldest brother, said, "I will go farther from home, out into the wide world. Somewhere there, surely, I can find work. Perhaps I shall even become rich."

His father shook his head. He was not so sure. Lino had a good heart, but he truly was lazy. "Go, my son," said the lame man. "Try your luck in the wide world. And may the Good God keep the wicked spirits away from you."

Lino walked far through the pampas grass. But nowhere did he find riches to take back to his parents. Indeed, often he had no more food in his stomach than he had had at home. He was feeling sorry and sad when he turned around.

But on his way back to his hut, he came upon a long, low rancho almost hidden in the tall pampas grass. At his knock, a strange-looking man opened the door. He was very tall, very thin, and his skin was dead white. His fierce eyes shone like two coals of bright fire, and he wore a little goat's beard.

Instead of a gaucho's usual loose shirt and baggy breeches, the Pale Man had on a long black coat and tight trousers like those seen in a city. A red cap was fitted tightly over his skull.

Lino was frightened by his eerie appearance, but he managed to say politely, "Señor, I look for work. I must earn a few pesos to buy food for my hungry parents."

"Well, there is work to be done here," the Pale Man replied. "But first I must ask whether you know how to read."

Lino's heart sank. Now he would surely be turned away.

"Alas, no, señor," he said. "I never had clothes fit for going to school."

To his surprise, however, the Pale Man seemed pleased.

"Good! Good!" he said. "Come in, young fellow, and I'll put you to work. Tomorrow I go away on a journey. You shall mind my rancho during the two days I shall be away. You shall feed my cows and my horses. And there is even more important work for you to do." He led Lino into three gloomy rooms in one end of the rancho. Each one was filled with piles and piles of old books.

"These musty rooms are to be aired and cleaned," he said. "So these books all are to be moved to the other end of the rancho. You must carry them there before I come back." And he rode away.

Now lazy Lino was not accustomed to this kind of work. And there were a great many books. By twos and by threes, he slowly picked them up. He had moved only half of those in the first room when his master came home.

"Go along, lazy fellow." His employer was cross. "Here is your pay!" And he threw a gold coin into Lino's old hat.

"Oh, that Pale Man was angry. I was afraid," Lino told his family, "but then he gave me the gold coin which bought this good beef for our supper."

As they sat round the table, Marco, the youngest of the three brothers, said, "That strange man must be a wizard. He could be the same wizard which caused our father's fall from his horse that broke his back." Then he added thoughtfully, "But, Lino, why did he say 'Good!' when you told him you could not read."

Neither Lino nor any other one at the table could think of a reason.

"It does not really matter," Luis, the middle brother, declared. "The man gave you a gold coin. Perhaps he will hire me, since I, too, cannot read. Perhaps he will give me another gold coin. I will go to his rancho."

All happened with Luis as it had with Lino. When he was asked if he could read, he made the same answer. "Alas, no, Señor. I never had clothes fit for going to school." So he was put to work, and his strange master went off on his journey.

Luis worked a little faster than Lino. He carried a few more books on each trip to the other end of the rancho. But he was only starting to work in the second room when the Pale Man came home.

"Go, lazybones!" he shouted. "You have done little better than the fellow who came here just a few days ago." His dark, angry eyes burned more fiercely than ever. Luis, too, was afraid when his master seized him by the arm and pushed him out of the door. "Here is your pay!" The Pale Man threw two golden coins down on the ground beside him.

These bought food for many days for the family, but even though no one was hungry now, young Marco declared that he wanted to seek out the rancho of this strange man whom he suspected of being a wizard.

His brothers laughed.

"How shall you who are younger do better than we?" Luis cried.

"The Pale Man will not hire you," Lino said. "You know how to read."

Marco went in spite of their warnings. And the strange rancho owner with the goat's beard and the fiery eyes opened the door to his knock.

"Yes, there is work here," he said for a third time. "But first tell me, young fellow, do you know how to read?"

Marco had thought well how he should answer, and he replied, "Look at my ragged shirt, Señor. Who would go to school in clothing like mine?"

Of course, this did not really answer the question, but the Pale Man seemed satisfied.

"Well then, come in," he said. "Mind my house, feed my animals, and move all these books while I am away."

As soon as his employer was out of sight, Marco explored the gloomy house. How eerie it was! How dark! How silent and big! Prickles of fear ran down his spine. But he somehow found courage to go to work.

He moved the books quickly. At the end of the first day he had emptied the second room. But in the third chamber he shook his head in dismay. There were twice as many books here as in the two other rooms together. He could never finish this task in time. So he stopped to read a page here and there in each volume he picked up.

In the second pile he came upon a little black book. It was old, very old, almost falling apart, and as Marco read its yellow pages, he gave an excited cry.

"This is a book of magic!" He spoke aloud. "I guessed right. The Pale Man is a wizard, the same wicked wizard who caused my father's fall from his horse.

"I do not know if this magic book is rightfully his, for there are other names written inside its cover," he continued, "but I shall take it away with me to protect myself and my family from more of his mischief. With this little black book of magic, I shall beat this wicked devil at his own game."

In his new-found treasure Marco found the words he needed to speak to move all the books in the wink of an eye. From it he also learned the wizard's trick of changing himself from one form to another. He tried this out by turning himself into a mouse. Then he said other magic words and lo, he was a dog. The spells worked for him as they, no doubt, worked for a real wizard.

The owner of the rancho was surprised when he came home that evening. His cows had been milked. His pigs had been fed. His horses had been watered. And every book had been moved.

"Hi-yi!" cried the Pale Man. "How can this be? However did you manage to move all the books?"

"They are moved, Señor. You can see that for yourself." Marco's words could not be denied, and the wizard did not know quite what to do. He was a little afraid of this youth who had completed a humanly impossible task.

"You shall be well paid," he said to Marco. And the youth replied pleasantly, "Pay me what you please, Señor. I shall be content." He did not say that he had already taken his pay in the little black book of magic which lay deep in his trousers' pocket.

"The brown horse in my barn shall carry you home, Marco," the wizard said then. "Load my white mule with these three bags of gold coins. And when you reach your rancho, let the beasts go free to find their own way back to me."

Marco was too clever to believe that the wizard was as generous as he seemed. He was sure there was a trick of some kind in the offer. He went around behind the rancho while he searched in the book of magic to find out what he should do.

From it he learned that the horse and the mule were evil spirits like their owner. So when he came to the barn, he was not surprised to find the brown horse snorting and rearing. He barely escaped being kicked to his death by the white mule.

"Beware of the Good God in Heaven, you devils!" he shouted.

At once the animals were quiet. The brown horse allowed himself to be saddled. The white mule did not move while the heavy bags of gold were put on his back. And Marco went home in triumph.

With the wizard's gold, Marco bought a better rancho for his family. Now they could have horses and cows. They could all buy new clothes in the city. Good luck now lived under their roof.

"But we must not be careless," he warned his father. "The wizard will try his best to recover his little black book of magic. Some Sunday he will ride here in the form of a gaucho. Dressed as a cowboy, he will ask for a race, and you must agree." This he had discovered by repeating a magic spell which told him what was to happen.

"I shall change myself into an old nag, a broken-down horse that can scarcely stand on his feet. You shall offer me for the race, my father.

When he sees the weak creature I shall be, the wizard will bet many gold coins on our race. But I shall win. Then he will wish to buy your old nag. Sell me, but take care, oh, take good care to take off my bridle before you give me up to him."

As Marco foretold, he won the race with the wizard's horse. The gold coins were paid, ten for winning the race and twenty as a purchase price for the nag. But, alas, Marco's father thought only of the gold coins he was getting. He forgot to take off Marco's bridle.

The wicked wizard stuck his sharp spurs into the sides of the aged horse. He beat it with his whip. His knowledge of spells told him that this nag was Marco, the youth who had taken away his little black book of magic.

Now, on his way home, the wizard stopped at the rancho of one of his evil friends. He tied the nag to a tree on the edge of a lake and went into the house.

A passing gaucho saw the weary old horse. The animal drooped, and panted for water. And the cowboy was sorry for it. He took off its bridle so that it might drink from the lake.

With a scream of anger, the wizard came running out of the rancho. But even more quickly Marco, the nag, jumped into the lake.

Once in the water, Marco spoke magic words that changed his form of a horse into that of a fish. He swam quickly away.

The wizard, however, turned himself into a shark. And he swam even faster. When Marco reached the other shore of the lake, the devil-shark was close on his tail.

"Let me now be a deer!" Marco called out, and he bounded away over the pampas. Loud barking behind told him that the wizard now was a swift hunting hound which could outrun any deer.

Only a bird in the air is safe from a hound, he thought. So he became a dove, flying high into the sky. A fierce hawk attacked him there, and of course this, too, was the wizard.

Before the hawk could kill the dove, Marco changed into a wee hummingbird so that he could hide himself under the wing of an eagle that was flying nearby. But the wizard now took on the form of a mighty condor, the biggest of birds. Flapping its great wings, the condor flew at the eagle.

High above the pampas the two birds fought fiercely. Then they swooped down over a fine house, Marco saw that a narrow window was open in a tower room. Still in his hummingbird form, he dropped from under the eagle's wing into the shelter of the tower. The condor pursued the tiny creature, but the window was hardly more than a slit in the wall. The great bird could not follow it inside the tower.

Marco had just time to take on his own form once more. With a loud voice he shouted, "Beware of the Good God in Heaven who protects me!" And the condor, in terror, flew swiftly away.

All this happened before the eyes of Rosa, the young daughter of the owner of this fine house. Marco thought he had never seen so beautiful a girl. It was not strange that she herself was pleased with such a brave young man. Nor that she should appeal to him for help.

"My father keeps me shut up in this tower," Rosa explained. "I do not blame him. He is only trying to keep me safe from a wicked wizard who wants me for his bride. My father is deeply in debt to this evil one who holds him in his power. Oh, good young stranger, help me to escape."

Marco remembered the spell which told of future happenings. And he said, "You shall buy your freedom from this devil with your jewels, dear Rosa. Give him your necklace and your bracelets. Give him all your rings except for one small golden circlet which you will wear on a chain round your neck. That small golden ring will be I myself, Marco, and this is what you must do with it."

The girl listened well. And she followed Marco's instructions to the smallest detail.

When the wizard came courting her, she poured a heap of gold and bright gems on a table before him. And she begged him to take them to pay her father's debts.

"These are not all of your treasures," the wicked wizard cried. "I must have also the little gold ring on that chain round your neck." His magic was strong. He knew the ring was Marco.

Rosa tossed the ring on the table as she had been instructed. It rolled off and as it fell to the floor it became a golden pomegranate which burst open and scattered its bright seeds hither and yon.

In an instant, the wizard changed himself into a rooster. He pecked at the seeds. He ate each one in sight. And he crowed, "Now at last I have the best of you, Marco!"

But one of the pomegranate seeds had fallen close to Rosa's feet. Luckily this seed was Marco, and as she pushed it under the table, he changed himself into a fox. With a leap, the fox sprang upon the rooster. He killed it even before it had finished its crowing.

"We are both safe now, dear Rosa," Marco said to the daughter of the rich man. He was standing before her in his own person, handsome and tall.

"Your father now is free from the power of the wizard," he said, taking her hand. "As my reward I shall ask him for permission to marry you, if you will only consent. I shall take you away to a fine house of our own. And with my little black book of magic, this devil shall never enter our door. No, not even if he should come back from the Other World in the form of a tall, thin man with a dead-white face, fiery eyes, and a little goat's beard."

Rosa said, "Yes," and her father gave his permission.

So the old people in Argentina tell the story of Marco and the little black book of magic. They say the two young people lived happily together for the rest of their lives.

If there is a lesson to be learned from this tale, one must compare Marco's adventures with those of his lazy brothers, Lino and Luis. This will show, surely, that it pays for a boy to go to school and learn how to read.

The Bottle Imp
by Robert Louis Stevenson

Robert Louis Stevenson, author of *Treasure Island* and *Dr. Jekyll and Mr. Hyde* (1850–1894), spent his last years on the South Sea island of Samoa, where he wrote his final work, *Island Night Entertainments*. The book included this bizarre tale of greed, love and a malevolent imp.

There was a man of the Island of Hawaii, whom I shall call Keawe; for the truth is, he still lives, and his name must be kept secret; but the place of his birth was not far from Honaunau, where the bones of Keawe the Great lie hidden in a cave. This man was poor, brave, and active; he could read and write like a schoolmaster; he was a first-rate mariner besides, sailed for some time in the island steamers, and steered a whaleboat on the Hamakua coast. At length it came in Keawe's mind to have a sight of the great world and foreign cities, and he shipped on a vessel bound to San Francisco.

This is a fine town, with a fine harbour, and rich people uncountable; and, in particular, there is one hill which is covered with palaces. Upon this hill Keawe was one day taking a walk with his pocket full of money, viewing the great houses upon either hand with pleasure. 'What fine houses these are!' he was thinking, 'and how happy must those people be who dwell in them, and take no care for the morrow!' The thought was in his mind when he came abreast of a house that was smaller than some others, but all finished and beautified like a toy; the steps of that house shone like silver, and the borders of the garden bloomed like garlands, and the windows were bright like diamonds; and Keawe stopped and wondered at the excellence of all he saw. So stopping, he was aware of a man that looked forth upon him through a window so clear that Keawe could see him as you see a fish in a pool upon the reef. The man was elderly, with a bald head and a black beard; and his face was heavy with sorrow, and he bitterly sighed. And the truth of it is, that as Keawe looked in upon the man, and the man looked out upon Keawe, each envied the other.

All of a sudden, the man smiled and nodded, and beckoned Keawe to enter, and met him at the door of the house.

'This is a fine house of mine,' said the man, and bitterly sighed. 'Would you not care to view the chambers?'

So he led Keawe all over it, from the cellar to the roof, and there was nothing there that was not perfect of its kind, and Keawe was astonished.

'Truly,' said Keawe, 'this is a beautiful house; if I lived in the like of it, I should be laughing all day long. How comes it, then, that you should be sighing?'

'There is no reason,' said the man, 'why you should not have a house in all points similar to this, and finer, if you wish. You have some money, I suppose?'

'I have fifty dollars,' said Keawe; 'but a house like this will cost more than fifty dollars.'

The man made a computation. 'I am sorry you have no more,' said he, 'for it may raise you trouble in the future; but it shall be yours at fifty dollars.'

'The house?' asked Keawe.

'No, not the house,' replied the man; 'but the bottle. For, I must tell you, although I appear to you so rich and fortunate, all my fortune, and this house itself and its garden, came out of a bottle not much bigger than a pint. This is it.'

And he opened a lockfast place, and took out a round-bellied bottle with a long neck; the glass of it was white like milk, with changing rainbow colours in the grain. Withinsides something obscurely moved, like a shadow and a fire.

'This is the bottle,' said the man; and, when Keawe laughed, 'You do not believe me?' he added. 'Try, then, for yourself. See if you can break it.'

So Keawe took the bottle up and dashed it on the floor till he was weary; but it jumped on the floor like a child's ball, and was not injured.

'This is a strange thing,' said Keawe. 'For by the touch of it, as well as by the look, the bottle should be of glass.'

'Of glass it is,' replied the man, sighing more heavily than ever; 'but the glass of it was tempered in the flames of hell. An imp lives in it, and that is the shadow we behold there moving; or so I suppose. If any man buy this bottle the imp is at his command; all that he desires—love, fame, money, houses like this house, ay, or a city like this city—all are his at the word uttered. Napoleon had this bottle, and by it he grew to be the king of the world; but he sold it at the last, and fell. Captain Cook had this bottle, and by it he found his way to so many islands; but he, too, sold it, and was slain upon Hawaii. For, once it is sold, the power goes and the protection; and unless a man remain content with what he has, ill will befall him.'

'And yet you talk of selling it yourself?' Keawe said.

'I have all I wish, and I am growing elderly,' replied the man. 'There is one thing the imp cannot do—he cannot prolong life; and, it would not be fair to conceal from you, there is a drawback to the bottle; for if a man die before he sells it, he must burn in hell for ever.'

'To be sure, that is a drawback and no mistake,' cried Keawe. 'I would not meddle with the thing. I can do without a house, thank God; but there is one thing I could not be doing with one particle, and that is to be damned.'

'Dear me, you must not run away with things,' returned the man. 'All you have to do is to use the power of the imp in moderation, and then sell it to someone else, as I do to you, and finish your life in comfort.'

'Well, I observe two things,' said Keawe. 'All the time you keep sighing like a maid in love, that is one; and, for the other, you sell this bottle very cheap.'

'I have told you already why I sigh,' said the man. 'It is because I fear my health is breaking up; and, as you said yourself, to die and go to the devil is a pity for anyone. As for why I sell so cheap, I must explain to you there is a peculiarity about the bottle. Long ago, when the devil brought it first upon earth, it was extremely expensive, and was sold first of all to Prester John for many millions of dollars; but it cannot be sold at all, unless sold at a loss. If you sell it for as much as you paid for it, back it comes to you again like a homing pigeon. It follows that the price has kept falling in these centuries, and the bottle is now remarkably cheap. I bought it myself from one of my great neighbours on this hill, and the price I paid was only ninety dollars. I could sell it for as high as eighty-nine dollars and ninety-nine cents, but not a penny dearer, or back the thing must come to me. Now, about this there are two bothers. First, when you offer a bottle so singular for eighty odd dollars, people suppose you to be jesting. And second—but there is no hurry about that—and I need not go into it. Only remember it must be coined money that you sell it for.'

'How am I to know that this is all true?' asked Keawe.

'Some of it you can try at once,' replied the man. 'Give me your fifty dollars, take the bottle, and wish your fifty dollars back into your pocket. If that does not happen, I pledge you my honour I will cry off the bargain and restore your money.'

'You are not deceiving me?' said Keawe.

The man bound himself with a great oath.

'Well, I will risk that much,' said Keawe, 'for that can do no harm.' And he paid over his money to the man, and the man handed him the bottle.

'Imp of the bottle,' said Keawe, 'I want my fifty dollars back.'

And sure enough he had scarce said the word before his pocket was as heavy as ever.

'To be sure this is a wonderful bottle,' said Keawe.

'And now, good morning to you, my fine fellow, and the devil go with you for me!' said the man.

'Hold on,' said Keawe, 'I don't want any more of this fun. Here, take your bottle back.'

'You have bought it for less than I paid for it,' replied the man, rubbing his hands. 'It is yours now; and, for my part, I am only concerned to see the back of you.' And with that he rang for his Chinese servant, and had Keawe shown out of the house.

Now, when Keawe was in the street, with the bottle under his arm, he began to think. 'If all is true about this bottle, I may have made a losing bargain,' thinks he. 'But perhaps the man was only fooling me.' The first thing he did was to count his money; the sum was exact—forty-nine dollars American money, and one Chili piece. 'That looks like the truth,' said Keawe. 'Now I will try another part.'

The streets in that part of the city were as clean as a ship's decks, and though it was noon, there were no passengers. Keawe set the bottle in the gutter and walked away. Twice he looked back, and there was the milky, round-bellied bottle where he left it. A third time he looked back, and turned a corner; but he had scarce done so, when something knocked upon his elbow, and behold! it was the long neck sticking up; and as for the round belly, it was jammed into the pocket of his pilot-coat.

'And that looks like the truth,' said Keawe.

The next thing he did was to buy a cork-screw in a shop, and go apart into a secret place in the fields. And there he tried to draw the cork, but as often as he put the screw in, out it came again, and the cork as whole as ever.

'This is some new sort of cork,' said Keawe, and all at once he began to shake and sweat, for he was afraid of that bottle.

On his way back to the port-side, he saw a shop where a man sold shells and clubs from the wild islands, old heathen deities, old coined money, pictures from China and Japan, and all manner of things that sailors bring in their sea-chests. And here he had an idea. So he went in and offered the bottle for a hundred dollars. The man of the shop laughed at him at the first, and offered him five; but, indeed, it was a curious bottle—such glass was never blown in any human glass-works, so prettily the colours shone under the milky white, and so strangely the shadow hovered in the midst; so, after he had disputed awhile after the manner of his kind, the shopman gave Keawe sixty silver dollars for the thing, and set it on a shelf in the midst of his window.

'Now,' said Keawe, 'I have sold that for sixty which I bought for fifty—or, to say truth, a little less, because one of my dollars was from Chili. Now I shall know the truth upon another point.'

So he went back on board his ship, and, when he opened his chest, there was the bottle, and had come more quickly than himself. Now Keawe had a mate on board whose name was Lopaka.

'What ails you?' said Lopaka, 'that you stare in your chest?'

They were alone in the ship's forecastle, and Keawe bound him to secrecy, and told all.

'This is a very strange affair,' said Lopaka; 'and I fear you will be in trouble about this bottle. But there is one point very clear—that you are sure of the trouble, and you had better have the profit in the bargain. Make up your mind what you want with it; give the order, and if it is done as you desire, I will buy the bottle myself; for I have an idea of my own to get a schooner, and go trading through the islands.'

'That is not my idea,' said Keawe; 'but to have a beautiful house and garden on the Kona Coast, where I was born, the sun shining in at the door, flowers in the garden, glass in the windows, pictures on the walls, and toys and fine carpets on the tables, for all the world like the house I was in this day—only a storey higher, and with balconies all about like the King's palace; and to live there without care and make merry with my friends and relatives.'

'Well,' said Lopaka, 'let us carry it back with us to Hawaii, and if all comes true, as you suppose, I will buy the bottle, as I said, and ask a schooner.'

Upon that they were agreed, and it was not long before the ship returned to Honolulu, carrying Keawe and Lopaka, and the bottle. They were scarce come ashore when they met a friend upon the beach, who began at once to condole with Keawe.

'I do not know what I am to be condoled about,' said Keawe.

'Is it possible you have not heard,' said the friend, 'your uncle—that good old man—is dead, and your cousin—that beautiful boy—was drowned at sea?'

Keawe was filled with sorrow, and, beginning to weep and to lament he forgot about the bottle. But Lopaka was thinking to himself, and presently, when Keawe's grief was a little abated, 'I have been thinking,' said Lopaka. 'Had not your uncle lands in Hawaii, in the district of Kaü?'

'No,' said Keawe, 'not in Kaü; they are on the mountain-side—a little way south of Hookena.'

'These lands will now be yours?' asked Lopaka.

'And so they will,' says Keawe, and began again to lament for his relatives.

'No,' said Lopaka, 'do not lament at present. I have a thought in my mind. How if this should be the doing of the bottle? For here is the place ready for your house.'

'If this be so,' cried Keawe, 'it is a very ill way to serve me by killing my relatives. But it may be, indeed; for it was in just such a station that I saw the house with my mind's eye.'

'The house, however, is not yet built,' said Lopaka.

'No, nor like to be!' said Keawe; 'for though my uncle has some coffee and ava and bananas, it will not be more than will keep me in comfort; and the rest of that land is the black lava.'

'Let us go to the lawyer,' said Lopaka; 'I have still this idea in my mind.'

Now, when they came to the lawyer's, it appeared Keawe's uncle had grown monstrous rich in the last days, and there was a fund of money.

'And here is the money for the house!' cried Lopaka.

'If you are thinking of a new house,' said the lawyer, 'here is the card of a new architect, of whom they tell me great things.'

'Better and better!' cried Lopaka. 'Here is all made plain for us. Let us continue to obey orders.'

So they went to the architect, and he had drawings of houses on his table.

'You want something out of the way,' said the architect. 'How do you like this?' and he handed a drawing to Keawe.

Now, when Keawe set eyes on the drawing, he cried out aloud, for it was the picture of his thought exactly drawn.

'I am in for this house,' thought he. 'Little as I like the way it comes to me, I am in for it now, and I may as well take the good along with the evil.'

So he told the architect all that he wished, and how he would have that house furnished, and about the pictures on the wall and the knick-knacks on the tables; and he asked the man plainly for how much he would undertake the whole affair.

The architect put many questions, and took his pen and made a computation; and when he had done he named the very sum that Keawe had inherited.

Lopaka and Keawe looked at one another and nodded. 'It is quite clear,' thought Keawe, 'that I am to have this house, whether or no. It comes from the devil, and I fear I will get little good by that; and of one thing I am sure, I will make no more wishes as long as I have this bottle. But with the house I am saddled, and I may as well take the good along with the evil.'

So he made his terms with the architect, and they signed a paper; and Keawe and Lopaka took ship again and sailed to Australia; for it was concluded between them they should not interfere at all, but leave the architect and the bottle imp to build and to adorn that house at their own pleasure.

The voyage was a good voyage, only all the time Keawe was holding in his breath, for he had sworn he would utter no more wishes, and take no more favours from the devil. The time was up when they got back. The architect told them that the house was ready, and Keawe and Lopaka took a passage in the *Hall*, and went down Kona way to view the house, and see if all had been done fitly according to the thought that was in Keawe's mind.

Now, the house stood on the mountain-side, visible to ships. Above, the forest ran up into the clouds of rain; below, the black lava fell in cliffs, where the kings of old lay buried. A garden bloomed about that house with every hue of flowers; and there was an orchard of papaia on the one hand and an orchard of breadfruit on the other, and right in front, toward the sea, a ship's mast had been rigged up and bore a flag. As for the house, it was three storeys high, with great chambers and broad balconies on each. The windows were of glass, so excellent that it was as clear as water and as bright as day. All manner of furniture adorned the chambers. Pictures hung upon the wall in golden frames: pictures of ships, and men fighting, and of the most beautiful women, and of singular places; nowhere in the world are there pictures of so bright a colour as those Keawe found hanging in his house. As for the knick-knacks, they were extraordinary fine; chiming clocks and musical boxes, little men with nodding heads, books filled with pictures, weapons of price from all quarters of the world, and the most elegant puzzles to entertain the leisure of a solitary man. And as no one would care to live in such chambers, only to walk through and view them, the balconies were made so broad that a whole town might have lived upon them in delight; and Keawe knew not which to prefer, whether the back porch, where you got the land breeze, and looked upon the orchards and the flowers, or the front balcony, where you could drink the wind of the sea, and look down the steep wall of the mountain and see the *Hall* going by once a week or so between Hookena and the hills of Pele, or the schooners plying up the coast for wood and ava and bananas.

When they had viewed all, Keawe and Lopaka sat on the porch.

'Well,' asked Lopaka, 'is it all as you designed?'

'Words cannot utter it,' said Keawe. 'It is better than I dreamed, and I am sick with satisfaction.'

'There is but one thing to consider,' said Lopaka; 'all this may be quite natural, and the bottle imp have nothing whatever to say to it. If I were to buy the bottle, and got no schooner after all, I should have put my hand in the fire for nothing. I gave you my word, I know; but yet I think you would not grudge me one more proof.'

'I have sworn I would take no more favours,' said Keawe. 'I have gone already deep enough.'

'This is no favour I am thinking of,' replied Lopaka. 'It is only to see the imp himself. There is nothing to be gained by that, and so nothing to be ashamed of; and yet, if I once saw him, I should be sure of the whole matter. So indulge me so far, and let me see the imp; and, after that, here is the money in my hand, and I will buy it.'

'There is only one thing I am afraid of,' said Keawe. 'The imp may be very ugly to view; and if you once set eyes upon him you might be very undesirous of the bottle.'

'I am a man of my word,' said Lopaka. 'And here is the money betwixt us.'

'Very well,' replied Keawe. 'I have a curiosity myself. So come, let us have one look at you, Mr Imp.'

Now as soon as that was said, the imp looked out of the bottle, and in again, swift as a lizard; and there sat Keawe and Lopaka turned to stone. The night had quite come, before either found a thought to say or voice to say it with; and then Lopaka pushed the money over and took the bottle.

'I am a man of my word,' said he, 'and had need to be so, or I would not touch this bottle with my foot. Well, I shall get my schooner and a dollar or two for my pocket; and then I will be rid of this devil as fast as I can. For to tell you the plain truth, the look of him has cast me down.'

'Lopaka,' said Keawe, 'do not you think any worse of me than you can help; I know it is night, and the roads bad, and the pass by the tombs an ill place to go by so late, but I declare since I have seen that little face, I cannot eat or sleep or pray till it is gone from me. I will give you a lantern, and a basket to put the bottle in, and any picture or fine thing in all my house that takes your fancy;—and be gone at once, and go sleep at Hookena with Nahinu.'

'Keawe,' said Lopaka, 'many a man would take this ill; above all, when I am doing you a turn so friendly, as to keep my word and buy the bottle; and for that matter, the night and the dark, and the way by the tombs, must be all tenfold more dangerous to a man with such a sin upon his conscience, and such a bottle under his arm. But for my part, I am so extremely terrified myself, I have not the heart to blame you. Here I go then; and I pray God you may be happy in your house, and I fortunate with my schooner, and both get to heaven in the end in spite of the devil and his bottle.'

So Lopaka went down the mountain; and Keawe stood in his front balcony, and listened to the clink of the horse's shoes, and watched the lantern go shining down the path, and along the cliff of caves where the old dead are buried; and all the time he trembled and clasped his hands, and prayed for his friend, and gave glory to God that he himself was escaped out of that trouble.

But the next day came very brightly, and that new house of his was so delightful to behold that he forgot his terrors. One day followed another, and Keawe dwelt there in perpetual joy. He had his place on the back porch; it was there he ate and lived, and read the stories in the Honolulu newspapers; but when anyone came by they would go in and view the chambers and the pictures. And the fame of the house went far and wide; it was called *Ka-Hale Nui*—the Great House—in all Kona; and sometimes the Bright House, for Keawe kept a Chinaman, who was all day dusting and furbishing; and the glass, and the gilt, and the fine stuffs, and the pictures, shone as bright as the morning. As for Keawe himself, he could not walk in the chambers without singing, his heart was so enlarged; and when ships sailed by upon the sea, he would fly his colours on the mast.

So time went by, until one day Keawe went upon a visit as far as Kailua to certain of his friends. There he was well feasted; and left as soon as he could the next morning, and rode hard, for he was impatient to behold his beautiful house; and, besides, the night then coming on was the night in which the dead of old days go abroad in the sides of Kona; and having already meddled with the devil, he was the more chary of meeting with the dead. A little beyond Honaunau, looking far ahead, he was aware of a woman bathing in the edge of the sea; and she seemed a well-grown girl, but he thought no more of it. Then he saw her white shift flutter as she put it on, and then her red holoku; and by the time he came abreast of her she was done with her toilet, and had come up from the sea, and stood by the track-side in her red holoku, and she was all freshened with the bath, and her eyes shone and were kind. Now Keawe no sooner beheld her than he drew rein.

'I thought I knew everyone in this country,' said he. 'How comes it that I do not know you?'

'I am Kokua, daughter of Kiano,' said the girl, 'and I have just returned from Oahu. Who are you?'

'I will tell you who I am in a little,' said Keawe, dismounting from his horse, 'but not now. For I have a thought in my mind, and if you knew who I was, you might have heard of me, and would not give me a true answer. But tell me, first of all, one thing: Are you married?'

At this Kokua laughed out aloud. 'It is you who ask questions,' she said. 'Are you married yourself?'

'Indeed, Kokua, I am not,' replied Keawe, 'and never thought to be until this hour. But here is the plain truth. I have met you here at the roadside, and I saw your eyes, which are like the stars, and my heart went to you as swift as a bird. And so now, if you want none of me, say so, and I will go on to my own place; but if you think me no worse than any other young man, say so, too, and I will turn aside to your father's for the night, and tomorrow I will talk with the good man.'

Kokua said never a word, but she looked at the sea and laughed.

'Kokua,' said Keawe, 'if you say nothing, I will take that for the good answer; so let us be stepping to your father's door.'

She went on ahead of him, still without speech; only sometimes she glanced back and glanced away again, and she kept the strings of her hat in her mouth.

Now, when they had come to the door, Kiano came out on his verandah, and cried out and welcomed Keawe by name. At that the girl looked over, for the fame of the great house had come to her ears; and, to be sure, it was a great temptation. All that evening they were very merry together; and the girl was as bold as brass under the eyes of her parents, and made a mock of Keawe, for she had a quick wit. The next day he had a word with Kiano, and found the girl alone.

'Kokua,' said he, 'you made a mock of me all the evening; and it is still time to bid me go. I would not tell you who I was, because I have so fine a house, and I feared you would think too much of that house and too little of the man that loves you. Now you know all, and if you wish to have seen the last of me, say so at once.'

'No,' said Kokua; but this time she did not laugh, nor did Keawe ask for more.

This was the wooing of Keawe; things had gone quickly; but so an arrow goes, and the ball of a rifle swifter still, and yet both may strike the target. Things had gone fast, but they had gone far also, and the thought of Keawe rang in the maiden's head; she heard his voice in the breach of the surf upon the lava, and for this young man that she had seen but twice she would have left father and mother and her native islands. As for Keawe himself, his horse flew up the path of the mountain under the cliff of tombs, and the sound of the hoofs, and the sound of Keawe singing to himself for pleasure, echoed in the caverns of the dead. He came to the Bright House, and still he was singing. He sat and ate in the broad balcony, and the Chinaman wondered at his master, to hear how he sang between the mouthfuls. The sun went down into the sea, and the night came; and Keawe walked the balconies by lamplight, high on the mountains, and the voice of his singing startled men on ships.

'Here am I now upon my high place,' he said to himself. 'Life may be no better; this is the mountain top; and all shelves about me toward the worse. For the first time I will light up the chambers, and bathe in my fine bath with the hot water and the cold, and sleep alone in the bed of my bridal chamber.'

So the Chinaman had word, and he must rise from sleep and light the furnaces; and as he wrought below, besides the boilers, he heard his master singing and rejoicing above him in the lighted chambers. When the water began to be hot the Chinaman cried to his master; and Keawe went into the bathroom; and the Chinaman heard him sing as he filled the marble basin; and heard him sing, and the singing broken, as he undressed; until of a sudden, the song ceased. The Chinaman listened, and listened; he called up the house to Keawe to ask if all were well, and Keawe answered him 'Yes,' and bade him go to bed; but there was no more singing in the Bright House; and all night long, the Chinaman heard his master's feet go round and round the balconies without repose.

Now the truth of it was this: as Keawe undressed for his bath, he spied upon his flesh a patch like a patch of lichen on a rock, and it was then that he stopped singing. For he knew the likeness of that patch, and knew that he was fallen in the Chinese Evil. [*]

Now, it is a sad thing for any man to fall into this sickness. And it would be a sad thing for anyone to leave a house so beautiful and so commodious, and depart from all his friends to the north coast of Molokai between the mighty cliff and the sea-breakers. But what was that to the case of the man Keawe, he who had met his love but yesterday, and won her but that morning, and now saw all his hopes break, in a moment, like a piece of glass?

Awhile he sat upon the edge of the bath; then sprang, with a cry, and ran outside; and to and fro, to and fro, along the balcony, like one despairing.

'Very willingly could I leave Hawaii, the home of my fathers,' Keawe was thinking. 'Very lightly could I leave my house, the high-placed, the many-windowed, here upon the mountains. Very bravely could I go to Molokai, to Kalaupapa by the cliffs, to live with the smitten and to sleep there, far from my fathers. But what wrong have I done, what sin lies upon my soul, that I should have encountered Kokua coming cool from the sea-water in the evening? Kokua, the soul ensnarer! Kokua, the light of my life! Her may I never wed, her may I look upon no longer, her may I no more handle with my loving hand; and it is for this, it is for you, O Kokua! that I pour my lamentations!'

Now you are to observe what sort of a man Keawe was, for he might have dwelt there in the Bright House for years, and no one been the wiser of his sickness; but he reckoned nothing of that, if he must lose Kokua. And again, he might have wed Kokua even as he was; and so many would have done, because they have the souls of pigs; but Keawe loved the maid manfully, and he would do her no hurt and bring her in no danger.

[*] Leprosy.

A little beyond the midst of the night, there came in his mind the recollection of that bottle. He went round to the back porch, and called to memory the day when the devil had looked forth; and at the thought ice ran in his veins.

'A dreadful thing is the bottle,' thought Keawe, 'and dreadful is the imp, and it is a dreadful thing to risk the flames of hell. But what other hope have I to cure my sickness or to wed Kokua? What!' he thought, 'would I beard the devil once, only to get me a house, and not face him again to win Kokua?'

Thereupon he called to mind it was the next day the *Hall* went by on her return to Honolulu. 'There must I go first,' he thought, 'and see Lopaka. For the best hope that I have now is to find that same bottle I was so pleased to be rid of.'

Never a wink could he sleep; the food stuck in his throat; but he sent a letter to Kiano, and about the time when the steamer would be coming, rode down beside the cliff of the tombs. It rained; his horse went heavily; he looked up at the black mouths of the caves, and he envied the dead that slept there and were done with trouble; and called to mind how he had galloped by the day before, and was astonished. So he came down to Hookena, and there was all the country gathered for the steamer as usual. In the shed before the store they sat and jested and passed the news; but there was no matter of speech in Keawe's bosom, and he sat in their midst and looked without on the rain falling on the houses, and the surf beating among the rocks, and the sighs arose in his throat.

'Keawe of the Bright House is out of spirits,' said one to another. Indeed, and so he was, and little wonder.

Then the *Hall* came, and the whaleboat carried him on board. The after-part of the ship was full of Haoles[*] who had been to visit the volcano, as their custom is; and the midst was crowded with Kanakas, and the forepart with wild bulls from Hilo and horses from Kaü; but Keawe sat apart from all in his sorrow, and watched for the house of Kiano. There it sat, low upon the shore in the black rocks, and shaded by the

---

[*] Whites.

cocoa palms, and there by the door was a red holoku, no greater than a fly, and going to and fro with a fly's busyness.

'Ah, queen of my heart,' he cried, 'I'll venture my dear soul to win you!'

Soon after, darkness fell, and the cabins were lit up, and the Haoles sat and played at the cards and drank whisky as their custom is; but Keawe walked the deck all night; and all the next day, as they steamed under the lee of Maui or of Molokai, he was still pacing to and fro like a wild animal in a menagerie.

Towards evening they passed Diamond Head, and came to the pier of Honolulu. Keawe stepped out among the crowd and began to ask for Lopaka. It seemed he had become the owner of a schooner—none better in the islands—and was gone upon an adventure as far as Pola-Pola or Kahiki; so there was no help to be looked for from Lopaka. Keawe called to mind a friend of his, a lawyer in the town (I must not tell his name), and inquired of him. They said he was grown suddenly rich, and had a fine new house upon Waikiki shore; and this put a thought in Keawe's head, and he called a hack and drove to the lawyer's house.

The house was all brand new, and the trees in the garden no greater than walking-sticks, and the lawyer, when he came, had the air of a man well pleased.

'What can I do to serve you?' said the lawyer.

'You are a friend of Lopaka's,' replied Keawe, 'and Lopaka purchased from me a certain piece of goods that I thought you might enable me to trace.'

The lawyer's face became very dark. 'I do not profess to misunderstand you, Mr Keawe,' said he, 'though this is an ugly business to be stirring in. You may be sure I know nothing, but yet I have a guess, and if you would apply in a certain quarter I think you might have news.'

And he named the name of a man, which, again, I had better not repeat. So it was for days, and Keawe went from one to another, finding everywhere new clothes and carriages, and fine new houses and men everywhere in great contentment, although, to be sure, when he hinted at his business their faces would cloud over.

'No doubt I am upon the track,' thought Keawe. 'These new clothes and carriages are all the gifts of the little imp, and these glad faces are the faces of men who have taken their profit and got rid of the accursed thing in safety. When I see pale cheeks and hear sighing, I shall know that I am near the bottle.'

So it befell at last that he was recommended to a Haole in Beritania Street. When he came to the door, about the hour of the evening meal, there were the usual marks of the new house, and the young garden, and the electric light shining in the windows; but when the owner came, a shock of hope and fear ran through Keawe; for here was a young man, white as a corpse, and black about the eyes, the hair shedding from his head, and such a look in his countenance as a man may have when he is waiting for the gallows.

'Here it is, to be sure,' thought Keawe, and so with this man he noways veiled his errand. 'I am come to buy the bottle,' said he.

At the word the young Haole of Beritania Street reeled against the wall.

'The bottle!' he gasped. 'To buy the bottle!' Then he seemed to choke, and seizing Keawe by the arm carried him into a room and poured out wine in two glasses.

'Here is my respects,' said Keawe, who had been much about with Haoles in his time. 'Yes,' he added, 'I am come to buy the bottle. What is the price by now?'

At that word the young man let his glass slip through his fingers, and looked upon Keawe like a ghost.

'The price,' says he; 'the price! You do not know the price?'

'It is for that I am asking you,' returned Keawe. 'But why are you so much concerned? Is there anything wrong about the price?'

'It has dropped a great deal in value since your time, Mr Keawe,' said the young man, stammering.

'Well, well, I shall have the less to pay for it,' says Keawe. 'How much did it cost you?'

The young man was as white as a sheet. 'Two cents,' said he.

'What?' cried Keawe, 'two cents? Why, then, you can only sell it for one. And he who buys it—' The words died upon Keawe's tongue; he who bought it could never sell it again, the bottle and the bottle imp must abide with him until he died, and when he died must carry him to the red end of hell.

The young man of Beritania Street fell upon his knees. 'For God's sake buy it!' he cried. 'You can have all my fortune in the bargain. I was mad when I bought it at that price. I had embezzled money at my store; I was lost else; I must have gone to jail.'

'Poor creature,' said Keawe, 'you would risk your soul upon so desperate an adventure, and to avoid the proper punishment of your own disgrace; and you think I could hesitate with love in front of me. Give me the bottle, and the change which I make sure you have all ready. Here is a five-cent piece.' It was as Keawe supposed; the young man had the change ready in a drawer; the bottle changed hands, and Keawe's fingers were no sooner clasped upon the stalk than he had breathed his wish to be a clean man. And, sure enough, when he got home to his room, and stripped himself before a glass, his flesh was whole like an infant's. And here was the strange thing: he had no sooner seen this miracle, than his mind was changed within him, and he cared naught for the Chinese Evil, and little enough for Kokua; and had but the one thought, that here he was bound to the bottle imp for time and for eternity, and had no better hope but to be a cinder for ever in the flames of hell. Away ahead of him he saw them blaze with his mind's eye, and his soul shrank, and darkness fell upon the light.

When Keawe came to himself a little, he was aware it was the night when the band played at the hotel. Thither he went, because he feared to be alone; and there, among happy faces, walked to and fro, and heard the tunes go up and down, and saw Berger beat the measure, and all the while he heard the flames crackle, and saw the red fire burning in the bottomless pit. Of a sudden the band played *Hiki-ao-ao*; that was a song that he had sung with Kokua, and at the strain courage returned to him.

'It is done now,' he thought, 'and once more let me take the good along with the evil.'

So it befell that he returned to Hawaii by the first steamer, and as soon as it could be managed he was wedded to Kokua, and carried her up the mountain side to the Bright House.

Now it was so with these two, that when they were together, Keawe's heart was stilled; but so soon as he was alone he fell into a brooding horror, and heard the flames crackle, and saw the red fire burn in the bottomless pit. The girl, indeed, had come to him wholly; her heart leapt in her side at sight of him, her hand clung to his; and she was so fashioned from the hair upon her head to the nails upon her toes that none could see her without joy. She was pleasant in her nature. She had the good word always. Full of song she was, and went to and fro in the Bright House, the brightest thing in its three storeys, carolling like the birds. And Keawe beheld and heard her with delight, and then must shrink upon one side, and weep and groan to think upon the price that he had paid for her; and then he must dry his eyes, and wash his face, and go and sit with her on the broad balconies joining in her songs, and, with a sick spirit, answering her smiles.

There came a day when her feet began to be heavy and her songs more rare; and now it was not Keawe only that would weep apart, but each would sunder from the other and sit in opposite balconies with the whole width of the Bright House betwixt. Keawe was so sunk in his despair, he scarce observed the change, and was only glad he had more hours to sit alone and brood upon his destiny, and was not so frequently condemned to pull a smiling face on a sick heart. But one day, coming softly through the house, he heard the sound of a child sobbing, and there was Kokua rolling her face upon the balcony floor, and weeping like the lost.

'You do well to weep in this house, Kokua,' he said. 'And yet I would give the head off my body that you (at least) might have been happy.'

'Happy!' she cried. 'Keawe, when you lived alone in your Bright House, you were the word of the island for a happy man; laughter and song were in your mouth, and your face was as bright as the sunrise. Then you wedded poor Kokua; and the good God knows what is amiss in her—but from that day you have not smiled. Oh!' she cried, 'what ails me? I thought I was pretty, and I knew I loved him. What ails me that I throw this cloud upon my husband?'

'Poor Kokua,' said Keawe. He sat down by her side, and sought to take her hand; but that she plucked away. 'Poor Kokua,' he said, again. 'My poor child—my pretty. And I thought all this while to spare you! Well, you shall know all. Then, at least, you will pity poor Keawe; then you will understand how much he loved you in the past—that he dared hell for your possession—and how much he loves you still (the poor condemned one), that he can yet call up a smile when he beholds you.'

With that, he told her all, even from the beginning.

'You have done this for me?' she cried. 'Ah, well then what do I care!'—and she clasped and wept upon him.

'Ah, child!' said Keawe, 'and yet, when I consider of the fire of hell, I care a good deal!'

'Never tell me,' said she; 'no man can be lost because he loved Kokua, and no other fault. I tell you, Keawe, I shall save you with these hands, or perish in your company. What! you loved me, and gave your soul, and you think I will not die to save you in return?'

'Ah, my dear! you might die a hundred times, and what difference would that make?' he cried, 'except to leave me lonely till the time comes of my damnation?'

'You know nothing,' said she. 'I was educated in a school in Honolulu; I am no common girl. And I tell you, I shall save my lover. What is this you say about a cent? But all the world is not American. In England they have a piece they call a farthing, which is about half a cent. Ah! sorrow!' she cried, 'that makes it scarcely better, for the buyer must be lost, and we shall find none so brave as my Keawe! But, then, there is France; they have a small coin there which they call a centime, and these go five to the cent or thereabout. We could not do better. Come, Keawe, let us go to the French islands; let us go to Tahiti, as fast as ships can bear us. There we have four centimes, three centimes, two centimes, one centime; four possible sales to come and go on; and two of us to push the bargain. Come, my Keawe! kiss me, and banish care. Kokua will defend you.'

'Gift of God!' he cried. 'I cannot think that God will punish me for desiring aught so good! Be it as you will, then; take me where you please: I put my life and my salvation in your hands.'

Early the next day Kokua was about her preparations. She took Keawe's chest that he went with sailoring; and first she put the bottle in a corner; and then packed it with the richest of their clothes and the bravest of the knick-knacks in the house. 'For,' said she, 'we must seem to be rich folks, or who will believe in the bottle?' All the time of her preparation she was as gay as a bird; only when she looked upon Keawe, the tears would spring in her eye, and she must run and kiss him. As for Keawe, a weight was off his soul; now that he had his secret shared, and some hope in front of him, he seemed like a new man, his feet went lightly on the earth, and his breath was good to him again. Yet was terror still at his elbow; and ever and again, as the wind blows out a taper, hope died in him, and he saw the flames toss and the red fire burn in hell.

It was given out in the country they were gone pleasuring to the States, which was thought a strange thing, and yet not so strange as the truth, if any could have guessed it. So they went to Honolulu in the *Hall*, and thence in the *Umatilla* to San Francisco with a crowd of Haoles, and at San Francisco took their passage by the mail brigantine, the *Tropic Bird*, for Papeete, the chief place of the French in the south islands. Thither they came, after a pleasant voyage, on a fair day of the Trade Wind, and saw the reef with the surf breaking, and Motuiti with its palms, and the schooner riding within-side, and the white houses of the town low down along the shore among green trees, and overhead the mountains and the clouds of Tahiti, the wise island.

It was judged the most wise to hire a house, which they did accordingly, opposite the British Consul's, to make a great parade of money, and themselves conspicuous with carriages and horses. This it was very easy to do, so long as they had the bottle in their possession; for Kokua was more bold than Keawe, and, whenever she had a mind, called on the imp for twenty or a hundred dollars. At this rate they soon grew to be remarked in the town; and the strangers from Hawaii, their riding and their driving, the fine holokus and the rich lace of Kokua, became the matter of much talk.

They got on well after the first with the Tahitian language, which is indeed like to the Hawaiian, with a change of certain letters; and as soon as they had any freedom of speech, began to push the bottle. You are to consider it was not an easy subject to introduce; it was not easy to persuade people you were in earnest, when you offered to sell them for four centimes the spring of health and riches inexhaustible. It was necessary besides to explain the dangers of the bottle; and either people disbelieved the whole thing and laughed, or they thought the more of the darker part, became overcast with gravity, and drew away from Keawe and Kokua, as from persons who had dealings with the devil. So far from gaining ground, these two began to find they were avoided in the town; the children ran away from them screaming, a thing intolerable to Kokua; Catholics crossed themselves as they went by; and all persons began with one accord to disengage themselves from their advances.

Depression fell upon their spirits. They would sit at night in their new house, after a day's weariness, and not exchange one word, or the silence would be broken by Kokua bursting suddenly into sobs. Sometimes they would pray together; sometimes they would have the bottle out upon the floor, and sit all evening watching how the shadow hovered in the midst. At such times they would be afraid to go to rest. It was long ere slumber came to them, and, if either dozed off, it would be to wake and find the other silently weeping in the dark, or, perhaps, to wake alone, the other having fled from the house and the neighbourhood of that bottle, to pace under the bananas in the little garden, or to wander on the beach by moonlight.

One night it was so when Kokua awoke. Keawe was gone. She felt in the bed and his place was cold. Then fear fell upon her, and she sat up in bed. A little moonshine filtered through the shutters. The room was bright, and she could spy the bottle on the floor. Outside it blew high, the great trees of the avenue cried aloud, and the fallen leaves rattled in the verandah. In the midst of this Kokua was aware of another sound; whether of a beast or of a man she could scarce tell, but it was as sad as death, and cut her to the soul. Softly she arose, set the door ajar, and looked forth into the moonlit yard. There, under the bananas, lay Keawe, his mouth in the dust, and as he lay he moaned.

It was Kokua's first thought to run forward and console him; her second potently withheld her. Keawe had borne himself before his wife like a brave man; it became her little in the hour of weakness to intrude upon his shame. With the thought she drew back into the house.

'Heaven!' she thought, 'how careless have I been—how weak! It is he, not I, that stands in this eternal peril; it was he, not I, that took the curse upon his soul. It is for my sake, and for the love of a creature of so little worth and such poor help, that he now beholds so close to him the flames of hell—ay, and smells the smoke of it, lying without there in the wind and moonlight. Am I so dull of spirit that never till now I have surmised my duty, or have I seen it before and turned aside? But now, at least, I take up my soul in both the hands of my affection; now I say farewell to the white steps of heaven and the waiting faces of my friends. A love for a love, and let mine be equalled with Keawe's! A soul for a soul, and be it mine to perish!'

She was a deft woman with her hands, and was soon apparelled. She took in her hands the change—the precious centimes they kept ever at their side; for this coin is little used, and they had made provision at a Government office. When she was forth in the avenue clouds came on the wind, and the moon was blackened. The town slept, and she knew not whither to turn till she heard one coughing in the shadow of the trees.

'Old man,' said Kokua, 'what do you here abroad in the cold night?'

The old man could scarce express himself for coughing, but she made out that he was old and poor, and a stranger in the island.

'Will you do me a service?' said Kokua. 'As one stranger to another, and as an old man to a young woman, will you help a daughter of Hawaii?'

'Ah,' said the old man. 'So you are the witch from the eight islands, and even my old soul you seek to entangle. But I have heard of you, and defy your wickedness.'

'Sit down here,' said Kokua, 'and let me tell you a tale.' And she told him the story of Keawe from the beginning to the end.

'And now,' said she, 'I am his wife, whom he bought with his soul's welfare. And what should I do? If I went to him myself and offered to buy it, he would refuse. But if you go, he will sell it eagerly; I will await you here; you will buy it for four centimes, and I will buy it again for three. And the Lord strengthen a poor girl!'

'If you meant falsely,' said the old man, 'I think God would strike you dead.'

'He would!' cried Kokua. 'Be sure he would. I could not be so treacherous—God would not suffer it.'

'Give me the four centimes and await me here,' said the old man.

Now, when Kokua stood alone in the street, her spirit died. The wind roared in the trees, and it seemed to her the rushing of the flames of hell; the shadows tossed in the light of the street lamp, and they seemed to her the snatching hands of evil ones. If she had had the strength, she must have run away, and if she had had the breath she must have screamed aloud; but, in truth, she could do neither, and stood and trembled in the avenue, like an affrighted child.

Then she saw the old man returning, and he had the bottle in his hand.

'I have done your bidding,' said he. 'I left your husband weeping like a child; tonight he will sleep easy.' And he held the bottle forth.

'Before you give it me,' Kokua panted, 'take the good with the evil—ask to be delivered from your cough.'

'I am an old man,' replied the other, 'and too near the gate of the grave to take a favour from the devil. But what is this? Why do you not take the bottle? Do you hesitate?'

'Not hesitate!' cried Kokua. 'I am only weak. Give me a moment. It is my hand resists, my flesh shrinks back from the accursed thing. One moment only!'

The old man looked upon Kokua kindly. 'Poor child!' said he, 'you fear; your soul misgives you. Well, let me keep it. I am old, and can never more be happy in this world, and as for the next—'

'Give it me!' gasped Kokua. 'There is your money. Do you think I am so base as that? Give me the bottle.'

'God bless you, child,' said the old man.

Kokua concealed the bottle under her holoku, said farewell to the old man, and walked off along the avenue, she cared not whither. For all roads were now the same to her, and led equally to hell. Sometimes she walked, and sometimes ran; sometimes she screamed out loud in the night, and sometimes lay by the wayside in the dust and wept. All that she had heard of hell came back to her; she saw the flames blaze, and she smelt the smoke, and her flesh withered on the coals.

Near day she came to her mind again, and returned to the house. It was even as the old man said—Keawe slumbered like a child. Kokua stood and gazed upon his face.

'Now, my husband,' said she, 'it is your turn to sleep. When you wake it will be your turn to sing and laugh. But for poor Kokua, alas! that meant no evil—for poor Kokua no more sleep, no more singing, no more delight, whether in earth or heaven.'

With that she lay down in the bed by his side, and her misery was so extreme that she fell in a deep slumber instantly.

Late in the morning her husband woke her and gave her the good news. It seemed he was silly with delight, for he paid no heed to her distress, ill though she dissembled it. The words stuck in her mouth, it mattered not; Keawe did the speaking. She ate not a bite, but who was to observe it? for Keawe cleared the dish. Kokua saw and heard him, like some strange thing in a dream; there were times when she forgot or doubted, and put her hands to her brow; to know herself doomed and hear her husband babble, seemed so monstrous.

All the while Keawe was eating and talking, and planning the time of their return, and thanking her for saving him, and fondling her, and calling her the true helper after all. He laughed at the old man that was fool enough to buy that bottle.

'A worthy old man he seemed,' Keawe said. 'But no one can judge by appearances. For why did the old reprobate require the bottle?'

'My husband,' said Kokua, humbly, 'his purpose may have been good.'

Keawe laughed like an angry man.

'Fiddle-de-dee!' cried Keawe. 'An old rogue, I tell you; and an old ass to boot. For the bottle was hard enough to sell at four centimes; and at three it will be quite impossible. The margin is not broad enough, the thing begins to smell of scorching—brrr!' said he, and shuddered. 'It is true I bought it myself at a cent, when I knew not there were smaller coins. I was a fool for my pains; there will never be found another: and whoever has that bottle now will carry it to the pit.'

'O my husband!' said Kokua. 'Is it not a terrible thing to save oneself by the eternal ruin of another? It seems to me I could not laugh. I would be humbled. I would be filled with melancholy. I would pray for the poor holder.'

Then Keawe, because he felt the truth of what she said, grew the more angry. 'Heighty-teighty!' cried he. 'You may be filled with melancholy if you please. It is not the mind of a good wife. If you thought at all of me, you would sit shamed.'

Thereupon he went out, and Kokua was alone.

What chance had she to sell that bottle at two centimes? None, she perceived. And if she had any, here was her husband hurrying her away to a country where there was nothing lower than a cent. And here—on the morrow of her sacrifice—was her husband leaving her and blaming her.

She would not even try to profit by what time she had, but sat in the house, and now had the bottle out and viewed it with unutterable fear, and now, with loathing, hid it out of sight.

By-and-by, Keawe came back, and would have her take a drive.

'My husband, I am ill,' she said. 'I am out of heart. Excuse me, I can take no pleasure.'

Then was Keawe more wroth than ever. With her, because he thought she was brooding over the case of the old man; and with himself, because he thought she was right, and was ashamed to be so happy.

'This is your truth,' cried he, 'and this your affection! Your husband is just saved from eternal ruin, which he encountered for the love of you—and you take no pleasure! Kokua, you have a disloyal heart.'

He went forth again furious, and wandered in the town all day. He met friends, and drank with them; they hired a carriage and drove into the country, and there drank again. All the time Keawe was ill at ease, because he was taking this pastime while his wife was sad, and because he knew in his heart that she was more right than he; and the knowledge made him drink the deeper.

Now there was an old brutal Haole drinking with him, one that had been a boatswain of a whaler, a runaway, a digger in gold mines, a convict in prisons. He had a low mind and a foul mouth; he loved to drink and to see others drunken; and he pressed the glass upon Keawe. Soon there was no more money in the company.

'Here, you!' says the boatswain, 'you are rich, you have been always saying. You have a bottle or some foolishness.'

'Yes,' says Keawe, 'I am rich; I will go back and get some money from my wife, who keeps it.'

'That's a bad idea, mate,' said the boatswain. 'Never you trust a petticoat with dollars. They're all as false as water; you keep an eye on her.'

Now, this word struck in Keawe's mind; for he was muddled with what he had been drinking.

'I should not wonder but she was false, indeed,' thought he. 'Why else should she be so cast down at my release? But I will show her I am not the man to be fooled. I will catch her in the act.'

Accordingly, when they were back in town, Keawe bade the boatswain wait for him at the corner, by the old calaboose, and went forward up the avenue alone to the door of his house. The night had come again; there was a light within, but never a sound; and Keawe crept about the corner, opened the back door softly, and looked in.

There was Kokua on the floor, the lamp at her side, before her was a milk-white bottle, with a round belly and a long neck; and as she viewed it, Kokua wrung her hands.

A long time Keawe stood and looked in the doorway. At first he was struck stupid; and then fear fell upon him that the bargain had been made amiss, and the bottle had come back to him as it came at San Francisco; and at that his knees were loosened, and the fumes of the wine departed from his head like mists off a river in the morning. And then he had another thought; and it was a strange one, that made his cheeks to burn. 'I must make sure of this,' thought he.

So he closed the door, and went softly round the corner again, and then came noisily in, as though he were but now returned. And, lo! by the time he opened the front door no bottle was to be seen; and Kokua sat in a chair and started up like one awakened out of sleep.

'I have been drinking all day and making merry,' said Keawe. 'I have been with good companions, and now I only come back for money, and return to drink and carouse with them again.'

Both his face and voice were as stern as judgement, but Kokua was too troubled to observe.

'You do well to use your own, my husband,' said she, and her words trembled.

'O, I do well in all things,' said Keawe, and he went straight to the chest and took out money. But he looked besides in the corner where they kept the bottle, and there was no bottle there.

At that the chest heaved upon the floor like a sea-billow, and the house span about him like a wreath of smoke, for he saw he was lost now, and there was no escape. 'It is what I feared,' he thought. 'It is she who has bought it.'

And then he came to himself a little and rose up; but the sweat streamed on his face as thick as the rain and as cold as the well-water.

'Kokua,' said he, 'I said to you today what ill became me. Now I return to carouse with my jolly companions,' and at that he laughed a little quietly. 'I will take more pleasure in the cup if you forgive me.'

She clasped his knees in a moment; she kissed his knees with flowing tears.

'O,' she cried, 'I asked but a kind word!'

'Let us never one think hardly of the other,' said Keawe, and was gone out of the house.

Now, the money that Keawe had taken was only some of that store of centime pieces they had laid in at their arrival. It was very sure he had no mind to be drinking. His wife had given her soul for him, now he must give his for hers; no other thought was in the world with him.

At the corner, by the old calaboose, there was the boatswain waiting.

'My wife has the bottle,' said Keawe, 'and, unless you help me to recover it, there can be no more money and no more liquor tonight.'

'You do not mean to say you are serious about that bottle?' cried the boatswain.

'There is the lamp,' said Keawe. 'Do I look as if I was jesting?'

'That is so,' said the boatswain. 'You look as serious as a ghost.'

'Well, then,' said Keawe, 'here are two centimes; you must go to my wife in the house, and offer her these for the bottle, which (if I am not much mistaken) she will give you instantly. Bring it to me here, and I will buy it back from you for one; for that is the law with this bottle, that it still must be sold for a less sum. But whatever you do, never breathe a word to her that you have come from me.'

'Mate, I wonder are you making a fool of me?' asked the boatswain.

'It will do you no harm if I am,' returned Keawe.

'That is so, mate,' said the boatswain.

'And if you doubt me,' added Keawe, 'you can try. As soon as you are clear of the house, wish to have your pocket full of money, or a bottle of the best rum, or what you please, and you will see the virtue of the thing.'

'Very well, Kanaka,' says the boatswain. 'I will try; but if you are having your fun out of me, I will take my fun out of you with a belaying pin.'

So the whaler-man went off up the avenue; and Keawe stood and waited. It was near the same spot where Kokua had waited the night before; but Keawe was more resolved, and never faltered in his purpose; only his soul was bitter with despair.

It seemed a long time he had to wait before he heard a voice singing in the darkness of the avenue. He knew the voice to be the boatswain's; but it was strange how drunken it appeared upon a sudden.

Next, the man himself came stumbling into the light of the lamp. He had the devil's bottle buttoned in his coat; another bottle was in his hand; and even as he came in view he raised it to his mouth and drank.

'You have it,' said Keawe. 'I see that.'

'Hands off!' cried the boatswain, jumping back. 'Take a step near me, and I'll smash your mouth. You thought you could make a cat's-paw of me, did you?'

'What do you mean?' cried Keawe.

'Mean?' cried the boatswain. 'This is a pretty good bottle, this is; that's what I mean. How I got it for two centimes I can't make out; but I'm sure you shan't have it for one.'

'You mean you won't sell?' gasped Keawe.

'No, *sir!*' cried the boatswain. 'But I'll give you a drink of the rum, if you like.'

'I tell you,' said Keawe, 'the man who has that bottle goes to hell.'

'I reckon I'm going anyway,' returned the sailor; 'and this bottle's the best thing to go with I've struck yet. 'No, sir!' he cried again, 'this is my bottle now, and you can go and fish for another.'

'Can this be true?' Keawe cried. 'For your own sake, I beseech you, sell it me!'

'I don't value any of your talk,' replied the boatswain. 'You thought I was a flat; now you see I'm not; and there's an end. If you won't have a swallow of the rum, I'll have one myself. Here's your health, and goodnight to you!'

So off he went down the avenue towards town, and there goes the bottle out of the story.

But Keawe ran to Kokua light as the wind; and great was their joy that night; and great, since then, has been the peace of all their days in the Bright House.

Acknowledgments

Many people made this anthology.

At Thunder's Mouth Press and Avalon Publishing Group:
Thanks to Will Balliett, Don Weise, Linda Kosarin, Dan O'Connor, Neil Ortenberg, Paul Paddock, Susan Reich, David Reidy, Michelle Rosenfield, Simon Sullivan, and Mike Walters for their support, dedication and hard work. Special thanks to the patient and meticulous Maria Fernandez.

Thanks to Taylor Smith for securing permissions for the selections in this book.

At the Thomas Memorial Library in Cape Elizabeth, Maine:
Thanks to the librarians for their assistance in finding and borrowing books from around the country.

Finally, I am grateful to the writers whose work appears in this book.

Permissions

Bibliography

The selections used in this anthology were taken from the editions listed below. In some cases, other editions may be easier to find. Hard-to-find or out-of-print titles often are available through inter-library loan services or through Internet booksellers.

Baum, Frank L. *The Magic of Oz.* New York: Ballantine Books, 1984.

Birch, Cyril. "Magicians of the Way" from *Tales From China.* Oxford, England: Oxford University Press, 1961.

Carpenter, Frances. *South American Wonder Tales.* Chicago: Follett Publishing Company, 1969.

Duane, Diane. *So You Want to Be a Wizard.* New York: Harcourt Brace & Company, 1983.

Hodges, Elizabeth Jamison. "The Magic Muntr" from *Serendipity Tales.* New York: Atheneum, 1966.

Lang, Andrew. "Aladdin and the Wonderful Lamp" from *Arabian Nights.* New York: David McKay Company, Inc., 1946.

Lang, Andrew. "The Dragon of the North" from *The Yellow Fairy Book.* New York: Viking Press, 1980.

Le Guin, Ursula K. "The Bones of the Earth" from *Tales from Earthsea.* New York: Harcourt, Inc., 2001.

Lewis, C.S. *The Magician's Nephew.* New York: Scholastic Inc., 1995.

McGowen, Tom. *The Magician's Apprentice.* New York: Lodestar Books/E.P. Dutton, 1987.

McKillip, Patricia A. "Baba Yoga and the Sorcerer's Son" from *Dragons & Dreams: A Collection of New Fantasy and Science Fiction Stories* edited by Jane Yolen, Martin H. Greenberg and Charles G. Waugh. New York: Harper & Row Publishers, 1986.

McKillip, Patricia A. "The Harrowing of the Dragon of Hoarsbreath" from *Masterpieces of Fantasy and Wonder,* compiled by David G. Hartwell. New York: GuildAmerica Books/Doubleday Book & Music Clubs, Inc., 1989.

Nesbit, E. *The Phoenix and the Carpet.* London: Puffin Books, 1959.

Nesbit, E. *The Story of the Amulet.* New York: Viking Penguin, 1959.

Shakespeare, William. *The Tempest.* Edited by Peter Holland. New York: Penguin Books, 1995.

Sharp, Evelyn. "The Spell of the Magician's Daughter" from *Victorian Fairy Tales,* edited by Jack Zipes. New York: Methuen, 1987.

Stevenson, Robert Louis. "The Bottle Imp" from *Black Water: The Book of Fantastic Literature,* edited by Alberto Manguel. New York: Clarkson Potter Publishers, 1983.

Turner, Megan Whalen. *Instead of Three Wishes.* New York: Greenwillow Books, a division of William Morrow & Company, Inc., 1995.

Wrede, Patricia C. "The Sixty-Two Curses of Caliph Arenschadd" from *Book of Enchantments.* New York: Jane Yolen Books/Harcourt Brace & Company, 1996.